Helen
Grant

Also by Helen Grant:

The FORBIDDEN SPACES trilogy:
Silent Saturday
Demons of Ghent
Urban Legends

The Vanishing of Katharina Linden
The Glass Demon
Wish Me Dead

Helen Grant

URBAN LEGENDS

CORGI BOOKS

URBAN LEGENDS
A CORGI BOOK 978 0 552 56677 3

Published in Great Britain by Corgi Books,
an imprint of Random House Children's Publishers UK
A Penguin Random House Company

Penguin
Random House
UK

This edition published 2015

1 3 5 7 9 10 8 6 4 2

Penguin Random House is committed to a sustainable future for our business, our readers
and our planet. This book is made from Forest Stewardship Council® certified paper.

MIX
Paper from
responsible sources
FSC® C016897

Set in 12.5/15.5 pt ITC New Baskerville by Falcon Oast Graphic Art Ltd.

Corgi Books are published by Random House Children's Publishers UK,
61–63 Uxbridge Road, London W5 5SA

www.randomhousechildrens.co.uk
www.randomhousechildrens.co.uk
www.randomhouse.co.uk

Addresses for companies within The Random House Group Limited.
can be found at: www.randomhouse.co.uk/offices.htm

THE RANDOM HOUSE GROUP Limited Reg. No. 954009

A CIP catalogue record for this book is available from the British Library.

Printed and bound in Great Britain by CPI Group (UK) Ltd, Croydon CR0 4YY

For Sarah

1

'So all of a sudden the light goes out and she sees this dark shape coming towards her. He's getting nearer and nearer and she recognizes her boyfriend's face, only his hair is on end, which freaks her out really badly. And something's wrong because the body isn't like her boyfriend's – he's kind of heavy but this guy is thin and wiry. The next moment the head is just ripped from—'

'Oh, come on,' interrupted Ruben. 'This is just a variation of *The Hook*. It's old.' He rolled his eyes sardonically, his face underlit by the flickering orange flames.

There were four of them in the darkened tunnel, huddled around the fire, which burnt in a battered coffee tin. Light danced on damp walls spotted with uneven growths that spread like disease across the crumbling bricks.

Maxim slumped resentfully, the sullen glitter of his eyes obscured by overhanging clumps of hair. 'Fine. Someone else can tell one, then.'

No one was bothered by the silence that ensued; they didn't have that kind of bond. If the story was bad, that was the storyteller's problem.

The fire and the falling water talked softly in the

background. At last Zoë spoke. She was the only girl, light-boned and fox-faced, with hair dyed vivid red and pulled into a knot at the back of her head. She avoided the role of peace-maker as she would have avoided pink or frills, but she was getting bored; she didn't want to sit here all night watching Maxim sulk.

'Why don't *you* tell us another one, Thomas? Yours are always cool.'

She was looking at the big man opposite her, broad shouldered and hulking in his padded jacket and trapper hat. Thomas wasn't *likeable* exactly; there was a stillness about him, a suggestion of something suppressed, that gave her a sense of unease. Still, his stories were much better than every-one else's. Next time she was in a group and he wasn't there, she might retell one of them, pretending it was her own.

Thomas sat in silence for a few moments, and then he said, 'I'll tell you "The Angel Smile".'

There was a cracking sound followed by a tiny splash as Maxim sent a pebble skimming across the tunnel with bitter energy.

'Two people, one male and one female –' began Thomas.

A couple, thought Zoë.

'– went to explore an abandoned sanatorium at night. It was a big place, impressive in its day, but now it had been disused for over forty years.

'The explorers parked their car off the road, where the darkness and the overhanging branches of the trees would hide it. By the light of the moon the pair of them examined the fence that surrounded the grounds. They had brought bolt cutters, but they didn't need them, because part of the chain-link fence was pulled away from the metal gate posts, leaving enough space to climb through. This didn't strike them as suspicious, because they knew that other people had been here before. So they slipped through the gap and began to make their way uphill to the sanatorium.

'It was much bigger than either of them had expected, though they had seen photos of it online. There was one massive central building and two sweeping wings. With only moonlight to see by, you couldn't tell how dilapidated it was; how the paintwork was peeling and the shutters hanging off their hinges. It looked deeply forbidding.

'The main entrance was a set of double doors with reinforced glass panels and a heavy-duty chain and padlock fastened across them. They might have got through the chain with the bolt cutters but it would have taken a lot of time and effort, so they began to walk along the building, looking for an easier way in.

'Soon they found a door standing slightly open, only a centimetre or two. The door was heavy and the hinges were rusty, but with two of them leaning on it with all their weight they were able to push it open far enough to get inside.

'The boy switched on his torch and played the beam up and down the walls. They were in a stairwell, the stairs zigzagging up into the darkness above them. The steps were covered in debris, as though someone had tried to clear things out from the upper floors by flinging them downstairs. There were files, collapsed cardboard boxes, a metal clipboard, the splintered remains of a wooden chair – all of it thick with dust.

'"I'm not sure about this," said the girl, and her words

floated up the stairwell like air bubbles rising through murky water.

'"I'll go up to the first floor and look. You stay here," said the boy.

'So the girl stood at the bottom of the stairs and watched the boy pick his way up the first flight, carefully skirting the heaps of rubbish. When he came to the bend in the stairs and started up the second flight, she could still see the light from the torch, slowly moving upwards.

'After a minute she heard him say something – she couldn't tell what – and then heard a kind of scuffling noise. After that there was silence.

'The girl could still see a faint glow from the torch, but it wasn't moving any more. She called the boy's name, but there was no reply. Eventually she decided to go and see what had happened to him.

'She went slowly up the stairs. As her gaze came level with the first-floor landing she saw the torch lying there, at the end of a long gouge-mark in the dust, as though it had skidded across the tiles. The door to the first floor was off its hinges and she could see straight into the long dark tunnel of the corridor, but the boy was nowhere to be seen.'

Thomas paused for a moment, and in the silence Zoë drew in a shivering breath. Then he resumed.

'The girl said his name again, her voice wavering with fear. She knelt to pick up the torch. It felt slightly sticky but she couldn't tell why. She took several halting steps into the corridor, swinging the torch from side to side to rake the filthy walls with light.

'There were doorways on either side but she didn't go

4

through any of them. She kept to the centre of the corridor because she was afraid. That was her mistake. If she had looked into the first room on the left she might have seen who was in there, and if she had been very, very quick she might have got away. But she didn't look.

'The moment she passed that door, someone stepped out of the room behind her. Now she was cut off. He didn't bother to tread silently, so she heard his footsteps very clearly and turned round.

'Even in the dim light she knew immediately that it wasn't the boy she'd come with. This man was taller and heavier, with broad shoulders and muscular arms – and he was holding a crossbow. She didn't dare run away.

'She said, "Where's—?" and named the boy, but she didn't really want to know the answer.

'The man came right up close, pointing the crossbow at her. He didn't tell her where the boy was. Instead, he said, "You have a choice. I kill you, or you take the Angel Smile."

'The girl didn't know what the Angel Smile was, but she didn't want him to shoot her with the crossbow, so she said, "The Angel Smile."

'The man put down the crossbow, but it was too late to run away. He was close enough to reach out and grab her arm. He was very strong. She couldn't pull herself free. He drew out a very sharp knife and cut her twice, here, at the corners of her mouth. Then he let her go.

'The girl dropped the torch and put her hands up to her face. She could feel the terrible cuts, and the blood pouring out of them, but she didn't dare scream, even though she was almost dead with fright, because she was afraid the cut flesh

5

would tear. That is the Angel Smile, you see, when the new mouth runs from ear to ear.

'The man stood watching her. When she didn't scream, he said, "Do you want to see the boy?"

'The girl didn't say yes or no, because she didn't dare speak, but the man grabbed her arm and dragged her towards the open doorway. He picked up the torch and shone it into the room beyond.

'There was the boy, propped against the wall, stone dead. There was something sticking out of his eye, and his whole jacket and shirt were drenched with dark blood. That was what she had felt on the handle of the torch.

'The killer waited for her to scream and give herself the Angel Smile. But what neither of them knew was that the girl had a heart defect. She took one look and her overburdened heart gave out. She went limp in the killer's grasp and sagged to the floor. Soon the blood stopped flowing. So she never had the Angel Smile.

'The killer dumped both the bodies in the undergrowth in the grounds of the sanatorium, and they were never found. He left the car where it was, knowing that it would soon be covered in vegetation. Nobody has ever found that, either.

'But the killer was denied the satisfaction of creating the Angel Smile. So at night he still prowls around the deserted sanatorium and other lonely places with his crossbow and his knife, looking for a new victim to receive the Angel Smile. Places,' said Thomas, 'like this.'

At the end of the story there was silence for a minute or two. Zoë cast uneasy glances at the deep shadows encroaching on all sides. She was thinking about leaving, about having to walk through the dark tunnel on her own; that black maw was looking increasingly uninviting.

Then Ruben broke the silence, his tone deliberately challenging. 'So if the bodies were never found, and neither was the car, and the killer escaped, how did the story get out?'

They all contemplated that, and then Maxim let out a short laugh.

'It's a made-up story, idiot.' He shook his head. 'And you've just wrecked it.'

Zoë looked at Thomas, but he didn't say anything.

The group broke up pretty soon after that. Zoë made a swift decision and said, as casually as she could, 'Is anyone going my way?'

Only Thomas nodded. She looked at him and said, 'Don't tell me any more stories on the way, OK?'

Thomas inclined his big head. He said, 'One was enough.'

Together, they vanished into the dark.

2

When the doorbell rang at eleven p.m., Gregory Verbruggen was surprised: not because of the lateness of the hour (he was practically nocturnal himself, being a web designer with a lot of clients in other time zones) but because hardly anyone ever visited him at home. Gregory didn't encourage it. About seventy-five per cent of his friends were online – ironic or swaggering usernames with cartoon avatars – and the others were people with whom he did things that might have been called illegal. Gregory didn't think of these things as *wrong* – he didn't hurt anyone, or damage anything, after all – but he was not stupid. He knew that the authorities wouldn't see things his way. Breaking into people's houses when they were away was trespassing, even if you did a bit of maintenance work while you were in there, as a kind of payment for enjoying the place. It wasn't like that was the end of Gregory's involvement, either. He was the one who'd set up an entire web forum, disguised within an innocuous-looking bird-watching site, so that members could exchange information: where there was a villa empty, and how to get inside. The Koekoeken, they'd called themselves – the cuckoos; the birds who invaded other birds' nests.

Gregory had got a huge kick out of the Koekoeken while it lasted, but that was all over now. Fred, the guy who'd started the group and got Gregory in to do the techie stuff, had shut the thing down overnight – a while back now. He'd got antsy about someone hassling other members and told Gregory to delete the whole site. Gregory had done it, reluctantly, and now he was back to exploring the places he could find on his own or with a few trusted acquaintances.

He wondered whether it was one of them pressing so relentlessly on the buzzer. It seemed unlikely, given that he never invited anyone here. Nor was it likely to be a girl; Gregory didn't *have* a girlfriend. Most likely it was a drunk who'd got his block numbers mixed up, or someone from one of the downstairs flats who'd lost their key. He considered ignoring it altogether, but the repetitive noise was intrusive. He thought he'd go down to the street door and tell whoever it was to fuck off.

He left the flat door open and went downstairs. His footsteps rang out on the stairs. Outside were the sounds of passing traffic; inside the block was silence. Everyone else was out, or asleep. Gregory ran a hand over his tawny hair, so that it stood up in clumps.

The ground floor was in darkness, because the light bulb had blown a week before and nobody could be bothered to change it. As Gregory stumbled down the hall he heard the buzzer sounding again in his flat upstairs.

He was seriously pissed off now. He crossed the last couple of metres and opened the street door.

The man who stood outside on the step, silhouetted against the yellow light from the streetlamps, was tall, broad-shouldered and muscular. He was big enough to deter Gregory from swearing at him; big enough to make Gregory start closing the door again. Too late. A brawny shoulder was against it.

'Gregory?'

When Gregory didn't immediately respond, the man said, 'Ringslang.'

Grass snake – that was Gregory's Koekoeken username. They'd all gone by usernames, most of them creepy-crawlies: insects, spiders, reptiles. It was a way of keeping the risk of being identified to a minimum.

Gregory said, 'What do you want?'

'It's me. Wolfspin.'

Wolfspin? For a moment Gregory's mind drew a blank, but then he remembered. Wolfspin – the wolf spider. That was one of the names used by the Koekoeken, though he didn't think he'd ever known the guy personally. He'd been a friend of a friend – a girl he'd actually met once or twice. Briefly he wondered what had happened to her: when women were rare in your limited social circle, you noticed when you hadn't heard from one of them for a bit.

'Look,' he said, keeping his voice neutral because he didn't want to piss this guy off, 'what do you want? If it's about—'

'The Koekoeken,' finished Wolfspin. He had pushed the door further open now and was easing himself into the hallway. Gregory noticed again how bulky he was; he made the space look narrow as he shouldered his way in, blocking the light.

'I don't do that stuff any more,' Gregory told him. 'The group has folded. The forum's been deleted.'

'I know,' said Wolfspin. 'That's why I'm here.'

Gregory rubbed his chin nervously. He heard the door close behind Wolfspin, shutting out the street. Now the only light came from the floor above, seeping down the staircase. He wished he could see the visitor's face.

'Look . . .' he began again.

Perhaps Wolfspin had detected his nervousness – realized that feeding it wasn't going to help him get what he wanted. He remained where he was, not trying to invade Gregory's personal space any more than he had, and when he spoke his voice was softer, almost affable.

'Gregory,' he said. 'Or would you rather Ringslang?'

'Gregory is fine. But—'

'I just need five minutes of your time, Gregory. I'm trying to contact someone. A former member.' A regretful tone came into Wolfspin's voice. 'And now the forum has gone . . .'

It entered Gregory's head to tell Wolfspin that he'd deleted all his own records too. Although the big man hadn't done anything that you could really call threatening, he gave Gregory the creeps. It was debatable whether Wolfspin's desire to locate whatever person he was after was going to be reciprocated. Still – *five minutes*. It was probably worth giving up the time to get this guy out of the block and back onto the street.

Gregory thought that after Wolfspin had left, he might email the person the big man was looking for and just mention the fact. He was confident he would have their details; he'd deleted the forum all right but he hadn't wiped any of the information from his own private records. You never knew when something like that might come in handy

– like now, when it was going to get Wolfspin off his back.

'OK,' he said reluctantly. 'You'd better come up.'

He turned and led the way back up the stairs to his flat. He was conscious of Wolfspin's heavy tread behind him. Gregory looked at the closed doors of his neighbours' flats as he passed them, but there was still no sign of life – no strip of yellow light under the door, no muffled sounds of voices or music playing.

They reached the open door of Gregory's flat.

Gregory turned, and for the first time he saw Wolfspin properly – not just the shape of the man outlined against the yellow light of the streetlamps. He couldn't help himself: he recoiled.

Gregory swallowed, his mouth dry. Suddenly he was very sure that he didn't want Wolfspin inside his flat; that it had been a mistake even to open the door. At the same time he dared not let his nervousness show. He didn't want Wolfspin to see his fear. Instinctively he felt that the big man would take advantage of it. He entered the flat, and Wolfspin followed. The door closed with crisp finality.

Gregory found that he didn't like having his back to Wolfspin. He led the way down the hall, half turning all the time, as though to check that the big man was following him, that he hadn't got lost somewhere.

The flat had two bedrooms, and Gregory used one of them as his work space. He paused at the doorway, hinting that Wolfspin should stay out in the hallway while he, Gregory, searched for the information he wanted.

'Who are you looking for?' he asked.

Wolfspin was looking past him, into the confined space of

the room, as though he thought whoever it was might actually be hiding in there. Then his head turned and he looked at Gregory, his eyes as dark and expressionless as a shark's.

'Kris Verstraeten. The one who called himself Schorpioen. And Honingbij – whatever her real name is.'

Schorpioen and Honingbij. Gregory knew who they were the moment he heard the names, though he did his best not to let the knowledge show on his face. Kris Verstraeten, yes, and Veerle De Keyser. He remembered those names because he'd heard them repeatedly on Fred's lips, along with a lot of angry and frightened invective. They were the two who'd rattled Fred so badly he'd had the Koekoeken website closed down.

'That's two people,' said Gregory carefully.

'Yes.'

Gregory felt that he should challenge Wolfspin, that he should ask him why he was so keen to get hold of Kris Verstraeten and Veerle De Keyser, if he wasn't close enough even to know both their real names. But he looked at Wolfspin and he couldn't do it. Looking at Wolfspin made him feel cold all over; it made his palms clammy with perspiration. He thought he would give the man what he wanted, thus shunting the problem onto Kris and Veerle – regrettable for them, but at least he could give them some advance warning. He would email them as soon as Wolfspin had gone, and let them know who was looking for them. Then he would forget any of this had happened. If the door-bell went at eleven p.m. again, he would ignore it.

'I'll have to look in my records,' he said to Wolfspin. He

could hear the unevenness in his own voice and inwardly cursed himself. 'You want – what? – email addresses?'

'Email addresses, real names, home addresses, everything,' said Wolfspin.

'I don't think I have home addresses,' Gregory started to tell him, but Wolfspin was already turning away, scanning the hallway in an insolent manner as though hoping to find somewhere comfortable to lounge while Gregory got him what he wanted.

Gregory went into the room, relieved at any rate that Wolfspin wasn't coming in with him and hanging over his shoulder the entire time, as he had quite expected him to do. The thought of coming into closer physical proximity with Wolfspin was repugnant, and it wasn't just the way he looked. There was a wrongness, an *otherness*, about the big man that made him want to cringe. He wondered again what on earth Kris and Veerle had done to make Wolfspin so very eager to find them.

He went over to his workstation and pushed the wireless mouse with his fingertips so that the iMac sprang into life. Then he began to click his way through files, looking for the one with the list of Koekoeken members. What had he named it? Something innocuous, because you could never be too careful . . .

Gregory located the file and opened it. As he had tried to say, it was a list of usernames, real names and email addresses. No home addresses. All the same, he knew where a few of them came from, more or less, simply because everybody was ultimately joined to everyone else. To be accepted as a member of the Koekoeken, you'd had to be put forward by two existing members. Gregory knew nothing about Veerle De Keyser beyond a web-based email address and her name, but he knew that Kris Verstraeten came from Overijse. He clicked again to print the list.

Now that Gregory had found the list, his attention disengaged from the iMac and he began to wonder what Wolfspin was doing. A glance over his shoulder showed an empty doorway, so the big man wasn't waiting there. Then he heard a sound from the little kitchen that was diagonally across the hallway. It was a familiar sound, a distant clash like percussion. Wolfspin had pulled out the kitchen drawer, with some force.

What the fuck—?

Gregory tried half-heartedly for indignation, but all he was feeling was a sudden and terrible dread. His mind was skittering across the contents of that kitchen drawer with the same speed as Wolfspin's strong fingers were undoubtedly rummaging through them. He wasn't worried about the spatula or the wooden spoon or even the corkscrew. What he was thinking about was the knives.

He pushed back his chair and got to his feet, not forgetting to rip the printed list out of the printer tray, with some idea of placating Wolfspin by presenting it to him.

Before he got to the doorway, Wolfspin was in it. Gregory's gaze slid from that terrible face to the fist that held the longest and sharpest of the kitchen knives. Dread exploded into terror. Gregory stumbled backwards, almost falling over the chair.

'Hey,' he said weakly. 'What are you doing? There's no need for that.'

The sheet of printed names escaped from his fingers and drifted to the floor between them. Gregory stood frozen, his back to the chair and the desk, and watched Wolfspin stoop to pick it up.

'No street addresses,' said Wolfspin, and his voice was as grim as the fall of an executioner's axe.

'I don't have them,' gabbled Gregory. 'Just the email addresses and the names. The girl, Honingbij, her name is Veerle De Keyser. That's all I can tell you.'

'That's not enough.' Wolfspin came closer, and the knife came up; he moved the blade from side to side, so that the light from the desk lamp flashed golden on the metal and ran up the wall like the flight of vermin.

'It's all I know,' pleaded Gregory. He was so terrified that he thought he might fall down, or even pass out, and then what would Wolfspin do to him with that knife? 'Look,' he said desperately, 'it's Fred you want, not me.' He didn't care whether he was dropping his friend in it or not; at that moment he would have offered his own mother to Wolfspin if he had thought it would keep that brutal triangle of steel away from his flesh. 'I just did the techie stuff. Fred's the one who had to approve everyone who joined. Fred knows far more about it than I do. Ask Fred. I can give you his address – his number—'

'I *have* asked Fred,' said Wolfspin. He studied the blade. 'He couldn't give me the addresses.'

Gregory stared at him then – at those cold dead eyes that were like holes punched into the cover of some black and stinking oubliette. Fred was dead. He *knew* that. Wolfspin had visited him, wanting the same information he was trying to get from Gregory, and now Fred was dead.

'Please,' said Gregory, and found that he was weeping with fear. 'I don't *have* any addresses, not for anyone. If I did, I'd give them to you. I'll tell you everything I can.'

'I know you will,' said Wolfspin as he closed in.

3

It was evening when Veerle De Keyser returned to the house where she had grown up. It was mid-August, just over a year since she had left it, and at past eight p.m. the sun had still not set. The great bulk of the medieval Sint-Pauluskerk with its high tower threw a long shadow parallel to the street. Each of the tall marble grave markers threw its own shadow too, a long dark streak against the yellowing grass, as though each one carried its own trail in its slow progress from past to future.

Veerle was alone. She had come from Ghent by train and then by tram and finally by the local bus, carrying a single small case that had wheels so that she could pull it along when she had to walk.

Her father, Geert, had offered to drive her down. This was unlike Geert; he was so direct himself that generally it was enough to say something to him once – you didn't need to labour the point, and neither did he. All the same, even though they had agreed that Veerle would travel on her own, at the last minute Geert had asked her again. Wouldn't she prefer it if he drove her? Wouldn't she prefer—?

Geert had stopped there, as though he had caught himself

18

about to say something hurtful, and in a way Veerle thought perhaps it would have been. She couldn't stay in Ghent. Even if Anneke, Geert's girlfriend, hadn't made her promise to go, she would have done so.

Veerle thought that if she had confided in Geert, and told him about the promise Anneke had extracted from her, he would have released her from it. He would have been angry about Veerle's repeated truancy, which Anneke had covered up for her in exchange for her agreement to leave, but that would probably have been a drop in the ocean compared to the other things he already knew about, such as Veerle's being embroiled in a *murder* case, and the fact that she had dismally failed to obtain her ASO diploma from school. The trouble was, he would also have been very angry with Anneke. Veerle couldn't see a happy outcome to a scenario where she continued to live with her father and his girlfriend after dropping a bomb like that into the situation. If Anneke had been out to get Veerle before, now it would be open warfare.

That wasn't the only thing, though. Veerle had begun to feel like a human lightning rod, attracting trouble wherever she went, bringing it down on the heads of those around her. She wanted to reboot her life, to reset it to two years earlier, before the Koekoeken, before the fire in the old castle, before the move to Ghent and everything that had happened there. Before Kris Verstraeten.

Do I really wish I'd never met him again? she had asked herself, sitting on the train from Gent-Sint-Pieters to Brussel-Zuid, her eyes still damp from the parting with Geert. She looked into her own heart, but she might as well have been looking down a bottomless well; she had no idea what the answer was.

Moving back to the village, to the house on Kerkstraat, was drawing a line under all of it.

She couldn't entirely slot back into her old life, of course. She would be living alone in the house she had shared with her mother. Her old friends from high school would have completed their studies and left. But that, Veerle thought, was for the best in some ways. There was at least some hope of her passing unnoticed. She would go back to school and re-take her final year, and this time she *would* get the diploma she needed to go on to college or university. She would keep house for herself in the place on Kerkstraat, she would study hard, she would visit Ghent occasionally. Geert wasn't the only one there, after all. There was also Bram, the boy she'd met while she lived in the city – the boy who'd taken her up onto the rooftops and shown her a completely different Ghent from the one thronged with shoppers and tourists. She wasn't entirely sure where she stood in relation to Bram. She knew what *he* wanted; he'd told her he loved her, after all, and in a moment of weakness she had said it back. But she'd never really rooted Kris Verstraeten out of her heart, and that had always stood in the way of her and Bram. Besides, getting her life back on track was the important thing now.

That was the plan, and it was the only practical one, and yet as she stood on the doorstep of her old home in the dying light and worked her key into a lock that was stiff with disuse, Veerle wished that she didn't feel so *empty*. She looked into the future and felt like a robot following a preordained track to complete a series of mechanical tasks.

The key turned at last, and she was able to push the door open. Her first impression was of coolness. The inside of the house was almost cold, in spite of the warm summer weather. The hallway, which had no windows, was also rather dark. The house smelled familiar, but there was a faded quality to the mixed scents of furniture polish and cleaning products, like the dead perfume of dried flowers.

Veerle dragged the bag inside and switched on the hall light.

Home.

It didn't really feel like it, although it wasn't as bad as it might have been. Most of the furnishings had been cleared out after Claudine's funeral, when Veerle moved to Ghent, but some of the larger items had remained, and Geert had supplemented them with plunderings from IKEA. He'd also had the boxes of Veerle's things that had come with her to his flat in Ghent delivered back to the house. Veerle was pretty sure that if she went into her old bedroom she'd find that stuffed rabbit on the bed again – the one her mother had persisted in putting back there, wherever Veerle hid it.

Veerle smiled a little sadly at the thought. *If the rabbit's there, she'll have won at last.*

She left her bag in the hall and wandered through the house, checking every room. Some had been mothballed altogether, because there wasn't enough furniture left to fill all of them: the dining room and her mother's bedroom were both empty, the shutters pulled down. In the bathroom, a faint stain had developed under a slowly dripping tap.

Veerle went into her own room last. She saw that Geert had gone to the trouble of making up the bed, or maybe he had asked someone else to come in – one of Claudine's friends, perhaps. As expected, the rabbit was propped up on the pillow. Veerle ignored it and went over to the window. The shutters were up but the window was closed, and the room was a little musty. She opened the window and leaned out, resting her arms on the sill.

From here you could see the church, and right into the graveyard – in fact you couldn't *avoid* seeing them; they took up most of the view. It hadn't bothered her when she was a child, having a bedroom that looked straight out onto a churchyard. In fact, sometimes she'd even gone in there to play, wandering around amongst the gleaming marble slabs and peering at the photographs in their oval frames. Her favourite picture was of a pretty young woman of about twenty-five. She'd been too young then to think about what they meant; about what death had done to the families of the people in the photos. At other times she had made chains out of the daisies that grew in the grass between the graves.

Veerle looked down from the window and tried to think about that; to see the Sint-Pauluskerk and the churchyard through a warm haze of nostalgia.

It wasn't working, though. She looked at the church in the dying light of the sun and suddenly the bell tolled once, marking the quarter-hour. In the cool evening air the sound had a brittle quality, as though it had shivered the silence into sharp fragments.

Such a familiar sound, and she'd almost forgotten it in her year away. There was only one day in the year when that bell didn't toll, and that was Silent Saturday, the day after Good Friday. And then the chain of thought led her inevitably to that Saturday eleven years before when she and Kris Verstraeten, then aged seven and nine respectively, had climbed the bell tower to see whether the myth was true – whether the bell had flown away to Rome.

She didn't *want* to think about that day. There was nothing pleasantly nostalgic in it at all. Nothing but horror. The bell had still been there, that was the first thing. So their parents and all the other adults in the village had lied. And then they had looked down from the tower and seen Joren Sterckx, the child killer, the child *hunter*, walking towards them with his victim in his arms. It was a horror that had been shared by the whole village; it was the worst day in the community's history.

The windowsill was cold under the bare skin of her wrists and hands. Veerle pulled her head in and closed the window. She was turning her back on the view over the churchyard when she felt her mobile phone vibrate in her jeans pocket.

Incoming email, she guessed. Geert, checking whether she'd arrived? Or Bram? Odd that, whichever it was, they hadn't simply phoned, but in a way she was grateful. She didn't feel like talking to anyone right now.

Veerle slid the phone out of her pocket and thumbed the screen. The message was from an address that began *gregoryverbruggen.*

Gregory? She was almost sure she didn't know anyone called Gregory. She wasn't even going to bother looking at the email, but then she saw the subject and for a few seconds she didn't do anything at all – didn't read the message, didn't delete it – just stared at the screen.

Koekoeken reunion.

So this Gregory, whoever he was, had to be one of them – the Koekoeken, the group she thought had been dissolved – and now that she thought about it, she was sure she'd heard a Gregory mentioned before. Hadn't he had something to do with setting up or running the Koekoeken? She supposed that was how he knew how to contact her, since the forum had long since been deleted.

It didn't matter who he was, though. Veerle had no intention of going to a reunion, or even of replying. The idea of it gave her an unpleasant hot skin-crawling feeling akin to guilt.

The Koekoeken thing is over. I have to get on with my life now.

Her thumb hovered over the tiny screen. She felt oddly upset at the intrusion into her life. Looking out of the window at the churchyard, she had felt a deep melancholy, but now she felt as though she had been got at. Still, it was tempting to read the message anyway, just to satisfy her curiosity.

Don't, she said to herself. *Don't look at it. Don't reply. The Koekoeken are history. You don't want to know.*

She made herself delete it without reading it.

4

The last week of August was warm and sunny. Veerle took the bus into the town, to the Administrative Centre, and re-registered as a local resident. The Centre was crowded with foreigners. In spite of the notice in the foyer advising every-one that all business had to be conducted in Dutch, most of them seemed to be trying in English or French.

Veerle listened in for a little while, but soon she became absorbed in her own thoughts, remembering the other times she had been in here with Claudine, her mother. Being here again didn't *hurt*, exactly. Losing her mother had been so terrible that she didn't think anything could actually make it *worse*. All the same, it was strange to be here alone. Now she could come in and do everything without translating any of it for anyone. In theory it was easier, but it still felt strange.

When she had finished she went to the little Carrefour super-market and bought food. That felt strange too. She could have bought nothing but croissants and Coke if she wanted, and lived on those. There was nobody to stop her.

Afterwards, walking up the street to the bus stop with both hands full of bags, she looked ahead to the corner and saw a young man with his back to her standing and talking into a mobile phone. He had unruly dark hair and a leather jacket, and for a moment she thought, *Kris.*

That was all she had time to think and feel: one pang of shock, not long enough for her to decide whether she was glad to see him or horrified. Then he turned, and she saw that of course it was not Kris at all. The face was heavy-jawed and slab-like, not sharp-boned and aquiline like Kris's.

Veerle walked up the street towards him and tried not to think about it; about whether she wished it was him or not. He had his back to her again now, talking urgently into the phone, but when she was almost level with him he swung round and gave her a casual unfriendly glance, as though he suspected her of trying to eavesdrop.

Veerle looked at his sullen, overfed face and wondered why she had thought even for a split second that he could possibly be Kris.

Because you wanted him to be?

She squashed that thought instantly. All the same, as she turned the corner and walked the last few metres to the bus stop, she was chewing her lip, thinking.

What if I do meet him?

No, she thought. *In all the years between the time his family left the village and the night I met him in the castle, I never saw him even once. There's no reason to think I'll ever run into him again. He lives in Overijse, after all.*

Veerle was barely at the bus stop when the familiar white-and-yellow De Lijn bus appeared, swinging its blunt nose round the tree that stood on the corner. She put down some of the bags and stuck out her arm.

The bus was the one that ran all the way to the airport. She paid and settled herself in a window seat, the sun hot on the side of her neck. She'd been on this bus the night she met Kris again. It had been a bad evening; she'd had an argument with someone at the climbing wall, an expat who'd had a go at Veerle's English without being able to speak a word of Flemish herself. It had ended with Bart, the owner of the wall, throwing Veerle out. She'd got on the bus in a furious mood, miserable and frustrated, realizing that she'd lost one of her only escape routes from the suffocating atmosphere at home. If it hadn't been for that row, she might not have done what she did. But she'd been at her wits' end.

The bus had stopped on a quiet stretch of road opposite an old and derelict castle. Veerle had looked out of the window into the dark, and seen a light burning there, where there should have been only black night. Before she really knew what she was doing, she had been off the bus and walking briskly across the castle grounds, determined to find out what the light was, set on adventure.

She had gone into the old castle, and what she had found inside was not a ghost, a phantom light, but Kris Verstraeten. And that was how it had all begun – joining the Koekoeken, the mysterious group who explored deserted buildings; visiting the opulent homes of absent expats; finally confronting a killer who was stalking the explorers for his own sadistic amusement. It had all stemmed from that moment. If she had not had the row with Bart she would have been on a later bus – she would have been in a calmer mood and might not have leaped off like that, drunk with frustration and anger.

And now? Veerle wondered. *If the same thing happened now, would I still get off the bus and investigate?*

As if in answer to her silent question, she felt her mobile phone vibrate in her pocket. When she pulled it out and read the name *gregoryverbruggen* again, it was all she could do not to throw the phone the length of the bus. She felt a kind of sudden and horrified repulsion, as though she had caught someone stalking her.

What, is he reading my mind?

She forced the feeling down. Pure coincidence, that was all it was – pure coincidence that she'd been thinking about the Koekoeken just before the email came in. Then she read the email subject: *You need to contact me now.*

No, I don't, she said to herself. She looked at the words again and wondered whether to read the message, in case there really *was* something she needed to know. But she couldn't think of one good reason why a member of the Koekoeken whom she had never met would be ordering her to contact him. As for bad reasons . . . *Don't go there*, she told herself sternly. *Don't read it, don't get sucked in. You're not doing that stuff any more, remember?*

It wasn't any use, though. She'd made herself delete the first email without reading it, but she couldn't withstand the gnawing of curiosity twice. Veerle thumbed the little icon to open the email.

It read: *You need to get in touch now. This is happening. You could be next.*

There was a picture attached. On the screen it was tiny, a pattern of dark and light that at first made no sense. Then Veerle saw that it was a hand, the flesh bleached white by flash – or was it entirely the flash that gave it that unnatural pallor? The lower surfaces had an ominous purplish tint, the colour of bruises, as though the blood had pooled there. There were fragments of other things too – some kind of untidy-looking plant frond and a chunk of stone or perhaps concrete. The dark patches did not dwell only in the shadows. Something that appeared almost black in the photograph was splattered and smeared onto the ragged leaves and the rough stone; it had run between the upturned fingers and dried there, leaving a black residue like tar.

A dead hand, thought Veerle, and something seemed to fall away beneath her; her stomach lurched nauseatingly. She exited the email as though the sight of that photograph could somehow infect her, and before she thought about what she was doing she had deleted it. She stuffed the phone back into her pocket and stared out of the bus window, trying to tell herself that it was just a stupid prank. But her heart was thumping.

Later, when she was home at the house on Kerkstraat, standing in the kitchen and quenching her thirst with a long draught of iced tea, Veerle tried to rationalize what she had seen.

A hand. Just a hand. Anyone could have taken a photo like that. That stuff that was splashed around all over the place could be fake blood or paint or anything. Tomato ketchup. Or maybe it's just a still from some stupid film.

She wasn't really convincing herself.

There was the message too. *You need to get in touch now. This is happening. You could be next.* On the face of it, Gregory was warning her of something. But what? The first message, the one she'd deleted without reading, had been titled

Koekoeken reunion. But the Koekoeken no longer existed. When she'd got home she'd booted up her laptop and run an online search for www.koekoeken.be, but nothing had come up. The group hadn't been mysteriously resurrected. Even if it had, under some other name, she had nothing to do with it. All Gregory could possibly have was her name and the email address he had written to.

A prank, she thought. But it wasn't funny. It wasn't even just stupid, a joke that had fallen flat. It was ominous. *This is happening*. That wasn't the same as saying, *Someone is doing this*. It didn't exclude the possibility that the writer was responsible. And *You could be next* could be read as an actual threat.

Don't reply, Veerle told herself. *If he's trolling you, replying will just encourage him.*

She wished she could have discussed it with someone, but the only person was Kris, and she hadn't talked to him for months, not since she stopped taking his calls.

Ignore. And if he does it again, block his emails.

She did her best to put the incident out of her mind, but when her mobile phone suddenly rang she almost jumped out of her skin. She looked at the little screen with trepidation.

It said *Bram De Wulf*.

Relieved, Veerle thumbed the green button and put the phone to her ear.

'Hi, Bram.'

'Hi,' said Bram's voice in her ear. 'Are you at home?'

'Yes,' said Veerle. She took another swig of the iced tea, looking out of the kitchen window towards the church, its grey stone walls golden in the sunshine.

'How is it?'

'It's OK,' Veerle told him. *Apart from the creepy emails.* She tried to push that to the back of her mind.

'That's good,' said Bram. After a moment he added, 'I'd like to come down and see the place.'

'Well . . .' began Veerle, and then she wasn't sure what to say. She was conscious of the seconds slipping past while her mind freewheeled, failing to gain traction on the issue. Bram would be noticing her hesitation. She said, 'I should get the first few days of school over.'

Veerle didn't miss the brief silence before Bram replied. She wondered what he was thinking, wishing she had said something more enthusiastic.

'That's why I rang,' said Bram smoothly. 'First day back is tomorrow, right?'

'Monday,' said Veerle, relieved to be back on safe territory.

'You ready?'

'I suppose,' said Veerle. She added, 'How's Ghent?'

'Come back for a weekend and you can see for yourself.' Maybe Bram realized that he was not going to get the reply he was hoping for, because he hurriedly went on, 'It's still hot. Sunny. Still full of tourists.'

'Do you still go up on the rooftops and watch them wandering around photographing everything with their digital cameras?' asked Veerle. She hadn't missed much from her life in Ghent but she had loved being up on the rooftops with Bram. It had been the one place that really had felt like home.

'Yeah,' said Bram. 'It was more fun when you were there, though.'

Veerle felt a sudden rush of warmth towards him.

He gets it, she thought. The need to step sideways out of everyday life, to get away from people who never wanted anything from you or themselves but safety – safety, duty and boredom. The need to surf for a while on the crest of a wave of adrenalin. To *live*. She thought she could stand any amount of graft, catching up with missed schoolwork, just so long as she could have a few stolen moments like that.

Then she thought about those emails, the ones from Gregory Verbruggen, and her mood went from warm to cold in an instant. *I'm not doing that stuff any more. It's trouble, and I've had enough of that.*

She chatted for a few minutes more and then she said, 'Bram, I should go. I'm sorry, I've got loads to do before Monday.'

'You'll come to Ghent soon, though? Look, I know you want to get back into school, but how about one weekend after that?'

'Um . . . maybe.'

'I'll take that as a yes. OK, I've got to go too. Love you.'

Veerle let out a pent-up breath. 'Me too.'

That was safe; it wasn't really saying *I love you* but it wasn't *not* saying it, either. She thumbed the red button to end the call. Then she stood there for a while, still staring out of the window at the church.

I've got loads to do.

The rest of the day was empty.

5

The man with the knife was waiting in the deep shadows at the side of a building, looking across the street, where the light from the streetlamps tinted everything amber. The light was a nuisance; it created a wide border around the building he was aiming for, like a moat he was required to swim across, with the arrows of potential glances falling all about him.

In the end, though, there was nothing for it but to move. No car had passed down the street for the past twenty-three minutes, and he hadn't seen a pedestrian for much longer than that. The town was sleeping.

Still, he pulled the hat low over his eyes, and kept his head down as he crossed the road. Anyone who did happen to gaze sleeplessly from an upstairs window would be able to give no better description than a *tall, broad-shouldered man in a dark coat*. The knife was out of sight, nestled close to his body.

He had to damage the street door a little to get inside the building. Luckily there was no deadbolt. It was a matter of weighing up the relative risks of someone inside the building hearing him and someone coming down the street and seeing him. He worked quickly, and soon he was inside, moving cautiously towards the staircase, listening for the telltale sounds of someone waking up and considering whether to investigate. There was nothing.

It went against the grain for him to creep about like this, like a craven thief in the night. He would have liked to descend upon his target like a berserker, to obliterate him.

All in good time, he reminded himself.

Slowly he ascended the staircase to the first floor. There was a timed light switch on the wall at the bottom, with an illuminated button in the middle to show its location, but he didn't touch it. There was just enough of that amber light coming through the front windows for him to see his way. He counted twelve steps, and then he was on the small first-floor landing.

There were two doors, one on either side, and an expanse of wall between them adorned with a spray of pressed flowers in a frame. There were brass flat numbers on the doors, a *3* to the left and a *4* to the right.

He stood there for a moment, listening, and when he was satisfied that nobody was stirring, he went to the right.

There was a tiny nameplate on the centre of the door, underneath the brass number. He took a miniature torch from his pocket and trained the tiny beam on the name. It was the same as the one downstairs next to the fourth buzzer button from the top. He had checked that one, casually, a week before.

Verstraeten, Kris.

The man with the knife – whose name was not applied as crudely as an address label but instead described what he was – De Jager; *the Hunter* – leaned close to the door and placed his cold cheek and ear against the polished wood. There was no sound of movement from inside flat number four.

He drew back and studied the lock. Fortunately for him – although not for the apartment's occupant – it was a simple pin tumbler lock. There was no deadbolt. He was not much concerned about whether there was a chain on the other side; as well as the knife he had lightweight bolt cutters inside the coat.

De Jager took out a bump key and a screwdriver. He glanced around once but there was no sign that anyone was awake; no telltale line of yellow light under either apartment door. He slid the key carefully into the lock, withdrew it a little, and then struck it sharply with the handle of the screwdriver, and the door opened.

There was no chain, which was foolish, although it wouldn't have slowed him down much anyway.

He waited silently for several moments to see whether anyone in apartment number four, or possibly in number three on the other side of the landing, was stirring. Still nothing.

He pushed the door open with a gloved hand, far enough to reveal the dim outline of a hallway. A faint and mottled light spilled out from a doorway to the right: the yellow glare of a streetlamp, filtered through lace kitchen curtains, he surmised. Swiftly he stepped inside and drew the door closed behind him.

The hall had some kind of hard flooring that gleamed slightly where the light touched it, but there was a runner in the centre, and he stepped onto that to muffle his footsteps.

The apartment could not have more than two bedrooms.

From where he stood, sliding a hand into the dark carapace of the coat to retrieve the knife, he could dimly make out five doorways. Kitchen, bathroom, sitting room, and two bedrooms, or perhaps one bedroom and a study. There was nothing to suggest that *Verstraeten, Kris* shared the apartment with any other person – the girl, Veerle, for example – but all the same De Jager proceeded with care; two sets of ears might pick up what one set slept through.

He passed the door through which the light spilled, and saw that his surmise was correct. It was the kitchen, the surfaces untidily loaded with the detritus of bachelor living. His nostrils flared, taking in a faint aroma of stale cooking that made his lip curl. There was something animalistic about it, as though the apartment's occupant were some rough creature slumbering amidst the bones of its last feast. It would not even be a pleasure to kill him; it would be like putting down an unwanted animal. First, though, he would get the girl's address, even if he had to carve it out of Kris's brain with the knife.

Opposite the kitchen was a room so small it was hardly a bedroom, more of a cupboard. No one slept there; it contained a cheap desk and chair. A closed laptop slumbered under the craning neck of an angle-poise lamp.

He didn't get as far as the fourth and fifth rooms. The second room on the left was the main bedroom. The door had been left confidently open. The roller shutters were down. If they had been completely closed, the room would have been pitch dark and there would have been no way to pick out anything inside it without his torch, but they had not been lowered to their full extent. There were still spaces between the slats, each of them pierced with a series of little round holes, so that the light from outside was projected across the room in strings of yellow dots. They ran across the bed as though chaining the occupant into it.

De Jager's flesh was absolutely cool and dry where it grasped the handle of the knife. He wasn't perspiring at all.

There was a large rug covering most of the floor in this room and he stepped onto it with care, approaching the bed with the knife raised like the blade of a guillotine poised to descend. He wanted to see Kris lying there, defenceless in sleep. He wanted to see the dark hair, the aquiline nose, the sharp lines of his cheekbones, the dark eyes sealed in slumber. The eyes had seen too much. Perhaps when he had finished with Kris he would carve them out altogether.

The thought seemed to run like a nerve impulse from his brain to his hand and into the knife, so that the tip of it shivered with the desire to cut.

However, there was no time to relish that moment of gazing upon his victim. De Jager didn't make a sound, not so much as a sigh or the tiniest creak of a floorboard, but Kris Verstraeten woke up all the same. Perhaps some deep instinct, the sixth sense that makes a watched animal aware of scrutiny, alerted him. He started, as though an electrical current had passed through him, and then began to sit up, his right hand tightening on the bedcover as he made to throw it back.

He never completed the gesture. De Jager was on him like a tiger, launching himself bodily onto the bed. He had intended that Kris should wake with a knife at his throat, that he should spill all the information De Jager needed before dying, but now Kris had woken prematurely and his reactions were fast, considering that he had been roused from sleep. He fought back, understanding that he was fighting for his life, and subduing him was taking more force than anticipated.

At last De Jager succeeded in kneeling on Kris's chest, crushing the breath out of his lungs. His eyes were adjusting to the almost-darkness now and he could see the stricken face staring up at him, the gaze taking him in. He stared back, for a long moment. Then the knife swept swiftly and brutally from left to right, and arterial spray fanned across the wall behind the bed.

When he had finished and backed away from the bed, breathing heavily, the hacked thing lying on it amongst the twisted covers was still and wet. De Jager went over to the window and closed the shutters completely, and then back to the doorway and switched on the main light.

He was drenched with the crimson effluent of Kris Verstraeten's dying.

6

Victor was twelve and he had his first packet of cigarettes in his pocket. He also had a lighter, a plastic one. Victor had swiped the lighter from the display behind the till in the little Carrefour supermarket in Tervuren, the same one Veerle had visited for her groceries. He had bought a packet of sweets, the cheapest he could find, just a few cents, and when he handed over the change to the girl on the till he had deliberately dropped some of it. While she was fishing it off the floor underneath the cash register he had grabbed the nearest lighter. By the time she sat up, looking at Victor with no very good grace, he was smiling apologetically and the lighter was safely in the pocket of his shorts.

He'd stolen the pack of cigarettes from his stepfather. He'd been watching for an opportunity for a while. No use taking them from the coffee table in the sitting room or the cluttered spot on the kitchen work surface where he sometimes dumped them along with his car keys. It would be too obvious that someone in the house – namely Victor – had taken them.

This morning, however, while his stepfather was still in bed, no doubt snoring like a pig, Victor had gone into the little front garden with some vague idea of shooting passing cars with his water pistol, and had looked through the driver's side window of the car and seen the cigarettes sitting forgotten on the dashboard. A quick glance at the upstairs front window showed that the shutters were still down. Victor went swiftly and silently back into the house and lifted his stepfather's car keys from the kitchen. A minute and a half later the keys were back where they had been and the cigarettes were in Victor's pocket.

He hadn't smoked any of them right away, of course. Far too risky. He'd hidden them until after lunch, when he had to go out with the Scouts, and then he'd slipped them into the side pocket of his shorts. By that time his stepfather had stopped cussing about his lost cigarettes and gone out to buy some more.

It was his stepfather who'd suggested the Scouts in the first place. Victor wasn't keen. It was a little too energetic and group-focused. Victor's idea of a good time was to slip off somewhere with a single trusted friend and make some serious mischief – like the time they'd set fire to some bins behind the chip shop. But Victor's stepfather thought he ought to be doing something hearty and boyish (ignoring the fact that there were girls in the troop too), or maybe he just wanted to get Victor out of the house more often.

Anyway, here he was, dressed in knee-length shorts and the despised beige shirt, high-stepping his way determinedly through the undergrowth. All the other Scouts had dispersed to other parts of the woodland that adjoined Tervuren park. They were working in little groups, because they had to share the limited number of GPS units. Victor didn't have a GPS unit but he didn't care. The rest of them were looking for a couple of geocaches hidden in the park, but Victor didn't care about those, either. He was going to find a quiet place amongst the trees and smoke as many of the cigarettes as he could.

Here. He squatted down, feeling for the pack, but he never got as far as taking them out of his pocket.

Shit, he thought, looking at the thing that was sitting under the nearest tree, half hidden by overhanging weeds. If he wasn't mistaken, it was a geocache – the exact thing the rest of the Scouts were currently hunting for. A small, heavy-duty plastic box with a clip-on lid, the contents cocooned in a plastic bag for additional protection from damp. The GPS co-ordinates of all the geocaches were recorded on the geocaching website. Entering the co-ordinates into your GPS unit told you more or less where each geocache was, but actually *finding* it was the fun part – assuming you were into that stuff. Sometimes the geocache would be large and relatively easy to locate, but others were tiny or camouflaged, and then it was a whole lot more challenging. Once you'd found the geocache you opened it and signed the logbook, and you could take something out, so long as you had something to put in to replace it.

Victor eyed the box with disgust. That was an end to his plans. If one of the geocaches was here, it could only be a matter of time before this part of the woods was swarming with eager Scouts. He put out a hand and tipped the box towards him.

Now that he'd found the thing, he might as well open it, he decided. If there was anything worth having, better that he, Victor, got it than one of the others. He wasn't going to replace it, though. What could he have put in there anyway? A plastic lighter and a packet of cigarettes were the only things in his pockets and he wasn't donating either of those.

Victor picked up the box with both hands and worked at the clip with his thumbs until it popped up. Then he put it down on the ground and lifted the lid.

It didn't look like a very interesting geocache. He couldn't see a log book, just the little bundle swathed in plastic. Perhaps the log was simply a roll of paper buried somewhere inside that. Victor fished it out of the box and began to pull off the rustling layers.

Even before he got to the thing that had been so carefully wrapped, Victor began to have misgivings. It felt odd; he couldn't quite have said why, except that he was having problems working out what it was that he was unwrapping. Then the smell reached his nostrils, faint at first but growing stronger with every turn of the plastic he unwound from it. He wondered whether someone had actually been stupid enough to put a *sausage* inside the geocache. Then he saw what was inside the wrapping, and for a single instant he really *did* think that was what they had done. A second later he realized what he was holding, and dropped it on the ground.

He looked at the thing, studied it until his eyes grew round and his mouth twisted in disgust.

All the same, Victor was made of stern stuff. After he had recovered from his initial shock, he began to see the possibilities of his find. Although he considered it uncool to run around in a pack with the other Scouts, panting like a dog in his enthusiasm to be first to find a geocache, he could see very plainly that this discovery was going to make him something of a celebrity.

A few minutes later he was haring through the woods, hurdling clumps of weeds in his zeal to find some of the other Scouts and lead them back to the spot where the thing still lay nestled in long strands of grass.

A further forty minutes passed before the Scout master, searching with slight stirrings of anxiety for his vanished flock, found most of the Scouts clustered around the gnarled tree trunk, staring at something on the ground. Some of them were chattering excitedly and nudging each other; others stood silently staring with their knuckles pressed to their mouths. The vegetation was trampled almost flat for perhaps three metres around the epicentre of their attention.

The Scout master approached and saw a plastic box upended on the ground, and next to it a crumpled plastic bag. He barked a few irritable words at the nearest Scouts; it was fifteen minutes after the time at which they should have returned to the start point, after all. Then he stepped close to the plastic bag and looked down.

Nestled on the crumpled folds like a peculiarly unappealing takeaway item was a human finger. Judging from its appearance and the unappetizing odour that seeped upwards from it, insinuating itself into the Scout master's unwilling nostrils, it had been separated from its owner for some time.

The Scout master ordered all the Scouts to move away

from the putrefying item on the ground, and called the police, but it was plain that little evidence was to be gathered from the scene. Not only was the vegetation trampled flat but the plastic box later proved to have fourteen different sets of fingerprints on it – all of them Scout-sized.

7

A group of four sat inside the derelict theatre, among the skeletal remains of padded seats and the mouldering rags of crimson velvet curtains. It was not the same four who had met in the tunnel. The big man, Thomas, was there; fox-faced Zoë was not, nor Maxim or Ruben.

They sat in the near-dark. A little light filtered in from the street outside, and besides, lighting a fire in here would have been risky, both for fire and for detection, so they didn't bother. Two of them smoked, the cigarette ends making tiny spots of glowing orange light. Those who were into photography had taken enough pictures, so now they were just sitting around chatting. Chatting, and retelling the urban legends that circulated amongst them like bad news.

'The Angel Smile, pah – heard that one a hundred times,' said the skinny one called Laurens.

Thomas didn't say anything.

The girl, Tina, took the cigarette from her lips with a swift sharp gesture. 'Have you seen the photograph?'

'What photograph?'

'The one they say is of the Angel Smile girl.' Tina held the cigarette away from her, staring at Laurens in the dark.

The other three felt so much as saw Laurens shrug. 'No.'

'It's on all the urbex websites. Well, it's all over the net, actually.'

'What does it show?' said Thomas in his flat voice.

Tina eyed him. 'Not much. A hand. And a load of – I don't know, weeds and old bricks and tiles. It could be anyone's hand. It's very pale, pretty much white, but that could just be the flash.'

'That's all?'

'Well, they say there's blood, but it looks kind of black. It could be oil or paint – or anything, really.'

Jonas said, 'I've seen that. It's crap. Anyway, if it were real the police would be onto it. There'd be something in the news.'

'Forget the Angel Smile,' said Laurens. He considered. 'Have you heard the one about the Burnt Guy, how he got burnt?'

'No,' said Jonas and Tina together. Thomas just shrugged.

'OK, well, this is definitely true, because I heard it from Zoë. Her cousin is in the police. Or maybe it was her friend's cousin, something like that. Anyway, it definitely happened.'

'It always *definitely happened*,' said Tina ironically.

'You want to hear it or not?'

'OK,' she said coolly. She touched the cigarette to her lips again.

'Well, there was this derelict castle not all that far from Brussels. It was hundreds of years old and nobody had actually lived in it for ages so it was just shut up. The door was locked and some of the windows were shuttered. The castle was in the middle of quite large grounds, and all the trees and grass had grown up around it. Everybody had pretty much forgotten it was there.

'Only sometimes people went in there. Not thieves, because there was nothing much left to take. Tramps, looking for a place to spend the night. Or people like us, exploring for the hell of it.'

'And sitting around telling stories.'

'Yeah. Anyway, there was this one couple who liked to go there quite often; I don't know why.'

'We can guess why, Laurens,' said Tina, snickering.

'Yeah, well, whatever. They used to go there quite a bit, and now and again they'd find stuff, like an empty bottle or something, but they never thought anything of it. They just thought it was other people poking around, like they were. They didn't know that someone was watching the place, just biding his time.

'The guy who was doing the watching was an escaped murderer and he was just waiting for a chance to pick them off in turn. You see, ordinarily they both turned up together, and then it was too risky. If he killed one, the other might have got away and raised the alarm. So he just kept watching them, and waiting for the day when they arrived at different times. Then he'd kill whoever arrived first, and leave the body lying in the hall, where the other one would find it. That was his plan, you see. He wanted the second one to come in and find their loved one, their girlfriend or boyfriend, dead on the floor. He was going to savour the moment, let them see what he'd done, before he killed them too.

'For ages he didn't get a chance. They always arrived

together, or one right after the other. Then one day the girl got held up somewhere and came late.

'The boy turned up at the castle at the agreed time. He had no reason to suspect anything. The girl was not outside the door waiting, but he didn't think anything of that. He went inside to see if she was already there. When he couldn't see her, he started calling her name. He didn't realize that the murderer was in there, armed with a meat knife and a crossbow. Standing in the middle of the hall shouting some-one's name was the worst possible thing he could have done. He never even knew what hit him. The crossbow bolt struck him with so much force that it almost went right through him. There was this much of it sticking out of his back.'

Laurens held up both hands, perhaps twenty centimetres apart.

'He was horribly wounded, but he wasn't dead, not yet. The murderer came out and kicked him a bit, and when he saw that the bolt hadn't killed the boy he was going to shoot him again, at point-blank range. But then he started to think that it might be more fun for the girl to come and find her boyfriend actually dying. She wouldn't run because she'd want to help him. Maybe he would come out and show him-self, let her see him striding towards her with the loaded crossbow. She'd have to make a decision then. Would she stay with the boyfriend, knowing that she was going to get a cross-bow bolt in the chest as well? Or would she make a run for it and try to save herself, knowing that she was leaving the guy to a horrible death? He thought this idea was just . . . sweet. He didn't care about their feelings. He didn't even understand them. He just liked the idea of watching her having to decide, like a kid torturing ants or something.

'So he went back to wherever he'd been hiding and waited. He'd got some petrol stashed there too, so that he could burn the evidence afterwards. He could do what he liked with them, and nobody would know because the most they'd ever find was bones, burnt black. Now he'd shot the guy and he was just waiting for the girl, so he went up and down the hall a few times with the petrol can and made sure everything was soaked.

'The problem was, the girl turned up when he was right at the other end of the hall. She had more sense than the boyfriend. She didn't walk in and start shouting the place down. Instead, she crept in quietly and had a look around. There was the boy, lying on the floor with this great long crossbow bolt sticking right through him, and blood spreading out around him.

'She clapped her hand to her mouth but she didn't scream. If she had, the murderer would have been there in a second, and that would have been the end of them both. She knew he must be in there somewhere. Her boyfriend hadn't shot himself, so there must be someone lurking in the castle somewhere. So she started dragging the boy outside.

'It was risky doing that too, because every time the end of the crossbow bolt scraped on something, it was churning up the boy's insides like a spoon stirring cake dough. But what else could she do? So she dragged him out of the door, but then she heard the murderer coming.

'So she's crouching there outside, holding onto this unconscious guy with twenty centimetres of carbon rod sticking out of his back, and she knows she has about two seconds to decide what to do. It's just like the murderer wanted – she's having to make this really agonizing decision. Only she doesn't do what he thought she'd do. She doesn't decide between staying with the boyfriend and running for her life. She decides to go back into the castle. Basically she's running back into danger, not away from it.

'She was going to try to get the murderer away from the boy so that he could crawl away, if he hadn't bled to death by then. That was the plan. But once she was back in the castle she smelled the petrol. Then she knew what the murderer was planning. Quick as a flash it came to her. She ran for the staircase, thinking that if she got up to the top, she could drop a light down into all that petrol and burn the guy to a crisp. Then she'd climb out of a window and down the wall, or maybe climb out into one of the trees that were growing right next to the castle walls. Hell, maybe she'd just jump out and hope she didn't break her neck. Anything would be better than whatever the guy with the crossbow was planning.

'So she ran to the stairs and started up them, and the whole time she was waiting for a crossbow bolt to hit her, and fumbling in her pockets trying to find the matches. Meanwhile the murderer was running after her, and shit, he was fast. He was halfway up the stairs before she managed to drop the match.

'The girl heard the petrol go up with a great roar and ran for her life along the upstairs landing. She thought she could hear the murderer behind her, thundering over the floorboards, gaining on her all the time. He'd be mad now, boiling with rage, and if he caught her God only knew what he'd do to her. She didn't dare look round. She kept running until she ran out of places to run to. Then she darted into one of the rooms and slammed the door behind her, sliding the bolt across to lock it.

'There was only one way out. The girl opened the window and climbed out. Then she did her best to climb down the castle wall. She climbed part of the way, and then she slipped and fell. But she survived. And her boyfriend survived too, because someone had seen the fire in the old castle and called the emergency services.

'The murderer couldn't escape the inferno. When the girl bolted the door behind her, she shut off his only escape route. He died horribly, roasted to death in the flames that consumed the whole building. When the firemen were eventually able to enter the smoking ruins, they found his charred body amongst the blackened bricks and fallen beams. It was so badly burnt that it was impossible to identify it.

'So the murderer was dead, but that wasn't the end of him. Because he died in terrible pain and rage, his spirit couldn't move on. He wasn't tied to the old castle, either, because it had burnt to the ground. Instead, his angry ghost haunts dark lonely places. Places like this. He hides in the deep shadows, watching and waiting. Longing to kill.

'If you are in the wrong place at the wrong time, he will take you. The last thing you will ever see is his burnt face, the empty eye sockets charred and crumbling . . .'

At the end of Laurens' story there was a short silence. Tina drew heavily on her cigarette, so that the tip glowed redly in the dark. She let out a breath. Then she said, 'So the other stories about the Burnt Guy doing all this stuff – murdering people and so on – all that is supposed to have been done by a *dead* guy?'

Laurens caught the sarcastic tone in her voice, even if he couldn't see her face clearly. 'It's an urban legend, not a news flash,' he said defensively.

'Well, it's not scary if it couldn't really happen,' Tina told him coolly. 'And dead guys don't go round killing people.'

'You're right,' said Thomas, and all three of them looked at the dark patch amongst the darker shadows where the big man sat. 'It's not scary if it's a story about some dead man, a ghost. But,' he went on, 'that's not the real end of the story, you know.'

'That's what Zoë told me, and it was her cousin it came from. Or friend's cousin, or whatever,' said Laurens sullenly. 'What's with her, anyway? I haven't seen her recently.'

Nobody was interested in that.

'Whatever she told you, it was only half the truth,' said Thomas. He paused for a moment, judging whether he had their attention or not. Then he went on, 'It's true about the castle, and the man with the crossbow, although he had his own reasons for being there. He wasn't just some random maniac, but that story can wait for another time. But he *was* waiting for that particular couple, the girl and her boyfriend.

'The boy came first, as you said, and took a crossbow bolt in the shoulder. Then the girl came, and tried to drag him away. But there was not enough time, so she went back into the castle and confronted the killer. She thought she could hold him off by threatening to set light to the petrol on the ground floor, and escape through one of the upstairs windows. What she didn't know was that the man with the crossbow also had an escape route planned, and a safer one than throwing himself from an upstairs window. In one of the upstairs rooms there was a window that looked out directly onto an adjacent section of roof, and at the end of that it was only an arm's length to a great tree that stood close by.

'So he was not afraid to pursue her. In fact, it was not she who lit the petrol. He did it, so that it would be impossible for her to go back. The flames roared, leaping up the staircase after them, almost licking at their heels.

'The girl ran, and as you said, she bolted herself into one of the rooms and tried to climb out of the window and down the wall. In her haste she fell, but she survived, as did the boyfriend, exactly as you described.

'The killer lingered too long, battering at the bolted door. Nearly, very nearly, he left it too late to make his escape. The wooden floorboards were charring through from underneath; the air was thick with smoke. A section of floor gave way and the fire erupted up through the hole. It caught at him, like a persistent supplicant plucking at his sleeve. His clothing went up, turning a compact dark figure into a screaming, leaping column of flames.

'He threw himself onto the smoking boards and rolled over and over, but the damage was done. Only adrenalin enabled him to follow the escape route he had planned, out of the window, along the roof and into the tree. He fell rather than climbed down from its branches. His outer clothes were smoking rags, his exposed skin horribly burnt.

'Another minute in the flames and he would have died of his burns. As it was, he dragged himself painfully away into the darkness and lay for a long time like one dead.

'He awoke to agony. Only a superhuman will to live enabled him to move at all, to seek help. He went to a crooked doctor he knew, and bought his silence and healing with threats. Later, he killed the man to ensure that he never went back on his promise of secrecy. That was much later, however. It took the burns a long time to heal, and the scarring was terrible. His face was frightful to look at; his hands were claws. The skin was pink and shiny, as though fire still glowed within the tortured flesh.

'He could live with the disfigurement itself. He had no interest in appearing attractive to other people. However, his appalling looks meant that he could no longer pass un-noticed amongst the herd of humanity. Nobody would care to be alone with him; anyone who looked into that grisly face recoiled. Even those who were kind or sensitive enough to conceal their horror at his scars would never forget seeing them. Nobody could see him pass by or linger in some quiet spot without remembering him long afterwards. So his ability to hunt and kill was heavily curtailed.

'And he wanted revenge. He thought of the girl and her boyfriend. If they had behaved as they were supposed to, they would both be dead now, dead and burnt. Instead, they were both alive and recovering, and he was disfigured.

'That was not the only reason for wanting to hunt them down. Both of them had seen him. The girl had had a particularly clear view of his face. His face had changed since it went through the fire, that was true, but she knew what he had looked like before. She had given a name to his old face. If she were clever and persistent enough, she might unravel the secret of his identity and his whereabouts.

'So now he hunts them, *de verbrande kerel* – the Burnt Guy. He looks for them in all the forbidden places where people like them go – the railway tunnels, the deserted hospitals and derelict factories; places, in fact, like this abandoned theatre. Those he catches alone, he kills. It was he who killed the couple in the story of the Angel Smile. But so far he has not caught the two he is looking for. So his anger grows and he does not stop.

'Take care,' said Thomas grimly, 'that he does not catch *you.*'

After a moment Tina said, 'OK, that was better. That was . . . creepy.'

'You think it was better?' muttered Laurens resentfully. 'There were holes all over that story.'

'Like what?'

'Like, whose was the body they found in the burnt-out castle, if the killer got away?'

Tina clicked her tongue in irritation. 'There was no body if he survived.'

'Zoë said there was.'

'Yeah, well, she also said there was a dead guy wandering around killing people. She was just talking crap.'

'Well,' remarked Thomas in his calm authoritative voice, 'there *was* a body. That part of the story was true.'

Now he had everyone's attention again, even Laurens's. He really was an amazing storyteller, thought Laurens grudgingly. You could never really pick holes in his tales; he had an answer for everything, as though the whole thing had really happened and he'd been there.

All the same, he had to take the bait.

'So whose body was it, then?'

'A tramp's. Just someone with no name and no home. People like him passed through the old castle from time to time. It was somewhere dry to sleep – or drink.

'The man with the crossbow knew there was a risk of running into down-and-outs in the castle. He'd seen evidence of their occasional presence. Empty bottles, mostly. He wasn't interested in them. There was no sport in running down someone who could barely stand because of drink and neglect.

'The tramp died because of poor timing. He'd been asleep, or maybe dead drunk, in one of the ground-floor rooms, before the killer even arrived. Eventually he woke up, and lurched out into the hallway.

'The killer himself was at an upstairs window, watching the gate in the wall that ran around the castle grounds, waiting to see whether the girl and her boyfriend would arrive together or singly. He saw the boy slip through the gateway and start across the overgrown lawns. He was alone. So the killer slipped downstairs to lie in wait.

'Before he was halfway down the hall, the tramp came staggering out of one of the rooms. The killer didn't hesitate. He grabbed the man from behind and slashed his throat right across. Before the blood had stopped pumping, he had dragged the body into a room and closed the door. Then he hefted the crossbow and went to shoot the boy.

'You know what happened next. And when the castle had burnt to the ground, and the ruins were no longer too hot to enter, the body of the tramp was discovered, charred to blackened sticks.

'The girl had heard the killer's screams of pain, so she assumed that he had died, and since they had a body, the police assumed it too. But it was the wrong body. The real killer is still out there – hunting.'

'Neat,' said Jonas.

Laurens let out a sigh that might have expressed weariness, or perhaps disgust. He began to get to his feet, dusting down the front of his jeans with his hands. Everything felt gritty in these places. 'I've gotta go,' he said.

Tina was grinding out her cigarette very carefully on the bare metal skeleton of a chair. After a moment she said, 'Me too. You coming, Jonas?'

Thomas got up too. There was no point in anyone remaining behind. They had seen what there was to see, taken a few photographs, exchanged a few stories. It was time to go.

They went out the way they had come in, through a side door that led into an alley. It would look suspicious if four of them trooped out of the alleyway all at once, so Jonas and Tina went first, and Laurens waited behind with Thomas. He was still feeling resentful about the story.

My version was better, he said to himself.

Verdomme, but it was cold out here. He put his hands into his armpits. He said nothing to Thomas. They waited for Jonas and Tina to vanish from sight.

Laurens assumed that Thomas felt the same mild dislike for him that he felt for the big man. After all, why else would he deliberately show Laurens up, by supposedly improving on his story?

He was surprised, therefore, when Thomas said, 'Do you want to come on somewhere else?'

They were almost at the mouth of the alley. Yellow light streamed in from a streetlamp. Laurens looked up at the big man's face. It was smooth and impassive, like a head carved of alabaster.

Illogically, he found himself thinking of the killer in the story, with his features seared into ugly ridges and patches by fire. Perhaps it was the contrast between that imagined face and this unmarred one that made him think of it.

He was preparing to say *No, thanks* when Thomas patted the front of his own jacket with a hand that was as unblemished as his face.

'I've got some . . . stuff.'

Laurens squinted at him. For a second he considered the idea that the big man's interest in him was more than friendly. But he rejected it. He'd seen him once before, chatting up one of the girls. He probably just wanted to sell something.

Laurens said, 'What have you got?'

8

At the beginning of September Veerle went back to school. It was a little strange, getting ready on her own, leaving the house and locking the door behind her, walking to the bus stop. In some ways Ghent still felt real to her; this was like stepping back into a past much further away than a single year. It was familiar and yet not familiar. Here came the bus, with the same number and destination on it that it had always had, but the faces inside were different. Oh, she recognized some of the people who had been in the years below hers, but even then, there were changes. Someone had put on a growth spurt and looked much more than a year older; someone else had had long hair cut short in an elfin style. Kids who had still been messing around and giggling with their friends the last time she'd seen them were now doing their best to look cool and nonchalant.

Veerle pushed her way down towards the back of the bus but there was nowhere left to sit. She held onto one of the poles and stared out of the window, deliberately not making eye contact with anyone. The bus pulled away; she tightened her grip on the pole. She waited to see whether anyone would say anything, either to her or about her.

Nobody did, as far as she could tell. Veerle began to relax a little.

That was the pattern for the day. Her new form teacher welcomed her in a sympathetic but low-key way. Perhaps Geert had asked the staff not to make a fuss, given that there were so many things about her recent life best left undiscussed. Nobody took an excessive or prurient interest in her presence. Probably, Veerle realized, she was a half-familiar face to most of her classmates; they'd have seen her travelling on the bus when she last lived here. She was less interesting than a total stranger would have been. At the same time, those who had known her well enough to bombard her with questions, like her friend Lisa, had all moved on. Nobody asked her about her mother, about her year in Ghent, about why she had gone or why she had come back.

Veerle supposed that once she got to know people she'd have to make decisions about what she was going to say. That, however, was in the future. For the present she would concentrate on catching up with her schoolwork and letting life drop back into some kind of normal groove.

At lunch time she realized that she had been clenching her left hand while taking notes with her right one; the scar that ran across the palm was beginning to ache. She went into the girls' toilets and dry-swallowed one of the over-the-counter painkillers she kept at the bottom of her bag. She stood in the locked cubicle for a few moments, needing to prolong the feeling of being alone; to psych herself up before she went out and faced the rest of the school day.

Psych myself up against what? she asked herself. This was normality. If there was no particular excitement, no prospect of climbing anything or breaking into anything or stealing kisses with anyone, well, there was also no danger. No one lurking in the shadows, hugging something sharp and gleaming to themselves. No one following at a distance, half glimpsed, drawing ever closer. No evil stink of petrol curling like tendrils of gas into her shrinking nostrils. The last email from Gregory flashed across her mind, the one with the photo, but after a few nights' sleep and no further communication it was easier to dismiss. *A sick joke.* She'd done the right thing by not responding. This was real life: school, and work, and later on shopping and homework and cooking, all of it quite safe.

Safe, she thought, mulling the word over in her mind. It wasn't something she'd ever aspired to be.

Veerle slid back the bolt, opened the door and stepped out. The bell was ringing; everyone else had gone. She looked across the room and saw her reflection in the big mirror that ran the length of the wall. Someone had turned the strip lighting off and the daylight filtering through the thick glass blocks that served as windows was almost green. She looked like a ghost of herself: thinner, and paler, her skin tinted an unhealthy shade by the dim light. A statue, a girl made of verdigris. She turned away and headed for the door.

Two weeks passed uneventfully. By the third Monday, life had dropped into a routine.

At the end of the school day Veerle went off to the bus stop with everyone else. There was nothing she needed from the town. Things were going well, she judged; she was catching up on the school work fairly easily. It wasn't as though she'd missed the entire year, or anything; she simply hadn't had her eye on the ball. All the same, she was tired today and had the beginnings of a headache. Maybe she wouldn't bother to cook; she'd go to the *fritkot* and buy some chips. Then perhaps she'd call Bram. It would be a luxury to talk to him after a day of superficial chat with people she still didn't know that well.

Veerle wondered what she'd say if Bram raised the topic of coming down for the weekend again. It wasn't something that was going to go away. Bram lived in Ghent, Veerle back in her village in Vlaams-Brabant, some seventy kilometres and several hours' journey apart by a combination of tram, train and metro. It was a trek if you didn't stay over.

She was thinking about that as she stood waiting to get on the bus. There was a crush around the door, as though it was the last bus out of a disaster area and everyone was desperate to get on. Veerle didn't really care if she had to stand up again, so she just waited, all the time mulling over the situation with Bram. She was angry with herself for failing to arrive at a decision. *How can I not know my own mind?* she thought. She shook her head as if to clear it, and glanced round.

And that was the moment when she saw him. He was perhaps a couple of hundred metres away, coming this way at a brisk pace, his long legs scissoring across the reddish pavement.

Kris, she thought with a sudden shock, and then immediately, *No, it can't be.*

She remembered the day she had seen someone standing on the corner near the Carrefour supermarket, and briefly taken him for Kris Verstraeten – until he turned round and she had seen that he was nothing like Kris at all; her mind had simply been playing tricks on her. Maybe it was happening again – maybe she was going to keep on 'seeing' Kris for a while, just as she had sometimes thought she recognized a familiar face in Ghent when she first got there, even though she didn't know a soul apart from Geert and Anneke. The mind played tricks like that, always trying to find familiar landmarks in things.

Suddenly she was almost at the door of the bus. The bottleneck had cleared. She was tempted to look back again, to see whether it really was Kris Verstraeten striding down the street towards her – *no*, to reassure herself that it *wasn't* him – but the last few people behind her were edging forward impatiently, pushing against the bag on her back. Veerle climbed onto the bus, and almost immediately they were shoving their way on behind her. The hydraulic doors closed with a hiss and a clatter. With a rumble the bus prepared to move off.

Veerle couldn't help it then; she had to look. She was sealed inside the bus now, anyway; whether it was Kris or not made no difference. There was no seat between her and the window, simply a section of grey plastic moulding covering the wheel arch. She leaned over and looked out – and froze.

It is Kris.

There was no possibility of a mistake this time. They were only a couple of metres apart, separated by the plate-glass window; Kris's dark eyes stared straight into her widening ones. There was a tight, closed look on his face. Veerle guessed that he was angry with himself; he had intended to catch her before she got on the bus, but he had arrived a minute too late.

He didn't try to shout to her, or make any kind of gesture. It would have been impossible to do so without attracting the gaze of dozens of interested eyes. Instead he stood there on the pavement, holding her gaze until the bus moved off and she slid from his line of vision. Veerle couldn't see what he did after that, but she imagined him stalking away, his movements stiff with annoyance and frustration. And then – what?

If Kris had worked out that she was back at school here, and that she was taking the same bus home as she always had, then he must have worked out that she was back in the old house in Kerkstraat. So it wouldn't be very long before he turned up there. Veerle considered. If he waited for the next bus he could be in the village half an hour after she was. If he had other transport – if he had borrowed his cousin Jeroen's old car again – he could be there a lot sooner.

I could put the shutters down and just not answer the door. Pretend to be out.

But did she want to do that? That was the thing.

There was an argument that said she'd have to talk to him sooner or later. They'd not been alone together since that terrible day in Ghent when they had stood upon a rooftop high above the ancient streets and faced a killer, an old man armed with a great triangular blade and an insane grudge. It had not been just the two of them up there, facing him, it had been three, but after it was all over there had only been two. The old man had made a suicidal rush at them, and the force of his attack had carried him and the third person clean over the parapet and into thin air; to certain death on the cobble-stones far below.

That third person had been Hommel – Kris's ex-girlfriend, Veerle's rival.

Veerle and Hommel had looked into each other's eyes in the split second before the old man cannoned into Hommel and took her over the edge, and Veerle had seen that Hommel *knew*. She knew that she was dead, and she knew that it was because Kris had chosen to shield Veerle instead of her.

Veerle thought about that moment, about the look she and Hommel had exchanged, far more often than she would have liked. It had come back to her often at the beginning – at all times of day and night; she relived it, and the sense of respon-sibility was crushing. Now she thought about it less frequently, but it seemed that she read more into it as time went on. In Hommel's pale eyes she now saw not only the consciousness of approaching death but also reproach. An accusation.

Veerle was not sure she could see Kris, speak to him, while she felt the gaze of those eyes on her.

And then there was the simple fact that she had promised Geert she wouldn't see Kris again. Geert had been stalwart all through the storm that had engulfed Veerle after Hommel's death. He had protected her from Anneke's hostile interest. He had asked her what she, Veerle, wanted to do about school, and respected her decision to try to finish the year in Ghent. But she had lost too much ground; she dismally failed to attain her diploma.

When Veerle had then proposed to return to the village

and repeat the year at her old high school, Geert had listened to that proposal earnestly too. He was grieved to see her leave Ghent, but he respected her efforts to get her life back on track. The one point upon which he was completely firm was Kris Verstraeten.

Geert didn't see what Kris had done as protective or brave, nor was he gratified that Kris had favoured his daughter at the expense of someone else. All Geert could see was that Veerle had been in appalling danger again, that once again she had come very close to dying, and that Kris Verstraeten was involved.

He made his agreement for Veerle to move back into the house on Kerkstraat dependent on her promise not to see Kris. And Veerle, who was tired and injured and tormented by guilt, had promised.

She was over eighteen now, and if she had given the matter serious consideration she would have realized that Geert couldn't really impose any such condition on her. At the time, however, she hadn't been able to imagine re-starting a relationship that had been dyed in the blood of someone else. So she had given her word.

I won't see Kris again. I promise.

All this was going through Veerle's mind as the bus rumbled and rattled back to the village.

I can't see him.

She bit her lip.

What can he possibly have to say to me, anyway? 'I love you'? That's the problem.

The thought made her wince. She wanted to get home, get into the house and lock the door. Lock out Kris and the past and everything that had gone so horribly wrong. She would drag out her school books and get down to the studying she so badly needed to do if she were ever to get her diploma. She would put on her headphones while she worked, and play something very loud – loud enough to drown out the sound of the doorbell, or of knocking.

I can't see him, she thought.

I won't see him again. I promise.

9

When Veerle got off the bus in her village, she could see no one on the street except a few other students dispersing towards their homes.

Veerle crossed the road and walked quickly up Kerkstraat, skirting the wall of the graveyard. As she walked, she burrowed into her pocket for her house keys; she had them in her hand before she was within ten metres of the front door. Once inside, she pushed the bolt across, then hesitated, feeling foolish.

It's Kris, not the Incredible Hulk. And anyway, maybe he won't come.

In the end she left the bolt drawn across.

Veerle put her school bag down in the hallway and went into the kitchen to get herself something to drink. All the time she was in there, she was keeping an eye on the window. There were lacy curtains, not something she would have chosen herself but a leftover from before, and it was easier to see out than to see in. She opened the fridge and took out a carton of juice, fetched a glass from the cupboard and filled it. Each time she turned away from the window, to get the juice from the fridge or return it afterwards, she was conscious of it behind her — the street outside, the space where she was half expecting to see a familiar figure appear.

Veerle took a mouthful of juice, watching the square of window. The street was deserted, the afternoon sunshine golden on the churchyard wall.

At last she made herself turn away again. Go upstairs, that was the thing to do; there wasn't a huge amount of school work to do, but there were one or two things she could look over. Upstairs in her room she wouldn't have a view into the street unless she actually went and hung out of the window.

Veerle went back into the hall to get her school bag, still carrying the half-full glass of juice. It was cool and dim here, calming in a rather sober way, like walking through a silent cloister. She was just about to pick up the bag when the front doorbell rang with sudden and jarring violence.

Veerle jumped so hard that the glass slipped from her fingers and smashed on the floor at her feet, spraying fruit juice across the tiles.

She stared at the closed front door, open-mouthed, her heart thumping. There was no way whoever was outside hadn't heard that, she knew.

Whoever? You know *who it is.*

Veerle took a step backwards, and shards of glass crunched underfoot.

What am I going to—

Abruptly the blaring of the doorbell ceased and there was a loud and rapid double blow on the panels of the door.

'Veerle?'

If there had been any shadow of doubt in her mind about

who was outside, the sound of her name in that familiar voice removed it. It crossed her mind that she could avoid the issue, at least for now; she could go upstairs and pretend – in spite of the sound of the glass breaking – that she was not home. She could stay there silently in her room until he had gone. That was probably what Geert would have expected her to do.

Instead, she began to move slowly towards the door, saying nothing, scanning the floor carefully so as to avoid the larger pieces of glass and the spreading pool of spilled juice.

'Veerle?'

Kris was shouting, but he didn't sound angry – not yet. His voice was urgent – he *really* wanted her to open the door – but it had not occurred to him yet that she might decide not to do so.

Veerle heard him bang on the door again. She was so close now that she could put out a hand and touch the door. She could feel the vibrations of his blows on the outside of it. The doorbell sounded again.

Veerle touched the bolt. The metal was very cold. With infinite care she slid it back – not making a sound, promising nothing. Her fingertips trailed almost thoughtfully down the door, aiming for the latch. She was still telling herself that she didn't know whether she was going to open it or not when the sound of the doorbell abruptly stopped. Silence crowded in on her, as thick as fog.

Veerle waited. Perhaps half a minute passed. Still she heard nothing. She leaned in to the door and placed her cheek against the polished wood, listening. Was Kris on the outside doing the same, his face just centimetres from hers? She closed her eyes for a few seconds, opened them again.

Then she pulled back, turned the latch and opened the door.

He hadn't left, as she had half thought he might have. He was standing there, just a metre away, looking just the same as ever: the dark hair falling untidily over his temples, the sharp aquiline features, the bold eyes. His brows were drawn together and there was a barely suppressed urgency in his stance, in the way his hands were held tensely at his sides.

Two pieces of knowledge assailed Veerle at the same time: firstly, that she had broken her promise to her father, and secondly, that nothing had changed. She still looked at Kris and felt that impulse towards him, like the gravitational pull of a black hole, dragging her inexorably to some kind of psychological event horizon after which she could no longer perceive such things as common sense, guilt – and promises.

'*Verdomme*, you *are* here,' said Kris, and the look of frank dismay he gave her hit Veerle like a slap in the face.

She began to shut the door again, but before she could pull it closed Kris was half inside, blocking it with his body. Veerle had to step back or come into actual bodily contact with him. She retreated into the hall, glaring at him furiously, and Kris came right inside, closing the door behind him. He stood looking at her with no joyful expression on his face; in fact he looked downright horrified.

'Why did you come back from Ghent?' he demanded.

His tone was so rough that Veerle's temper was piqued. She stood her ground, folding her arms, but she said nothing. She simply looked at him mutinously. There was nothing in his tone that invited confidences.

Kris didn't wait for a reply anyway; his head was turning as he took in the hallway with the cheap new console from IKEA, the telephone on it, and the open door leading through into the kitchen, where utensils and crockery were visible on the table.

He said, 'You're living here again,' in a tone of incredulous horror.

Finally he seemed to become aware of Veerle's silence. His gaze left the open kitchen door and swung round to settle on her. For a moment they just stared at each other.

Veerle was fighting down a feeling that was threatening to overwhelm her – a black wave of emotion, not merely disappointment but misery and anger. Had Kris really come here, had she really broken her promise and let him in, just for him to tell her he didn't want her here? Still she said nothing.

'Why didn't you answer any of my calls?' Kris said finally.

There were many possible replies to that, including *Why do you care, since you don't seem pleased to see me?* and *What do you think you're doing, marching in here like this?* In the end, however, Veerle told him the truth.

'I didn't know what to say.'

Kris looked at her carefully for a moment, his expression not unkind, but then he said, 'Look, you can't stay here.'

'What?' Veerle's temper flared. 'You can't say that. What right have you got to tell me what to do?'

Kris stepped up close to her and actually took her by the shoulders. 'You have to go back to Ghent.'

'The hell I do.' Furious, Veerle shook him off. 'Why have you even come here? Just to tell me to go away? You know what you can do.'

'Veerle—'

'What?'

'I'm not telling you to go away. I'm telling you it's not safe here.'

It took a few moments for Kris's words to sink in, and then Veerle just stared at him.

You could be next, the email from Gregory had warned her. All of a sudden there was a cold feeling of apprehension in the pit of her stomach.

'What do you mean, *it's not safe here?*' she said slowly. She gazed up into his face, and now that she was looking at him, *really* looking, she saw no hostility, no desire to push her away in his expression. She saw concern and urgency.

'Look, can we go and sit down in there or something?' said Kris, tilting his dark head towards the open kitchen door.

Veerle didn't move. 'What do you mean?' she repeated stubbornly.

'Veerle—'

'I'm not sitting down, Kris. Tell me what you mean.'

Kris sighed heavily. 'OK. I think he's back.'

'Who . . . ?' Veerle didn't finish the sentence, but Kris supplied the answer anyway, though his words were superfluous; Veerle knew before he even said them.

'De Jager.'

10

'The Hunter?' Veerle spoke through lips that felt numb. All the indignation had gone; a chill was upon her, like the chill of approaching mortality.

Kris looked down at her and the expression in his dark eyes was sombre. 'Yeah, I think it's him.'

No, Veerle wanted to say. *I don't believe you. I don't want to hear any more.* But she had a terrible sense of inevitability, a feeling of grim expectation satisfied that was so strong it was almost like relief.

He's back, Kris had said; but for Veerle he had never really gone away. All those nights after the fire at the castle and the fall that had broken her: she had lain there with the blunt bodkins of pain stitching an evil tapestry all over her body, and the heat of summer and the closed windows making the air thick and sour, and every time she had slipped into a restless sleep, there he had been. Joren Sterckx. De Jager. An ogre armed with a crossbow and a knife so huge and sharp that the mere sight of it slicing through the air made her limbs go weak, as though she were a marionette and he had hacked through the strings.

So the story hadn't ended for her that night with his apparent death in the fire.

Sometimes, when she was feeling particularly low, terrible fears slithered through her mind, taking forms too grotesque to be described to anyone else. She, Veerle, was the only one who had clearly seen the killer who called himself De Jager; she had identified him as Joren Sterckx, the 'child hunter'. Joren Sterckx, as the police had told her over and over with weary patience, was dead – yet she had seen him. It was no great leap from that to thinking that he might have survived a second time, though the *how* of it was more than she could imagine. If he had, Gregory's latest message made grisly sense, although how Gregory knew was another matter. It was too much to take in all at once.

She glanced up at Kris. 'I think maybe I'd like to sit down after all.'

They went into the kitchen and sat on either side of the little table. It was strange, Veerle thought; this was the first time they had ever done this. Her mother had never made Kris welcome in the house when she was alive.

She said, 'Tell me everything.'

'There's no good way to say this,' Kris told her. 'I think someone's trying to kill me. And that probably means . . . us.' He leaned towards her across the table. 'Look, there are a lot of Verstraetens in the phone book. And some bad stuff has been happening to them – the sort of things that would happen if someone was going right through the book trying to find one particular Verstraeten.'

'Things?' repeated Veerle. 'Like what?'

'Break-ins . . . mostly.'

'Mostly?'

'And . . . a couple of deaths. One Kris Verstraeten and one

Koen Verstraeten. The guy called Koen was just listed in the phone book as *Verstraeten, K.* So, you know . . . if someone was looking for a *Kris* . . .'

'What happened?' asked Veerle. There was a hard little knot in the pit of her stomach, like a fist tightening.

Kris sighed. 'The one called Koen Verstraeten was quite an old guy, nearly eighty. They think he had a heart attack. Someone seems to have broken into his house, and he woke up and found them inside and – *wham*. Died of shock in his own hallway with his pyjamas on. Whoever broke in didn't lay a finger on him.'

'And the other one?'

'Yeah, the other one.' Kris hesitated. 'The one called Kris Verstraeten – well, he wasn't so lucky. Someone broke into his flat too, and I guess he didn't hear them getting in because they found him still in bed – what was left of him.' He looked down, and then looked up, into Veerle's eyes. 'Whoever killed him used a knife – pretty thoroughly.'

'Shit.' Veerle stared at him in horror.

'Yeah. Verstraeten is getting to be an unlucky surname.'

'How do you know all this?'

'The police. They came to talk to Jeroen, you know, my cousin, the one who has the maid service for rich expats. They were talking to anyone listed as Verstraeten in the phone book.'

'Did they come to see you?'

Kris shook his head. 'No, the flat's in my mother's name so it's her surname in the White Pages.' He shrugged. 'She's got a new partner and she practically lives at his place, but we've never changed the listing. It still says Hemeleers in the book. I guess that's just as well.'

'What did they say to Jeroen?'

'They asked him if he'd seen or heard anything suspicious, stuff like that. And whether he knew any reason why someone might be targeting people with the surname Verstraeten. They told him to call them if he noticed anything out of the ordinary.'

'Has he?'

'No. He's crapping himself now because of what the police said. If he thought there was anything going on, he'd tell them like a shot. He's terrified.'

'I don't blame him,' said Veerle, thinking of what he had just told her about his namesake, the other Kris Verstraeten. *Whoever killed him used a knife – pretty thoroughly.* She thought about the photo Gregory had sent her, the black splashes and streaks on the pale flesh and the vegetation. She shivered. 'Look,' she tried, 'maybe he was after this other guy with the same name, whoever did this. Maybe it has nothing to do with you. Or me.'

Kris was shaking his head again. 'No, it definitely has something to do with me. Did you see that thing in the news a few days ago, about the Scouts who found a human finger when they were out geocaching in Tervuren park?'

'No . . .' Veerle stared at Kris. 'That's – horrible.'

'Yeah. Well, the police weren't naming anyone, but there was a lot of stuff about it maybe coming from a local murder victim and there aren't all that many of those. So I'm pretty sure that it was the other Kris Verstraeten's finger.' He rubbed his face with one lean hand. 'The thing is, about a week ago I got an email.' Kris was looking down as the word *email* crossed his lips, so he didn't see Veerle react. 'No text or anything, just a string of numbers.'

Veerle looked at him uncomprehendingly. 'Numbers?'

'Yeah.'

'You mean a phone number?'

'No.' Kris shook his head. 'I knew right away that it wasn't a phone number. It didn't start with a zero, and there was a full stop and a couple of commas. I didn't *know* what it was – maybe just some kind of stupid spam message – so I would have ignored it, only . . .'

'Only what?' Veerle demanded.

Kris let out a long sigh. 'It was from Gregory.'

Veerle stared at him, pressing her hand to her mouth. That terrible sickening feeling washed over her again, the one she'd had when she received the email from Gregory. She stared for so long that Kris thought she hadn't understood.

'You know,' he said. 'Fred's tech guy, the one who set up the Koekoeken website for him; the one Fred told to shut the whole thing down after we went to see him that time.'

'Yes,' said Veerle tightly. 'But why was he sending you strings of numbers?'

'He wasn't, that's the point,' Kris told her. 'It wasn't him. It came from his email address, but it wasn't Gregory.'

'How can you be so sure?' Veerle asked him, and now Kris was looking at her very strangely, as though she was the one person in the entire world who had failed to take in some significant fact.

'Because Gregory's dead,' he said. 'Veerle, didn't you know?'

'No,' said Veerle. She touched her brow with cool

fingertips, rubbing distractedly. None of it seemed to make sense. 'I don't understand what you're telling me,' she said. 'Look, I had a couple of emails from him too.'

'Saying what?'

'I don't know about the first one. I didn't read it. But the other one . . . it had a kind of warning in it – and a photo.'

'Of what?'

'A hand, that was all you could really see – and some stuff splashed around. It could have been blood, but you couldn't really tell. It had dried and it looked nearly black. I couldn't tell. I was hoping it was just a sick joke . . .'

'I don't think so,' said Kris.

They looked at each other.

'No,' said Veerle. 'This is crazy. It doesn't make any sense. Gregory is sending emails, but it can't be him because he's *dead*?'

'It was his email address,' said Kris grimly. 'But unless they have wifi in the afterlife it wasn't Gregory who sent the message.'

'Maybe someone hacked his account.' Veerle didn't want to think about who might do that, but unpleasant ideas were popping up all over her mental landscape like evil imps.

'Maybe,' said Kris, 'but I don't think so. I think Gregory gave them the login details just before he died.'

'But why would anyone want them?'

'Maybe because they didn't want to use an address that could be traced back to them.' Kris sighed heavily. 'The numbers were GPS co-ordinates – you know, the longitude and latitude of a place. I wouldn't have thought of it, only the kids who found the finger were geocaching in the park. So I checked. There are websites where you can put in the co-ordinates and it tells you where they are – the address or whatever. I put the numbers from the email in, and it came up with some place in Tervuren park.'

He waited for Veerle to say something. When she didn't, he went on, 'I can't prove it, because the police aren't telling people exactly where they found that finger, but I think those co-ordinates were for wherever it was hidden.'

No, thought Veerle. She wanted to scream it. *No, no.* This was not supposed to be happening.

'This has to be someone playing a sick joke,' she insisted. 'Anyway, you got the email *after* they found the finger. *Anyone* could have worked out roughly where it was. It doesn't mean they had anything to do with *putting* it there.'

'That's true,' said Kris. 'But—' He fell silent, as if something had occurred to him, something he didn't want to put into words.

Veerle gazed at him, and suddenly her mouth was dry. 'You said Gregory was dead. Did he just die, in an accident or something?'

'No.' Again Kris was silent for a moment, then he burst out, 'Why did you come back, Veerle? Why didn't you just stay in Ghent? You can't live here, in this house, on your own.'

'What happened to Gregory, Kris?' cut in Veerle sharply. She had a terrible feeling that she really didn't want to know, but she had to ask. 'If it wasn't an accident, then what?'

'There was a fire,' said Kris. He spoke fiercely, sounding almost angry. 'It started in Gregory's flat, which was at the top of the block.'

'So he died in that?'

'No,' said Kris, shaking his head. 'He was dead before that. Didn't you see any of this on the news, Veerle?'

'I don't look at it.' That was true enough. Veerle had had enough bad news to last her a lifetime; the thought of opening a newspaper or scanning a news website and reading about more crime, more murder, more violence, was appalling. It was kind of compelling if you'd never been affected by any of it, but once you'd seen someone you knew die, once you'd seen them pushed off a rooftop to plummet to their death on the cobblestones – then you didn't want to hear about any more of that stuff, not if you wanted to sleep at night.

'Well . . .' Kris seemed reluctant to go on. 'The flat was burnt out. Everything gone, or ruined. And Gregory – well, the body wasn't all in one place. They found . . . remains – in one of the bedrooms – and the kitchen, and the bathroom. Whoever set fire to the flat tore him apart first, Veerle.'

'Oh God!'

'And then someone emails me using Gregory's address. And I think . . . maybe the reason pieces of Gregory were found all over his flat is that whoever killed him tortured him first, to get something out of him. Like email addresses and names. Maybe a *list* of names. Or maybe . . . just two.'

'Shit,' said Veerle. She covered her face with her hands, as though trying to shut the whole horrible idea out. Then she took her hands away and looked at Kris, wanting to persuade him that what he had surmised was wrong. 'You remember what Fred said, that time we went to see him at the gallery in Brussels? People like the Koekoeken get involved in all sorts of stuff. Maybe Gregory was mixed up in something we don't know anything about. This doesn't have to be about us.'

Kris was shaking his head again, his face very grim. 'Yes, it does. The email sent to me directly links Gregory – who's dead – with the discovery of that finger. Which belonged to someone who had exactly the same name as me.'

'You don't know that. You said yourself, the police weren't giving the name out. They just said a murder victim.'

'This isn't the city. There aren't that many murders around here. It's obvious.'

Veerle began to shake. 'No,' she said again. 'This can't be happening. This has to be some kind of horrible joke.'

'Veerle . . .'

'I've only just started back at my old school. I'm supposed to be getting my life on track. I'm supposed to be concentrating on passing my diploma this year, not – not . . .' She clenched her fists, her expression wild. 'I'm not even supposed to be *seeing* you. I promised Dad I wouldn't. He wouldn't have let me move back if I hadn't.'

Even through her turmoil Veerle saw Kris flinch at that. He opened his mouth to say something and then thought better of it.

After a few moments she spoke in a calmer tone. 'Why us, Kris? If it's something to do with the Koekoeken, there were maybe forty people involved. Why would anyone come after us?'

'Because we saw him,' said Kris simply.

'You mean Joren Sterckx?' said Veerle flatly.

'Whoever he was. He called himself the Hunter. *De Jager.*'

'For the last year everyone's been telling me he was dead,'

said Veerle, not without bitterness. 'The police thought I was nuts. They didn't come out and say it, but you could see they were thinking it. The crazy girl who saw Joren Sterckx when she was a kid and couldn't stop seeing him on every street corner ever since.'

'Does it matter who he was?' asked Kris. 'The point is, you saw him. You could identify him.'

'Yes, it *does* matter. How do you think it feels, having people look at you like you are completely insane? And anyway, the police won't believe me now if I start saying he's back again. I'm the last person on earth they'd listen to.'

'Veerle, just . . . Please, go back to Ghent. Go back to your father's place.'

'I can't! *Verdomme*, Kris, do you ever listen to a word I say? I came back here to make a fresh start. I can't go back there. He has his own life, with Anneke and Adam.'

'He's still your father. And you'd be safer there.'

'Look . . .' began Veerle. She shook her head, as though trying to shake off pestering flies. 'Look, I have to think about this. I can't just throw everything over and go back to Ghent, just like that.' She clasped her hands in front of her, squeezing the fingers together as though crushing something between them. 'Supposing it's all true,' she said. 'Supposing somehow Joren Sterckx – or De Jager or whoever he is – *is* back, and he *did* kill Gregory and got his hands on every single piece of information Gregory had about the Koekoeken – how bad is that, Kris? He has our usernames, right? And our email addresses. But that's all. He doesn't have our actual addresses.'

'No,' said Kris reluctantly. 'But everyone had a rough idea where the other members came from – the ones they had direct contact with, anyway. Gregory might have known I'm from Overijse.'

'Who would know that?'

'Well, the two members who vouched for me, for a start. Daniel – you don't know him – he's moved away now anyway. And . . . Hommel.'

The name descended between them like a portcullis.

Mixed with the terrible upswell of emotion she always felt when she thought of Hommel, Veerle felt a small sad twinge of surprise. She had always assumed that it was Kris who had introduced Hommel to the Koekoeken, not the other way around.

Just another thing I didn't know about whatever went on between them.

'She and I vouched for you,' Kris was saying. 'And I haven't told anyone where you come from.'

And Hommel's not going to, thought Veerle bitterly.

She said, 'So *if* someone is looking for us, they don't have our home addresses. Your name's not in the White Pages and neither is mine. Mum's name is still listed – it says Charlier, not De Keyser. There's no easy way to find us.'

'Maybe not,' said Kris. 'But this is a guy who's prepared to kill someone to find out.'

'Or it could still be someone's sick idea of a joke,' persisted Veerle. She leaned forward, gazing earnestly into Kris's face. 'Supposing it was . . . *him.* De Jager. Supposing by some miracle he escaped the fire and the body was somebody else's, somebody nobody has missed, which is a bit far-fetched to start with . . .' She was running on rapidly, so that the words were tumbling out of her breathlessly. She went on,

'Supposing he *did* kill Gregory, and he's also the one stalking people called Verstraeten, and he *did* send us those emails. Why would he do that? It doesn't make sense. He can't get at us through emails. We're hardly going to write back with our home addresses, are we? So all he's done is put us on our guard. What's the point of that?'

'I don't know,' Kris snapped back. Then he sighed heavily. 'I don't know,' he repeated in a softer voice. 'But I wish you weren't here on your own. In case.'

'I'll be OK,' said Veerle.

'Couldn't someone else stay here with you for a while?'

Bram, thought Veerle. *He means Bram.* Immediately she felt her cheeks burning and prayed she wasn't actually blushing. When the moment had stretched out far too long in silence, she blurted out, 'No. I mean . . . not really.'

Kris studied her, his expression unreadable.

At last he said, 'So you promised your dad. Is *that* why you didn't answer any of my calls?'

'No,' said Veerle immediately, and then found she couldn't say anything more; the right words simply wouldn't come. She couldn't look Kris in the eye and say, *Hommel died because you chose to protect me.* It was too monstrous. It wasn't even fair anyway, because Kris and Hommel would never have been on that rooftop in the first place if she, Veerle, hadn't called Kris when she went into the building. But the fact remained that Hommel was dead. Veerle couldn't say to herself, *Getting back with him won't change anything*, or worse, *Hommel would have understood.* Sometimes a little voice at the back of her mind would try to say those things, and Veerle had come to despise it; she thought that voice had a wheedling, self-interested tone to it. So she said nothing, although the silence was like biting on something bitter.

At last Kris said, 'OK.' Veerle saw the shadow that passed across his face and knew that he took her silence as rejection.

Impulsively she said, 'I've broken my promise already.'

Kris smiled wryly at that. 'You have.'

They stared at each other, and although there was still something there between them, some unseen barrier, there was more warmth in the looks they exchanged.

'How did you know I'd be on the school bus?' asked Veerle.

'I didn't. I came on the off chance. I tried calling the land-line at your dad's place, and each time I got his girlfriend, so I just hung up.' He shrugged. 'I guessed that if you were still living there, sooner or later it would have been you who picked up the phone. You know, I called here in the summer but the shutters were down – nobody home.'

'I was probably still in Ghent then.'

'Well, anyway, I thought if you were back here but living somewhere else I might catch you at school. And I nearly did.'

'Kris . . . do you really think we're in trouble? You really think *he's* back?'

Kris nodded sombrely. 'Yeah. I don't know how that's possible, but . . . yeah. And even if it isn't him, look at the facts. Someone's breaking into the homes of people with my surname, and some of those people are winding up dead. And it looks like the same person who's doing that is sending emails from a guy who was cut into pieces and burnt along with everything he owned. That's trouble, all right.' He sighed. 'And I think it's worse than that. I think back then De Jager was just hunting random members of the Koekoeken, whoever happened to be in a convenient place at the right time. But I think this is personal. I think it's about us.'

11

The room was dull; it was almost offensively dowdy. The wallpaper was a faded 1970s design that sat awkwardly with the cheap modern furniture. The only picture on any of the walls was a print that had been bleached by the sunlight so that only shades of blue remained; it was like looking at a landscape through endless freezing rain. None of this mattered very much to the occupant of the room. The house was a façade, a mask; a place to sleep that outwardly conformed with convention, a smooth shell that contained the pulsating creature within.

De Jager stood by the large window that was the only attractive feature of the room, and gazed out at a slanting triangle of field, a tangle of woodland. No human figure ever passed across that prospect. From that point of view, the house, though old-fashioned, was perfect. De Jager looked out at a landscape as devoid of human life as the moon, and deliberated.

Kris Verstraeten and Veerle De Keyser.

He considered those names, and the fact that he was compelled to consider them was an irritant. He didn't care to consider prey as an opponent.

He was used to interacting with the ones he hunted – to a certain extent. An accomplished hunter knows how to predict the reactions of a given creature; how to channel its movements in the direction he wants, driving it towards the bow or the pit or the guns. De Jager was very accomplished. He drove his victims before him by stealth or persuasion or threat, and they always ran the way he wanted them to, down the narrowing path that led to death. Their very predictability fed his desire to slaughter them. Anything as stupid as that deserved to die.

And now these two were proving elusive. De Jager had actually shot Kris Verstraeten with a crossbow bolt, the night of the fire in the old castle. The bolt had punched right through Kris's shoulder, probably collapsing a lung, certainly causing enough pain to incapacitate him. On a whim De Jager hadn't finished him off then. He'd left him on the worn and dusty floor, and gone to prepare for the arrival of the girl. It was rare for De Jager to feel regret about anything; his belief in his own infallibility was too strong. Yet he regretted not killing Kris then.

The girl, Veerle, had turned up, and incredibly she had managed to escape him as well, by climbing down the side of the building like a monkey. That was bad, but what was worse was that she had had a good clear look at him from the upstairs gallery of the castle. They had stared at each other, he looking up with confident impassivity, she gazing down with horrified recognition on her face. And then she had named him. *Joren Sterckx.*

De Jager knew that if she looked into it – as she certainly would if she hadn't already – she would find out that Joren

Sterckx had died in prison of cancer nearly a decade before that evening in the castle. If she made enough fuss about what and whom she claimed to have seen, the police would probably check that, and they would tell her that Joren Sterckx was indeed stone dead.

If she left it there, all well and good. But she wouldn't leave it there; he was convinced of that. She would keep working away at the problem like a particularly irritating woodworm boring away at an ornate piece of furniture. She would wonder how a dead man could be walking about a decade after his own demise; how he could be killing people. And there was a risk that eventually, limited though her perspective undoubtedly was, she would solve the mystery of his existence.

That would be a very serious problem. That would be an end of anonymity, an end of available resources. If the police realized that she wasn't a delusional hysteric, they'd be crawling all over the case. They might locate one of his previous hideouts, where grim things lay hidden, to be unearthed if anyone dug deep enough. Then the Hunter would become the hunted. All because of some idiot girl who had refused to die when she should have.

De Jager felt an unfamiliar sensation: a hot and toxic pressure, like a storm front building up on some strange planet where the atmosphere is made of sulphur dioxide. Anger. He was unused to it; when he killed he felt a cold satisfaction rather than seething fury. The anger fed on itself; the very fact that he was experiencing the emotion fed it. It was as though Veerle De Keyser had *infected* him with this feeling that spread through every atom of his being like a fast-replicating virus. He was determined to root her out, to obliterate her. He would ensure that her destruction was not only total, but slow, so that both he and she could appreciate every degree of pain she passed through on her way to annihilation. It would be spectacular.

The problem remained, however, that he had still not discovered her current whereabouts.

Gregory had told him that Kris Verstraeten lived in or near Overijse, and although there were a great many Verstraetens in the White Pages, he was confident that sooner or later he would find the one he wanted. It was regrettable that two of them had died, especially the one he'd had to kill, because that sort of thing attracted attention.

He remembered that night in the dark flat, where chains of light had fanned across the room from the slits in the roller shutters, and he had knelt on the struggling figure in the bed with the knife ready in his fist. He had seen, too late, that this Kris Verstraeten was not the one he wanted. The man was too old, too heavy, with coarse features quite unlike the aquiline ones he had expected. But if he could see that, then the Kris Verstraeten in the bed could see him too – could identify him later. So he had struck with the knife, again and again, until his clothes were heavy and his skin warm with blood. Then he had taken the finger, hacking at the joint until he was able to wrench it free. The finger would make fine bait, he had thought. It would show Kris Verstraeten he meant business. It was simply a pity it had been found by a bunch of Scouts before Kris had a chance to see for himself how serious matters had become.

Of course, the murder had been reported in the press,

especially coming so close after the death of Koen Verstraeten, the fool who had died in his pyjamas of a massive heart attack after one look at the intruder in his home. The police were closed-mouthed about their investigations, but De Jager knew that if they had any sense they would talk to other Verstraetens in the area; they would put them on their guard. They might even give some minimal protection to any other K. Verstraetens.

It was prudent, he thought, to try to draw Kris and Veerle out in other ways for the time being. He would send more emails from Gregory's address, trying to provoke either one of them into a response. Gregory had given him the login details, as he had given every other piece of information stored inside that wooden head of his. De Jager had also lifted Gregory's laptop before he torched the flat. That way, even the sender's IP address led towards the dead man, in so far as it could lead to anyone.

He could also try to locate Veerle. De Jager stared out at the corner of field, at the ragged border of trees, but he was not seeing them. His mind was running through options with savage speed, like a thief rifling through cupboards, looking for valuables.

Gregory had told him next to nothing about the girl: only that name, Veerle De Keyser, and the email address. De Jager believed him when he said that was all the information he had. Gregory's face had been crimson and wet; he had been juddering violently with shock and pain. De Jager didn't think he had it in him to lie. If Gregory could have told him any small thing to take the pain away and shovel it onto Veerle instead, he would have done it. Too bad De Jager was going to finish the task with him, whether he had the information to give or not.

Since then, he had spent a lot of time thinking about the Koekoeken. When the group was still active, he had taken a strong interest in the details of the properties they visited. It was more enjoyable to hunt in a sprawling villa than in a tiny apartment where the pursuit was of necessity short and sharp. It was preferable to choose locations that were fairly isolated, to reduce the risk of interference by nosy neighbours. He had selected his hunting grounds with care, and in the process he had developed a good mental map of them. The majority were in Brussels itself or in the districts to the east, stretching as far south as Sint-Genesius-Rode and as far north as Vilvoorde. It would be quite possible to travel down from other cities in Flanders to explore any of these places, but unlikely, he judged. Every city had its urban explorers, but the Koekoeken were unique, depending on a very specific type of local knowledge. To gather enough of that knowledge to be able to trade with other people, they had to be fairly local, which meant Brussels or east of Brussels.

Then there was the fact that, in the few words they had exchanged that night in the castle, as in her contributions to the web forum, Veerle had spoken Flemish. It would have been hard to identify a particular local accent since she had mostly been screaming things like *Go away or I'll light it* and *Didn't you check? Klootzak!* at the top of her voice, but it was safe to conclude that she was a Flemish speaker, which meant that she was more likely to be living in one of the Flemish-speaking districts than the capital.

De Jager had narrowed it down further than that. She was

involved with Kris Verstraeten, and Kris lived in or near Overijse. It was not impossible to live in Vilvoorde and have a relationship with someone who lived in Overijse, but it was more probable that they lived within close travelling distance of each other. She might, for example, live in Tervuren or one of its satellite villages, or in Overijse itself.

He had searched the White Pages for those areas and found dozens of De Keysers – even some V. De Keysers. He had checked out a few of them, standing casually outside houses to see who went in or out, even breaking into one or two and rummaging through photographs and papers, looking for any proof that this was where Veerle lived. So far he had failed to find her.

He had run a few online searches as well, in case she had appeared at a school event or won a competition and managed to get her photograph in the paper. Nothing. He had tried looking at the coverage of the fire at the castle, of his own supposed death, but Veerle was not named, nor a domicile given; she would have been under eighteen at the time, he guessed, and it wasn't as if she had been convicted of anything.

The room darkened slightly; a cloud had passed over the sun. Across the wedge of open field the branches of the trees were buffeted by wind, a precursor to rain, and sure enough, the first fat drops came exploding onto the windowpanes. Within a couple of minutes it was raining heavily, and the view beyond the window had dissolved into grey streaks.

Rain.

That was what had given him the key to the puzzle. *Silent Saturday.* It had rained that day, the day of the murder, the one that had led to the name of Joren Sterckx being reviled the length of Flanders. The killer had walked up a muddy track across some allotments, heading towards the church spire that dominated the village, the bloody body of a child in his arms.

She had been there. She *had* to have been there. He had considered the matter from every angle, and the more he considered it, the more convinced he had become. How old was Veerle now? Eighteen, perhaps, or nineteen? At the time of the murder she would have been about seven years old.

De Jager thought that if you went up to any random person of eighteen or nineteen and asked them to describe the appearance of Joren Sterckx, the child hunter, in any detail, they would have struggled. It wasn't as though there was any coverage of the case in the media these days; since the killer had died in prison there were no lawyers clamouring to get him out, no protestors insisting that he stay where he was, no artist's impressions of him sitting in an appeal court, listening intently.

Of course, the case remained notorious; for Veerle's village, it was the most appalling day in its history, a nuclear explosion that had obliterated centuries of peaceful living in an instant. You couldn't live there and not know about Joren Sterckx; about the way he had hunted down and killed a young child, and worse, taken trophies from the body. But would you recognize him if you saw him?

There were photographs of Joren Sterckx on Wikipedia; De Jager had looked at them himself. But they were grainy pictures, scanned in from the newspaper coverage; it wasn't as if his family were going to supply anyone with a smiling studio portrait, after all. And they had been taken over a decade ago; if he were alive now he'd have been about thirty.

No. If Veerle had recognized the man on the ground floor of the old castle as she stood there gazing down from the gallery, if she had named him with such utter conviction, it was because she had seen him before. She was from his village.

De Jager turned away from the window. He was sure now that he would find her.

12

They came singly, stealthily, moving over the uneven ground carefully in the darkness, visible as no more than faint beams dancing across the surface of the rubble like marsh lights. The old factory was not easy to visit; it was too close to streets lined with bars and scruffy apartments where even at this hour the occupants were still active, arguing and fighting or hanging out of windows and doorways to have a last smoke. It was worth coming, though; the factory was under a death sentence. Already the building was critically wounded; the machinery that stood silently behind wire security fences had torn into the flank of it, so that its floors stood open to the elements, a doll's house for Titans. In a week or two there would be nothing to visit. Last chance to see.

Xander was one of the last to arrive. He hated leaving his car, which was one of his two great loves – the other being this, the exploring – in an area like this. He was afraid of coming back to find that keys had been dragged down the side, or the tyres slashed, or that the car had vanished altogether. He drove around for a while until he found a place that was at least half satisfactory, parking right under a street-lamp close to a twenty-four-hour pharmacy. Then he walked to the factory site, a compact figure in jeans and leather jacket.

In spite of the need for caution, it wasn't physically difficult to get inside. There were a number of places where the fences were down. Signs warned the passer-by to keep out, that the site was dangerous, but Xander was so indifferent to such warnings that he hardly noticed them. He stood for a moment outside the perimeter fence, listening. He glanced left and right, but there was nobody in sight, not *outside* the fence, anyway. He stepped over one of the fallen sections, and then he was inside.

He took the tiny torch out of his pocket, switched it on, and began to follow the pale beam across a jagged surface of broken bricks and chunks of cement. It was a shame he couldn't photograph the place by daylight. But there was no chance of that; even without the risk of being seen by the demolition workers, there was the distinct possibility of being caught indoors when the bulldozers moved in. That would be very unpleasant indeed.

He glanced up at the building looming above him. The concrete sections showed as paler patches in the darkness, the openings that represented doors or simply breaches in the walls as black places. As he came closer to the near wall, he trained the torch beam on it and saw that there were sections of brick, the edges ragged and crumbling as though gnawed by gigantic rodents.

Xander's face remained impassive, but there was a tight effervescent feeling under his breastbone. His breathing was coming a little faster and he became conscious of a pulse beating in his neck. The sensations were not entirely unpleasant; this was what he came for, after all. The danger. The rush.

As he followed the wall he saw that he was approaching a doorway. The door itself was gone, and the lintel was exposed, giving the opening a raw look. Xander slipped the compact camera out of his pocket and took his first photograph.

Flash. For a split second the doorway was illuminated, bleached white, the blackness within suddenly given depth and dim form. Xander looked at the picture on the little screen at the back of the camera. It looked like a photograph taken underwater – a corridor inside the wreck of a ship.

He stepped through the doorway, looking cautiously ahead, and far inside the building he saw the faint beam of another torch slide across a slanting section of ceiling. Good; at least one other person was already here. Xander didn't call out, though. The meeting was for later; now he wanted to explore a little for himself, take more photographs.

He moved further inside, sometimes pausing to take a picture. *Flash.* A metal door and, beyond it, an office desk on its side. *Flash.* An internal window, the panes opaque with filth and the metal frames brown with rust. *Flash.* A rack of things that looked strangely like round cheeses but were probably pottery moulds, girded around with metal bands.

The photographs were not perfect. The flash had a tendency to bleach things at the front of shot and let everything at the back drown in murk, but on the whole Xander was satisfied with them; they were atmospheric, at any rate.

He saw light at the periphery of his vision. A gruff greeting came out of the darkness. Xander lifted the torch and saw that it was someone he knew, a guy called Jonas.

'It's you,' said Jonas, coming up to him. 'I thought maybe it was Thomas.'

'No.'

'The others are through the back there. There's a bit where the workers used to sit and hand-paint stuff.'

'Really?'

'It's cool. There are still posters up. Coffee cups on the benches.'

Xander shrugged. That didn't sound particularly interesting to him. He liked to take shots of ruined architectural features – crumbling walls, broken windows. A visible look of decay. Coffee cups were not really his thing. He went with Jonas anyway, though; he liked to hear the tales the others told, even if he didn't believe them.

He followed Jonas past racks and racks of items so thickly covered with dust that you could hardly tell what they were. Soon, when the bulldozers had finished, they would be nothing at all. They would be dust themselves.

The 'others' turned out to be two people huddled together, using a wooden pallet as a place to sit. Xander looked at the faces dimly underlit by torches, and recognized Ruben and Tina. Not Thomas, though.

Ruben and Tina were studying something. A smartphone; he could see the glow of the screen. As Jonas and Xander came up, Ruben dug Tina in the ribs with an elbow.

'Ask Xander. He's the expert on photos.'

'Ask me what?' said Xander.

'Are these for real?'

Xander took the smartphone and looked at the photograph displayed on it. 'What's this?'

'Download. It's all over the urbex sites.'

'Who took it?'

A shrug. '*Meneer* Username. Your guess is as good as mine.'

'What's it supposed to be?' asked Xander, although he could see perfectly well what was in the picture. The colours were dark and rich; he suspected that the picture had been doctored using a digital photography app. The borders had a vignette effect that made them look antique. The subject was a rectangular chunk of stone, leaning at a slight angle. It was old, and the surface was covered with lichen and moss, so you couldn't really see what was underneath any of it, but all the same it was pretty clear what the stone was. It was a grave marker. Slung carelessly over the stone was a man's casual jacket.

That was about all there was to see. It was possible to pick out a little background texture suggesting overgrown grass, but otherwise it was just a photograph of someone's jacket, hanging on a gravestone.

'The dead hitchhiker,' said Tina, sounding bored.

'I don't see anyone dead,' said Xander, but already his thumb was working on the touch screen, bringing up the next photograph – and there it was. Long grass raked across the picture, and amongst it, crushing some of the blades flat, was a hand whose fish-belly whiteness proclaimed that there was no longer a heart pumping blood around the system.

Seemingly, Xander reminded himself. This was a photograph of a hand in some grass. So what?

He looked up, scanning the others' faces. 'Why do you want to know if these are for real? Anyone can snap a hand in some long grass.'

'Have you looked at the others?' asked Ruben.

Xander sighed inwardly, and carried on tabbing through them. Another shot of the gravestone, taken from a different angle and further away. A photograph of a single shoe, lying on its side against a low metal railing topped with blunt ornamental spikes. The one after that was more obviously sinister. It seemed to show someone lying on their back in that same unkempt grass. The figure was backlit, so it was hardly more than a silhouette, but you could see that the head was flung back, the mouth gaping open.

Still, thought Xander, *it's probably just someone messing about. I could get someone to do that – Jonas or someone – and take an identical pic, no problem.*

The next picture though . . .

It gave Xander a start, sending little prickles of shock shooting through him, although almost as soon as he had reacted, he knew that what he was looking at was probably a mock-up, same as the other photographs. This time the photographer had closed in on the recumbent person and shot them at close range, using a flash.

You couldn't see the whole of the face – just one eye, the cheek, the crease running down from the side of the nose, and the jaw. It had that ghastly white looming-up-at-you look, caused by the flash going off. The eye was half open. A photograph is essentially static, a moment in time, so you could not expect to see movement in that eye, but all the same there was something about it that suggested fixedness.

All this was mildly unpleasant but Xander had seen worse stuff online, and he knew he could have faked any of it relatively easily.

What made him stare at the picture, with a cold slithering sensation in the pit of his stomach, was the flies. There were two of them, squat, bristly, greenly metallic insects with reddish compound eyes. They stood out against the dead-white skin like jewels. Xander was pretty sure they were blow flies, sometimes called carrion flies.

He imagined the sensation of those tiny feet on the sensitive skin of the face – the vibrating buzz maddeningly close to the ear and eye. Even if those flies didn't happen to prefer the company of the dead, he didn't think a live person could lie there motionless for very long with *those* crawling over his face.

That was the last photograph.

Xander handed the phone back to Ruben.

'Well, what do you think?' Ruben asked him.

Xander found himself shrugging. He said, 'Pretty much anything can be faked.'

That was true, at any rate. All the same, the picture had disturbed him. He was slightly on edge, and when someone loomed up out of the darkness behind him, brushing against his shoulder as he pushed his way past, Xander almost jumped.

It was big Thomas, clad in a thick jacket, a woollen hat pulled low over his forehead, nodding a greeting.

There was a little shuffling as Tina and Ruben moved along the edge of the pallet. There was a slight reluctance to sit next to Thomas. Everyone recognized his status as narrator of the most chilling urban legends, but that didn't mean they wanted to snuggle up to him while he was telling them. They made just a little too much space for him at the end.

'Quinten not coming?' asked Tina.

'Yeah, he said he would,' said Ruben.

'Well, he's not here.'

Xander said, 'Thomas, you were the last one in. Did you see Quinten?'

'No,' said Thomas.

The chat began after that, with Quinten's no-show soon forgotten. For a while they debated the photographs of the guy lying in the graveyard. *The dead hitchhiker* – that was what everyone was saying. They all knew the story, or some variation of it. A man driving along a lonely road picks up a hitchhiker. They were agreed on that, though not what the hitcher was like.

'It was a guy.'

'It was a young girl, with long dark hair.'

'Then after the guy has dropped the hitcher off, he finds a jacket in the car,' said Tina. 'And when he tries to return it, he finds out that the person died two years before.' She managed to inject a strong note of incredulity into her voice.

'That doesn't work,' objected Jonas. 'How would the jacket end up on the gravestone?'

Xander said, 'No, it's like this. It's a cold night, and the hitcher borrows a sweater or a jacket from the driver. When he gets out of the car, he forgets to hand it back. But later they find it draped over a gravestone and the person buried there is the hitcher.'

There was a rumble of approval at this, followed by some

discussion about other hitchhiker stories. There was, for example, the one about the girl who picks up a little old lady, but notices during the journey that her passenger has hairy hands . . .

Eventually they ran out of steam. Xander wondered whether one day they would run out of stories altogether. There had to be a limit to the number of tales you could tell about people who later turned out to be dead, nasty domestic accidents and creepy-crawlies laying eggs in people's hair or flesh.

As usual, though, Thomas didn't let them down. The story he related was once again a variation on a theme: the child playing hide-and-seek in a church who accidentally shuts himself in a coffin; the bride who hides in an old chest during the wedding reception in a castle and can't open the lid again. What made Thomas's version particularly spine-chilling was the fact that he set it in a deserted factory – 'Much like this one,' he told them, his deep voice resonating through the darkness.

'The factory was a long way from here, but like this one, it was old. Over the decades the owners had added to it, without bothering to pull down the original parts. So now it was like a maze. Some of the older areas were still in use, but some had been shut up or used to store lumber. As the factory site grew, it became necessary to squeeze in further buildings, sheds and walkways, so that the spaces between them became narrower. New workers had difficulties finding their way around, so the old hands had to guide them. Sometimes, for fun, they would misdirect them, so some gormless apprentice of seventeen would find himself in a room full of rusting machinery when he'd been hoping for the canteen or the WC.

'Eventually the company that ran the factory fell on hard times. The economic climate had worsened, and there was no longer a market for the type of expensive porcelain they manufactured. So the decision was taken to close the old factory. Because it was such a labyrinth, nobody wanted to buy it as it was, so the plot was sold to developers and the factory was scheduled for demolition . . . like this one.

'Of course, there are always people like us, who go in and look around before the place is gone for ever. On this particular evening a young man came to take some photographs. The demolition was due to start the following day, so this was his last chance, and although he hadn't found anyone to come with him, he wasn't going to pass up the opportunity. So he slipped through a gap in the fence and went into the old factory.

'It was disorienting being inside it in the dark. The place was such a rabbit warren that he wasn't confident of recording everything. Luckily the yellow light from the distant street was visible through the open door and windows, so he could always tell which way led back to the outside. He wasn't really worried.

'He went around with his camera, taking photographs of everything he could, climbing over pieces of furniture and ducking his head to go under low beams.

'A few times he thought he heard movement elsewhere in the labyrinth, but that didn't bother him, either. He was used to passing other explorers on his way in and out of places like this. Generally there wasn't an issue. He'd once come across a guy carrying pieces of antique carved wood out of a ruined chateau, which you weren't supposed to do – it was strictly take only photos, leave only footprints and don't even leave those if you have any sense – but even then he'd said nothing. There'd been no confrontation.

'After a while he came down a flight of concrete stairs that had no banisters; they had been demolished or stolen. He found himself in front of a pair of heavy metal doors. There were tracks leading in through the doors, so that things could be pushed in and out easily. It was an industrial kiln.'

Thomas paused, letting his words sink in, and then he went on.

'He began to take photographs, the flash working like a strobe, and then suddenly he felt a terrible blow on the back of his head, and the darkness closed in.

'He awoke a little later in the pitch dark. His head was throbbing, the pain so bad that he felt nauseous. What had happened? It entered his head that perhaps he had walked into something in the dark. But no – he was sure the blow had come from behind. He hadn't walked *backwards* into anything. His fingers found a huge tender swelling on his scalp. The hair was slick with something sticky. Automatically he brought his fingertips up to his face, but of course he couldn't see a thing.

'Had the streetlamps outside the factory gone out? The darkness was so complete that it was like having been struck blind. He'd brought a small torch with him, but when he felt in his outside pocket it was gone. Had he been carrying it when he struck his head? He couldn't remember. Everything was hazy. Perhaps he had dropped it on the floor.

'Then he thought: *the camera*. He'd definitely been holding that. It had to be around somewhere. If he'd dropped it, it might have smashed, but there was still the memory card inside it, with all his photographs of the factory stored on it. Besides, if it was still working, he could set off the flash and try to see which way was out by its brief light.

'He began to feel about on the dusty floor, cautiously at first, then with increasing urgency. Why was it so dark? It didn't matter how much time passed, his eyes weren't acclimatizing to it. *I should be able to see the doorway. It wasn't that dark out there. There was a window right opposite.*

'He had a paranoid moment of wondering whether he really *had* been struck blind. He fought down the panic that threatened to well up at this idea. He kept feeling about on the floor, but he couldn't find the camera or the torch. He found one of the tracks that ran the length of the kiln, though, and now he could orient himself a little. Crawling along with the fingertips of his left hand following the cold metal, he moved painfully in the direction that he hoped led to the doors.

'The effort was much greater than he had expected. The pain from his head was appalling and his limbs felt leaden with exhaustion. If he had been able to think more clearly he might have diagnosed concussion, but his brain was a fog of pain and tiredness. All he could think about was getting to the door, and out.

'A metre or two brought him to a cold metal wall. *The wrong end,* he thought. He sat there for a while, and the only thing he could see was the faint sparks that danced in front of his eyes, but they were inside his head, not outside. Then he began to creep back the other way, still following the track.

'He was cautious because he was afraid of running into something again. His head felt as though it would explode if it struck anything else; it felt like a giant blister, swelling with painful pressure. So it was not his head but his outstretched fingers that first felt the barrier at the other end of the kiln.

'Cold, unyielding metal. He didn't understand it at first; didn't *want* to understand it. He crouched there and put both hands up, running them over the hard surface. Had he somehow run up against the side of the kiln instead of the end? But then he found the narrow crack running vertically up from the floor, and as he traced it with his fingertips he knew what he was feeling. The kiln doors had been closed.

'How was this possible? He hadn't closed them himself; even through the fog of concussion he knew that. They were heavy doors, at least ten, perhaps twenty centimetres thick, and they seemed very firmly closed. Hard to imagine that they had swung shut on their own.

'He pushed at them, but they didn't budge. It was like trying to push down a brick wall. He put the flat of his hands against the metal and shoved, and when that didn't work he hauled himself painfully up and tried putting his shoulder to them.

'Nothing. The doors remained closed, the darkness total. At last he lost control and burnt out all his remaining energy by slamming his hands against the metal, screaming and begging in a voice that was getting wilder and wilder.

'When he had worn himself out, he lay on the floor, panting, and he thought he heard a faint noise from outside. A footstep? He was about to cry out, but something stopped him. Had someone done this to him – had they locked him in, fastening the latch on the outside of the doors?

'It occurred to him that this was an industrial kiln, capable of reaching temperatures that would roast him alive. Surely the power was off long since? But still he was tormented by visions of the whole place heating up like a crematorium. Would he hear gas jets firing, or would it simply get hotter and hotter? He lay on the floor and cried with fear.'

Tina drew in breath in a little hiss that sounded clearly in the cold still air.

'But the kiln never heated up,' said Thomas, 'and if there was anyone outside it, they left without a sound. The night cold closed in. Death came, but very . . . *very* slowly.'

When Thomas had finished speaking, there was silence for a few moments as the others contemplated his words.

Shortly after that, the meeting broke up. By agreement they didn't all leave together; although it was very late and the neighbourhood wasn't particularly respectable, if they poured out into the street like a teeming horde of rats, someone might notice.

Xander was the last to leave, because he wanted to take a few more photographs. He kept moving about, humming to himself tunelessly under his breath to keep nerves at bay.

Damn Thomas. His stories were so realistic, so horrible, it made him feel uncharacteristically nervous afterwards. Why had Thomas had to choose to set the latest one in a factory just like this, of all places? It was almost not fun any more. *Actually*, he said to himself, *it really* isn't *fun*. His skin was prickling as he moved about in the dark. He was seriously spooked.

Only his determination to get the photographs he wanted

kept him inside the old factory at all. He couldn't imagine uploading the ones he had tomorrow and having to admit to people that he had only shot half the factory because he had been too frightened.

Xander stepped through a doorway that was no more than a square hole in a featureless wall, and moved past some pallets stacked with items that might have been overturned bowls but were so thickly coated with dust that they appeared almost furry. Then he stopped where he was, and stared.

A rectangular structure, taller than he was, with metal doors, tightly closed. Xander didn't think he'd ever seen an industrial kiln before, but he was pretty sure that was what it was. There were two metal-rimmed tracks running out from under the doors, just like the ones in Thomas's story.

Xander looked at those closed doors, at the implacable metal surface with that one thin line down the middle of it, and he felt his heart thumping. Suddenly his mouth was full of a clinging sour wetness and he had to swallow.

Fuck you, Thomas, he thought furiously. He didn't want to be this afraid. His hands moved restlessly on the camera he was still clutching between them. He was torn between making himself go on, past the kiln, and turning tail right now.

Supposing . . . he thought, but he didn't want to go any further with the ideas that were slithering out of the darkest parts of his imagination. Thomas's story was made-up crap. Great made-up crap, but still made-up crap.

All the same, he went a little nearer to the kiln, looking at those closed doors. There was a latch all right, and he put his hand on it, testing it. Either it was very stiff, rusted shut in some place he couldn't see, or there was some trick to it he couldn't master. It wouldn't budge. Xander was slightly disgusted to realize that he was relieved about that.

Forcing himself into an act of bravery he really didn't feel, he leaned forward and pressed his right ear to the cold metal surface. He listened. He stood there for perhaps twenty seconds, hearing nothing at all, and then, just as he was about to pull away from the door, he heard the tiniest sound from within.

It was so slight, so brief, that he wasn't even sure he had heard anything. He couldn't have said whether it was a scuffle or a scrape or even a groan.

Xander struck the metal lightly twice with the flat of his hand, waiting to see if there was an answering sound. Then he listened again, but he heard nothing.

Perhaps, he thought, he had imagined the sound. Perhaps it had come from outside the kiln – a rat scuttling away over the bricks, or dust falling from the ceiling.

Thoroughly spooked now, he backed away from the kiln. Then he retraced his steps, heading back towards the door he had come in by. *To hell with the photographs.*

Xander made it to the doorway, and then it was a short but irksome route to the broken section of fence, doing his best not to fall over the bricks and chunks of concrete that turned the ground into an obstacle course. He put the camera back into his jacket pocket and brushed brick dust off the sleeves.

All the way back to the car he kept thinking about the kiln. Had he heard anything – or not? Then he was back at the place where it was parked under the streetlamp. The pharmacy seemed to be closed, twenty-four-hour or not.

The streetlamp was still shining down brilliantly on the car, and by its yellow light he could clearly see the scratch marks made by keys on its gleaming flank. Xander forgot about the kiln.

The next day, and for days after that, the wreckers and excavators and bulldozers moved in. The old factory crumpled in on itself, and was finally reduced to a pile of rubble.

It was another month before anyone realized that Quinten had vanished.

13

For several weeks after Kris's visit, Veerle's thoughts kept returning almost obsessively to the things he had told her. Outwardly, life went on as normal. She got up every morning, raised the shutters to let in the morning light– sometimes sunshine, more often the grey miasma of autumn. She took the De Lijn bus to school and spent the day working as hard as she could; diligently taking notes, her dark head bent over the desk, or answering questions. The faces in her classroom were coalescing into personalities: Mathis, the class clown; Finn, who was a bit too fond of himself but so laid back that you couldn't really mind; Emma, who was quiet but pleasant, and sometimes lent Veerle things in class. Veerle thought that Emma could become a good friend in time.

Geert called her to say that her little brother Adam had said his first word. At least, he and Anneke thought so. The word had been *Papa* or (Geert admitted) possibly *gaga*. Veerle had smiled a little at that, but she was pleased for her father. She had ended the call with a promise to visit soon so that she could hear this portentous utterance for herself.

Sometimes she walked into Tervuren after school and picked up a few groceries before taking the bus the rest of the way back to her village. She would walk up Kerkstraat, past the great bulk of the church, and let herself into the house. Then she would spend the evening cooking, completing her coursework, surfing the internet. At last she would let the shutters down again and go to bed.

That was her outward life. Inwardly, her thoughts seethed like swarming insects, crawling all over every aspect of the situation, testing and probing.

She had not seen Kris since the afternoon he came to the house. He had left not long after saying that terrible thing. *I think it's about us.* There was nothing else to say after that. It was the white flash of bare bone – it was the grin on the skull. She couldn't discuss what to do until she had understood that, and even then, she wasn't sure whom she should be discussing it with. Perhaps only herself.

Kris had stood up, and she had got to her feet too. She had gone with him to the front door, moving automatically like a person in the grip of a horrible but very realistic dream, her face drawn with shock. She had not expected Kris to touch her. She still remembered the night on Bijlokevest when she had thought he might kiss her one last time, but she had seen him turn his collar up, his face impassive, and turn away. So she was surprised when he turned and embraced her, pulling her close to him. Her face was pressed into the warmth of his bare neck.

'Just be careful,' she heard him say into her hair. 'If anything happens, call me. Or call the police. OK?'

Veerle had nodded, and he had released her. A moment later he was gone, and she was closing the door behind him, shooting the bolt across. Acting mechanically, she locked the door with the deadbolt too. After a moment's thought she went through the house to the back door and checked that that was locked as well. She took the key out of the lock altogether and laid it on a shelf, away from the door. Then she had stumbled back to the kitchen, the thoughts already rising in buzzing clouds, like flies from a stinking carcass.

And so it had been ever since. On the bus, at school, in her bed at night – it was always with her. And yet she couldn't come to any conclusion about what to do.

Gregory was dead. That was a fact. After Kris had gone, she had booted up her laptop and gone online to see for herself. The story was there, on several news sites, accompanied by various quotes from the police about possible lines of investigation, all covering the fact that they didn't have a single suspect.

Still, Veerle supposed, someone other than De Jager could have killed Gregory. The emails, those were ominous. Under no circumstances was receiving a message from a dead man anything other than sinister – and Gregory wasn't just dead. He had been butchered.

Was it possible, she wondered, that it really *was* just a sick joke? She couldn't see *how*; it wasn't likely that a webhead like Gregory would share his login details or choose a password that was easy to guess. The emails continued to prey on her mind.

Then there were the two K. Verstraetens who had died, at least one of them actually killed.

If I knew two other V. De Keysers living in this area had been murdered, I'd be worried. No, I'd be more than worried. I'd be shit scared.

She'd checked that online too, but all she'd found was a reference to a burglary in which the victim's surname was De Keyser. That could have been something or absolutely nothing.

Veerle could see why Kris had come to the conclusions he had – why he'd gone to the trouble of tracking her down and sharing his suspicions. She thought about Kris, about the promise she had made to her father, already broken. She thought about what Bram would say when she told him about the visit. *If* she ever told him.

He'd be annoyed, she thought – and suspicious. He'd always been uneasy about Kris, thinking that there was still a spark between him and Veerle. And, Veerle knew, he was right. She couldn't deny it. She saw Kris and she still wanted him. The fact that she wasn't going to do anything about it – *couldn't* do anything about it, with the ghost of Hommel standing between them like a sentinel – wasn't going to be enough to keep Bram happy. Bram wanted the whole of her, not half.

No; Bram would be suspicious. He might actually think that Kris had made up the story of the email as an excuse to approach Veerle again. After all, it had worked, hadn't it? She wouldn't have opened the door, wouldn't have heard him out, if it hadn't seemed so urgent.

When this thought occurred to her, Veerle had a dizzying moment as she wondered whether these hypothetical suspicions she was attributing to Bram could possibly be true. A feeling as hot and poisonous as guilt suffused her.

No, she said to herself, pushing the idea away determinedly. *You know Kris would never, never do anything like that.* Her confidence in that belief solidified around her; ground that had seemed to tilt like a fairground ride was suddenly firm beneath her feet again. All the same, she had shocked herself. Had it got to the stage where she didn't really trust *anyone*?

Not long after Kris's visit, Bram had called her. He hadn't just phoned; he had Skyped her from his digs in Ghent. Veerle had known he would call – he still wanted an answer to his question about when she was coming to Ghent – and she had been determined to answer, and to act as normally as possible. However, she was slightly dismayed that he hadn't just phoned her mobile. It was hard enough trying to sound nonchalant over the phone, but twice as hard to look it over a video link. She had tried, anyway.

Bram's familiar face had appeared on the screen, blond hair falling untidily over his blue eyes.

Bram had his back to the wall in his room; if he turned himself and the laptop round so that he had his back to the window, would she be able to spot the Belfort tower looming over the surrounding buildings? She felt a rush of something that was not as pleasant as nostalgia.

Bram was looking at her with a welcoming grin. Veerle tried to smile back as carelessly as possible, but the smile felt unnatural, as though her face were some stiff clay being pressed into a grimace by brusque fingers.

Right up until the very last moment, she had not made up her mind whether to tell Bram everything. Now she found she simply couldn't do it. Kris's revelations had left her feeling exhausted; rehashing it all with Bram didn't feel possible. She couldn't think of any good way to tell him that she had spent over an hour with Kris, either.

'Are you OK?' Bram had asked her, and she had tried to pep up that artificial smile.

'Yeah,' she said, brushing the hair back out of her eyes with one hand and taking the brief opportunity to drop her gaze. 'I'm just a bit tired.'

'How is it going?'

'School? It's all right. I mean, I've covered most of the work before, just not well enough.' Veerle shrugged. 'I'm catching up OK.'

'So it's all right?'

'I guess so.'

'Caught up with anyone you know?'

Only Kris.

'Not really. They were all in the year below me.'

I've just lied to him, Veerle thought dismally. But what could she have said? She hadn't really got it straight in her own mind, that meeting with Kris.

Nothing happened, she reminded herself.

She began to ask him questions, wanting to put the matter of Kris and her concealment of the meeting behind her, and Bram had been pleased, telling her all about his day, about his coursework, about a new place that had opened up, which he'd really like to take her to when she visited. Then he had pressed her to say when she would come, and once again she'd put him off. The excuses were wearing thin, she knew that; soon she'd have to agree to go or risk a breach between them. But that meant staying over at Bram's . . .

When they'd hung up, Bram had said, 'Love you,' and Veerle had fudged it again, saying, 'Me too.' She *did* care about him – he was more than lovable – but she wasn't *in* love . . .

not yet. Bram was always wanting to move much faster than she did; she wished she could slow things down.

She remembered Kris saying, *Veerle, just . . . Please, go back to Ghent.* How would it be if she took him at his word?

She had sat there for a very long time, bathed in the dying rays of the sun streaming through the window, thinking. She had come to no conclusion that night; only that she was not going to rush back to Ghent, not for one night to see Bram, nor permanently because of what Kris had told her. Part of her hoped that the leaden feeling of dread that had descended on her after she heard what Kris had to say would dissipate after a night's sleep, the way a nightmare never feels as bad after a second, dreamfree night.

It didn't, though, and since then she'd had that horrible feeling, as though her brain were an ants' nest, teeming with busy and ceaseless activity.

At last she came to a decision. The problem, she thought, was the same one that had dogged her in the past: pieces of information that could be put together in a certain way to create one particular picture, but could just as easily be random. Maybe De Jager was around again. Maybe someone was just playing a very sick joke. Maybe Kris— But no, she wasn't even going to consider *that* option.

She could consider the details she had for ever and she wouldn't manage to work it out, any more than you could finish a jigsaw with only half the pieces. No; she was going to have to do some poking about of her own.

Veerle decided to pay Fred a visit.

14

The following Saturday morning Veerle got up early and caught the bus that left the village shortly after eight-thirty. She knew that there was no particular hurry; businesses like Fred's art gallery frequently didn't open until late in the morning. Perhaps he wouldn't open up at all on a Saturday, but she was prepared to risk that. The restless thoughts that had tormented her all week were reaching a crescendo; she had to do *something*.

By nine she was on the number 44 tram, pulling away from Tervuren on its half-hour journey to Brussels. Once she had settled herself into one of the single seats by the window, her shoulder bumping the glass lightly as the tram swayed along, she hauled out her mobile phone and turned it off. If Bram rang her she would only have to think up some fictitious reason for the expedition, and if Kris rang her it would be worse – she was trying to verify his story, after all. At Montgomery she got off the tram and descended into the metro. She was heading for Porte de Namur, which meant a single change.

She was a little tense, because she knew that Fred wouldn't be pleased to see her; there would probably be a scene. But

Veerle wasn't going to let that stop her. She had faced a lot worse, after all. Fred wouldn't do anything more than shout at her.

She had thought about what she would say. Fred would know all about what had happened to Gregory, obviously. She would ask whether anyone had approached *him*, or whether he'd had any odd messages or calls. And she would have to press him on the topic of the Koekoeken membership. Did he still have a list? Fred was the only living Koekoeken member she knew of, apart from Kris, but there must be dozens of others. Did he have any contact with any of them? He must, she thought; a thing like the Koekoeken spread organically and the first members must have been people he knew personally. Fred hadn't wanted to know when she and Kris had visited him last time; he had blustered, trying to deny that there was anything sinister going on, and when they had persisted, his response had been to close down the web forum. Never mind that this would only make the killer move on. Now, Veerle thought, she would try to insist that he take the situation seriously. If he still had a list, then the chances were De Jager was on it, concealed by some other name.

Her pace quickened perceptibly as she strode along, the ideas developing in her mind. Supposing the emails had been nothing more than a sick and opportunistic joke? It was still true that people who got into the Koekoeken were most likely into other things with an element of risk to them. If Fred could tell her that Gregory had been mixed up in something else which had probably been the thing that had got him killed, then Veerle could sleep soundly at night again – or as soundly as she ever did, these days.

She turned down a side street, and then made a second turn onto the street where the gallery was. She picked it out with ease: the white stucco stood out amongst the other more sombre buildings. Her heart sank as she approached it, though. The large and gleaming glass window was veiled behind a security cage.

Too early, Veerle told herself. *Maybe he opens at eleven, or noon.*

She crossed the street, moving unhurriedly now, not wanting to draw attention to herself. The window was caged all right, but she now saw that the door was not. There was a security shutter, but it was in the raised position, poised over the doorway like the blade of a guillotine waiting to descend. The inexpressive eye of the CCTV camera stared down at Veerle.

Although the window was caged, it was still easy enough to see the displays behind the glass. It had been a year since Veerle had last visited the gallery with Kris, so it was not surprising that the lace-like bowl and the ugly chunk of carved stone she had last seen had gone, replaced by two etiolated wire sculptures of figures that might have been humans or aliens. Veerle thought that they were possibly even uglier than the stone block.

She looked up at the security camera, and then at the door itself. At first sight the raised shutter had suggested that someone was inside – that they had just unlocked the door for the day but had not got as far as lifting the cage over the window or opening the gallery to customers. Now she began to think otherwise. There was a letterbox attached to the wall by the door, and it was stuffed with post, the flap wedged open by the thick sheaf of letters, like a roast hog with an apple in its jaws. Veerle looked down and saw others piled on the doorstep too. Some of them had a pale wrinkled look which showed that they had been sitting there for some time, that rain had spattered them at some point. The step itself was bone dry, as was the pavement, so it hadn't happened recently.

She looked at the CCTV camera again. She had a strong feeling that the glass eye was blind, that even if it was working, there was nobody to look at what it recorded.

Veerle pressed the buzzer, still looking up towards the lens. Fred had to let her in, if he was inside, so there was no point in hiding her face. She didn't hold out much hope, however. The drift of abandoned letters told its own story.

After a minute of fruitless pressing on the buzzer, she pushed at the door with the flat of her hands, but of course it was locked. Veerle pressed her face to the glass and peered inside. It was very dim in there. No lights were on so the only illumination came from the door and the windows, which were mostly blocked by screens forming the backdrop to the wire figures.

She could make out a number of plinths with objects on them, and more of the wire sculptures. There was a chair by the wall, an overdesigned thing made of leather and chrome, and next to it a glass-topped unit with a slippery fan of brochures on it. There was no sign of anyone inside – no sign anyone had been in there *recently*.

Veerle bit her lip.

Perhaps he's moved on.

But that didn't make sense. She looked at those wire

sculptures. Ugly though they were, someone had *created* those. It wasn't likely that Fred would move his business or indeed his private life away from the gallery and leave someone's work sitting there until the next tenants arrived.

Veerle pressed the buzzer again, but it was half-hearted this time. She didn't think there was any chance that anyone would answer.

After that she stepped back out of the doorway onto the street and looked around.

Somebody must know where he is.

The shops on either side were just as expensive and exclusive looking as the gallery itself. Both were lit, indicating that someone was inside, but still she hesitated to go in and quiz the occupants about Fred's whereabouts. She couldn't imagine getting a friendly hearing: a teenage girl in jeans and boots and a scruffy-looking jacket.

As she stood there she saw a saleswoman appear at the window of one of the shops, all coiffed hair and tailored clothing. The woman gave Veerle a very dirty look. *No point in asking in there,* Veerle thought.

As she was standing there, wondering what to do, she saw a door open on the other side of the street. It was a service door, squeezed in between two shops just as grandiose as these ones. A woman of perhaps sixty emerged, holding a broom. She was stout, moving slowly as though the effort of carrying the broom out into the street had left her breathless, and clad in a dingy floral overall.

Veerle crossed the road and went up to her. 'Excuse me?' she said in French. Although she always used Flemish with her friends and at school, Veerle had grown up with a

Francophone mother, so her French was fluent and almost without accent. In spite of this, she half expected a rebuff. The way the woman was huffing and puffing was not suggestive of a cheerful disposition.

The older woman surprised her, though. First she looked at Veerle as though she had only just noticed that there was another person nearby, and then her wrinkled face broke into a pleasant smile.

'You know the gallery over there?' said Veerle, pointing. She tried a smile herself. 'I'm looking for the owner, Fred.'

The expression that fleetingly crossed the woman's face did not escape Veerle's attention. Well; that was no surprise. Fred had been so high handed on the one occasion Veerle had met him that she couldn't imagine him having time to be polite to his neighbours' cleaners.

Still, the old lady quashed whatever opinion of Fred had been rising to her lips. She leaned on the broom and looked at Veerle carefully. 'What do you want with him?'

Veerle should have been prepared for that question. She hesitated, various options suggesting themselves in rapid succession. Friend? Relative? Godchild? But any of those would have some idea where he was. Instead she said, 'I'm looking for work.'

When that got her a doubtful look, she added, 'I'm an art student.'

The old woman was shaking her head. 'I think you've wasted your time. He's not going to employ anyone. He's gone off.'

'Gone off?'

'Oh yes. No one's seen him for weeks. In fact, it might be a couple of months now. I lose track.'

It wasn't difficult for Veerle to show a disappointed expression. She said, 'Do you have any idea where?'

The old woman shook her head. 'No. I don't believe anyone does.'

'Is the gallery closed down?'

'It is now. But there's going to be trouble about it. He went off without leaving a key with anyone, and without sending all those masterpieces back to their owners. Already a couple of them have been here, ringing the doorbell and banging on the door.'

'Really?'

'Oh, yes.'

'And nobody has any idea why he went off, or where?'

The old woman looked at Veerle, rubbing her withered lips together. 'Probably money trouble.' She leaned forward conspiratorially. 'Who would buy any of the things in that gallery? All of them as ugly as the seven deadly sins.'

At that, Veerle couldn't help herself. She laughed.

The old woman grinned, pleased. She went on, 'People have been there because of unpaid bills too. But there's never anyone there. He must have been a spendthrift, that man. After he'd gone he left the upstairs lights burning night and day for weeks. I suppose they've cut off the power now.'

She rattled on, not noticing that her audience's mind was elsewhere.

Veerle was standing there, nodding agreement, but her mind was running on what the old woman had told her about the lights. She had a very ominous feeling about that.

The window was caged but the shutter on the front door was up.

And the lights were on for weeks. Night and day, she said.

The shutter on the door was up but the cage on the window was down. Just as if someone were getting ready to close up for night – only they didn't leave the gallery.

The lights were on for weeks, because nobody ever turned them off.

Maybe they didn't turn them off because they never left.

This was giving Veerle a very bad feeling indeed.

She thought about Fred, and she thought about Gregory and the very bad company he had found himself in. When she and Kris visited him Fred had been pretty arrogant, but she didn't believe he actually had the instincts to fight. Veerle doubted he would last half a minute in a direct confrontation with someone really brutal. *De Jager, for example.*

Fred was wary about who came into the gallery. As with other overpriced shops, the front door was normally locked and you had to get someone to buzz you inside. If Fred didn't like the look of you, you didn't get to come in. The only reason he had let her and Kris inside was to stop anyone else seeing them outside the gallery. He hadn't wanted his connection to the Koekoeken advertised.

So Fred would not have opened the door to De Jager, but there was one moment when the gallery was vulnerable, and that was when Fred himself was outside on the doorstep, preparing to lock up for the night. Then it would be possible for someone larger and stronger than him to force his way in, taking the art dealer with him, perhaps dragging him bodily, a meaty fist clenched in the fabric of that flamboyant purple shirt Fred wore.

Veerle had pressed her nose to the glass door and gazed into the gallery, and she had seen no sign of anyone inside. But, she remembered, there was a staircase leading to the first floor, where Fred had an office furnished with an expensive coffee maker and decorated with tasteful black-and-white photographs of his urban exploration. There was no way to see into *that* from street level. The only way to get a view into the office was from the upper windows of the building opposite, and even then it would be quite easy to block the view by pulling down the blinds.

A feeling of cold dread was seeping through Veerle, draining the colour from her face. Her imagination was presenting a scenario to her in which Fred was forced back through the door by someone who kicked it shut behind him, and dragged the protesting art dealer up the stairs. Once inside the office, out of sight of prying eyes, that someone could have done anything to Fred, anything at all that might make him cough up what he knew. Fred would probably have spilled his guts pretty quickly, but that wouldn't have helped him; alive, he could describe his attacker. So at some point he had had to die. His assailant had at last let him go, a savage dog dropping something it had torn and shaken to bloody death, and Fred had landed on the gleaming floor with the finesse of a falling bag of cement.

After that, the killer had only to descend the stairs and let himself out of the gallery, locking the door behind him and taking the keys away with him. The body was locked in, and everyone else was locked out. For a few days nobody would think anything of the closed gallery. Perhaps they would see the lights burning and think that the owner was working night and day on his accounts, or stocktaking or something.

Eventually the post had started piling up. The letterbox became full and the postman started leaving things in the corner of the doorway instead. Still nobody would have jumped to any extreme conclusions; people sometimes went away for a week or two, forgetting to cancel the mail delivery. And all the time Fred would be lying upstairs on the polished floor, his dead eyes staring into nothing and his tissues slowly dissolving into a puddle of decay from which any forensic evidence would be increasingly difficult to retrieve.

How long? wondered Veerle.

The lights might have gone out because the power had been cut. But perhaps the bulbs had died, or a fuse had blown. If Fred paid all the regular bills, power and rent and water, by direct debit, the bank would carry on paying out until funds in the account ran out. That might be a long time, considering the price tags on the artworks in the gallery. The angry artists whose work was imprisoned inside were a different matter, but they wouldn't just break in – couldn't, perhaps, since the window cage was down and the door locked. They might send threatening letters, but those would pile up on the doorstep with everything else.

Hold it, Veerle said to herself. *You're letting your imagination run away with you. Perhaps he really* did *just leave. Perhaps he took all the cash out of the business and flew off to somewhere sunny. You don't know.*

But she looked up at the first-floor windows above the gallery and thought that she *did* know.

She glanced at the old lady and found that she had stopped talking. She was looking at Veerle a little strangely.

'Are you all right, dear?' she enquired, but her tone was a little stiff. Veerle guessed that she had caused offence by her obvious inattention.

'I'm sorry,' she said as warmly as she could. 'I'm just . . .'

'Disappointed?' said the old lady. She sniffed. 'It's a shame about the job you were after, but you wouldn't have wanted to work there.'

She turned, and began to sweep the pavement with short, brusque movements.

'Thank you,' said Veerle to her back. She glanced at the gallery one more time, and then walked back towards the metro station.

15

De Jager sat at the table in the dowdy kitchen with the laptop open in front of him. It was dusk and the room was dim, the screen bathing his heavy features in a bluish light so that his face hung like a Halloween lantern in the murk. He was looking at the website for the White Pages, the telephone listings for Belgium.

There were eleven De Keysers and eight Dekeysers listed for the village. De Jager was not dismayed by this. He was confident that he could winnow his way through them until he found the right one. *If* she was listed there, of course – and that all depended on her circumstances. It was a shame she hadn't taken the bait of the emails from Gregory's account. She could have saved both of them a lot of time.

Briefly he closed his eyes, remembering. He'd had a clear view of the girl that evening at the old castle. He had seen her run across the hall and climb the stairs. She had stood at the top, leaning over the wooden rail of the gallery so that she could shout abuse at him. Finally he had pursued her along the upper corridor, while she fled silently and the flames roared.

How old is she?

He was the Hunter. He was used to gauging the age, the sex, the approximate weight or indeed height of his prey, judging how best to subdue them, how much force would be required. He made himself do it now, recreating the scene in his mind with as much intricate detail as possible. He supplemented his hunter's judgement with the deductive skills of a tracker.

De Jager thought that Veerle was – or had been, the night he saw her – between sixteen and nineteen years old, perhaps 1.65 metres tall, with a slender athletic build – ideal for climbing out of windows and down walls, not so good for fighting off someone heavier, and armed.

Assuming she had been in the village the day Joren Sterckx was seen striding through it with the bloody body of a child in his arms, and assuming that this was indeed how she had recognized him, she could not have been too young at the time of the killing. A child of two, for example, would not have recalled anything. So Veerle had probably been at least six or seven at the time, possibly several years older. This would mean that now she must be at least seventeen and possibly as old as twenty-one or twenty-two.

This presented possible difficulties. At seventeen Veerle would by law still be in full-time education, probably at a local secondary school. She would probably be living with her parents, in which case she might be at one of the nineteen addresses listed in the White Pages, depending on whether it was her father's name or her mother's that appeared.

At nineteen or more, however, she had a great many more options. She might have left education and gone straight into a job, in which case she could still be living at home but she might also have a flat of her own. She might have left the village altogether and gone to university.

In either of those cases it would still be possible to find her through her home village, as long as he found a member of her household. People always told De Jager what he wanted to know in the end. It simply took longer with some than it did with others. This did not bother him; in fact he tended to prefer it when it look a long time.

And if none of this led him to Veerle?

He could enquire amongst other people in the village, not just those at the key addresses – people who might know where she was, or where she had gone. That was not his ideal method, because it was risky; if his assumptions were correct, and Veerle's village was *his* village, there was a danger that someone would realize who he was. He had an idea how he might get around that problem, however, though he filed it away for future reference.

De Jager looked at the names on the screen. His large fingers rested on the rim of the keyboard. After a few moments he began to type. One forefinger skated about the mouse pad, then clicked.

He had covered this ground before, but there was no harm in trying again. He searched for Veerle's name, then Kris's, trying slight variations in spelling. He tried entering their email addresses, in case those were linked to some kind of listing. Nothing. It seemed that neither Kris nor Veerle had any presence on social media, nor had either of them won a prize, been placed in a race or represented their school or workplace. As far as online presence went, the pair of them might never have existed. Either they led humdrum technophobe lives or they were *very* careful. He suspected it was the latter.

After a little thought he checked the inbox of Gregory's email account too. As anticipated, there was nothing except a couple of spam messages. Nothing from Veerle. Kris hadn't replied to his email containing the GPS co-ordinates, and De Jager hadn't really expected him to – not since that idiotic troop of Scouts had stumbled on the cache.

He had hoped that that opening salvo would grab Kris's attention – would convince him of the seriousness of his, De Jager's, intentions. Once the dialogue had been opened he was confident of luring Kris in, with a combination of bait and barbed threats. Now, however, it was debatable whether Kris understood the message at all. There would be nothing to find at that spot in the park, unless it was a length of warning tape marking the spot where the cache had been. The papers hadn't named the owner of the finger, assuming they had worked out whose it was.

No matter. There was plenty of time for Kris Verstraeten. If he found Veerle first, De Jager thought, he might have something *really* alluring as bait – something Kris wouldn't be able to resist. He'd send a time as well as the location, and then he'd be sure of meeting face to face.

He went offline and shut down the laptop. It was really dark in the kitchen now. Night. In the village, shutters would be descending; people would be fortifying themselves against the darkness.

He could have gone out to make a start on the nineteen names in the White Pages; people were wary of opening their doors to unexpected visitors at night, but on the other hand, wherever the shutters *weren't* down you could see right inside; you could see people moving about in the brightly lit interiors. He might spot Veerle in her sitting room, oblivious to the wrath that was about to descend on her.

He decided against it, though. It could wait for tomorrow. Tonight he had other prey.

16

On Sunday morning Veerle awoke to the sound of the church bell striking the hour. Drifting up into wakefulness, she began to count the number of times it rang, but she was not sure whether she had missed some. She reached over and pressed the button on top of the alarm clock by her bed, so that the dial lit up. It was nine a.m.

It felt strange to be lying here in the house with the bell striking outside and absolutely no sound within except her own breathing. With the roller shutters down it was very dark, but since this *thing* had come up, this horrible, frightening and possibly paranoid thing about De Jager, she didn't like to sleep without putting them down. She lay there for a little while, thinking about other Sunday mornings, when her mother had still been alive.

Claudine attended mass regularly, but she never went to the Sint-Pauluskerk on the other side of the street. She went to a French-speaking church in a nearby district. Sometimes she had tried to get Veerle to accompany her. Occasionally she had, but more often she had stayed at home. Sometimes she had lain in bed as she was now and listened to Claudine moving about.

Her mother generally made heavy weather of everything; Veerle would hear her pad down the landing on leaden feet, as though she'd had to force herself to get up. Sometimes there would be a heavy sigh as she reached the head of the stairs. Then she would descend slowly, with a series of thuds on the wooden treads. At the time all this had irritated Veerle, but now she smiled rather sadly into the darkness. If she waited until Claudine had gone out before she got up, she always found breakfast laid out for her when she went downstairs. That, she thought, was typically Claudine: a thorough pessimist who never forgot to care for you. It was strange that after all their struggles they had finally made peace.

At last Veerle switched on the bedside light and sat up. A feeling was coming over her, an unpleasant feeling that was seeping into her consciousness like chilly damp. The night before, she had come to a decision.

I have to finish it with Bram.

It had come to her when she was sitting on the tram on her way back to Tervuren, hugging herself more for reassurance than warmth, her shoulders hunched, her hands twisting restlessly. The visit to the gallery had shocked her. She had no proof that anything had happened to Fred. She wouldn't have thought of going to the police on a hunch, a wild surmise, not when they already thought she was the Girl Who Sees Dead Murderers, but she thought she knew what they would find if they ever did break in there.

Fred is dead. I know he is. Like Gregory is dead.

She hadn't liked Fred one bit – there was nothing to like: he was rude and arrogant and cowardly. But knowing what had happened to Gregory, she found that she was actually sorry for the art dealer. She wished she could have believed that he was in Mauritius, drinking cocktails with fruit in them and soaking up the sun. But she was sure he wasn't.

Trouble was coming. She could smell it, like the scent of smoke from a distant conflagration. Veerle thought that if the trouble was half as bad as she expected, it was no good running back to Ghent. The house on Kerkstraat couldn't be sold, not without a lot of investment that Geert couldn't afford, so the only option would be to move back in with Geert and Anneke and Adam. The thought that De Jager might track her there, that he might come within fifty kilometres of her tiny half-brother, made Veerle feel nauseous. She shivered, turning away from her fellow passengers, and in the window the reflection of her pale features was like a death's head, the skull and crossbones on a bottle of poison.

That's what I am, she thought. *Poison. Anyone who touches me now . . .*

That wasn't the reason why she had decided to finish with Bram, although when you came to think of it, it was a perfectly good one.

I'm not being fair to him, she thought.

She'd kept postponing going back to Ghent, but now she hadn't seen him for well over a month and it was obvious she had to make a decision: end it or commit to the relationship fully. Anything else was selfishness. It was just . . .

Veerle sighed. Bram was kind and easy-going – and yes, she admitted it, so good-looking that anyone in their right mind would want to go out with him. When he'd kissed her, she couldn't help responding, but that was part of the problem. She liked him – liked him a lot – of course she did, and Bram knew that too, and he thought that they were going down one particular path, whereas Veerle knew that she was going somewhere else altogether.

When she first returned to the village she'd thought she'd seen Kris in the street in Tervuren. And when she had opened the door to him and he had said, *Verdomme, you* are *here*, in a tone of such obvious dismay, something had shrivelled up and died inside her. The feelings she had about that were bleak and terrible ones, but they filled her heart. The road she was taking was steep and difficult and it ran through darkness and thorns, but she was going to take it anyway because she knew no other way.

She got out of bed and went to raise the shutters. The room filled with the lurid grey light of an overcast morning. The bulk of the great church was a black shape against the sky.

Veerle went over to the desk, sat down and opened her laptop. As she booted it up, she was wondering whether it was too early to call Bram. The thought of what she had to say was tormenting her; she wanted to get it over with. She chewed her lip, wondering how to open the conversation. There was no good way to say it.

But Bram was not online yet.

Veerle leaned back in her chair. She could call him on his mobile, she supposed, but if he was still asleep it seemed needlessly mean to wake him up for the kind of conversation they were inevitably going to have. Her gaze drifted down the list of contacts, and she saw then that although Bram was not online, Kris Verstraeten was.

The thought of calling Kris instantly presented itself.

I have to tell him about Fred.

Still she hesitated. They hadn't made any definite arrangement to speak to each other or see each other again. And she couldn't face any further attempts to persuade her to pack her bags and go back to Ghent. She told herself that this was because nobody, not even Kris, was going to boss her around, but the fact was, it hurt when he so obviously wished her elsewhere. All the same, this wasn't something she could keep to herself. Of all the people in the world, Kris would understand the significance of Fred's disappearance.

Veerle sat forward, gazing at the screen.

He might not be there anyway. Maybe he just left his laptop on.

Her fingers hung poised over the keyboard for a moment, and then she typed, *Are you there?*

Yes, came the reply almost instantly. *What's up?*

I went to see Fred, typed Veerle.

There was a long pause. Then: *Go to video call.*

No, she sent back.

Why?

I only just got out of bed.

Another pause. Then, *I'll come over later.*

Veerle looked at the screen, pushing her hands into the dark hair that threatened to fall over her eyes. She wondered whether breaking her promise to her father a second time made it any worse than doing it once. Maybe not. The promise was already broken; now she was just quibbling about the degree.

OK. When?

12. OK?

Yes.

Veerle waited, but there was nothing after that. She stood up, leaving the laptop open, and went downstairs to make herself some coffee. When she came back up, holding the luxuriously warm mug in two hands, Kris had gone offline.

Bram was still obstinately offline too. He remained offline after she had drunk the coffee, got dressed in jeans and a T-shirt and made herself some breakfast.

Late sleeper, she thought. She wished he wasn't; the coming conversation was one she wanted to get over with.

At half past ten she cracked and tried Bram's mobile phone, but it went straight to voicemail.

Has he vanished off the face of the earth? Veerle thought impatiently, and then she remembered Fred, who seemingly had, and hastily turned her thoughts elsewhere. The morning was going to drag if she spent it waiting for Bram to wake up, so she fetched her school bag and started on some coursework.

Once she went downstairs for more coffee. Otherwise, she worked through until five past twelve, when the doorbell rang.

It had to be Kris, but Veerle automatically glanced out of the bedroom window before she went down to open the door. Sure enough, there he was, stepping back to look up at the house.

Veerle hastily left the window and went downstairs. It took her a little time to open the front door: she had used the deadbolt as well as the pin tumbler lock, and shot the bolt across. Eventually she had undone everything and she opened the door.

'Hi,' said Kris, stepping inside. He leaned in and kissed Veerle briskly on the cheeks, the greeting of one friend to another. Then he was moving past her, into the house.

Veerle had not expected the kisses, and warmth rose to her face. She reminded herself that it didn't mean anything; she would have kissed Claudine's strident friend Berthe or her own friend Lisa if she had met them. All the same she was touched.

They went into the kitchen and took a seat on either side of the table.

'Do you want some coffee or something?' asked Veerle.

Kris shook his head. He went straight to the point. 'Tell me about Fred. Why did you go and see him? Was it about Gregory?'

'Yes. Only I didn't actually see him. He wasn't there.' Veerle hesitated. Then she said, 'Look, I may as well come out and say it. I did go because of what you told me about Gregory. I thought – well, I was *hoping* – that maybe there was some other explanation. Like Gregory was mixed up in some other stuff, and that was why . . . whoever did it did the things they did to him.'

'That wouldn't have explained the email.'

'A sick joke, maybe. I don't know. I just . . . didn't want it to be De Jager.'

Kris sighed, running a hand through his dark hair. 'I don't want it to be him, either. But I have a bad feeling.'

Veerle looked down. 'The other thing is – supposing it is him, then he might be traceable through the Koekoeken.

I mean, he was one of them. He must have been, because he turned up at the castle that night after we posted that message on the web forum. Nobody except the Koekoeken could have seen that message. Now Gregory's dead and everything he had was burnt, the only person who might still have a list of all the members is Fred.'

'He wouldn't have given it to you even if he did have it,' commented Kris. 'You saw what he was like, that time we went to talk to him. He doesn't want any trouble – doesn't want to know. He'd probably burn it himself before he handed it over.'

'I know,' said Veerle heavily. 'But I was going to try to persuade him.' She looked at Kris. 'I mean, this is serious. This is not just *Maybe something is happening to a bunch of people we don't really know – and maybe not.* This is someone coming after us. You and me.' She let out a long breath. 'If he didn't co-operate I was going to threaten to go to the police and tell them he'd been involved all along.'

Veerle was relieved to see that Kris did not look offended at what she had done, with its implication of checking up on his story. If anything, he looked admiring.

'They wouldn't have believed me even if I did,' she added. 'They think I'm slightly nuts anyway. But Fred wouldn't know that.'

'So what happened when you got there? He was out, or just not answering the door?'

'He was' – Veerle shrugged – 'gone. There was a kind of grille over the window but the security shutter on the front door was up, as though someone had just gone in or out. The door was locked. I know because I tried it. But I didn't really think he was there anyway. The letterbox was full of post and there was a heap of it on the doorstep too. Half of it was kind of wrinkly from getting wet so I think it had been there for ages.'

'So what did you do? Did you just come straight back?'

Veerle shook her head. 'There was this old lady brushing the pavement so I asked her if she knew where Fred was. She said he'd disappeared. Hadn't been back for weeks. Maybe even a month or two. Nobody knows where he went.'

Veerle stopped. She had seen the expression that crossed Kris's face when she said the word *disappeared*.

When Kris spoke there was a grim edge to his voice. 'Where did the old lady think he had gone?'

'She thought maybe he had money worries and did a runner.'

'But . . .'

'But she also said that after he vanished, the lights were on in the office for a long time. Day *and* night. They went out in the end but that might have been the power being cut off.'

'And nobody had checked?'

'I don't think so. I mean, she'd probably have known. She seemed kind of . . . sharp-eyed. She'd noticed the lights on.'

Kris smiled faintly at *sharp-eyed* but his air remained sombre. 'This *is* about us. Maybe it's about *all* the Koekoeken – I don't know. But that includes us.'

'I know,' said Veerle. 'I just . . .' Her voice tailed off. *I just don't want it to be.* The life she had planned out for herself – the diligent schoolwork, the housekeeping for herself – seemed to be dissolving like some kind of improbable dream. She wanted to snatch at it, to wrap herself in it again.

'Maybe Fred *has* done a runner,' she said uncertainly.

'Veerle, you know he hasn't. And even if he had, at least three people are dead. Two with my name . . . and Gregory. This isn't going away.'

'So what are we going to do?'

'I still think you should go back to Ghent,' said Kris firmly.

Veerle leaned forward. 'I can't. And anyway, if De Jager is back and he's going to the trouble of torturing people to death to find the ones he's after, do you think he's going to stop because I've moved seventy kilometres away? Suppose he comes looking for me there? My half-brother is only a baby, Kris. I can't risk it.'

'You could stay with Bram.'

'Are you crazy? He can't fight off De Jager, either. And anyway – it's finished with Bram. I mean—'

Veerle stopped short, realizing that she had come out and told Kris for the first time that there *had* been something going on with Bram, and conscious that it was not strictly accurate to say that it was finished. It *would* have been finished if Bram had been online this morning, and it would be over before the evening, but at present it was a unilateral decision, not yet communicated to Bram.

For a moment neither Kris nor Veerle said anything. Then Kris said, 'If it's him, nobody can fight him. Only the police, maybe.'

'Kris, I've already told the police who I think he is, and given them a description. They didn't believe me.'

'Maybe we need to get them more evidence.'

'What? Try to lure him out by using ourselves as bait again?' Veerle stared. 'No. No way.' She pushed back her sleeve and showed him the scars. 'Remember what happened last time?' Her temper was kindling now. 'He shot you with a *crossbow*, Kris. Remember that?'

'Of course I do,' Kris snapped back. 'That's not what I'm suggesting. I just think we could do a bit of investigating ourselves. There must be a reason why you recognized him, Veerle. Maybe he didn't die in prison after all.'

'How could we prove that?'

'I don't know. But we could at least *try* to find out.' Kris considered. 'If we could get a better photo of him than the crappy ones in the papers, you could take a really good look at that too. Maybe something would strike you – I don't know, some detail.'

'You think maybe I'd realize it wasn't him I saw?' said Veerle, not without bitterness.

'If Joren Sterckx really is dead, then it *wasn't* him, was it?' Kris told her reasonably.

'OK,' said Veerle after a pause. She sat back, letting out a long breath. 'I guess we have to do something other than sit here and wait to see if De Jager comes looking for us.'

'Veerle . . . you shouldn't be here on your own, you know. In case.'

'I don't have much option,' she pointed out. 'I told you, I can't go back to Ghent.'

'I could stay here with you for a while.'

Veerle's jaw dropped. She stared into Kris's dark eyes but she was too stunned to try to read his expression. When she tried to speak her mouth was dry; she had to clear her throat.

'What are you suggesting?' she managed to ask.

'Just that.' Kris shrugged. 'I could stay here so you're not alone if anything . . . odd happens.'

'Ah . . .' Veerle found that she was actually lost for words. It wasn't the fact that she was now completely disregarding the promise she had made to Geert; it wasn't even the practical question of accommodating another person in the house. She was thinking about the hours and hours she and Kris would be spending in each other's company if he did what he proposed. She felt an almost uncontrollable urge to say yes, and yet she knew it would be like asking someone who has crawled across a desert to sit amongst fountains of clear sparkling water without slaking their thirst. It wasn't the promise she had made to her father that held her back – it was the promise to herself. All the same, she couldn't quite bring herself to say no. The word was stuck in her throat, choking her.

When she failed to produce anything that sounded like a coherent reply to the suggestion, Kris put out a hand towards her, saying, 'Look, Veerle, what happened in Ghent—'

He didn't get any further. The doorbell buzzed like an angry wasp.

Who the hell is that? thought Veerle.

She and Kris looked at each other.

'Are you expecting someone?' he said. He spoke casually but there was a slight edge to his voice.

'No,' said Veerle, shaking her head. For a moment she remained where she was, at the kitchen table. Then abruptly she stood up, pushing back her chair. 'We're getting paranoid,' she said. 'It's not likely to be – you know, *him* –

ringing the bell in the middle of the day. It's probably just one of the neighbours wanting something.'

This was undeniably possible, but still, Kris stood up and went with her to the door. The doorbell buzzed again as Veerle was fumbling with the latch.

'Hold on,' she muttered under her breath. *Why so impatient?* Then she managed it, and she opened the door.

It was Bram.

Seeing him there on her own doorstop was such an unexpected shock that it took Veerle a second to understand that it was really Bram. The neutral words of greeting that she had been preparing to say died on her lips. Dimly she was aware of Kris at her shoulder.

Bram had been about to say something too – probably *Surprise!* – but the words curdled in his throat. Veerle saw the expression on his face go from cheerful and slightly self-conscious expectation to blank shock before it hardened into something far grimmer. A flash of colour snagged her gaze; she glanced down and saw that he had brought flowers, a bright sheaf of them wrapped in cellophane. The sight of those, more than the sight of Bram's outraged face, almost broke her heart.

At her shoulder she felt Kris react; she heard the angry word that hissed out of him like steam.

Veerle stepped out of the doorway, towards Bram. 'Bram—' she began.

'No,' said Bram, in a hard voice quite unlike any tone she had heard him use before. He flung away the flowers, not caring where they fell.

'Bram, I know what you're thinking—'

'Do you?' he shot back with heavy irony. 'Then you'll know that I've wasted my time coming all this way. I never had you down as a cheat, Veerle.' His gaze moved briefly to Kris. 'Seems to me you two deserve each other.'

'Will you let me speak?' burst out Veerle.

'I don't want to hear it,' snapped Bram. 'I'm not blind. I can see what's going on.'

'Maybe you can tell me then,' said Kris coldly. 'Veerle, you told me you'd finished with him. So what's he doing here with a bunch of flowers?'

'Finished?' repeated Bram with a dangerous note in his voice. 'You told him that, did you, Veerle?'

Veerle was beside herself. 'Bram, I was going to talk to you. I just—'

'Really? When? Whenever you got round to it?' he said with biting sarcasm. His handsome face was made ugly by a scowl. 'I guess it didn't really matter when, did it? Because you thought I was in Ghent where I wouldn't have any way of knowing what you were getting up to.'

'Veerle?' That icy voice in her right ear was Kris's. 'You said you'd finished with him.'

Veerle pushed her fingers into her hair, clutching handfuls of it. She felt like screaming, the rising pressure within her accelerated by the guilty knowledge that this could have been avoided, if only, if only . . .

'I meant . . .' Words failed her. 'I don't *know* what I meant.'

'Run out of lies?' snapped Bram tightly.

'*Someone's* lying here,' said Kris, and the deadly chill in his voice was worse than the heat in Bram's.

'I tried to call you,' said Veerle to Bram.

'Save it,' he told her. His eyes flickered contemptuously over her and Kris. 'You told him we were finished. Well, as of now, we are.' He shook his head angrily. 'I can't believe you'd be such a b—'

Veerle might have forgiven him the word he used then. She could see the corrosive look of hurt in his eyes. But Kris lunged at him. Bram stepped back, and the next moment the pair of them were grappling with each other on the pavement.

'Stop it!' screamed Veerle.

Behind her a window went up with a bang. 'What's going on?' said an indignant female voice. That was Mevrouw Peeters, one of the neighbours; Veerle knew without looking round. A moment later there was a second report as another window was thrown up, and this time it was a male voice demanding to know what the hell was going on.

This brought Kris and Bram to their senses. They separated reluctantly, glowering at each other like tomcats.

Even without the angry retorts from the neighbours Veerle was conscious of them glaring down at her, of the avid gaze of Mevrouw Peeters and the surly one of the man further down.

Disaster. If Geert had asked any of the neighbours to keep an eye on Veerle, she supposed it would be no more than minutes before they were on the phone telling him there was a fight taking place on his daughter's doorstep, and giving him a minute description of both protagonists. Veerle didn't think Geert could make her come back to Ghent whatever she did, but she was horrified at the thought of being caught breaking her promise.

Her tenuous grip on her rising temper slipped away.

'Get lost, both of you,' she blurted out – so vehemently that in spite of their barely suppressed anger both Bram and Kris looked shocked. 'Idiots – fighting! As if there wasn't enough shit flying around already. Why don't you just go away? Go!' Her voice was rising to a shriek.

'Veerle—' began Kris.

'Get lost. I don't want to see either of you again! Just – just – *go away*!'

Veerle marched into the house and slammed the door so hard that it jumped in its frame. Her face was burning with the humiliation of being seen by the neighbours. She shot the bolt across with trembling fingers. Then she folded her arms and went into the kitchen, realized she could still see Kris standing outside through the window, and went upstairs to her room instead.

A couple of minutes later the doorbell buzzed twice in quick succession. Veerle swept her hands through the books spread out on her desk. Her fingers closed on her MP3 player. She jammed the headphones onto her head and turned up the music as loud as she could. Then she sat on the bed, her back to the window, hands clenched into fists on her knees.

She wasn't even sure *what* she was feeling: anger at Bram or Kris or herself or at the neighbours for poking their noses in; shame at being thought to have lied deliberately; misery at having hurt Bram. All of it was churning about inside her and she might as well have tried to identify individual pieces of debris being borne along by a flash flood. She was drowning in a hot tide of emotion.

Veerle sat there for a long time, hugging herself, letting the music block out anything from outside. Gradually the temperature of her mood began to drop. A leaden calm crept over her, insidious as hypothermia. She stood up and went slowly to the window. When she looked down into Kerkstraat there was no one there. It seemed even the neighbours had drawn their heads back in again.

Veerle took off her headphones and laid them on the desk. Then she picked up her mobile phone and looked at it. No missed calls. It looked as though Kris and Bram had taken her at her word.

She rubbed the smooth edge of the phone with her thumb, thinking.

Who do I call?

Bram? She had meant to finish with him today anyway.

Only not like this, she thought. *Not with him thinking I meant to string him along.* The memory of Bram's face, the hurt on it solidifying into anger, was terrible to think about.

But Kris . . . Kris had been angry too; she had heard the ice in his voice. And he also thought she had lied about finishing with Bram.

If I'd been able to get hold of Bram this morning it wouldn't have been a lie, thought Veerle. *And none of this would have happened.* Verdomme, *why didn't I tell him before?*

She turned the phone over and over in her fingers. *Who do I call? Do I call anyone?*

At last she decided to call Bram – or at least, to call Bram first. Bram deserved to hear the truth – if he would listen to it. Up until that morning he had thought he and Veerle were an item, after all. And, Veerle thought with a miserable pang of guilt, he had travelled for hours from Ghent to see her, and ended up leaving without even setting foot in the house. So she called him, but Bram wasn't answering his mobile. The phone didn't even ring; it went straight to voicemail.

Veerle didn't think Bram's phone had run out of charge; she thought he had switched it off on purpose. She recalled vividly the day in Ghent when she had tracked a murderer to the building where he was squatting, and had tried to call Bram because she dared not go in alone. Bram had been angry that day too; when he arrived at the cathedral as arranged and found that she was not there, he had assumed that she'd stood him up. He had gone off in a state of resentment and turned his phone off for hours – all day and all the next night for all she knew, since before the end of that afternoon things had gone so horribly wrong for Veerle that she was not thinking about calling anyone but the police.

She wondered how long the phone would be off this time. *Perhaps he's got the right idea,* she said to herself. *If we speak now we're going to say things we regret.*

That left the question of whether to call Kris, and if so, what to say to him. *Someone's lying here,* he had said in that icy tone; should she call him to explain herself, to tell him that she had been about to finish with Bram, that she *would* have finished with him if she'd been able to get through to him that morning? It piqued her to think of doing that.

We're not going out so he has no right to cross-question me about Bram.

All the same, she couldn't let him walk away. He had been at the house because he and she were chained together by something more savage and urgent than love. De Jager was coming for them, and there was no one to turn to except each other.

When she called Kris, though, he wasn't answering, either. The first time, the phone rang twice before going to voice-mail; the second time, it didn't even ring.

No, thought Veerle. She stared down at the phone in her hand, at the tiny screen innocent of message or missed call alerts.

I don't want to see either of you again! she had shouted.

After a few minutes she went downstairs, the phone still in her hand. She went down the dimly lit hallway and opened the door, although a long time had passed since she had slammed it against Kris and Bram. She didn't really expect to find anyone outside, but she still looked. The flowers Bram had brought her were still scattered on the pavement, a bright fan of colour against the grey. One more thing for the neighbours to notice; she'd managed to provide them with a fascinating little drama today. Veerle knelt and picked up the flowers, then carried them into the house.

She went into the kitchen, and there was the chair Kris had used, standing at an angle to the table. She wondered what to do with the flowers, realizing that the kitchen equipment Geert had bought her from IKEA didn't extend to a vase. Eventually, for the lack of any better idea, she put the flowers in the sink.

The phone didn't ring, and when she tried Kris half an hour later there was still no answer.

Veerle stood at the window with the phone pressed to her ear and looked out at the great grey bulk of the Sint-Pauluskerk. If she moved far enough to the right, she could see the tower piercing the sky. More than eleven years ago, she and Kris had climbed that tower together and seen the worst thing in their young lives. Together.

A year ago, she and Kris had faced the same horror – together – and nearly died. *Now*, she thought, *it's still out there but we're not together. De Jager is coming for me, and I'm alone.*

17

The storytellers met after dark at the abandoned hotel. This time there were three of them: Tina, Ruben and Maxim. They were expecting Thomas too, but at twenty minutes past the meeting time he had still not shown up. None of them were all that sorry, especially not Tina: Thomas was a little creepy, the way he told those stories in such detail and with such intensity but said so little the rest of the time. OK, a *lot* creepy. All the same, Tina shrugged off the thought of him quite easily. As far as she was concerned, about ninety per cent of men were creepy anyway, in one way or another.

The hotel stood beside an ill-lit stretch of road rarely used since the nearby motorway had been built. It was a large, square building made of brick punched through with tall windows that had mostly been boarded up. The ones on the ground floor were a riot of colour, spray-painted with fluorescent tags. There was a car park that was shrinking with the encroachment of vegetation, and a big portico supported by slender columns that had once been smooth and pale as milk but were now discoloured with streaks of brown and green. The portico led nowhere; there had been a door once but it had been bricked up. The way in was through a window at the rear of the building, where the boards had been prised away from the frame.

'It doesn't look much,' said Tina, her voice infused with disdain. She was fidgeting for a smoke, turning the cigarette over and over in her long fingers.

'It's supposed to be amazing inside,' said Ruben. 'There's a ballroom with mirrors and stuff. One of the chandeliers is still hanging.'

Tina shrugged. 'Let's go, then.'

'What about Thomas?'

'He'll find us if he turns up,' said Maxim. 'There's only one way in.'

They climbed through the window. Ruben was the first to go in, and he shone his torch on the frame to check that there were no shards of glass sticking out. It was clear, so he climbed inside, smelling mould and thick layers of dust. He imagined that this was how an Egyptian mummy would smell – of dry and aromatic decay.

As the others climbed in, he trained the beam of light on the interior. The room they were in was nothing special. As it was at the back of the hotel, Ruben suspected it was a store-room. Now it stored nothing except a single broken-backed chair and what at first appeared to be huge pallid curled leaves; on closer inspection they proved to be strips of wallpaper.

The door was open, and beyond it was blackness. Ruben approached it cautiously, sweeping the torch beam back and forth, checking for broken floorboards or sagging ceilings. The room opened onto a corridor that led to the front of the hotel, passing other doorways that sagged open like hungry mouths. Halfway along it were double doors, perhaps marking the border between the guests' territory and that of the staff. Now one of them was off its hinges, leaning against the shabby wall. Ruben, Maxim and Tina followed the corridor to the hotel lobby. A panelled wooden reception desk stood to one side, a dusty bell still adhering to its upper surface like a tarnished limpet. More impressive was the staircase that curved round to an upper floor, the elegance of the design still obvious in spite of missing banisters and the ubiquitous dust that coated everything like felt.

'This is good,' said Maxim, and even Tina, the cynic, nodded.

They ascended the sweeping staircase with care. On the first floor they found the room someone had told Ruben about. It wasn't quite a ballroom but something optimistic on a smaller scale. Mirrors speckled thickly with black lined three of the walls; the fourth contained a row of boarded-up windows.

They all stared up at the chandelier suspended above them. It must have had hundreds of hanging crystals, all now opaque with grime; it looked like an inverted bush bristling with dusty leaves. Another chandelier lay lopsidedly on the floor further down the room, where it had fallen. Tina wandered over and picked up a stray crystal, brushing it with the pad of her thumb to clean it. It was finely made and she was faintly surprised that it had not been worth anyone's while to remove the chandeliers when the hotel closed. She let the piece drop. *Take only photographs*, she reminded herself.

The three of them spent some time exploring the rest of the hotel, but eventually they drifted back to this room, where they broke out a little bottle of brandy that Tina had brought. They sat cross-legged on the bare boards and passed it between them. Tina was still itching for a smoke but everything was tinder dry in here; she put the cigarette in her pocket for later.

'You see the latest one?' asked Maxim. None of them needed to ask, *The latest* what?

'Fake,' said Tina decisively.

'How can you say that?'

'They're all fake,' Tina told him.

'What's your rationale?' asked Ruben.

Tina gave her habitual lazy shrug. 'They have to be. Look, if it was just one photo I might believe whoever took it just came across a murder and decided, you know, to take a snap and post it online. But nobody's going to stumble across – I don't know – six or seven different killings, are they? It's not probable.'

'Maybe it's not just one person posting them,' suggested Ruben.

'Yeah, well,' said Tina, 'it's still not likely, is it? I mean, how old are you, Maxim? Thirty, thirty-one? You ever see a dead body in all that time?'

'Fuck off, I'm twenty-six. But no, since you ask.'

'So,' said Tina.

'That doesn't prove anything,' said Ruben. 'Maybe the person posting the pictures killed them all.'

'Oh, come on.'

'It's possible.'

'They're fakes. They *have* to be. I mean, look, who's going to go to the trouble of killing a load of people just to illustrate a bunch of urban legends?'

'Maybe it's the Burnt Guy,' suggested Maxim facetiously.

'On the basis of what?' said Tina.

'He's a psycho.'

'Intelligent rationale.'

'Anyway, the place in those pictures – I read on a forum that it was a kiln. You know, a big one, an industrial one.'

'So?'

'He's the *Burnt* Guy.'

'He got burnt in a fire in a castle, dummy. Not a kiln. If you were inside a kiln, you'd be roasted. You wouldn't go around murdering people, because you'd be dead.'

There was silence for a while after that. Eventually Tina said, 'It's cold in here.'

'Are we going to do a legend or are we going to forget it?' asked Maxim.

'If Thomas were here we'd have one,' Ruben pointed out.

'So? Anyone got a new one?'

'I have,' said Tina. She had too, and it was a good one. She'd heard it from Thomas himself, another night, when neither Ruben nor Maxim had been present, though she saw no need to mention that. It was a good story; it practically *deserved* to be pinched.

'There was this girl,' she began, 'who was homeless, or maybe she'd run away from home. She'd taken her German shepherd dog with her because she didn't want to leave him behind, and also for protection. She was travelling around with just the dog and a rucksack with her stuff in, and spending the night wherever she could. Sometimes she would stay over with a friend, but when they got tired of having her there and chucked her out, she would find a deserted building and doss down there. She tended to avoid places in the middle of the city because there were too many druggies and weirdos in those. Instead she went for places that were a bit out of the way . . . like this one,' added Tina with sudden inspiration. She reached out for the brandy, took a swig and handed it to Ruben.

'So one night she broke into this really big old building at the side of a road. She wasn't sure what the building had been – either a hotel or maybe someone's home, back when people still had enormous mansions and loads of servants. Now it was deserted, but the roof and the windows were still intact so it was dry, and warmer than being outside. The girl went upstairs to find a place to sleep, and the dog followed her.

'Eventually she found a room that was small enough to feel cosy and it actually had a bed base in it. Not the whole thing with the mattress and everything, but better than sleeping on the floorboards. It was fairly comfortable. So she lay down there and the dog settled down on the floor next to the bed, and she put out her torch and went to sleep.

'She slept for a while and then suddenly woke up with a start, her heart thumping like crazy. There'd been a noise, quite close by. She didn't get off the bed or put the torch on, though. She figured that if there was someone in the building, the best bet was to stay silent in the dark, and with a bit of luck they'd go away without ever knowing she was there.

'So she lay there, hardly daring to breathe, and after a while she heard this dripping sound. Just that. *Drip . . . drip . . . drip.* She couldn't hear rain outside and she knew she hadn't heard a tap dripping or anything like that before she went to sleep. The sound really gave her the creeps. She wanted to check that the dog was nearby, so she leaned out of bed and whispered, "Here, boy." The dog snuffled a little bit and then came and licked her hand a couple of times. The girl felt safe then, so she curled up again and went back to sleep.

'The next morning she woke up and there was sunlight coming in through a hole in the shutters. She sat up, and right away she could see that the dog wasn't there in the room with her. She tried calling out, "Here boy, come here," in a low voice, but she didn't really want to shout the place down because the noises the night before had spooked her a bit. Anyway, the dog didn't make an appearance, so after a little while she got off the bed and went to look for him.

'He wasn't in the hallway, but another door leading into a bathroom stood half open. She thought maybe the dog had gone in there looking for something to drink, so she pushed the door right open. Then she stood there in the doorway and just screamed and screamed.

'The dog was hanging from a rail by its neck, stone dead, its fur matted with blood. On the tiled floor under it there was a big pool of congealed blood that had dripped from the body during the night. That was the *drip . . . drip . . . drip* she had heard.

'And on the wall, written in big straggling letters with the dog's blood were the words: *Humans can lick too.*'

For a few moments after Tina finished her story there was silence. Then Ruben laughed.

'So it wasn't the dog who licked her hand in the night, then.'

'Obviously not,' said Tina with heavy irony. She held out her hand for the brandy with a somewhat weary air.

'Maybe it was the Burnt Guy,' suggested Maxim slyly.

'You're obsessed with the Burnt Guy,' Tina told him.

'He's always the one, though,' said Ruben. 'I mean, a lot of those stories, they tell them everywhere. The Angel Smile, they have that in the US and Japan and a whole load of other places. But the Burnt Guy, he's *local*. He actually comes from *Belgium*.'

'He comes from bullshit land,' said Tina.

'Don't say that,' Maxim warned her, putting on an overdone tone of menace. 'If you diss him, it'll be you he comes for next.'

'Yeah, right,' said Tina. She shook the bottle, turned it upside down, but it was empty.

It occurred to her that this whole scene was becoming tedious. Maxim and Ruben were immature, a couple of little boys in grown-up bodies, and Laurens, who wasn't much better but was at least good-looking, hadn't turned up to anything for ages. There was never enough to drink unless she brought it herself, and then everyone else pinched it. Also, she was *dying* for a smoke now. She wanted to get outside into the open air and draw some carcinogens into her grateful lungs.

The session broke up. Maxim went first. Ruben lingered with Tina in the room they had first entered, amongst the autumnal drifts of wallpaper scraps.

'Do you want a lift?' Ruben asked her.

'No, thanks. I've got the bike.' Tina suspected that, given very little encouragement, Ruben would make a pass at her, and she really couldn't be bothered; she'd pretty much decided she wouldn't be hanging out with any of this lot again anyway. So she turned her back on him and climbed out of the window, moving with casual grace. As soon as her boots touched the ground outside she was feeling in her pocket for her lighter.

Verdomme, there was Ruben at her shoulder again. 'You want me to walk you to your bike? It's pretty dark.'

'No, Ruben.' Tina lit a cigarette, inhaled and then blew out smoke like a dragon. When Ruben didn't immediately move, she said, 'Really. No.'

Ruben got the message. He didn't bother to say goodbye, just turned and stalked off into the dark. Tina watched him go, then she turned and walked the other way.

The bike was parked between bushes a little way up the road – not too far, but well hidden. Anyone just driving by wouldn't spot it under all that overhanging vegetation. Tina walked up the left side of the road, and as she went she heard Ruben drive off in the other direction, his battered car rumbling ominously. The sound faded into the distance. Tina stopped and turned, but the tail lights had already vanished round a bend in the road. She took another long drag at the cigarette and turned back towards her bike.

She was perhaps twenty metres away from it when someone stepped out of the bushes in front of her. The nearest streetlamp was behind him so his face was in shadow, but there was no missing that physique – the height, the broad shoulders, the meaty arms.

'Hello, Tina,' he said.

18

The phone rang six times.

'*Met* De Keyser.'

'Good evening. May I speak to Veerle?'

A pause – of confusion or perhaps suspicion. 'Who?'

'Veerle. Please,' he added as an afterthought.

There was a *click* as the person at the other end of the line hung up.

De Jager looked at the list of De Keysers and Dekeysers that he had copied from the White Pages. It was mostly a waste of time telephoning – he had concluded that from his initial attempts to locate Kris Verstraeten. The fact that there was more than one Kris Verstraeten in the relevant area meant that the only way to be one hundred per cent sure of the identification was to see the target in person.

He had already spoken to one Veerle De Keyser who sounded about ninety-five years old. Of the other De Keysers he had spoken to, a number of the calls had been in-conclusive, like the one he had just made. The person had probably hung up because there was no Veerle there, but there was always the remote possibility that they simply didn't want to admit that Veerle was there.

He was going to have to get rid of the phone soon anyway, in case anyone tracked the number. It wouldn't lead back to *him*, obviously, but it did lead back to a theft. Public call boxes weren't ideal, either: there were fewer and fewer of them, and those there were tended to be helpfully located right next to railway stations and bus stops, places that were full of nosy people with nothing better to do than listen in.

There was no substitute for going and looking – and that meant more time, and a lot of stealth. In a village, especially a village like the one he had grown up in, people noticed things. De Jager dressed in a nondescript manner but he couldn't help his physical appearance marking him out. A scarf over the nose or a hat drawn down low wasn't going to solve that particular issue. He would have to keep the whole thing very low key.

That was no problem, though. He *was* going to find Veerle, sooner or later. The experience would be all the sweeter because of the long anticipation. Sweeter for him, that is; it wasn't going to be sweet for Veerle.

He scanned the list again. He wasn't a believer in hunches. To be a good hunter and tracker you needed to observe, deduce and anticipate, not listen to irrational convictions.

Where is she? he said to himself.

He knew the village intimately – of course he did; he had done most of his growing up there. Every single street listed in the White Pages for the various De Keyser households was known to him. The De Keysers were spread out randomly across the village, as you would expect: some located close to the centre with its lopsided square, church and handful of shops, some located much further out. There was even one solitary *De Keyser, H.* living up a farm track on the very perimeter of the village.

Of course, any of them could have been in the village centre on Silent Saturday all those years ago, when a killer strode through the pouring rain with a dead child in his arms. That was where the shops were, the bakery, the church, the only bar. The bus stop was near the church. The red post box was there too. There was any number of reasons for people living on the edge of the village to be there in the centre. All the same, De Jager decided to start with the ones living right in the heart of the village. If those people had been living at the same addresses eleven years ago, some of them could have looked out of their own windows and seen Joren Sterckx pass through the village with his victim.

There was a *De Keyser, J.* living on a street parallel to the village square and a *Dekeyser, P.* living on the square itself. He could pick one, park somewhere nearby and watch to see who went in or out.

De Jager looked at his watch. It was a little after three.

If Veerle were still attending high school – and this was by no means certain – she would have to be in the town, since the village itself had only a nursery and a primary school. Lessons would be finishing any time now, and then she would probably take the bus home, arriving in the village around four. He might save himself a lot of legwork by waiting to see who got off the bus. If Veerle were amongst them, he would know that she did indeed belong to the village; he might see the direction she took on her walk home and deduce from that which of the addresses was hers; if he were lucky he might even be able to follow her right back to the house.

He did not allow himself to become excited at this prospect. There was too much that might go awry, too much that might not fit. She might have moved away in the last decade; she might never have lived here at all, although he was convinced that she did. She might have left school, in which case she would not be coming home on the four-o'clock bus. However, it was logical to check.

He left the dull-looking red-brick house that was his current base and drove towards the village. It was a clear, bright day with a cool edge to the air. The dry weather was good; none of the high-school students would be swaddled in hooded raincoats and scarves. He expected to pick Veerle out easily – if she were among them.

Near the church there was a handful of parking spaces, all of them empty at this time of day. De Jager backed the car into one of them. As he reversed in, he could see the façade of the great Sint-Pauluskerk reflected in the rearview mirror. He felt no nostalgia at the sight of the familiar building. He felt nothing.

He took a map out of the side pocket and unfolded it ostentatiously. Sitting in a parked car watching school kids get off the bus would be suspicious – it might draw attention. Sitting in the car studying a map as though diligently plotting his route would be quite acceptable, and there was the added benefit that the map acted as a screen behind which he could conceal himself.

On the passenger seat lay a dark coat, folded neatly. Hidden in the folds, invisible to any passer-by who might casually glance into the car, was an ebony-handled Japanese boning knife with a contrasting buffalo-horn ferule. It had cost several hundred euros online.

De Jager did not expect to use the knife today. His desired outcome was to locate Veerle's home with precision. How he proceeded after that depended on her living circumstances.

He had not yet located Kris Verstraeten; he had only the email address. Therefore the ideal thing would be for Veerle to vanish without trace. De Jager would then offer Kris a meeting at a place and time specified by himself, baiting the hook with a promise of information about her whereabouts. It would be easy to make Veerle disappear if she lived alone. He had taken down plenty of people as young and fit as her.

On the other hand, if she were living in the bosom of a large family, other considerations would come into play. Killing all of them would be too conspicuous, although it did have certain attractions as a project; De Jager had never picked off every single member of a family before, so it had the same allure as bagging a particularly rare hunting trophy. He could take Veerle when she was alone, but to do that he would have to understand the family's schedule – the times when Veerle was vulnerable, when no one else was around. That would mean more time, more patience, more subterfuge.

No. He did not expect to use the knife today. It rested quietly between the folds of black woollen cloth, a dark promise for the future.

The bell in the Sint-Pauluskerk rang a quarter to the hour. Nobody passed the parked car on foot. Some traffic went past: a handful of cars, a tractor with a trailer full of muddy-looking root vegetables. There was no sign that anyone had taken particular notice of De Jager's car. Nobody slowed; he did not see any of the drivers turn their heads his way. Beside him, the boning knife slumbered.

Shortly after the church bell had struck four times, a yellow-and-white De Lijn bus came slowly up the road from Tervuren. From his vantage point in front of the church De Jager saw it slow as it approached the junction, then swing its nose round the corner with ease, like the head of a mallet describing an arc through the air.

It was crammed with high-school students. They were pressed up against the big windows like specimens crammed into a preserving jar – arms, shoulders, even one face was flattened against the glass. The bus drew to a halt opposite the church, not twenty metres from where De Jager sat watching over the top edge of the map. The doors opened with a hiss and a clatter, and discharged perhaps a dozen students onto the pavement. Then the bus moved off and De Jager was able to see them.

The group of three boys he was able to discount immediately. One of two girls walking away from him caught his attention briefly: the hair was slightly the wrong shade, a little too light – he remembered Veerle having very dark hair – but hair colour was easily changed and the girl had that slender physique and an energetic stride that suggested athleticism. She turned, however, to check for traffic before she and her friend crossed the road, and he saw that it was not Veerle. Her face was far rounder than Veerle's, the mouth small and prim.

His gaze veered away from her, sliding past a couple with arms entwined and a skinny boy with mousy hair and spectacles, hunched over as though already at home in spirit, crouching over a keyboard. He saw a knot of students dispersing, a mixture of girls and boys, and amongst them he picked out a slim girl with dark hair falling over her face.

In spite of his habitual sangfroid he felt a quickening of interest, a little kick of adrenalin. The triumph would be very great if he had found her this easily, simply through calculating the probability that she would be in this particular place at this time.

It was impossible to get a good look at the girl's face. Either she was shy or she didn't want to engage with the other students. She kept her head down, the shining cascade of hair obscuring most of her features, and held a thick file to her chest like a shield. De Jager folded the map but he never looked away long enough for the girl to vanish down a side street without him seeing.

He kept his movements slow and unhurried as he started the engine and indicated to turn out of the parking space. No point in rushing; a scream of tyres would only draw attention to him. He saw the girl – Veerle? – turn to go down a street that ran alongside the church.

Kerkstraat, he thought. No De Keysers lived there, according to the White Pages, but there was a household with that name on one of the residential streets at the other end. She could be using Kerkstraat as a cut-through.

De Jager waited for the girl to get a good distance down the street before he followed her. As luck would have it, the street was narrow and there were a number of cars parked along one side, with wheels on the pavement, so the girl was having to walk in the road itself. There was no way to pass a pedestrian safely in the narrow space, so he was able to follow her in the car with apparent civility, neither sounding the horn nor trying to squeeze by. The girl didn't look round, seemingly oblivious to the car behind her. A white cable snaked from a pocket to earphones hidden under the fall of dark hair, and De Jager guessed that she was unaware of his presence.

So tantalizingly close. He could have floored the accelerator, and within seconds she would be dead, a mangled and bloody mess dragged under a couple of tonnes of steel and aluminium, the tyres tracking blood up the road. How satisfying to feel the uneven jolts as the car went over her body, grinding the bones grittily against the tarmac, pulping the flesh so that the red ran out of it like juice from a squeezed lemon . . .

He had no conscious intention of doing it, not in broad daylight, but his foot moved almost convulsively on the pedal and the car lurched forward in a sudden toad-like spring. Now the girl *did* hear something over the music flowing into her ears. She half turned, and then she jumped.

The dark hair swung back from her face and De Jager saw that it was not Veerle at all. This girl was thin-faced, almost horsy, with plump lips like the petals of an overblown flower. She was nothing like Veerle De Keyser.

De Jager raised a hand to apologize for startling her, keeping his head down to conceal his face, and when she stepped back between two cars, he passed her carefully and drove off down the road, remaining within the speed limit.

His actions were carefully controlled, but inside he was dismayed by the blast of angry frustration that had swept through him when he saw that the girl was not Veerle.

Nothing touched him – that was the normal course of things. He planned, he tracked, he hunted and killed, all without emotional engagement. If he felt anything it was a cold satisfaction, a pride in his own objectivity. He rose *above* the prey; he didn't wallow in the filthy trenches of emotion with them.

The girl had somehow affected him in spite of that. The boyfriend, Kris, was one of the only two people De Jager had ever tried and failed to kill, but that had been a slight error of judgement; it had nothing to do with Kris's actions. Veerle, however, had faced him deliberately, and she had escaped. She had run back into danger when all logic dictated that she should run away from it. She had taunted him. She had fled, weak and unarmed. And she had got away. De Jager felt an unfamiliar soreness over that, as though he were a statue that had begun miraculously to come to life, the cold marble turning to feeling flesh. He wanted to understand how Veerle had done this. He wanted to be alone with her for a long time, so that he could take her apart minutely, wrench and rend and dissect her until he had found that elusive quality, whatever it was.

De Jager drove away, his hands tight on the wheel. His patience was failing.

It could take him an age to find Veerle De Keyser like this. He was determined to find a faster way.

19

Veerle waited until the bus had left the stop opposite the church, and then she pressed the STOP button. The bus travelled to the eastern outskirts of the village, and then it came to a halt at a stop that overlooked a field of maize. Veerle was the only one to alight. She stood on the pavement, shouldering her school bag and feeling somewhat self-conscious as she watched the bus depart with a rumble and a last flatulent emission of exhaust fumes. When it had disappeared round the corner, she turned and headed back towards the village.

The walk felt longer than she had expected. It was a dull route, passing first the maize field and then a long hedge and finally a series of uninteresting houses.

This is stupid, she said to herself.

She was tired and a little thirsty, and the extra walk was beginning to feel like a useless piece of paranoia. As she approached the village centre, she took a right-hand turn down a road so narrow that it was little more than an alley, the cobbles shiny with age. There was a weathered brick wall running along one side, higher than her head. When she judged that she had reached the right spot, she took the bag off her shoulders and threw it over the wall, listening for the rustle that told her it had landed safely in the bushes on the other side. Then she stepped up to the wall, felt carefully for holds, and began to climb. It was not difficult; the pointing between the bricks was crumbling and in places had all but vanished. She only needed to take a couple of steps off the ground and she could reach the top of the wall with her hands. Then she managed it with ease. She sat astride the wall, her legs swinging, and looked down into the garden.

Her bag was there, cushioned in the foliage. It had snapped a slender branch on the way down, but other than that you could see at a glance that the garden had been undisturbed for months. Veerle herself never went further than the back doorstep when she wanted to put rubbish out to await collection day. If she had felt any concern about anyone trespassing, it evaporated.

She slid off the wall and dropped to the ground inside the garden. Then she retrieved her bag from the bush and picked her way to the back door, feeling in her jeans pocket for the key.

I couldn't do this with two bags of groceries, she thought, and smiled to herself, thinking of lobbing boxes of eggs and cartons of juice over the wall. It *did* feel ridiculous, coming into the house this way, but also reassuring. A little over a week had passed since the row with Kris and Bram without her speaking to either of them, and Veerle was horribly aware that she was alone.

Is he really out there? she asked herself, almost obsessively. She wanted to believe that it was all paranoia, but at heart she *knew* it wasn't. She thought De Jager was out there, all right, and she also thought that he was looking for her. The house on Kerkstraat was still listed in the White Pages as *Charlier, C.*, but that might not prevent from him finding her. Kris had done it, after all; he had deduced correctly that she was back in the village after seeing her board the bus outside the school.

Whenever she thought about that she felt a sickening, vertiginous feeling that transcended fear; it was the numb shock of approaching annihilation, the long-stretched-out moment of an unavoidable car crash. She would think about Gregory, and about the deserted gallery with its lights on day and night, and dread would settle on her like sickness.

The only way to live with it was to do something practical to try to ward off the impending evil. So she had spent a lot of her spare time trying to research the Joren Sterckx murder, and she had eventually hit on the idea of varying her route home. It was a small defence, but it was something; it made her movements harder to track. The first day she had stopped off in the town to buy groceries anyway, so she'd got back to the village late. The next, she'd got off the bus two stops early and walked through three fields to the village centre. Tonight she'd overshot her normal stop and climbed into the back garden over the wall.

Tomorrow . . . she thought, but she was running out of ideas. *I'm probably wasting my time anyway,* she said to herself. *If De Jager's looking for me, climbing over the garden wall isn't going to stop him.*

Tomorrow she'd go back to her old route.

20

The house was cool and silent when she let herself in. Veerle stood inside the back door for a few moments, listening. Nothing, of course. She put her school bag down in the hall and went into the kitchen to make herself a snack.

As she stood at the counter she was very aware of the window looking out onto Kerkstraat. The lace curtains were pulled right across, but once the daylight started to fail and she had the lights on inside, anyone standing out in the street would be able to see right in. Veerle paused from what she was doing, making herself an open sandwich, and stared out.

The street was deserted. The sun was sinking in the sky; the shadows were lengthening, and where the sunlight fell it gilded what it touched. A sparrow flew down and perched on top of the churchyard wall, but there was no other movement to be seen. On the other side of the wall the occupants of the churchyard slept soundly.

Veerle looked down, peeling a slice of cheese out of the packet with the side of a knife, and then looked up again, at the window. She was aware of a distinct thread of apprehension in her thoughts, a minor tributary flowing into the greater stream of her consciousness. If she were to look up and see someone standing there, outlined against the evening sunshine . . .

She found herself struggling against a compulsion to lower the roller shutters and block the view.

No, she told herself. *That's paranoia. You're getting like Mum was.*

That thought was enough to stop her letting down the shutters. Her mother's anxiety had overshadowed both their lives in the years leading up to Claudine's death. Claudine had been afraid of muggers, of sudden life-threatening illnesses, of freak accidents, of life outside the safety of home. The shutters had always gone down before nightfall, and all the doors had been locked and bolted. Veerle could barely recall a time when her mother *hadn't* been like that, although she did remember playing outside on her own when she was very small. The day she went into the church and met Kris Verstraeten – Silent Saturday – was not the first time she had gone there alone.

Veerle suspected that the day of the murder had triggered something in her mother. When news of the killing of a child had spread, Claudine had realized that her small daughter was not in the house, and had panicked. She'd had no way of knowing that Veerle was in the bell tower of the Sint-Pauluskerk with Kris, hysterical but otherwise unharmed. When Veerle had appeared, still crying with terror, Claudine had been so overwrought that she had slapped her. Veerle couldn't remember any of this; Kris had told her about it much later. He and his mother had witnessed the slap; Kris's mother had given Claudine an earful for it.

In the years that had followed, Veerle's parents' marriage

had broken down. Geert had left for his native Ghent. Claudine had retreated further and further into a protective shell, consumed by a hundred different anxieties. She had fortified the house with care every evening. She had discouraged Veerle from going out at night, and finally she had locked her in her room one evening to stop her meeting Kris.

Don't let me get like that, Veerle said to herself. Living with someone who thought about nothing but her fears had pushed Veerle the other way. She had *deliberately* taken up dangerous pursuits, like rock climbing.

And the Koekoeken.

Veerle glanced at the window again.

I'm not putting the shutters down. He'll have won then – Joren Sterckx or De Jager or whoever he is. He got Mum, and now he'll have got me too, even if he never finds me.

She finished making the sandwich, poured herself a glass of orange juice and carried them both upstairs to her room, leaving the downstairs shutters open.

While she was eating the sandwich she booted up her laptop. She'd run so many online searches for 'Joren Sterckx' that his name came up automatically in the search box as soon as she typed J.

There were pages and pages of links to articles about him: newspaper archives, true crime sites, even a Wikipedia entry. Veerle had been through dozens of them, searching for details that would tell her that Joren Sterckx really was dead; that whatever or whoever she had seen, it wasn't him.

Most of the articles were about the murder he had committed, the boy he had killed over a decade ago. Nobody was very interested in the killer dying of cancer during his prison sentence. What they were interested in was the crime itself. Compared to many killers, Joren Sterckx wasn't prolific. You couldn't call him a serial killer. He had that one murder to his name. What horrified and fascinated people was the nature of the murder.

The victim was an eleven-year-old boy called Karel Adriaensen. Veerle had no memory of Karel, although she must have seen him in Joren Sterckx's muscular arms as she gazed down in terror from the bell tower. She didn't remember him from school, either – he had been four years older than her, after all – but she had seen a photograph of him. The reports always used the same one.

Karel was an ordinary, slight-looking boy with thick brown hair cut in an unflattering style, and a freckled face. He had a rather startled expression in the photograph, as though he had been taken unawares. His lips were open, his eyes slightly widened.

Karel had gone out to play in the village with a group of schoolfriends that day, as he had done many times before. When the others went home, Karel had lingered, or perhaps he had simply taken his time, dawdling on the way back to the little house he shared with his parents and sister to avoid being roped into helping with the preparations for his grand-parents' visit on Easter Sunday. Thus he had been alone, quite alone, when Joren Sterckx found him.

It had been impossible to persuade Joren to describe what happened next. He refused to speak to anyone about it, not the police, nor his lawyer, nor his family. The investigators had managed to patch it all together, though, from the trampled grass and the broken twigs of bushes, the trail of blood and the discarded weapons.

If Joren Sterckx had simply wanted to kill Karel Adriaensen, he could have done it quite easily. He was very much bigger and heavier. He could have strangled the young boy, or struck him on the head, or beaten him. Instead he took Karel to a copse near the allotments, and as the rain began to fall he drew out a knife and stabbed him in the calf of the right leg, deeply enough to cause pain and limping, not deeply enough to cause a major haemorrhage.

Karel had been shocked and terrified, and naturally he had tried to get away. And Joren had let him. He had stood – or perhaps even sat – in the deep shade of the copse, with the raindrops filtering down through the branches of the trees, and watched Karel Adriaensen try to run away from him with one leg damaged and bleeding. After a while he had followed the terrified and stumbling boy and had struck again, but not mortally. He had slashed at the back of Karel's left knee, and watched him fall to the ground.

The rain had been coming down hard now, reducing visibility and turning the world grey. The houses on the edge of the allotment some hundreds of metres away were drowned in the downpour. Anyone who might have been lingering on the allotments would have hurried home. Soon the earth itself was greyish and muddy, the soil with its heavy clay content sucking at the soles of Joren's shoes as he stood over his victim. Still he did not strike the death blow. He watched Karel Adriaensen try to get up and sprawl in the mud again. The second time, the boy managed to stagger a few metres before he fell down. Soon his clothing and skin were slick with mud. Only the red that leaked from his wounds was not the colour of the hungry earth.

At last Karel had tried to crawl away on his stomach, and then Joren Sterckx had crouched beside him and struck again, wounding him in the arm. After that it had been a slow process of attrition, as Joren let the wounded boy crawl a little further before striking once more. Karel's struggles to get away had become weaker and weaker. Finally there was a blow to the side of the neck.

Some time after that, Karel Adriaensen had died, there in the mud, with the rain diluting his crimson blood and plastering his brown hair flat to his skull.

That was bad, that was unimaginably bad, but what was worse was that Joren Sterckx had taken trophies. That was why they had described him as hunting down his victim; it was not just the slow measured pursuit but also the hunting trophies he had taken. Joren had produced a second knife, one with a serrated blade, and he had hacked at the prone body, carving off souvenirs for himself. Karel's mother had had to be taken out of the courtroom while that part of the story was being related. It was not at all clear whether Karel had been dead when Joren Sterckx did this; there was some reason to think that it had caused his death, his heart giving out from exhaustion and pain.

Veerle hated reading the reports of the killing. Karel Adriaensen had been older than she was, but that had been over eleven years ago; now he looked incredibly young. She wanted to cry for him. When she read the details she thought, *If he's still out there somewhere, the evil bastard who did that, then whether he's after Kris and me or not, I want him found.*

183

Now she skipped over the reports of what Joren Sterckx had done to his victim. She didn't *want* to relive the whole thing again. She had gone over and over it until she was sick to her stomach, but she hadn't found anything to tell her how she might have seen the killer a decade after he died. Now she wanted to go further into the aftermath, to the trial and Joren's subsequent committal to prison.

There must be something, she thought. *Some clue . . .*

Refining the search to include the word *trial* brought her a new set of links, including one melodramatically titled *Blind hate: also dumb.* That was from a true crime site.

Veerle clicked on the link and found a long report of the trial, lovingly embellished with speculation by the writer. There needed to be speculation, because Joren Sterckx had refused to explain or justify himself. He had refused even to discuss the murder. He had uttered not one single word during his extensive questioning by the police, and he said nothing in court, sitting instead like a monolith, a carved idol with an impassive face and a dead soul.

He didn't even tell the Adriaensens why he'd done it, thought Veerle, and she felt that hot anger kindling inside her again. At such times she felt recklessness sweeping over her. She couldn't live with the outrage she felt when she thought about what he had done; she wanted to hunt down the Hunter herself. Then she would think of the monstrous bulk of him – taller than she was and twice the weight – and the remorseless brutality, and her heart would fail her. She would swing back the other way into cold, creeping dread, the fear that turned every creaking floorboard, every distant footstep, into a horror.

Veerle put her head in her hands, threading her fingers through her dark hair, and closed her eyes for a few moments. Then she made herself open them and read on.

Joren's lawyer had had an impossible task. Still, he had done his best to argue that his client was severely disturbed or insane. It was the only possible hand he could have played, and predictably, it failed.

Although the killing was not the act of a normal person, the cold-bloodedness with which it was carried out and the apparent planning involved in taking two different blades to the scene of the crime went against him. Joren Sterckx was borne away to prison, dull, mute and unresisting in spite of his size and strength, there to die of the tumour that was already growing like a dark seed inside him.

The writer of the article finished it off with a small journalistic flourish by saying that the body parts Joren Sterckx had taken had never been found. Perhaps, he managed to imply, Joren had eaten them.

Veerle pressed her hand to her mouth when she read that. She clicked to exit the article and go back to the search results. The list of links was reassuringly clinical, a list of headlines without the detail she had just read.

He ate them?

She really didn't want to think about that. She didn't want her mind to skip back to the evening in the castle when she had opened the door and found Kris on the dusty tiles, pierced through with a crossbow bolt. Better to let her mind swerve round that, not thinking about what De Jager or Joren Sterckx or whoever he was might have done if he had carried his plan through.

Veerle tried another search, putting *died + prison* first and then the name, *Joren Sterckx*.

Nothing new. She had read most of these articles already. She tried again, with his name and the word *funeral*.

The number of results was much smaller than for the murder itself. One article reported that no church had been willing to receive the mortal remains of the notorious Joren Sterckx, the 'child hunter', into their churchyard. The killer's body had been cremated.

Veerle tried some others but basically that was it. Joren Sterckx had been cremated nearly a decade ago, mourned by no one. If his ashes had been scattered somewhere special, nobody was saying where. The article mentioned the fact that he had died without ever explaining his actions on that Silent Saturday. It did not mention the missing body parts.

Veerle sat back in her chair. She knew more now than she had ever wanted to know about the Silent Saturday murder (*he ate them*), but she was still no nearer to finding out whether Joren Sterckx really had died. The papers said he had. There was no doubt in any of the reporting, no dubious references to anything being 'alleged' or 'supposed'. The police had told her repeatedly that he had died, and it wasn't as if she hadn't pressed them on that particular point; once or twice she had been almost hysterical about it. But could you really believe *anything* if you hadn't seen it with your own eyes – if you hadn't seen him packed into his coffin and loaded into the crematorium; if you hadn't seen them firing up the gas jets?

I saw him alive, she thought.

She stared at the screen for a while, and when she got tired of that she leaned back and stared at the ceiling.

How could he still be alive?

It was only in films that convicted killers were approached by shadowy authorities and offered freedom in exchange for some dubious role as a spy or assassin. Veerle simply couldn't swallow that idea.

Mistaken identity?

That seemed so unlikely as to be almost impossible. Joren Sterckx's appearance was distinctive: taller than average, broader across the shoulders than average. And anyway, someone would have had to identify the body. Consider deliberate misidentification and you were back into Hollywood territory.

What now? thought Veerle. She leaned forward again and closed the laptop. There was only so much that you could do online. After a while you started getting like the person who had written the true-crime article: you started speculating and building theories on evidence so flimsy that a sneeze would have blown it away.

I need to talk to people who might know something, she thought. The question was who. After the fire in the castle, the police had come to talk to her in hospital, and later she had been to the police station to sign her statement. Veerle could remember the policewoman who had done most of the talking. She supposed it would be possible to go to the police station and ask for her. But what could she possibly say? *Can you call the prison and the crematorium for me and ask whether it was really him they burnt?* You didn't have to be a genius to see how laughable *that* was.

I wish Kris was here, Veerle thought. She hated to feel alone, the solitary shipwreck survivor with a shark circling. And between them they might come up with some idea that she had missed on her own.

Those weren't the only reasons she wished he was there, though. She wished he would put his arms around her again like he had that day he had followed her from school.

If you knew that you had hardly any time left to live, you'd want to make everything right with the people you love the most.

That was the truth. She was going to try to find De Jager before he found her. She would fight him if she could. But in her heart she knew that it was like shaking her fist at a tsunami.

Think, she said to herself sternly. *Who can you talk to?*

21

At six a.m. the following Saturday morning Veerle's mobile went off, shrilling like a large and angry fledgling.

Veerle was hauled from the depths of sleep to wakefulness in an instant, like a diver who has surfaced fast enough to risk the bends. The phone was on the bedside table, but the room was dark and she was disorientated. She fumbled for the phone and felt it skid away from her clutching fingers. A moment later it hit the floor and fell silent.

Veerle sighed and felt for the light switch instead. Yellow light bloomed and she blinked, wrinkling her nose. Then she leaned over the side of the bed and fished the phone up off the floor.

Dad? she thought, squinting at the tiny screen. Geert usually called on Saturdays, sometimes a little earlier than she would have liked, because he was up at the crack of dawn with Adam, her half-brother. She glanced at the alarm clock. *Not this early.*

The phone burst into life again in her hands, trilling insistently.

Kris Verstraeten said the caller detail.

Veerle pressed the touch screen to accept the call and

clamped the phone to her ear. There was a tight feeling in her throat, an excitement she tried to tamp down. She waited for Kris to speak.

'Veerle?'

She heard the urgency in his voice, and all of a sudden her stomach was in free fall. *Something's happened.*

'Yes?'

'Shit.' Veerle heard Kris exhale heavily. 'Thank God.'

'Kris? What's the matter?'

It was a moment before he answered. The silence was filled with a rustle and then a creak; Veerle suspected that Kris had thrown himself back into a chair.

He said, 'I've had another email from Gregory.'

'Oh.' Veerle had no other words. The news was doing nothing for the unpleasant feeling in the pit of her stomach. She rolled onto her back, the phone still clamped to her ear, and pushed the hair away from her face with her other hand. She waited for Kris to tell her the rest.

'This one had a photo attached. It's . . . well, it's a girl with dark hair. I was afraid it was you. The picture's not great but I think that's deliberate. It could easily be . . .'

'. . . me,' finished Veerle.

'Yes.'

'Can you describe the photo to me?'

'I'll forward the email. It doesn't show much. You can see the girl is lying on something – it looks like tiles, maybe. All that's visible is a shoulder and the side of the face. The jaw and the ear. And dark hair. The hair is loose. You can't tell exactly how long it is, but I'd say at least as long as yours.'

'Well, does the email say anything?'

'Just the same as last time,' Kris told her. 'A string of numbers. I guess it's another grid reference.'

'You haven't checked it yet?'

'No. I saw the photo and . . . I wanted to call you first.'

Veerle sat up and swung her legs out of the bed. 'I'm going to start up my laptop. Can you send it?'

She padded barefoot across the room and sat down at the desk, switching the phone to left hand, left ear, so that she could use her right hand to boot up the machine. After a minute or two she had the email in front of her, and the attached photograph.

'That's . . . a bit freaky,' she said into her mobile, looking at the photo. It was exactly as Kris had described it, only there was something almost indefinably dreadful about it. The exposed skin was very pale, the sickly blue-white of a fish belly – but that might be the result of flash photography. You could take a photo of a live person and it would look like that. No, thought Veerle, it was the tiles – they had been white but now they were grubby, gritty, smeared with filth. Nobody would want to lie down on those. Nobody with long hair like that would want it to come into contact with that grimy surface; you'd be brushing out dust and dead insects for days.

'I'm checking the grid reference now,' said Kris's voice in her ear.

'There wasn't any other text?' asked Veerle.

'No.'

She waited.

'It's a town in Luik. Wait, I'm going to try to zoom in.'

Hurry up, hurry up, thought Veerle. She tapped the desktop impatiently with her fingertips. 'Kris?'

'It's just some derelict building. The windows are all boarded up. A lot of graffiti.' Veerle could almost hear the frown in Kris's voice. 'It's by a road.'

'You don't recognize it?'

'No. I don't think I've ever been near that town.'

'Well, why did he send it, then?'

'Same reason he sent the last one, I guess,' said Kris grimly. 'To tell us something is there.'

Thinking about *that* gave Veerle a peculiar tight sensation in the chest. 'You mean like the finger? You think there's a *body* there?'

'It would . . . make sense.'

'But *whose*? And why is he telling us this?' Veerle could hear her own voice rising but she was unable to stop it. 'This is sick. If there really is a body there . . . it's just—' She shut up abruptly, biting her lip, hands curling into fists.

'I think . . .' began Kris reluctantly. 'I think he expects us – or me, anyway – to go there. It's Saturday. There's the whole weekend ahead. If I was going to have a look, I'd probably do it today or tomorrow.'

'And then what?'

'And then maybe he just sits there and waits for me to turn up, whoever he is.'

We know who he is, Veerle said to herself. *Or what he is, anyway. The Hunter.*

Aloud, she said, 'But you're not going to go, are you?'

Kris paused just long enough to send an icy stab of fore-boding through Veerle, and then he said, deliberately, 'No. I'm not.' He sighed heavily. 'I think we should talk to the police. *I* should, anyway. You don't have to get involved.'

Veerle didn't reply for a moment. She leaned on her elbow, thrusting her fingers into her dark hair. She was conscious of a certain sense of relief. *Talk to the police.* It made sense. That was the responsible thing to do – the sensible thing to do. Rushing off to investigate something like this yourself was a completely *insane* idea. Nobody in their right mind would entertain it.

But after that initial wave of relief came a troubling question.

'What we are going to tell them? You'll have to say how you knew Gregory.'

'Friend of a friend,' said Kris.

'But why would someone be sending you grid references to dead bodies?'

'I'll have to play innocent on that one. I could say I think it's someone playing a prank but I'm just reporting it to be on the safe side.'

Veerle thought about it for a few moments.

'Kris, they're going to work out pretty quickly that this is the third time we've been' – Veerle hesitated – 'in trouble. There was the fire in the castle and the . . . thing in Ghent.'

'I know,' said Kris grimly. 'That's why I think you should stay out of it. If they see both of us are mixed up in this, they're going to get a whole lot more interested in us. Plus, it might get back to your dad. If they talk to him, he's going to know we've seen each other.'

This was undeniably true. The thought of Geert knowing that she had broken her promise was appalling; it made Veerle hot with guilt. She said, 'Look, maybe we should think about this a bit more. Sleep on it or something.'

'Veerle, we can't do that. He's almost certainly bargaining on the fact that this is Saturday so I – or we – will go over there this weekend, maybe today. *If* we go. So if we tell the police now, and they send someone down there, there's just a slim chance they might catch him. If we spend all week discussing it, that's not going to happen.'

Veerle sighed. 'OK. When are you going to do it?'

'I'll wait till nine and go to the station. I'll print this stuff off and take it with me.'

'Will you let me know what they say?'

'Of course.'

Suddenly there was silence between them. Veerle thought, *We haven't talked about what happened that Sunday.*

'Kris,' she said eventually, 'do you want to come over here afterwards, to the house?'

'Are you sure you want me to do that?' he asked. His voice was perfectly even, without a trace of bitterness, but still he asked that question, and still Veerle winced under it.

'Yes,' she said.

'OK, I'll come.'

Veerle took a deep breath. 'Kris, last time – I didn't know Bram was coming. He didn't tell me, he just turned up. And I did mean to tell him I wanted to finish but I couldn't get hold of him.' She hesitated. 'And I still can't. He won't take any of my calls.'

'Well, I'm sorry,' said Kris in that level tone, and she couldn't tell whether he was saying, *Sorry for lungeing at him like that*, or *Sorry for not believing you*, or even *Sorry, it's too late for explanations.* 'Look, I'll see you later, OK?'

'OK,' Veerle said. 'Good luck,' and then she ended the call. She looked at the time display on the laptop. It wasn't even half past six. All the same, she couldn't imagine going back to sleep now. She got to her feet with a sigh and went to get dressed.

22

'They didn't bloody believe me,' said Kris savagely.

He was standing in the hallway of the house on Kerkstraat, a tall lean figure clad in his habitual black, except that the leather jacket had been replaced with a pea coat Veerle hadn't seen before, presumably to present a smart front to the police. Kris hadn't got as far as the kitchen or the sitting room before his indignation burst out. His sharp-boned features were set in a scowl. Veerle could feel the angry energy rolling off him in waves.

'They didn't believe you?' she repeated incredulously.

'Well, they didn't take me seriously.' Kris pushed his way past her and went into the kitchen. He threw himself down on one of the kitchen chairs, but he was too wound up to relax; a second later he was sitting forward, his whole posture stiff with suppressed tension.

Veerle sat opposite him, her face serious. 'Tell me what happened.'

'I was down there for hours. I went in just after nine and spoke to someone on the front desk. I explained it all to her, and then they left me waiting for bloody ages until the right person could come and talk to me. I swear he wasn't doing anything, either. He was just having his morning coffee and *chocoladebroodje*. He had crumbs on his shirt when he eventually came out.'

Veerle let out a hiss of annoyance at that.

'So I had to go through the whole thing again with him, but I could tell right away that he just wasn't interested. I showed him the photo and the email, and he hardly looked at them. And then he said, "You're probably the fifth person who's come in with stuff like this".'

'What?!' Veerle could hardly believe her ears.

Kris nodded curtly. 'Yes. I guess he meant to the police in general, not that particular station. But apparently they've had a load of calls from people about pictures like that one. There's this thing on the net. Killings from urban legends.'

'What does that mean?'

'You know, those stories that are always going around. The ones about psychopathic babysitters and vanishing hitch-hikers. They're always supposed to be real – they happened to someone's cousin or their brother's girlfriend's mother or something, only if you ask questions you can never pin any of it down to an exact person.' Kris shook his head. 'Anyway, someone's been posting photos on some of the urban exploration sites, and they're supposed to show people who have died in those legends, at real urbex locations.'

Veerle didn't bother to say *That's ridiculous*; she knew better than anyone that a deserted building is an excellent place to go hunting if your prey is human. All the same, she was dismayed by what Kris was telling her. She was beginning to see why the police hadn't listened to him.

'The photos are probably fakes, just someone messing

about, that's what he said,' Kris went on. 'It'd be easy enough to do. They always show something but not quite enough. Just a hand or whatever.'

'And who posts them?' asked Veerle.

'No one seems to know. Some anonymous username, I guess, and then the pictures get reposted all over the place. They're on Facebook and Hyves, for God's sake.'

'Well, did you tell him who sent you the email? I mean, whose account it came from?'

'Yeah. And since it didn't seem to mean much to him, I told him it was the same Gregory who was found dead in his burnt-out flat.'

'He must have taken *that* seriously, surely?' said Veerle. She was beginning to feel a horrid fascination for the way in which the unnamed policeman had managed to brush aside things that seemed appallingly sinister to her.

But Kris was shaking his head. 'A prank, he reckoned. He said someone probably just hacked the account. It goes with the pictures – photos of people who are supposedly dead, sent from a murder victim. A sick joke, he said.' Kris's brows knitted together in a ferocious scowl. 'Everything he said seemed to be implying that there was a lot of time-wasting going on.'

'So aren't they going to check it out?' asked Veerle. She wanted to know the answer to that particular question very badly. It wasn't so much the issue of whether they ran into De Jager; she thought it was unlikely. In her imagination he had almost supernatural powers of cunning and deceit – she couldn't see him falling into the hands of a couple of bored constables with a torch. No; she wanted to know that the police were going to check out that abandoned building in Luik, because that meant Kris wouldn't try to do it himself. She could feel *that* possibility insinuating itself at the forefront of her consciousness like the stealthy protrusion of a venomous snake from thickly clustered leaves.

Kris said, 'Yes, he said they'd get it checked out.' His tone was leaden. 'But that was only because I kept on and on about it. And he said he'd have to contact the police in Luik and get them to look into it. He couldn't handle it because it's in another province. And that's all going to take time. If they don't get round to it until after tomorrow, I'm betting there won't be anything to find.'

'But they *are* going to check it?' asked Veerle.

Kris shrugged. 'He said they would. But I wouldn't bet on it.'

Veerle looked at him very earnestly. 'Please tell me you're going to leave it up to them, though.'

She saw Kris's jawline tense and sensed his frustration, but at last he said, 'Yes. If we can get out of this one without anyone trying to shoot us with a crossbow, then fine. Maybe the police *will* go today.'

'Is there any way we can know?'

Kris shook his head. 'I asked if I could come back and find out what they'd discovered, but he said no. He said if they did find anything I'd be seeing it in the paper, and if they didn't find anything I should think myself lucky I wasn't in trouble for wasting their time.'

'Shit.'

'Yes.'

For a little while they sat in silence. Then Veerle said, 'What do you think will happen when you – we – don't turn up at that place in Luik?'

Kris had been looking down, brooding, but now his head came up and the gaze of his dark eyes was on her. 'It's not going to go away,' he said.

'No.'

'He'll probably wait a bit and try again. Or maybe he'll check out a few more addresses listed to Verstraeten.'

'Or De Keyser,' said Veerle.

'We don't know that – yet,' said Kris. 'You could still—'

'I'm not going back to Ghent,' Veerle cut in sharply.

'Veerle—'

'No, Kris. Don't try to persuade me because I'm just *not*. Anyway, you think it would stop him coming after me? We've been over this before.'

They glared at each other and it occurred to Veerle, dismally, that once again they were at loggerheads; Kris had been trying to suggest what might be safer for her, and she had snapped at him.

She said, 'Look, that Sunday, before Bram came—'

Verdomme, *why did I mention that?*

Veerle made herself go on. 'We were talking about doing a bit more digging. You said so yourself. Not acting as bait again but *researching*. I've spent a lot of time on that this week, reading old articles online. It's all there, all the details of what Joren Sterckx did to that kid on Silent Saturday, but it still doesn't tell us how I came to see him walking around when he's supposed to be dead. I think we need to try something different.'

Kris studied her. 'Like what?'

'I think we should try talking to people in the village.'

'The police probably talked to them, back when it happened,' said Kris mildly.

'I know. But maybe someone would remember something they didn't think of before. Or maybe the police weren't asking the right questions. I mean, they *had* the killer. They didn't need to question the entire village about every detail to work out who did it.'

'OK,' said Kris slowly. 'Let's try that, though I'm betting some of them won't talk about it.'

Veerle's face fell. 'I suppose you're right. It wasn't exactly the best day ever in the village.'

'It's worth trying, though,' Kris told her. 'It's not like we can go and talk to Fred or Gregory. Did you have anyone in mind?'

'I thought if we could find out where the Sterckx family lived, we could see whether whoever lives there now knows where they moved to. And there are a few older people I know slightly. Mum never had many friends in the village because she couldn't speak Flemish, but there were one or two people she used to chat to. There was one guy whose wife was from Tournai and she used to talk to Mum in French. And I thought maybe we could try Mevrouw Willems. Do you remember her?'

'Yeah, I remember her. The head at the primary school – at least, she was for a while but then she left. That was before we went to Overijse. I thought she'd moved away.'

Veerle shook her head. 'No, I think she was sick or something. Anyway she still lives in the village somewhere so we could go and talk to her as well. She must have known pretty much every family with kids.' She shrugged. 'She probably taught Joren Sterckx when he was a kid too. She might remember something.'

'Yeah. Like he used to pull wings off insects or something. Or all his paintings were of hunters.'

In spite of the awfulness of the situation Veerle sniggered at that. Kris grinned back at her, the surly expression suddenly transformed, made handsome, and she felt it again, that old familiar pull towards him. She looked at his bold dark eyes, his aquiline nose, the sharp lines of his face. She thought about running her thumb along his cheekbone, pushing her fingers into his dark hair, pulling him close. Kissing him. The impulse was so strong that she had actually put her hands in her lap and clenched them together to stop herself before she realized what she was doing. She was sure the blood was coming to her face at the thought.

They ought to talk about what had happened the weekend before, she supposed. She owed him a proper explanation about what was going on with Bram. She owed *Bram* an explanation too, come to that, though he wasn't prepared to listen to one right now. And there was still the question of Hommel, the wraith who stood between her and Kris.

All of it amounted to a very heavy conversation indeed. And when Kris smiled at her, and she felt that tentative connection between them, like tendrils curling towards each other, she just didn't want to do it.

So instead, she said, 'Where shall we start?'

23

All the rooms in the house were painted white or shades of off-white: ivory, magnolia, cream. Mevrouw Willems, who moved about her home with studied care, had wanted it like that. She did not want her visitors – the daughter who came in daily, the doctor, the friend who came to read to her – to think of the house as a dim and gloomy cave. When she was expecting someone, she always put the lights on. Periodically she checked the bulbs, by placing a hand over them to see whether they were warm, but sometimes she forgot and when she pressed the switch the bulb would remain dead, unlit. She hoped that the white walls would make up for that – that the house would seem cheerful and bright to anyone who came to visit.

Mevrouw Willems herself moved about the house in almost-darkness, the eyes from which the light had faded preserved carefully behind tinted lenses. In spite of the blindness, she was acutely aware of all the small changes that took place in her environment: the patch of warm sunlight that moved across the sitting-room wall during the course of the day, the purr of the heating as it went on and off according to the pre-set times.

Her last cat had passed away years before and she had

never replaced her; silent weavings about the legs and ankles were too risky as her sight slowly slipped away. Still, she liked to have living things about her. There was a row of plants on the kitchen windowsill, and as her fingers touched the leaves, feeling for the spot where water should be applied to the earth in the pot, she caressed them tenderly, as she had once rubbed the old cat behind her soft ears.

She found her way around the house by memorizing the position of everything in minute detail, and by returning everything, once used, to its place. All those things had their own texture, their own sound. She could tell immediately which chair a visitor had chosen by the creak or the sigh it made as they settled themselves in it.

She had her weekly schedule carefully memorized too, since there was no point in writing it down anywhere, so she was a little surprised when she heard the doorbell ring. It was Thursday morning, and she was not expecting anyone until her daughter came in at lunch time. The postman had already been and gone; she had heard his footsteps on the gravel next door. She thought that that had only been a little while ago, but perhaps she had lost track of time; sometimes she did end up dozing a little. So she touched the hands of the little clock on the cabinet by the sitting-room door. No; it was only a little after ten.

Mevrouw Willems made her way out into the hallway, and went unhurriedly to open the front door. It was impossible to lunge like a mad thing to answer the doorbell, and besides, all her regular callers knew to wait. As she passed the light switch in the hall she reached out and put on the light. It flickered into life unseen above her head.

'Coming,' she called as the doorbell sounded again. She touched the door, felt for the little knob that undid the lock, and turned it.

As soon as the door was open, before her visitor had spoken a single word, she knew that it was someone she hadn't met before. Her daughter was short and plump, the doctor short and petite, the friend who read was of middle height and very thin. This person was tall and broad-shouldered; she could *feel* that by the hole he made in the cool air that moved all around him.

'Mevrouw Willems?'

The voice was unfamiliar but he had the local accent, or most of it.

'Yes. And who are you?' she enquired with a touch of the schoolmarm she had been.

'Kris Verstraeten.'

'Verstraeten?' She cast her mind back, wondering whether the name should mean anything to her. The family name was a common one – she must have taught dozens of little Verstraetens in her time. Was this one of them?

She really had no idea. It was impossible to keep track; so many had passed through the school, and even if she had had her sight, children changed so much as they grew. Time stretched them or inflated them or, more rarely, whittled them down. Family resemblances bobbed to the surface of childish features, and suddenly the round-faced little cherub had turned into the image of his ne'er-do-well uncle. The things she *could* perceive, such as tone of voice, changed just as much. And anyway, she tended to remember only the ones who had stood out in some way from all the others – the ones who had been spectacularly talented or spectacularly naughty.

Come to think of it, there had been one family of Verstraetens who fell into the latter camp . . .

'Yes,' said her visitor simply. 'I asked at the school and they said I would find you here. I was hoping to ask you about something. May I come inside for a few moments?'

'Well, I . . .' Mevrouw Willems stood there indecisively on her own doorstep. She preserved enough of the headmistress about her that she did not actively *fear* anyone, yet still she hesitated to allow her unexpected caller inside.

Anna wouldn't like it, she said to herself, thinking of her daughter, who was protective.

'What sort of thing?' she asked him, still holding onto the door, wondering whether to close it in his unseen face.

'I'm trying to trace someone who went to the school.'

'You know, I've been retired for nearly twelve years.'

'Yes,' he said. 'This would have been before that.'

'And the school told you where I live?' She couldn't think who would do that. She barely knew the two women – *girls*, she thought – who worked in the school office now. 'Whom did you speak to?'

'I'm not sure what her name was . . .'

'Was it the one who's always sniffing? Lotte Maes?'

'Yes, that was it. Mevrouw Maes.'

She considered. 'Are you police?'

'No,' he said. 'It's – well, it's a personal thing. If you'd let me explain . . . Please,' he added engagingly, and then she relented.

'Very well,' she said, stepping back. Then she added, rather self-consciously, 'I don't have much time, I'm afraid. My daughter is coming very soon.'

Already she was regretting her decision. His tread on the hall floorboards was heavy compared to her light footsteps; she had visions of him knocking things over or pushing things out of place. It was very important to her to know where each thing was with exact precision; otherwise it was impossible for her to get about easily.

'The sitting room is on the left,' she said, closing the front door carefully. Mevrouw Willems waited to hear that he had turned into the room, and then she followed, tracing the line of the wall with her fingertips, touching the wood of the doorframe as she followed him in. She heard a creak as he settled himself in one of the chairs, and she identified it as the French-style fireside chair, the one upholstered in worn velvet the colour of dusty roses. She herself took the high-backed leather armchair on the other side of the coffee table, feeling carefully for the arms before she lowered herself onto the seat.

'Are you completely blind?' asked Kris Verstraeten.

He spoke in a neutral voice, neither mocking nor pitying, but Mevrouw Willems was slightly piqued all the same.

'Yes,' she said, rather tartly. 'Otherwise I shouldn't have retired early. You wanted to ask me about this person you're trying to trace, Meneer Verstraeten?' She used the word Meneer ironically, lapsing back into the role of a headmistress dealing with a slightly irritating child. For any other visitor she might have offered coffee or tea, but this one had annoyed her. She felt his question had been rude.

He said, 'As I said, it's personal.' He paused. 'You will think me sentimental when I tell you. I am looking for a girl I knew.'

The corners of Mevrouw Willems' mouth turned up at that, but behind the tinted glasses, where her visitor could not see them any more than she could see him, her eyes were cool, the corners unwrinkled by smile lines. It was not possible to be the headmistress of a village school for several decades without coming to know a certain amount about human nature. Now that her eyes no longer served her, her ears were exquisitely tuned to nuances of tone. She thought that although Meneer Verstraeten said he was sentimental, he did not sound sentimental at all, or passionate, or eager. He sounded cold.

'Who was this girl?' she asked mildly.

'Her name is Veerle De Keyser.'

There was an expectant pause.

Mevrouw Willems said, 'And what did she look like, this Veerle De Keyser?'

Now it was his turn to hesitate. 'Thin,' he said at last. 'With dark hair.'

'Well,' said Mevrouw Willems carefully, 'that could describe quite a few of the girls who came through the school, you know.'

She heard him shift restlessly in the rose velvet chair. *Too heavy for it*, she thought to herself.

'Why do you want to find this particular one?' she asked him. The smile that did not reach her sightless eyes was still on her lips but she was listening for his unspoken reaction, and sure enough, there it was, the indrawing of breath through the nostrils. Her question had irritated him.

He didn't say as much, of course. He said, 'We used to be close but we lost touch. I can't forget her.'

Suddenly it came to the old lady. *Kris Verstraeten.*

She knew Veerle, all right. She'd recognized the name immediately, because there had been that very sad business a year or two ago, when Veerle's mother had been struck by a vehicle here in the village, and died. The father had gone some years before and Veerle had had to go too, after her mother died. Mevrouw Willems hadn't spoken to Veerle since leaving the school, but she knew what had happened anyway – you couldn't keep anything a secret in a small place like this.

She remembered the girl as a bit of a daredevil; once she'd climbed out of an upstairs window onto a section of the school roof. She was a curious contrast to her mother, who'd been one of those rather anxious parents. You had to wonder whether the child was so daring as a reaction to the mother, or whether the mother had become anxious as a result of the child's adventures. Mevrouw Willems had rather liked the child Veerle, though; she had spirit, which sometimes led to behaviour that had to be considered naughty, but she wasn't spiteful or destructive.

It was thinking about Veerle that brought Kris Verstraeten back to mind. She had seen them together on a number of occasions. Kris would have been a little older than Veerle, and she vaguely remembered that there was some concern about the two of them hanging about together. She couldn't call to mind any specific wrongdoing on his part, but she remembered the family very well, and they were all troublesome. Mevrouw Willems rather thought that one of the older ones had actually gone to prison for a short period. The issue of Kris's friendship with Veerle had thankfully passed away unaddressed because the Verstraetens had, to no one's great regret, moved out of the village.

There was Kris in her mind's eye: nine or ten years old, thin and energetic, with a mop of hair so dark it was almost black, and a ready grin.

'I know who you are!' she exclaimed.

In the moments that followed she heard nothing. She couldn't even hear him breathing; couldn't hear the chair creaking under his weight. Mevrouw Willems had the unnerving feeling that he had frozen there in the chair, glaring at her with angry eyes. Or perhaps he had arisen, his movements cloaked by her words, and was now frozen halfway across the space that had divided them, like a child playing that game, *Een, twee, drie – piano*. She turned her head this way and that, scanning for him. How could any person be so silent? Like a cat stalking its prey. She stuffed the yawning silence with her own words.

'You were that skinny boy, the one with the dark hair that looked as though it was never combed. And sharp little features, like a fox. Kris Verstraeten. I remember you. I remember you hanging around with the little girl too, Veerle.'

In spite of the indefinable unease his presence caused her, she couldn't quite keep the disapproval out of her voice.

'Yes,' he said, speaking without any inflection that would tell her that he was pleased or otherwise at her remembrance, but at least locating himself in the room. He was still there, seated in the rose-pink chair. 'That was her. Veerle De Keyser. I really want to find her.'

'That's rather sweet of you,' said Mevrouw Willems, but her

voice was almost as colourless as his. She felt very uncomfortable indeed now. She was regretting overriding her impulse to close the door in her visitor's face. *Anna wouldn't like it,* she had said to herself when debating whether to let him in. Now she thought that she didn't much like it herself. She wished she could remember exactly how long ago it was that Veerle had been at the school; she wished she could work out how old the girl would be now. But this unseen and toneless entity sitting opposite her in the rose velvet chair was making her so nervous that the thoughts were scattering like beads dropped onto a parquet floor, bouncing in all directions before skittering under furniture or dropping between cracks. What could he want with Veerle De Keyser? He didn't *sound* like a sentimental suitor, whatever he might say.

She cleared her throat. 'I suppose she must have changed since then. And you, Meneer Verstraeten? Would I recognize you if I could see you? Still so thin and such thick dark hair?'

'Yes,' he said, and now she knew he was lying. She couldn't tell everything about a person's appearance without her eyes, of course she couldn't, but she could estimate height and breadth and even weight by the feeling of the air around them and by the sound of their movements. Kris Verstraeten, if that was who this really was, was not thin any more. He was bulky, and she suspected that the bulk was muscle, because he sounded fit. He didn't breathe heavily when he moved. There was no telltale sound of cloth whispering against cloth.

She was careful not to let this realization show on her face. As headmistress she had seen her fair share of trouble over the years. It wasn't like a high school, of course, but still there were a few kids who were out of hand before they even got to the age of twelve. And then there were the occasional parents who didn't like something you'd done. Mevrouw Willems knew better than to let concern show on her features. She sat opposite him, apparently calm, and waited for him to ask her about Veerle De Keyser again.

'I've tried contacting some of the De Keyser families in the village,' he told her, 'but it's very slow work. If you could tell me anything . . .'

Mevrouw Willems considered, and in the distance she heard the church clock striking and knew that it would be nearly ninety minutes before her daughter arrived. She must say *something* – but what?

She did not believe in Meneer Verstraeten's declared sentiment. But if he wanted to find Veerle and he was not in love with her, nor even her friend, what did he want with her? She might tell herself that this was no concern of hers, but she had always despised people who did that sort of thing; who stood by letting all manner of things happen and said that it was nothing to do with them. She had no way of knowing what he really wanted with the girl, and having asked him, she could hardly ask again, but she did know that he was a liar, and that was not a good starting point.

Refusing point-blank to say anything at all was another possibility, but her heart failed her. Ninety minutes stretched out in front of her, a steep and perilous road with no friendly hand to support her. She had heard and felt how much bigger he was than her.

Her visitor became restless waiting for her to finish her pondering. She could hear him shifting in the rose velvet chair; it creaked under his weight.

Finally she said, 'I'm afraid I don't have an address for Veerle De Keyser, Meneer Verstraeten. Hundreds of children passed through the school while I was there, you understand. I can't possibly recall the personal details of all of them. But I do believe Veerle lived here in the village, with her mother only, and the mother's name was Charlier.'

That was safe, she thought; he could hunt for addresses listed to Charlier all he liked; Veerle had moved away to live with her father.

Anyone with less finely attuned ears would have missed the tiny hiss of satisfaction that greeted her words.

'Thank you,' he said, with the first hint of warmth she had heard since they sat down.

'You're welcome,' she said, nodding. 'And now, Meneer Verstraeten, you must excuse an old lady. I get tired very easily these days, you know.'

'I'm sorry,' he said immediately in that deadpan tone, and once again she had the sense of emptiness in the words, as though they were simply a metallic echo thrown back from cold damp walls.

Mevrouw Willems stood up, and she heard him do the same. His breathing was at her left shoulder as she led the way to the door, letting her fingers guide her along the hallway. She took care to show no outward sign of nervousness, but she had to use the wall: the visit had unnerved her so much that she was unable to concentrate on her mental map of the house. It slid away from her, corridors lengthening and the dimensions of rooms stretching. She thought there was a real danger she might lose her head and lead him into the kitchen instead.

At last she was able to open the front door and feel the cool autumn air rush in. She stood back to let him pass. He didn't pass, though; he stepped forward until he was level with her and then he stopped.

Mevrouw Willems sensed something passing rapidly through the air before her face; she could feel the wind of it on her skin.

'Meneer Verstraeten,' she said, summoning as much of her headmistress's severity as she could manage, 'it is pointless to do that. I cannot see it but I can certainly feel it. I told you I am blind. Kindly do not insult me.'

This time he didn't bother to reply. They stood there for a few seconds, the warmth of the house on one side of them and the cool air from outside seeping in on the other. Mevrouw Willems could hear cars passing along the road; she heard footsteps approaching on the pavement, perhaps twenty metres away.

Then she felt him touch her throat, just over the pulse point. The touch was extraordinarily light for such a big person. It had the irritating quality of an insect crawling over the bare skin. His fingertips were cold.

She held her breath, time sliding greasily past as his fingers lingered there. Then they were gone. He turned and she heard him striding briskly away, his footsteps resonant on the pavement.

Mevrouw Willems closed the door with hands that trembled, and pushed the bolts across. Then she felt her way to the downstairs toilet, wetted the little towel that hung there, and scrubbed at her throat; scrubbed until the skin was sore.

24

This time it was the old school, and there were only three of them: Thomas, Jonas and a young man called Filip. Their numbers had been thinner recently. The weather was getting colder, and as the winter drew in, it would be dark when work finished for the day. It wasn't just that, though. People were dropping out of sight – like that red-haired girl, Zoë, and Laurens.

With some of them, it might be nerves. There were all those stories that had been going round – and the photographs appearing online. People had been grumbling about those; Jonas had heard someone describe them as 'bullshit', but he had the impression that the indignation was put on to cover the fact that the speaker was genuinely unnerved.

Jonas was beginning to think he might pack in the exploring for a bit himself. For one thing, with the diminished numbers he seemed to be running into Thomas more and more frequently. The guy gave him the creeps. He knew the best stories, all right, and he was good enough to be an actor, but there was a coldness about the delivery which suggested that Thomas didn't care about the unfortunate protagonists of his increasingly gory tales. He had all the personal charm of a scientist cold-bloodedly conducting experiments on live things.

Filip didn't seem bothered by Thomas's lack of charisma, though. He was younger than the other two, and visibly impressed by the location. The school was not as old as some of the other sites, but it was in a good state of preservation. Not all the windows had been broken, and most of the fittings were still in place. There were girls' and boys' toilets, with rows of stalls, the doors coloured pink and blue respectively, and a long metal mirror still showing a dim reflection of anyone who wandered past the basins with their tarnished taps and brown stains from water that had long since dried up. There were white-tiled kitchens with stainless-steel units furred with dust. There were classrooms with roll-down chalkboards, some of them still faintly marked with the graffiti of lessons long past.

The three of them were sitting in what had once been the staff room. There were a few chairs in here, the seats splitting open so that the foam stuffing protruded. They sat on them anyway, because it was better than sitting on the floor, which was filthy. Filip had even found a chipped glass ashtray and was smoking self-consciously.

Thomas, of course, was telling the story, a fact that both fascinated and irritated Jonas. The big man seemed to have an unending supply of tales.

'This happened in Belgium,' he was saying. 'Not here in Flanders. A long way from here, in Wallonia, towards Arlon. There's a place there where the forest is full of abandoned cars. It's a graveyard of cars. In some places where there is a gap in the trees you can see lines of them, like a frozen river running through the landscape, a torrent of rusting metal. Everything is coloured brown with rust or green with moss and lichen. One day the forest will swallow them altogether.

'In the meantime, people like us visit the site. There are still things to find – steering wheels, tyres, dials. Or you could just take photographs. A lot of people do that.

'So one evening, along comes this American boy, maybe eighteen years old, with his camera. He's heard about the place. Supposedly the cars belonged to a bunch of American soldiers who had to leave them behind at the end of World War Two. The kid thinks it would be cool to take some photographs to show people when he gets home.

'It takes him a long time to find the right place, because he doesn't speak French. So he keeps stopping people, and either they can't understand what he wants or they don't want to speak English with him. Or maybe they aren't keen on people poking about on private land.

'Eventually he works out where the car graveyard is, though by now it's getting towards the end of the day. The sun is low in the sky. He comes across the first car and gets his camera out and takes a lot of photographs. He wanders further into the wood, snapping away. When they found his camera afterwards, it had over a hundred photographs on it.

'So he moves down between the lines of cars and he's leaning right into one of them, trying to focus on the dashboard dials, when he hears a metallic clang and looks up. There's someone maybe twenty, twenty-five metres away, coming in his direction. He seems to be in a hurry. Whoever he is, he's quite a bit older than the kid and he doesn't look like a tourist. He looks more like a local. The clang was the guy running into a car door that was swinging on its hinges, so it slammed shut.

'The American puts up his hands to show that he doesn't mean any harm. He's thinking the guy is the landowner, coming to run him off the land. But as the guy gets closer he sees that he doesn't look angry. He looks frightened.

'The man comes right up to the kid and starts telling him something really urgently. Only it's all in French, so the American can't understand a word of it. He tells the guy this in English but it doesn't make any difference. The guy keeps on at him in French, but now the kid is only half listening because he's trying to take a few more photographs while he still can. He's worked out that the older guy can't be the landowner because he seems nervous, not angry. He's probably seen whoever *does* own the place coming. Whatever the problem is, he probably doesn't have much more time to take pictures, so he decides to get on with it.

'The guy grabs the kid's arm and points away into the distance. The kid is annoyed but he looks anyway: he can't see a thing. He's getting fed up with being ranted at in French, so he pulls his arm away and carries on with what he was doing. Maybe he tells the guy to fuck off in English.

'The older guy gets the message. He says whatever it is he was saying to the kid in French one more time and then he's gone. He weaves his way in and out of the cars and then he vanishes under the trees.

'When he's gone, the kid stops trying to photograph the inside of the car and straightens up. He looks the way the older guy was pointing but he still can't see anything untoward. He can't hear anything, either. No footsteps, no dog barking, no more clanging of metal. So what was all the fuss about?

'He keeps going, moving up the line. Eventually he comes to a particular car that stands out from the rest. It's big, long, and it's stood up to the test of time pretty well. Most of the windows are covered with green stuff, so the glass looks like it has a coating of green felt, but they're all there. All the doors are shut. The tyres are covered in that green stuff too, but at least it still has tyres. Many of the other cars are just resting on empty wheel arches.

'The kid leans in and rubs at the green stuff on the driver's side window. It's hard to pick out much inside but it looks like most of it is still there: the dashboard, the steering wheel. He could sit in there and take a photograph from the *inside*.

'So he tries the door, and it opens quite easily. Everything's green in there too, either because there really is moss growing on it or because of the light being filtered through the green-stained windows. It smells a little uninviting, a lingering scent of damp and mould.

'He gets in anyway. He slides into the driver's seat and pulls the door shut. Then he starts to mess about with his camera, adjusting the settings. He takes a photo of the dashboard with flash but it comes out too bright. So he tries again without flash, and it's more atmospheric but you can't make much out. He thinks maybe it would work better after all if he opened the door, so he reaches for the handle, and as he does so, he hears a sound behind him, in the back seat.

'It's just a tiny sound – a creak as someone shifts their weight – but it's enough to tell the kid that he wants to get out of there *right now*. He grabs the door handle, but before he can get the door open someone lunges forward and grabs him round the neck. He panics and starts trying to fight, but whoever it is is much stronger than him.

'The camera falls into the foot well and the kid never sees it again. Someone will look at those photos, but it won't be him. The guy behind him has an arm around his throat and it's cutting off his breathing. He goes wild trying to break the grip, but it just makes matters worse because he uses up oxygen faster.

'Now he knows what the French-speaking guy was trying to tell him, but it's too late. He's going to pass out . . .

'Then the guy behind him slackens his grip, and all of a sudden he can breathe again. His head is swimming and his throat hurts but he's groping for the door, and then he glances behind him, and in his last seconds he sees why the guy let go. He had to let go to pick up the axe.

'It's a while before anyone finds the kid, but when they do, the door of the car is open, inviting you to look inside. The inside of the car isn't green like all the other stuff lying around in the wood. Not *only* green, anyway. It was red and now the red has turned brown. And the kid – the kid is all over the car. They find fourteen different pieces. The head is on the dashboard, where it would be staring through the windscreen if it weren't blind and the windscreen weren't opaque with green stuff.

'They never found the guy who did it, or the axe. Some people say he's still out there, haunting the car graveyard, waiting for another victim.'

Thomas had finished, and now he sat there impassively while Filip gabbled on about how cool the story was. Jonas had the impression that Thomas didn't care whether his audience thought the story was cool or not.

So why is he even here?

Not for the first time, he examined the unease he felt about Thomas.

The whole storytelling thing, the urban legends – he didn't know where that had come from. Probably not from Thomas. He'd heard plenty of other people relating them, though few with such chilling detail. Quite a lot of the tales going round were just recycled ones about the Burnt Guy.

Then there were the photographs; the ones that were supposed to show the victims of urban legends – some of the *same* legends he'd heard Thomas relate. Nobody knew who took those pictures, nor who uploaded them.

Supposing, he thought, *you put all these things together . . .*

And made what? That was the question.

Maybe nothing.

'Look,' he said at last, 'that was great, but I've got to go.'

He stood up, and to his dismay Thomas stood up too.

'Me too.'

Jonas snickered uneasily. 'We don't want to walk out of here hand in hand, you know.'

'That was not my plan,' said Thomas in his deadpan way.

'Well, good. Glad we got that one cleared up,' said Jonas, but he noticed that Thomas didn't sit down again.

Suddenly he really didn't want to walk back through the deserted corridors with the big man – not on his own. He glanced at Filip. 'You coming?'

'No,' said Filip. 'I'm going to stay here a bit longer. Take some snaps. It's amazing.' He went on for a bit like that, about how cool the site was, how he couldn't wait to upload some pics. Jonas could cheerfully have thumped him.

There was nothing for it, though. He'd have to leave with Thomas. He couldn't see any alternative that didn't sound stupidly indecisive or actually nervy, and he had an instinctive feeling that showing fear would be a bad idea; it would be like the struggles of the wounded fish that bring the sharks cruising around.

He said, 'Fine,' shoved his hands deep into his pockets and headed for the door, conscious of Thomas at his shoulder.

Outside the staff room, the hallway stretched away to darkness at the far end. Soft grey moonlight slanted down through the windows, picking out dark knots of rubbish on the dusty floor. Jonas and Thomas moved down the hallway together until at last the darkness swallowed them, and the sound of their footsteps faded to nothing.

Later, Thomas came back to find Filip.

25

The first attempt was almost useless.

Kris knew the house where the Sterckx family had lived, over a decade before. It was on a street not far from the village centre, but in an unfavoured location. A row of houses stared across a cobbled street at an open space containing the remains of four great greenhouses, the type used for growing grapes. If there were any vines remaining, they had either dried up and died or grown wildly out of hand. The greenhouses were clearly abandoned. The glass was mostly intact but the panes were opaque with dirt, and the area around was a forest of weeds, in which bits of rusting machinery and other detritus lurked like traps.

The Sterckx house did not look much better. Even before they tried knocking on the door, Kris and Veerle could tell that it was uninhabited. It was a compact-looking building with nothing relaxed or sprawling about the design, built of bricks unfashionably painted red with the mortar between them picked out in contrasting white. The shutters on all the windows were down, so that the house presented a blind aspect to the world. The driveway was relatively clear, but the lawn was a jungle. There was a wooden post by the gateway that might once have held a mail box, but there was nothing on it now.

They walked up the driveway and Kris knocked on the door in a desultory manner but, as expected, there was no reply. The door itself was tightly secured; it didn't even rattle when pushed. The house gave the impression that it had been abandoned for a long time. There weren't any advertising flyers on the step; even the deliverers of junk mail had given up.

After checking both sides to see whether any of the neighbours were taking an interest in their activities, Kris and Veerle went round the side of the house. Here they found an estate agent's board lying amongst the weeds. It was so faded by rain and sunlight that the words TE KOOP were almost illegible. The bottom end of the wooden stake on which it had been mounted was badly splintered, suggesting that it had been taken down by force. They stepped over it and went to examine the back of the house.

The shutters were down here too, but there was a back door with a glass panel in it, and that was unshuttered. By standing close to the glass, Veerle could see that a key was still in the inside of the lock. It would be possible to break in, if they weren't squeamish about smashing the window.

She looked around the rear garden. The spot where they stood was well screened by trees and bushes, the overgrowth working in their favour. She looked at Kris, telegraphing a question.

'We have to go in,' he said in a low voice. 'He's not here. I'd be willing to bet nobody's been here for years. But there might be something.'

'OK,' said Veerle. 'Are you going to do it?'

Kris nodded. He went back to the side of the house and fetched the estate agent's board.

'Keep back.'

He punched the stake through the glass pane in the door, turning his head away as he did so in case of flying shards. A couple of extra blows knocked out the pieces of glass that stood up in the frame like fangs, ready to slice into anyone who reached inside.

Kris dropped the stake and put his hand through the window, twisting the key to unlock the door. It took him a little while; the key was evidently stiff from disuse. At last he managed it, and the door opened.

They listened for a few moments, checking that nobody within earshot had heard the glass breaking and decided to come and investigate. All they could hear was the sound of a car passing along a road some distance away, and the harsh sound of a crow. Either nobody had heard, or nobody cared enough to come and see what was happening.

They went into the house.

Kris slipped a torch out of his pocket. With the shutters down, the only light came from the door through which they had just come, and as they penetrated further, that would be inadequate. He switched on the torch and it lit the interior with a faint pale light.

The room they had entered was some kind of utility room leading through into the kitchen. Both were empty. The kitchen had fitted units with an ugly yellow finish, but all the appliances had been removed, leaving dusty spaces like gaps in a row of teeth. The tiled walls were also yellow, with a floral design that surely dated back to the 1970s. Veerle pulled open a drawer that looked as though it had held cutlery, but it was empty. No kitchen knives or meat cleavers. She slid the drawer closed again. Her fingers left tracks in the dust on the yellow surface.

Kris led the way into a narrow hall lined with a dowdy wallpaper featuring knots of limp-looking roses. Even in the dim light from the torch Veerle could see paler patches on the paper where things had hung – photographs or prints or a mirror. Everything seemed dry – there was no smell of damp, no running stains on the walls – but there was a faint pervasive odour of something unpleasant that Veerle suspected was mouse droppings. The house was claustrophobically gloomy; she could feel it closing in like the contraction process of mummification. It was not difficult to imagine him growing up here – Joren Sterckx, De Jager, whoever he was.

It probably looked better back then, and with a bit of sunlight coming in, she reminded herself.

There were three other rooms on the ground floor: one that had almost certainly been the sitting room but now stood empty apart from an ugly gas fire, a dining room whose once polished boards showed the scratches of table and chair legs, and a narrow lavatory with a chipped sink.

'I suppose we should look upstairs,' said Veerle doubtfully. She and Kris had explored plenty of empty houses, but this was different. Those houses had been fun to visit; some of them had been downright opulent. There had been the thrill of possible discovery. She didn't feel that thrill now. She wasn't afraid; she really didn't think any living person had been in here for years, and she didn't believe anyone was about to turn up now. The house was simply depressing. It gave off the ugly, miserable stink of neglect. Veerle couldn't imagine anyone having a good time in here, ever.

'Yeah,' said Kris laconically, moving the torch beam over the flaking banisters of the staircase. He glanced at her. 'You can stay here if you like. I can't tell if those stairs are sound.'

'No,' said Veerle. 'I'm coming with you.'

She saw the corner of Kris's mouth twitch at that, but he said nothing. He started up the stairs, moving cautiously, testing each one as he went, and she followed. She left a little space between them, in case their combined weight should be too much for any of the aged timbers.

The treads groaned under their feet, but nothing gave way. The banisters lining the upstairs landing came into view, and then Veerle could see a strip of carpet so dusty that it could have been cut from grey felt. The wallpaper up here was a broad stripe, again pockmarked with lighter patches where pictures had been removed from the wall. It was very dark, now that the feeble light from the back door was so far behind them.

They found a cramped bathroom, the lavatory in a separate sliver of room next door. All the fittings were a dull pink, the colour of sunburn. There was a rail above the bath, but no shower curtain.

After that they entered what had probably been the master bedroom, although it hardly deserved the name. The worn carpet showed darker patches where furniture had stood, and deep indentations from the feet. A mirror with bevelled edges hung from a chain on one wall, overlooked by whoever had moved the other things out. Veerle could see herself reflected in it, and the back of Kris's head as he stood staring at the ugly textured wallpaper. She wondered whose reflection had last appeared in those silvery depths.

Kris made a brief sound of frustration. The house wasn't telling them anything. They'd known from the start that no one was hiding out here, but it looked as though the house really had nothing to say. It was empty, hinting at nothing of its former owners except a lack of interest in renovating.

What did you expect? she thought. *A forwarding address?*

All the same, it seemed lax not to look over the last couple of rooms. They wandered out of the bedroom and into the room next door. This was slightly smaller and there wasn't so much as a forgotten mirror in it; only two very large paler rectangles on the plain walls. At the corner of one, a drawing pin was stuck into the wall, a scrap of glossy paper impaled on it like a tiny butterfly transfixed by a pin.

A poster, Veerle thought. She prised out the drawing pin so that she could examine the scrap of paper by the light of Kris's torch. There wasn't enough of it even to suggest what the poster had shown. Still, a poster – that was the sort of thing you'd expect to find in the bedroom of a child or a teenager or maybe even a young adult.

Maybe this was Joren's room, she thought, and her throat tightened as though a cold hand had encircled it and squeezed. She found herself turning, scanning the entire room, checking that they were really alone, just the two of them, her and Kris. It was stupid – she knew that – but she couldn't help it. This, she realized, was the reason why the house was empty. You'd have thought that someone would have taken it after more than ten years, even if it was just some thrill-seeking ghoul, but the thought of sleeping in here, where *he* might have slept, was just impossible.

There's one more room, she reminded herself. *Don't work yourself up. Maybe this was the guest room and he slept in the other one.*

She couldn't wait to get out, though. She felt jittery waiting for Kris to finish looking around. Going anywhere without him wasn't an option; she hadn't thought to bring her own torch, and groping about in this place in the dark wasn't something she wanted to contemplate.

Finally Kris had satisfied himself that there was nothing to see. He went back out onto the landing and Veerle followed. The final bedroom was right at the front of the house. If the shutters had been up, there would have been an unimpeded view of the four abandoned greenhouses.

Kris went into the room, and Veerle followed.

For several long moments neither of them said a word. Veerle's eyes widened. Her nostrils flared as she drew in a breath, held it, let it out slowly. She turned to Kris.

'What does this mean?'

26

The bedroom was small, even smaller than the one they had just left. It was more of a box room. Like the other rooms, it was empty of furniture. There were no pictures on the walls, no lampshade on the dead bulb that hung from the ceiling, no curtains at the shuttered window. The carpet had been removed, leaving a bare wooden floor.

The only thing that told Veerle who or what the occupant of the room had been was the wallpaper. Fairy-tale characters drawn with the light touch of a cartoonist cavorted on a faded blue background. There were knights and ladies, strutting cats in thigh-length boots and cavalier's hats, fair beauties surrounded by jolly dwarfs, grinning ogres and fire-breathing dragons. A child's wallpaper. 'Why is there a child's room?' asked Veerle, staring at a knight on a prancing horse.

'There must have been a child,' said Kris.

'Yes, but who? Joren Sterckx wasn't a kid. He was – I don't know, nineteen or twenty or something.'

'Maybe he had a brother or sister?' suggested Kris.

'I don't remember one.'

'Me neither, but then I can't remember every kid in the

village from back then. It was a long time ago.' Kris shrugged. 'I can remember the ones I was friends with, but not all the others.'

'He couldn't . . .' Veerle considered for a moment. 'He couldn't have had a kid of his own, could he?'

'Joren?' Kris shook his head. 'I don't think so. He was old enough, but I can't see him as a dad. This is a guy who hunted a kid down and killed him. Anyway, wouldn't it have come out at the time of the trial?'

'I don't know. I mean, when all that stuff was in the papers after the fire in the castle, they didn't put my name in because I was under eighteen. Still a kid,' said Veerle ironically. 'So maybe they didn't mention *this* kid for the same reason. Protecting them or whatever.'

She followed the pale torch beam with her gaze as it moved over the illustrations on the walls.

'Perhaps this was Joren's room when he was little,' she said. 'Maybe he moved into the bigger one next door when he got older, and they never bothered to redecorate.'

'Maybe,' said Kris. He began to move around the room, examining the pictures on the wallpaper by the light of the torch, and Veerle stayed close because outside its beam everything rapidly dissolved into darkness.

She was so close to Kris that she could have reached out and touched his face, run a hand through his dark hair. It wasn't as though the thought hadn't occurred to her; in fact it was occurring to her with such persistence that her face was warm and there was a tight little sensation of excitement under her breastbone. But the house had a dampening effect; ill luck hung over it like a bad smell. Love expressed here would crumble into dust. Veerle put her hands in her jeans pockets and tried to hang back.

There was very little to see. There was no furniture, nothing on the walls, not so much as a single forgotten marble or Lego brick on the floor. The wooden windowsill under the shutters was scarred with a series of long scratches and gouges that might have been made with a penknife, but what did that mean? Any bored ten-year-old might have done that.

Then Kris said, 'Look at this.'

He squatted on the dusty boards, and Veerle knelt down beside him.

Kris trained the torch beam on one of the illustrations on the wallpaper, tracing it with his fingers. 'See?'

She did see. The picture he was touching was of a princess waving her handkerchief at a knight in armour as he rode out on his charger. The knight had the visor of his helmet raised, so that his face would have been visible – except that his face was gone. Obliterated. Someone had taken a sharp object and very deliberately scratched it out, ripping the paper and gouging into the plaster underneath. The same went for the princess. Underneath the pointed headgear with its swirling veil, there was a void for a face, a ragged patch of tatters and scrapes.

'And here,' said Kris, his lean hand sliding up the wall to rest on a mutilated picture of Puss in Boots, the face beneath the feathered hat scratched away. He began to point out others, but Veerle was already picking them out for herself. None of them occurred more than a metre above floor level, and all in that one part of the wall. She wondered why.

Perhaps that spot had been screened from view by a piece of furniture, concealing the damage from the adults in the house. Perhaps it had been the only spot that *hadn't* been covered by furniture, leaving the defacer free access. There was no way to tell now where the furniture had stood.

'Odd,' commented Kris.

'I think it's creepy,' Veerle told him. 'Who scratches out Puss in Boots' face?'

'A bratty kid,' said Kris.

'I don't know. It's nasty, the way just the faces are gone.' Veerle stood up. 'There isn't anything else to see, is there? Can we get out of here?'

They left the room and went downstairs again. At the back door, Kris paused.

'We should ask the neighbours if they know where the Sterckx family went. I guess they probably didn't advertise it, wherever they went, but you never know.'

'OK,' said Veerle. She squinted up at Kris, who was silhouetted against what seemed like dazzlingly bright daylight after the time they had spent indoors, in the dark. She said, 'Whose room was that, do you think? The one with the wallpaper?' She didn't wait for him to reply. 'It was Joren's, wasn't it? When he was a kid?'

'Maybe,' said Kris.

They let themselves out and Kris reached inside to lock the door behind them. There was nothing they could do about the broken windowpane, but somehow Veerle thought it would be a while before anyone discovered it. They picked their way self-consciously back to the gate, and then Kris nodded towards the house on their right.

'Let's start with that one.'

The house was a similar design to the one they had just left, but the walls had been whitewashed, perhaps in a conscious attempt to make it look less like the Sterckx house. The garden was neat, the lawn cropped to a tidy length, the flowerbeds meticulously weeded. Here and there twee little statues peeped out amongst the shrubs and flowers: a ceramic snail, a brace of gnomes.

They had to climb a short flight of steps to the well-scrubbed porch. Kris rang the bell; they could hear it buzzing inside the house. They waited.

After a few moments they heard the rattle of someone unfastening a security chain, and the door opened. A wan face appeared, the grey hair cut short in a practical but unflattering style. If it had not been for the peach acrylic sweater and the pendant, Veerle would hardly have known whether the face was male or female.

'Yes?'

'I'm sorry to bother you, *Mevrouw*,' said Kris politely, 'but the family who used to live next door – we were wondering—'

'No,' said the woman shortly, and closed the door in their faces.

'Thank you,' called Kris ironically. He and Veerle looked at each other.

'That went well,' said Veerle dryly. As they went back down the steps, she added, 'Shall we try the one on the other side?'

'Yeah.' Kris didn't sound optimistic.

The other house was new. The garden had a raw, un-finished look to it, the flowerbeds recently turned, saplings supported by stakes. If there had been a house here a decade ago, it had been knocked down and replaced by this one with its neatly painted walls and flawless window frames.

They rang the bell anyway, but if anyone was at home they weren't answering the door.

'Should we come back?' asked Veerle as they drifted back down the drive.

Kris shrugged. 'I don't think they'll know anything. This place is too new.'

They paused when they reached the pavement. If they each went their separate ways, they might just as well part here. Kris could walk to the end of the street and take a cut-through onto the main road, where buses ran back to Overijse; Veerle could go the other way, towards the village centre and Kerkstraat. She wondered whether to invite him back to the house for a while. That would certainly be over-stepping the boundary of their current investigative partnership, not to mention her promise to Geert. There was no particular reason to ask him back; she had a little more research to do before they could visit any of the other people they planned to see. Still . . .

'Kris—' she began, and then her mobile phone went off in her pocket.

Dad? Veerle thought, but she knew it probably wasn't Geert. He'd called that morning, as he always did on a Saturday, so he wouldn't be calling now unless something unusual had happened. As soon as *that* thought crossed her brain, she had to look and see who the caller was. She slipped the phone out of her jeans pocket.

Bram De Wulf.

Verdomme. Why did he have to call now, at this precise

moment, and after all this time? She didn't want to speak to him in front of Kris.

The phone trilled a second time in her hand, insistently. It would ring a third time, and then it would go to voicemail, she knew. She hesitated. Kris said, 'Go ahead. I'll call, OK?'

He turned and strode away across the street.

He knew.

Veerle was still watching him as she thumbed the green ANSWER CALL icon and put the phone to her ear.

'Yes?' she said.

27

'Veerle?'

'Bram.' Even as Veerle said his name, her gaze was follow-ing Kris as he strode towards the end of the road and the cut-through.

Shit, she was thinking. She was sure that Kris had guessed it was Bram calling. Another nail in the coffin of the rekindled relationship she'd promised herself and Geert she wasn't going to have. And now she had to talk to Bram with that conviction hanging over her, making her feel so self-conscious that she could hardly speak naturally.

'I tried to call you,' she said.

'I know. Eleven times,' said Bram.

'Was it eleven?' Now Veerle was really dismayed. He'd kept track? And just like that, it happened again: the ground that she had thought was firm beneath her feet was shifting again. She glanced away from Kris's retreating figure, then glanced back and he had gone, vanished into the cut-through. She was alone with the phone pressed to her ear and Bram seventy kilometres away listening to her down the open line. 'Bram,' she began, 'about the day you came here . . .'

'Yes,' he said, waiting.

'I'm really sorry that happened.'

'You're sorry?' Bram repeated. 'Veerle, does this mean you're back with him?'

'No.' That was the truth. Kris hadn't so much as tried to kiss her, apart from the brief touches on the cheek that everyone used for greetings. He hadn't embraced her since that first time he had come to the house on Kerkstraat to warn her. Veerle had thought about touching him, about running her fingers through that dark hair, about kissing him, but she hadn't done anything about it. She thought of it in the same abstract and yearning way she would have considered the glittering contents of a shop window if someone had said to her, *If you could have anything from that display, what would it be?* She and Kris were working together because they had to – because it might mean survival or not. 'No,' she said again. 'We're not back together.'

She sighed. 'Look, I called you all those times because I wanted to explain.' Abruptly, the words dried up. Was she going to tell him everything – all the things she and Kris knew, or suspected?

After a moment Bram said, 'Well, explain. I didn't want to hear it before but now I do.'

There was a chunk of brick wall on the other side of the road, in front of the derelict greenhouses. Only a chunk, perhaps two metres long, but enough to sit on. Veerle crossed over and sat down on it, racking her brains. She couldn't think of anything to tell him but the plain truth, but she was imagining his reaction.

'Look,' she said, 'the day you came up, Kris wasn't there for . . . a social visit. Some stuff has been happening here and we needed to talk about it, because it ... well, it affects both of us. I don't think we can ignore it.'

Bram didn't reply. Into the silence Veerle suddenly blurted out, 'De Jager's back.'

This time she heard a sharp hiss of intaken breath.

'De Jager? You mean the guy who attacked you in that old castle, before you even moved to Ghent?'

'Yes. I mean him.'

'Veerle . . .'

Don't say it, she thought.

'He's dead. You told me he was dead yourself. How can he be back?'

'I don't know how,' said Veerle tightly. 'I just know he is.'

'*How* do you know?'

'Because of the things Kris told me. And other stuff I worked out myself.'

'So you haven't actually *seen* anyone who might be him, or like him?'

'No. But, Bram, I'm not imagining this. Look, Kris came to see me because at least two people with the same name as him have been killed. One of them was cut to pieces in his own bed.'

'Shit,' said Bram.

'And then,' she said, 'whoever did that took his finger and left it somewhere, and sent Kris an email with directions to find it. Only someone else found it first.' She let out a long breath. 'I suppose it's possible someone with the same name as Kris could have been murdered and it could just be a coincidence – there are loads of people called Verstraeten. But the email – that shows it was about him.'

'Well, maybe it was,' said Bram slowly, 'but that doesn't mean it has to be about you too. You don't have to get involved.'

'But I *am* involved already,' said Veerle. 'It's not just Kris. *I've* had emails too. You know that group I belonged to before, the Koekoeken? The emails came from one of them, supposedly. From his email account, anyway. A guy called Gregory. And, Bram – Gregory's dead as well. Someone killed him and burnt his flat.'

'*Godverdomme*, Veerle, this is serious shit. Have you been to the police?'

'Kris went. They didn't believe him.'

'What?!'

'They thought it was some kind of hoax.'

'Shit.' There was silence as Bram considered. Then he said, 'The emails sent to you – were they the same thing? You know, directions to something?'

'No,' said Veerle. 'The first one I didn't even read. The second one was a kind of warning – only it sounded creepy, like maybe it was actually a threat and not a warning at all. It said, *This is happening, and you could be next*, or something like that. And there was a photo.'

'Of what?'

'Of a hand. And maybe blood, but you couldn't really tell. It just looked . . . wrong.'

'Did you reply?'

'No.'

'Well, maybe it really was a warning. You said they came from the same account, this Gregory guy's? Maybe whoever it is who's after Kris wants you to keep out of it. And maybe you should, Veerle.'

'I can't,' she said immediately. *Walk away and let Kris get it?* But she couldn't say that, not to Bram. Hurriedly, she went on, 'What if it isn't just a warning to keep out? What if he comes after me too?'

'Look, Veerle,' said Bram, 'supposing it *is* one of these Koekoeken. Maybe De Jager, though I don't see how, or maybe someone else with a grudge. Can they find you?'

'I don't think so. It was just usernames. The people who ran the group, Fred and Gregory, had email addresses and names too, but not home addresses. I guess Gregory would have known Kris was from Overijse because they knew each other slightly, but I never gave mine out to anyone. The only one who knew where I lived was Kris, and maybe Hommel, but she's . . .'

Dead.

Veerle didn't say that.

This time Bram was silent for so long that Veerle began to wonder whether he was still on the line. At last he said, 'You're sure this is real, Veerle? Not just some sick idiot messing around?'

'Yeah,' said Veerle grimly. 'I'm sure.'

'Then . . .' He hesitated. 'Come back to Ghent.' He must have heard the sharp intake of breath from Veerle because he hurried on. 'Just come back. If you can't stay with your dad and his girl-friend any more, you can stay here until you sort something out. You could re-enrol at school here. You could—'

'Bram, *stop!*' Veerle made herself lower her voice. 'I can't just move back. I have a life here. The house I grew up in is here. It's *home*. And anyway, if it's him, De Jager, he won't just give up. He'll keep trying to find me.'

'You could make sure he doesn't.'

'How?'

'De Keyser's a common name. There must be thousands of De Keysers in Flanders. He can't check them all, especially if he doesn't know where to start. Just leave, and don't tell anyone where you're going. Not the neighbours or the people in your class – and *especially* not Kris Verstraeten.'

'But—' Veerle was stunned. *Leave the village without telling Kris?*

'Veerle,' said Bram in a hard voice quite unlike his usual amiable tones, 'think about it. If this Gregory guy is dead, and' – he hesitated – 'so is Hommel, then the only Koekoeken members who actually know who you are are Kris and the other guy you said ran the group . . .'

'Fred,' said Veerle flatly. 'I don't think he's in the picture, Bram. He's disappeared.'

There was a pause as Bram digested that information. Then he said, 'So it's just Kris, then.'

'What are you saying, Bram?' asked Veerle in a brittle voice.

'I'm saying that if not one single member of the Koekoeken knows where you've gone, you'll be pretty much impossible to trace.'

'Bram . . .' Veerle was having real difficulty in keeping her voice down. 'You're telling me to run away and leave Kris to face this?'

'Isn't it what he told you to do? Pack up and move back to Ghent for your own safety?'

'Yes, but—'

'You don't owe him anything, Veerle.' Bram paused and then plunged on. 'Look at the facts. Mixing with him is

242

dangerous. Supposing you decide to stay in the village, and this guy keeps stalking you. What if Kris decides to draw him out by using you both as bait again, like that time in the castle?'

'That's totally unfair!' Veerle spoke much more loudly than she had intended. A bird fluttered out of the long grass behind her. Her fingers were tight on the phone. 'I agreed to go to the castle that night. Kris didn't make me.'

'What about what happened in Ghent? Don't tell me Kris didn't drag you into that one.'

'*Verdomme*, Bram! He *didn't*.'

'Veerle—'

'Shut *up*, Bram.'

After that, Veerle didn't trust herself to speak. The seconds slid by and there was nothing between her and Bram but the empty line.

At last Bram said, 'Veerle, I can't keep waiting for you for ever, you know that. But I guess we're still friends, aren't we?'

'Yes,' said Veerle, and now she really felt like crying, but she kept a lid on it.

'I'm telling you as a friend, don't get pulled any further into this. You don't have to stay there, especially not if you feel threatened. You could come back to Ghent. I know you want to finish high school but you don't have to do it there. You can come here, to my place, any time. No pressure. You can come here as a friend. OK?'

'OK,' said Veerle unsteadily. She rubbed at the corner of her eye with the heel of her free hand. She said, 'I think I should go.'

'All right. But the offer stands. Just come if you need to – or if you want to.'

'Thanks.'

Veerle ended the call and pocketed the phone. She stood up, looking around. The street was deserted. Kris was long gone. The house at which they had knocked showed no signs of life; the old Sterckx house looked as desolate as ever. She put her head down and walked home.

28

Veerle didn't see Kris that week. Nothing more had happened since he received the email with the photograph. There was nothing to suggest that De Jager was closing in on them. There was only the vague and persistent sense of time sliding past with no progress made.

It was now late October and the autumn holiday was fast approaching; she had a ton of coursework to do before school broke up, and she'd have much more free time afterwards. She *knew* it sounded ludicrous, setting school work against the threat looming over them. Still, this year in the village was supposed to be her chance to get her life back on track. She had to take that seriously.

That wasn't the whole story, though. The conversation with Bram had shaken her.

Mixing with him is dangerous.

Was Bram right? She didn't *want* to believe that. Kris had protected her on the rooftop in Ghent. Veerle couldn't believe that he would deliberately put her in the firing line.

All the same, there were three strikes against Kris now. Her mother had actually locked Veerle in her room to try to stop her meeting him. Geert De Keyser had first discouraged the relationship and then made Veerle promise not to see Kris. And now Bram was telling her that Kris was dragging her into danger.

Sometimes, in her darkest moments, she thought perhaps Bram *was* right. She'd got into the Koekoeken through meeting Kris. If that hadn't happened, she'd never have come face to face with De Jager at all. It was Kris who had suggested they use themselves as bait to lure the killer out into the open. They'd survived that encounter but they both bore scars.

Kris didn't force me to join the Koekoeken, she said to herself. I chose *it.*

She remembered that January night when she had looked out of the window of a bus into the darkness and seen a light where there should have been no light. Ninety-nine people out of a hundred would have ignored that light. They certainly wouldn't have got off the bus and gone to investigate. But Veerle was the one person who had. So she'd been exploring before she met Kris, before she'd ever heard of the Koekoeken.

And in Ghent, it hadn't been as straightforward as Bram made out, had it? The first time she'd laid eyes on the killer who'd called himself Joos Vijdt she hadn't been with Kris at all, she'd been with Bram himself. They'd spent an evening on the rooftops and then tried to climb down a service ladder into a yard behind some shops. The old man had run at Bram as he climbed down, brandishing a knife that only Veerle had seen, and Bram had had to lunge upwards, out of reach. Bram, who hadn't seen the blade, had been inclined to pass the incident off as a random attack by a nut or a druggie.

If things had been different – if the old man had been quicker or we hadn't seen him in time . . .

Then it wouldn't have been Kris who had 'dragged her into danger', if you wanted to put it like that – it would be Bram.

But what about now? Even if I could stay out of this, would I?

That was what it came down to; that was the question she asked herself a hundred times that week.

If I could walk away and leave Kris to face this, would I do it?

Claudine would have snatched her child away from him in an instant; she had told Kris to stay away from Veerle all those years ago, to stay away or she'd kill him. If Geert found out what was going on, he'd probably drive down from Ghent himself and start packing her stuff. And Bram had told her that mixing with Kris was dangerous.

But . . .

Veerle could hardly put it into words, even to herself. Saying that she loved him too much to walk away didn't cover it at all. Sometimes she wasn't sure it was love she felt; it was more like pain. There was nothing defined between her and Kris. They exchanged the polite kisses of platonic friends, that was all, and perhaps that was all there would ever be. Still, she couldn't walk away.

He protected me, she thought. She flinched from the memory of what had happened on the rooftop, and yet she made herself look at it, like someone unwrapping a sinister-looking parcel, afraid of what they will find inside it.

Kris chose to come when I called him. He chose *to protect me.*

That was the terrible thing. When she thought about Hommel's death she didn't dwell on the moment when the girl vanished over the edge of the roof; she thought about the moment when their gazes had met and she had seen that awful knowledge in Hommel's eyes. Hommel had known perfectly well whom Kris had chosen. The next instant she was gone.

Choice. That was what it came down to. She could choose to stand next to Kris and face what was coming, or she could choose to go, and save herself.

She thought about it all week, but really there was only one choice in the end.

I'm not running away. I'm staying with Kris.

29

They met at night. This time it was the sewers, and it was only two of them: Thomas and Maxim.

Maxim had half expected Ruben. Maxim hadn't seen him for a while – in fact there were a couple of times when he'd expected to see Ruben and he hadn't appeared – but he'd sent him a message with details of the meet. Ruben didn't turn up, though.

He and Thomas had waited for a little while, but Maxim sensed that the big man wanted to get on with it. Thomas didn't think Ruben would come, and the longer they spent hanging about, the more risk that someone would see them.

The meet was on a dingy street in Saint-Josse-ten-Noode. Much of the ground-floor frontage was taken up with garage doors or blank sections of wall, the rest with barred and shuttered windows. The streetlamps were spaced well apart, so Thomas and Maxim took care to keep to the shadows. At this hour there were hardly any pedestrians about, but there was no point in risking the attention of some busybody.

The way into the sewers was down a manhole capped with a metal cover. Thomas had brought an implement similar to a crowbar, concealed inside a sports bag.

On their walk through the streets, Thomas had filched a couple of traffic cones to place on either side of the hole when they were down; he didn't want to pull the manhole cover back over it when they were inside in case they couldn't open it again from underneath. Worse, some late returner might park on top of it: it was on the pavement, but plenty of people parked with two wheels off the road. Thomas explained all this in answer to Maxim's questions, using the same unemotional monotone he always did, whether discussing meets or telling stories of murder and mutilation.

None of these thoughts – about not being able to get out of the sewers again – had occurred to Maxim until Thomas pointed them out. Now he began to feel doubly apprehensive: not only was he increasingly aware that he knew very little about the hazards of negotiating the sewers, but he was also worrying about being trapped down there for ever. He opened his mouth to say something to Thomas, but when he met the gaze of those pale impassive eyes he couldn't do it. He saw less empathy there than in the black eyes of a lizard. He wished Ruben had come; two of them might have carried the point, suggesting a late-night drinking session some-where instead of a descent into the dark, but on his own he hesitated to cross Thomas.

How did I get myself into this? he said to himself miserably, folding his arms against the cold night air as he watched Thomas levering up the manhole cover. The black opening that was revealed did nothing to change the growing impression that this latest excursion was a very bad idea.

'Dark down there,' he commented, peering in.

Again those pale eyes turned to him, cold as stones. 'Dark up here,' grunted Thomas. 'It wouldn't make much difference going down at noon, and we'd be seen.'

The big man slipped the crowbar back into his bag. Now he produced a hard hat with a lamp attached to it.

'*Verdomme*,' muttered Maxim. He hadn't thought of that; all he'd brought was a torch. It was too late to talk Thomas out of it, though; he was already climbing into the hole, the flattened bag slung over his arm. When only his head and shoulders were protruding, he looked at Maxim and gave him a sharp nod. Then he turned his attention to the metal rungs that descended into the darkness below.

Maxim heard a series of metallic clangs as Thomas's boots hit each rung in turn, and then a distant syrupy splash. The light of the head lamp was a ghostly pale glow down there in the darkness. Maxim glanced left and right up the street, checking that there was no one in sight, hoping to see someone hanging around, because that would mean he didn't have to lower himself into this malodorous oubliette. The street was deserted. There was nothing for it but to follow Thomas.

The torch was a pain – he realized that now. He tried to climb into the hole clutching it in one hand, and couldn't hold onto the metal rungs properly. He tried holding it in his teeth instead, but immediately he thought he could detect a faint and mouldy flavour, transferred from his hands. Maxim risked taking a hand off the rungs for a moment and put the torch into his pocket instead. Then he carried on climbing down.

A couple of minutes later he was following Thomas along a passageway shaped like an inverted pear. The torch was back in his hand, but Maxim was sure he could still taste it on his tongue. He tried to train the beam on the wet walls and not on the fluid through which they were paddling.

'This place stinks,' he said to Thomas's back. The big man nearly filled the tunnel with his broad shoulders; he blotted out much of the light of his own lamp.

'It's a sewer.' The words floated back to him through the chill and malodorous air.

'I know,' said Maxim, and suddenly he stopped walking. He hadn't been sure he wanted to do this. Now he was sure he didn't. It was cold and dark and he didn't have a hard hat. Worse, it really stank, far worse than he'd expected. It wasn't just the offensiveness of the smell – he was starting to worry about sewer gas too. Wasn't it poisonous sometimes? It smelled toxic enough; he'd have put his hand over his mouth and nose but his fingers probably stank by now too.

Thomas stopped too, waiting.

'Hey,' said Maxim. 'I've changed my mind. I've seen enough.'

Thomas turned. In the cramped space it was hard to manoeuvre; the bag slung over his shoulder snagged on the rough-hewn wall and he stumbled forward clumsily, striking Maxim's extended right hand. The torch fell out of it into the tainted soup at their feet. For a couple of seconds the light was still visible under the surface, then abruptly it went out. Maxim swore.

'I'm sorry,' said Thomas in that same flat voice.

Maxim didn't bother trying to fish out the torch. It was dead. God knows, he'd have been dead himself if he'd been submerged in that muck. He wanted to tell Thomas to go fuck himself; he even opened his mouth to say it, but then he thought better of it. He was in Thomas's hands now and he had a strong feeling that he shouldn't piss him off. He had the only light, after all.

Instead, he said, 'I'd really like to get out.'

'You haven't seen anything yet,' Thomas told him. 'If we keep going this way, eventually we'll see the Senne, the river that runs under the city. The tunnels are huge.'

'I'd rather not—' Maxim began, but Thomas was already turning away, and most of the light went with him. He started off again, splashing doggedly through the sewer, and Maxim was forced to follow.

It seemed to Maxim that they followed the tunnel for a very long time, but it was hard to equate time spent splashing through the filthy water with actual distance. He wondered whether he could have found his own way to the open manhole if he'd turned back as soon as his torch was broken. It was too late now. They'd passed openings that led into other tunnels; if he tried to negotiate even ten metres on his own he'd probably get lost.

Occasionally they heard a deep vibrating rumble that swelled and then faded.

'Trains,' commented Thomas tersely.

At last the pear-shaped tunnel opened into a larger one with a walkway along the side, allowing them to keep out of the murky water that ran along the bottom. Thomas paused, letting the pale light from the head lamp travel over walls that were mottled with greenish patches.

'Not much further to the Senne.'

'Listen,' said Maxim. 'I don't want to see the Senne. It's just more smelly brown water, right?'

Thomas's pale gaze moved to him briefly. 'We can have the story here if you wish.'

'Story? You mean another urban legend?' Maxim couldn't quite believe his ears. 'No way. There's just no way. It's freezing in here and it stinks like hell. We're going back now.'

Thomas said nothing. He simply kept looking at Maxim in that impassive way. Then he reached up to his helmet with deliberate slowness.

Maxim realized what was coming. He started to say, 'Hey, don't do that,' but it was too late. Thomas switched off the lamp and plunged them both into darkness.

The blackness was absolute. The manhole, with its weak supply of street lighting filtering down, was so far behind them that it might never have existed.

Maxim almost let out a scream. He choked it back with a mighty effort of will. All the same, when he spoke there was a tremor in his voice. 'What are you doing? Put the light back on.'

He stepped forward, swinging his hands through the empty blackness. But his hands grasped nothing but cold air. Either Thomas had been further away than he judged, or he had stepped back silently.

'Thomas, put the fucking light on.' Maxim's voice was rising. He would have tried another lunge forward, but the dark was disorientating and he was terribly conscious of the edge of the walkway and the brown water moving sluggishly below. He strained to hear Thomas's movements. Common sense told him that Thomas was as blind as he was in this absolute blackness, but still he was tormented by the fear that the other man would creep away and leave him here in this dark labyrinth.

How long, he wondered, would it take him to die, tramping kilometres in the smelly dark, cold, hungry, thirsty but unable to touch the contaminated waters that flowed past? And that was assuming there were no flash floods or sudden plummets into freezing water.

Don't think about that, he said to himself, knowing that if he once gave in to the luxury of thinking about his plight he would drop over the edge into a black pit of panic.

'Put the fucking light on,' Maxim said again, as aggressively as he could. He took a step forward and the tip of his boot met empty air. The edge of the walkway. For one dizzying moment he rocked before regaining his balance and stepping back from the edge. His heart was racing and his own breath was loud in his ears. 'Thomas—!'

Maxim could have cried, actually *cried*. For a while, perhaps he did. Perhaps he called for his mother, who by that time of night was probably snoring softly under the dowdy yellow counterpane she still used. Perhaps he begged Thomas to bring back the light.

Eventually, however, there was no other option open to him.

'So tell me the *verdomde* story,' he sobbed, and Thomas did, his voice echoing eerily in the dark.

'This is a story about *de verbrande kerel*, the Burnt Guy. You may have heard the tale that has been going around, how the Burnt Guy became what he was, a scarred monster, scorched beyond recognition.

'The story goes that he got his burns when an abandoned

castle down around him. He had gone to the castle to meet two people, a young couple. Some people say he just liked to hunt human prey, and he chose that pair because he knew that they frequented the old castle. Others say that he had a reason to kill these particular people – and they are right.'

Thomas paused. 'You know this story, at least so far?'

'Yes,' whispered Maxim into the dark.

'Then you will know that the boy came to the castle first, and the Burnt Guy, who was not yet burnt, shot him with a crossbow. And later when the girl turned up, she found the boy on the floor, still living, but with the bolt right through him. So she dragged him outside and went back in to confront his attacker.

'The killer had doused the old building with petrol, meaning to burn it down after he had killed the pair of them, and as he pursued the girl he set light to it, intending to drive her before the flames. But the girl escaped by climbing out of a window and down the castle wall.

'There are different versions of what happened next. Some say the killer died in the flames and that his ghost haunts the lonely places he visited in life, searching for the two people he still blames and still wishes to kill. Certainly, a body was found in the ruins of the castle, charred beyond recognition. But an unidentified body could belong to *anyone* – a tramp, perhaps, who had happened to be in the wrong place at the wrong time.

'I have myself once related another ending to the story, in which the killer escaped the burning castle through an upstairs window, but was horribly burnt. In this version, the

Burnt Guy went to a crooked doctor, whom he later killed. He did not die of his burns but he was terribly disfigured. He could no longer hunt human prey, because his appearance attracted too much notice. If he were seen in a lonely place, people would remember him, shuddering. And people he met were reluctant to trust him, because they could read nothing but fire and pain on those seared features. In that version, the Burnt Guy still haunts lonely places but is not a ghost. He is a flesh-and-blood person, and he intends to catch up with the two people who escaped him.

'But both these endings are wrong. This is the true ending. The Burnt Guy did not die, and his face was not hideously burnt. He *did* escape through the window, but the only burns he received were to his left arm and back. None of these were visible when he was fully clothed, and once he had recovered he was completely unimpaired. His face was as clear and unmarked as mine is.'

Thomas paused again, and then he said slyly, 'But you cannot see mine, can you?'

Maxim whimpered softly in the darkness.

De Jager went on, 'The Burnt Guy did not think of himself as that, *de verbrande kerel*. No; he thought of himself as *De Jager*, the Hunter, because that was what he was. He was a higher creature, and he hunted those who were lower down the order of things than himself.

'His grudge against the boy and the girl was because they had ruined one of his hunting grounds. He had a fine system for tracking his prey, and they had discovered it, just as a dog will sniff something out. Now it is required' – Thomas had slipped from the past to the present tense without apparently noticing – 'that they be found and finished, according to the law of survival of the fittest.

'So the Hunter continues to seek those two, and all the time he is growing nearer and nearer. Now he is close – very close indeed.

'During the time spent tracking down that girl and boy, the Hunter has not been idle. He has continued to pursue his . . . activities.

'There are always people who like to explore forbidden places. Abandoned buildings. Old theatres. Disused factories. Sewers.

'There is a culture of storytelling amongst them: horror stories, urban legends. They tell of people like themselves who have stumbled into danger or met strange and horrible ends in places where their bodies may never be discovered. Sometimes photographs appear on urban exploration websites, and they say those are the ones it actually happened to.

'But nobody is ever certain whether those photographs are real or just hoaxes, just as nobody ever knows whether the stories are true. In a way it doesn't matter; the fact that the tales *could* and *might* be true is the important thing.

'Imagine how easy it was for the Hunter to insinuate himself into this environment. The stories he related, the pictures he posted online – all those *were* real, only nobody could be quite sure of that.

'In his previous experiences he never engaged closely with the prey. But a talented Hunter is always learning new skills. He can learn a bird call to lure the birds down, and he can learn to speak the language of those he preys upon, to camouflage himself amongst them.

'Are you following me so far?'

Maxim made a tiny inarticulate sound in the darkness.

'Good. So while the Hunter continued to search for the two people he wanted to destroy, he amused himself with the storytellers. Sometimes he hunted one of them down and then made their death into a story, an urban legend that he poured into the avid ears of the others. Sometimes he began with a legend and fitted the killing to it.

'And still, all this time, he was hunting the girl and the boy. He visited someone who had known of them, and spent a long time questioning him. The man died slowly and painfully, and he passed on some information, but it was not enough. The Hunter was able to send messages to the targets through cyberspace, but the messages did not lure them out into the open.

'The Hunter deduced from observations he had made that the girl probably lived in a particular village, so he made enquiries there. This time he did not have to kill anyone . . . yet. He learned the name under which the girl was living. He was confident that he would find her very soon. And once he had her, he would have the bait to hook the boy too.

'The Hunter thought that the acts of the girl and boy, who had evaded him for too long, deserved more than the killing shot.

'He thought of all the urban legends he had told and heard retold; stories that remained alive in the imagination of so many people, long after the protagonists had died. Then the idea came. He would create the greatest – and the worst – urban legend of all, and he would make the girl and boy live it. They would die in the darkest, loneliest and filthiest place imaginable, fighting each other and the Hunter. They would die slowly and painfully, tortured in ways that you would not want to imagine, until their own mothers would not recognize the mangled flesh they had become.

'Then, when they were both dead, the photographs would appear, to prove the truth of the story, so that nobody would doubt it, and the tale would be told over and over, for ever.'

Thomas was still breathing hard, and stirring restlessly in the dark.

'But to return to the urban explorers, the storytellers: the Hunter had picked off most of them, one by one. A young man who died in the cold interior of an industrial kiln, and was buried in the rubble when the factory came down. A young woman who was dragged back into the abandoned hotel she had just explored, and taken to a disused bathroom where the tiles ran red with her blood.'

Maxim made a terrible sound at that. In the dark, Thomas smiled.

'Yes, you knew her, that girl.'

He went on, 'The Hunter had almost exhausted the prey. Soon it would be time to move on. But one of those regulars remained – a young man, not very bright or resourceful, but still with that taste for forbidden places. The Hunter thought that he would use this person to test some elements of the plan he was formulating for the boy and the girl he was going to kill. There was a kind of artistry to it, using the very last explorer as a dry run for his most spectacular killing ever.'

If the atmosphere in the darkened sewer had not already

stunk to high heaven, Thomas's sensitive hunter's nose might have detected the scent of fresh urine.

He said, 'The young man had listened to all the ways in which others like him had died, and he never suspected the truth of the matter. So the killer was able to lure him to that lonely and evil-smelling place without too much difficulty. An apparent accident disposed of the young man's light. So when the Hunter put out *his* light too, the young man was alone in the dark with the killer.

'The killer began to relate a story, just as the explorers always did. And as the young man listened, it came to him gradually that *he* was the victim of the tale; that the story was being told to him by the killer, the one known variously as the Burnt Guy and the Hunter; that the story was about to end with . . . his own death.'

Maxim made inarticulate animal noises in his throat. He knew that he should make some attempt to save himself, but he was frozen to the spot, paralysed with fear between the unseen edge of the walkway and its drop into the filthy water, the impossible labyrinth of tunnels at his back and Thomas somewhere in the dark. Thomas, who was twice as big as Maxim and could probably have torn him apart with his bare hands, although almost certainly he had something much worse in mind. Feebly, Maxim groped behind him with his hands, hoping to touch the reassuring solidity of a wall, but his fingers met nothing but air.

In the pitch black Thomas shifted; Maxim heard the soft *whiff* of fabric rubbing together as he raised his arms. Then Thomas switched the helmet lamp back on.

The effect was dazzling, but short-lived. Maxim saw

Thomas, still standing a couple of metres away, and then the light flickered and went out again, plunging them back into darkness. Maxim heard a small sharp impact; Thomas had tapped the lamp. It came on again, fitfully, showing the big man with a hand still raised, and then out it went.

'No problem,' said Thomas's voice in the blackness. 'I have another torch in my pocket.' But he didn't put it on.

Maxim was thinking, *Was his voice nearer than before?* He wept.

Then he heard Thomas begin to laugh. The sound echoed off the wet stone walls. In the confined space it sounded as though half a dozen Thomases were laughing. The lamp flickered into brief life, and for a moment, after his eyes had processed the sudden blaze of light, Maxim saw Thomas's face – closer now, yes, and distorted with laughter, the eyes reduced to slits and the mouth a great gaping maw lined with strong white teeth. Then the light died again.

'Ha-ha-ha,' laughed Thomas, and as Maxim listened an idea came to him, a straw to clutch at.

'Thomas,' he quavered, 'are you fucking about with me?'

As the laughter ebbed he tried again, his voice a little stronger now. 'Thomas, you bastard, were you just messing around?'

'Yes,' came the reply out of the near darkness, and Maxim felt a wave of relief so strong that he thought his knees might actually buckle under him. 'Yes, I *was* messing around.'

There was a swift movement in the inky blackness.

'But now I'm not,' said Thomas, and the cold steel bit into Maxim's flesh.

30

Veerle tried to find the woman from Tournai, the one who had been friends with her mother when she was a child. But her husband, who was Flemish, had died. There was nothing sinister about that, not unless you considered an irresistible attraction to the *fritkot* with its double-fried chips a kind of culinary nemesis. Veerle remembered him as terrifyingly stout, his bulging belly as ominous as a sea mine. Evidently the mine had gone off, detonating his heart through too much cholesterol. His wife had moved back to Tournai, as Veerle discovered when she spoke to the new residents of the house. It would have been a long shot anyway. She hadn't lived particularly close to the road where the Sterckx house stood, nor even within sight of the spot where the killing had taken place on Silent Saturday, all those years ago.

Veerle decided to discount her. Mevrouw Willems was a much more likely source of information.

It wasn't difficult to find the former headmistress's house; in fact, pretty much anyone who had grown up in the village over the last three decades probably knew who she was and where she lived. It was a neat brick building on a street close to the square. The bricks were a smooth warm terracotta colour, giving a pleasant impression quite unlike the garish look of the red-and-white Sterckx house. There was a very small front garden defined by a low brick wall the same colour as the house. The garden was very neatly kept, with a selection of aromatic shrubs and fragrant flowers. The only sign that the owner was in any way less able than other residents of the street was a white metal handrail running from the pavement to the front door.

It was Saturday afternoon, the first day of the autumn school holiday and a week almost to the hour since Kris and Veerle had last met at the Sterckx house, when Veerle arrived to see Mevrouw Willems. She came alone. She had spoken to Kris that morning and he had offered to come, but Veerle had told him she would go by herself; she thought she might get less out of the old lady if they turned up mob-handed.

The autumn sunshine was bright in spite of the cool air. It reflected dazzlingly off the polished front windows of the house, so that Veerle was unable to glimpse anything inside. As she went up the garden path she could smell lavender quite strongly. She pressed the button for the doorbell and waited.

She stood there for so long that she began to think there was nobody home, but she didn't give up immediately; there was nothing else in particular to do and this was important. She couldn't think who else she would approach if the old lady couldn't tell her anything.

Eventually she heard footsteps slowly approaching the front door. There was a rattle and the door opened to the extent of the security chain inside. Veerle looked into the gap and saw smooth white hair and dark glasses.

She's blind, she realized. She'd known Mevrouw Willems had retired early on some kind of health grounds but she hadn't known what, or perhaps she simply hadn't remembered; she'd been so young when she had last seen the headmistress.

'Yes?' said Mevrouw Willems in a sharp, brittle tone.

'It's Veerle De Keyser. You might not remember me, but I used to go to the school in the village when you were the headmistress.'

Veerle didn't really expect her name to mean anything to the old lady, who must have overseen the primary school years of hundreds, if not thousands, of local children. But to her surprise Mevrouw Willems said, 'Yes, I remember you.'

Veerle said, 'I wanted to ask you about something. May I come in?'

There was a short silence during which Mevrouw Willems remained perfectly still, her face towards Veerle. Veerle could have sworn that the old lady was *looking* at her, and then she realized that she was; she was looking with her ears, not her eyes.

'Is there anyone with you?' asked Mevrouw Willems abruptly, and Veerle wondered whether that was what she had been listening for – the sound of a second person shuffling their feet or exhaling.

'No,' said Veerle. 'I'm on my own.'

The door closed and she heard the chain being unfastened. Then it opened again and she found herself looking at the former headmistress framed in the doorway. The old woman was smaller than she expected, although perhaps that was simply that she, Veerle, had grown so much – she was half a head taller than Mevrouw Willems now – and dressed very neatly in a skirt and twinset of a light blue shade. There was a gold locket on a thin chain around her neck and she wore small gold earrings with blue stones in them. It was hard to imagine that she had prepared her appearance without the help of a mirror.

'Come in,' said Mevrouw Willems, in a noticeably firmer tone than before, and she turned to lead the way into the house, touching the wall lightly with her fingertips. 'Would you like a cup of coffee?' she asked.

'No, thank you.'

Veerle was looking with interest at the interior of the house. It was incredibly light and cheerful; all the walls had been painted in shades of white or off-white, so that with the autumn sunlight streaming in through the windows the rooms almost seemed to glow. They went into a cosy sitting room, and immediately Veerle smelled flowers. There was a vase full of colourful blooms on a little table, set carefully out of the path Mevrouw Willems took between the door and the armchairs.

'Please, sit,' said the old lady, and lowered herself into a straight-backed armchair.

Veerle chose an ornate-looking chair upholstered in rose velvet. 'Thanks for seeing me,' she said.

For a few moments Mevrouw Willems did not reply. She sat upright in her chair, her pale hands that were wrinkled like muslin curled around the ends of the arm supports. Her eyes were hidden behind the dark lenses, but her posture suggested that she was considering something very seriously. When she spoke, however, her tone was light and businesslike.

'How can I help you, Veerle?'

'It's going to sound a bit strange, but it's about something that happened a long time ago.' Veerle clasped her hands in her lap, and squeezed them together. 'You remember Joren Sterckx, who murdered that little kid on Silent Saturday?'

'Of course I remember him,' said Mevrouw Willems brusquely. A slight air of disapproval had crept over her; perhaps she thought that Veerle had simply come out of some prurient desire to rake over old ashes.

'Well . . .' Veerle hesitated, then made herself push on. 'According to all the newspaper reports he died not all that long after he was sent to prison.' She saw the old lady dip her head in assent. 'Only . . . last year something happened that I can't explain, and now I'm wondering whether it's possible that there was some kind of mix-up or mistake and maybe he's still alive.'

'It sounds like some kind of television programme about true crime,' said Mevrouw Willems dryly.

'I know,' said Veerle. She looked down, at her hands. 'I know it sounds crazy but I do have a reason for asking.'

'And why don't you tell me what that reason is?'

Veerle sighed. 'It might take a while. It's complicated.'

'Nevertheless,' said Mevrouw Willems.

'OK. On the day he did the murder – Silent Saturday – I actually saw him. I was in the bell tower of the Sint-Pauluskerk. I went up there to see whether the bell really had flown away or not – you know, like they tell little kids it does.'

Veerle didn't mention Kris. She could see from Mevrouw Willems' face that the old lady was sceptical about the direction this story was taking, perhaps thinking that Veerle was a thrill-seeker or a fantasist. Telling her that she had sneaked into the bell tower, which was supposed to be off limits, wasn't helping, even if it was a necessary part of the story, so she saw no reason to drop Kris in it as well.

'Anyway,' she went on, 'I looked out and saw him walking through the village with that little boy – Karel – in his arms. I didn't remember it for ages, though. I suppose I blotted it out because I was so upset. But I did see him, so I guess the memory was in there all the time.

'Then last year, in the spring, this thing happened. You know *het rode kasteel,* the old castle, the one between here and the airport? It burnt nearly to the ground. It was on the news. Well – I was there when it happened. I used to go there with a friend sometimes, just to explore. We didn't steal anything or do any damage. We were just looking around.'

That wasn't the full story, either, but Veerle was so used to presenting the version *without* the Koekoeken in it that she hardly had to think about what she was saying.

'And that particular evening, the one when the castle burnt down, there was someone already inside when we got there. He had a crossbow and a knife.' Veerle felt self-conscious saying *that*; it really did sound like a TV programme. But it was the truth.

'He shot my friend, and he tried to shoot me, but I got away by climbing out of a window. After the fire they found a body in the ruins and they said it was the killer, but they couldn't actually identify it. But I saw him. I was the only one who got a good look at him before the fire. And I'm *sure* it was Joren Sterckx.'

'Why are you so sure?' asked Mevrouw Willems sharply.

'You didn't remember seeing him on Silent Saturday, did you?'

'No,' admitted Veerle. 'But when I saw him – I was standing on the upstairs landing and looking down and I had a really clear view of him. It just came back to me at that moment. I recognized him.'

'Don't you think perhaps it was the fear coming back?' asked Mevrouw Willems. 'Perhaps you felt the same as you did when you were a child. It was the feeling you recognized, not the person. Joren Sterckx would have been dead for nearly ten years by then, Veerle.'

The use of Veerle's name was meant to be sympathetic, but it made Veerle bristle a little; she was so used to not being believed that the feeling of being humoured was difficult to bear.

'It wasn't just the fear,' she said, trying unsuccessfully to keep the resentment out of her voice. 'It was him, or else it was his double.'

'Whoever it was, didn't you say they found his body in the ruins? Does it really matter, if he's dead?'

'Yes.' Veerle's chin came up. She bit her lip. It was terribly tempting to blurt out the whole story – to say that the reason she needed to know about Joren Sterckx was that she thought he was back again, with more lives than a monster in a horror film. That was no good, though – that was only going to sound even crazier, and it couldn't lead anywhere good. If what she suspected was true, it might not even be safe for Mevrouw Willems in her dark world to know anything about it.

Instead she said, 'I can't put it behind me. The police and

everyone else think I imagined it. I know what I saw but I also know it's impossible. I want to know the truth.'

'My dear, what makes you think that I can tell you that?'

Veerle sighed. 'I was hoping you could tell me something about the Sterckx family, and about Joren. Anything. We – I – went to the place where they used to live but it's obvious nobody's lived there for years, maybe not since the murder. One of the neighbours just refused to talk at all, and I think the others have only just moved in, because the house is new. I'd like to find out where they went if I can. Or if you can't tell me that, maybe you can tell me something about them – about the family, and Joren himself. I mean, I guess he went through the school here, the same as the rest of us.'

'Oh yes,' said Mevrouw Willems. 'I remember him going through the school all right.' She shook her head. 'I can't tell you where the family went, though, or even if all of them are alive. Meneer Sterckx, Joren's father, was quite a bit older than his wife. An old father. And that was ten, eleven years ago. Mevrouw Sterckx wasn't terribly strong either, from what I remember. What Joren did broke them. Nobody was surprised when they moved away. They may have changed their name too, which would make them very difficult to find, although perhaps they didn't bother. There are plenty of people with the name Sterckx in Flanders. They wouldn't have stood out.'

'What was Joren like when he was at school?'

'Well, of course, he was only at the village school until he was twelve or so. A lot can happen after that.' Mevrouw Willems considered carefully. 'He was rather troublesome, I remember that. And not terribly bright.'

'Troublesome?' prompted Veerle. She felt a cold stirring in the pit of her stomach at that one word. It was impossible not to have visions of what *that* might mean.

But Mevrouw Willems didn't come out with tales of class-mates abused or knives carried into the playground. She said, 'He was very easily led, you know. If there was some mischief going on, he'd usually be in the middle of it, but I don't believe he was the ringleader. He wasn't bright enough for that. I don't know whether you'd say that kids who egg the others on to do naughty things have *leadership qualities* exactly, but whatever it is they do have, Joren hadn't got it. I'm fairly sure he took the blame for things other children had done sometimes.'

Veerle stared at the old lady, wishing that she could see further than the bland dark lenses of her glasses. This didn't match what she knew of Joren Sterckx at all. Easily led? She wondered whether it was possible for a few years to work such a transformation on someone's personality that they would change from a rather dull-witted boy who was drawn into troublemaking to a grown man with a taste for hunting down and killing those smaller and weaker than himself. The man she had seen in the old castle, the killer who had pursued her through the burning building carving savage chunks out of the air with a knife – she couldn't imagine him as a child with no worse trait than being easily led. She couldn't think of De Jager as anything other than born tainted.

She said, 'He doesn't sound like the sort of person you'd expect to do what he did.'

'No,' said Mevrouw Willems. Her head moved to meet the

sound of Veerle's voice, giving the impression that she was able to see her. 'It was a shock when we knew what he had done. A terrible, terrible thing. If it had been his brother, I'd have been less surprised. I suppose it proves that you cannot judge by appearances, nor what you think you know about a person. It comes down to what can be proved in a court of law.'

Veerle hardly heard the last part of this.

'Joren had a *brother*?'

'Yes.'

'Older or younger?' Veerle's heart was thudding now. She had a vague queasy feeling, something like excitement's ugly sibling.

'Younger,' said Mevrouw Willems.

'Do you know how much younger?'

'About eight or nine years, I would think. Don't take my remark about being less surprised as an accusation. He was an unpleasant child, but far too young to do anything as brutal as what was done to that poor child Karel. All the same, he's probably the only member of the family you can be sure is still living – unless there was some accident, I suppose.'

Veerle's mind was racing. She thought about the last bedroom she and Kris had visited in the deserted house that had once been the Sterckx family home. The childish wallpaper – that would have been the younger son's room, then. And the scratched-out faces in the wallpaper – who had done that? Had the younger boy done it for unfathomable reasons of his own, or had Joren done it, out of spite towards his sibling?

'What was his name?' asked Veerle as calmly as she could.

'Kasper.' The old lady's lips pursed disapprovingly. 'As I say, not a pleasant child. Perhaps I should not express such an opinion. Still, you did ask me for anything I knew about the Sterckx family. Considering what Joren did, and what Kasper was like, something was very wrong in that house.'

'What did Kasper do?'

Mevrouw Willems thought for a little while before she replied. 'I can't tell you that Kasper went about hitting the other children, showing all the signs of turning into a brute like Joren must have. It was more subtle than that. When he was at the school there were some incidents.' She sighed. 'Of course, there are always incidents. People think children are innocent little angels, but many of them aren't at all.'

Veerle waited for the old woman to go on.

'And Kasper, well, it was very hard to catch him at any wrongdoing, but whenever there was something going on, he tended to be there, on the edge, and that happened a bit too often to be coincidence. Mostly it wasn't anything too serious. These were primary school children, after all. They had fights, but it wasn't like they were great big youths carrying knives. There was one incident when a child tried to gouge another one's eye, but it wasn't Kasper who did it. As I say, not all children are angels.' The old lady paused. 'There was one time – one of the younger teachers found a group of them in a corner of the playground, all gathered around something. She went to see what they were doing, and they had an animal. I believe it was a rabbit. I suppose it belonged to someone in one of the houses next to the school and it had escaped and got through the fence. Kasper was there that time, right in the middle of the group. The rabbit was lying on the ground, either dead or nearly dead. They'd . . . hurt it.'

'Oh—' Veerle remembered who the old lady was just in time and bit back the expletive. 'And Kasper did that?'

'That was the strange thing,' continued Mevrouw Willems. 'When the teacher surprised them, she said Kasper looked up at her, and his face was – well, she described it as *horrible*, although she was young and rather given to exaggeration. She said he seemed absolutely furious to see her. Not at all ashamed or guilty.

'The others all looked shocked and horrified, but Kasper just seemed angry that she had caught them. So she made them come to see me. She was so upset that she just marched them all into my office. I can remember it quite clearly. Even then my eyesight wasn't good, but I could tell that Kasper wasn't reacting in the same way as the others. They were almost silent, heads down, waiting for trouble, and some of them were snivelling. But not Kasper. He didn't do anything as obvious as swagger, but he walked in quite calmly, not moved at all. He was the only one who wasn't upset.

'But one of the other children owned up. I don't remember the child's name any more. He wasn't someone who'd been in trouble before. I think he was just one of those mousy children who sit in a corner or at the back and get on with their work, trying not to be noticed. I wouldn't have put him down as someone who would torture animals – not in a million years. But he insisted he'd done it.

'He kept his head down nearly the entire time, looking at the floor and swearing he'd killed the rabbit. He only looked up once. As I say, my eyesight wasn't good, but I'm fairly sure he glanced at Kasper. Then he looked down, and he didn't look up again. It didn't matter what we asked him or the other children; the story never changed. Kasper hadn't done anything; this other boy had.'

Mevrouw Willems lapsed into silence.

'But you think Kasper *did* do it?' prompted Veerle.

'I really don't know,' she said, sounding a little weary. 'But I'm quite certain he had something to do with it.' She patted the arms of her chair with her pale hands. 'That's all I can tell you about the Sterckx family, really. I never got to know the parents very well. The father never came to school meetings and the mother was in ill health, so quite often she didn't come, either. I had the impression they didn't mix much with other people in the village – although of course, after the murder, nobody was going to admit to friendship with them anyway. I very much doubt you'll find anyone to give you a forwarding address.'

She fell silent, and they sat for a few moments in the sunlit room, with the scent of flowers filling the air, each preoccupied with her own thoughts.

Kasper Sterckx, thought Veerle. She didn't remember a boy of that name, but then he would have been a few years higher up the school than her. If he was eight or nine years younger than Joren, she supposed he would have been about twelve at the time of the murder, almost ready to make the leap to high school. Now, he would be in his twenties. A man.

Is it possible it was him I saw in the castle? she thought. A brother might look closer to a person in appearance than any other human being, although there was no guarantee of it. *How can I find out?* She had a few photographs from her primary school days, but nothing that would have shown a child from another year, and even if she could lay hands on one with Kasper in it, would it really tell her anything? Over ten years had passed since then. People changed a lot in a decade, especially if they did most of their growing up over that time.

Veerle was suddenly fidgeting. She wanted to call Kris, to share the information, to think whether the revelation of this new name, Kasper Sterckx, brought them any further in their investigations. She shifted on the rose velvet seat.

'Thank you for telling me all this,' she said finally. 'I suppose I should go.'

Mevrouw Willems seemed a little restless too, now that the interview was coming to an end. Still, she didn't make any attempt to stand up. Instead she sat moving her hands over the fabric of the arms of the chair, smoothing it with her fingertips.

At last she said, 'I wonder if there is something I should mention to you.'

'Please,' said Veerle, though her mind was still full of calling Kris, and what she should tell him first. In her mind she was already out of the front door and hurrying down the street, pulling her mobile phone from her pocket.

'It really is a little strange, but you're the second person who's called wanting to ask about someone who was at the school when I was headmistress.'

'Really?'

'Yes, and you see, the other person who called was asking about *you*.'

'Me?' Veerle's jaw dropped. 'Who was asking about *me*?'

'He said his name was Kris Verstraeten.'

'What . . . ?' Veerle leaned forward, clutching the ornate arms of the chair. 'That can't . . .' Her voice tailed off. She thought, *She must mean he came round here in the summer, before I moved back, to see if she knew where I was.* 'When was this?' she asked.

'I suppose it was about nine or ten days ago.'

'Ten days . . . ? Are you sure?'

'Well, it might have been nine.'

'It couldn't have been longer? Like in the summer holidays?'

'No, definitely not. It was quite recent.'

Veerle sat back in the chair. She felt stunned, as though someone had slapped her round the face. She couldn't think of a single reason why Kris would have come to Mevrouw Willems within the last two weeks to ask about her, and done it secretly too. It didn't make a bit of sense. He hadn't said anything about having seen Mevrouw Willems when they talked about this visit, either – and yet he must have known that the old lady would tell Veerle she had seen him.

At last she said, 'What did he want to know about me?'

'You do know him, then?' asked Mevrouw Willems, and Veerle sensed a faint note of anxiety in her voice.

'Yes,' she said.

'He wanted to know if I knew where you lived. He said – let me think – it was something like, *We used to be close but we lost touch* and *I can't forget her.* He said it was sentimental of him, and I particularly remember that because – if you'll forgive me – he didn't seem a very sentimental person to me.'

There was a long silence. Veerle gripped the arms of the chair. *Don't jump to any conclusions*, she told herself. *Maybe the old lady just lost track of time, and Kris did come, in the summer.* But she didn't really believe that. She didn't think Mevrouw Willems was getting forgetful or confused, not at all. In fact the old lady seemed extremely sharp.

Her mouth was very dry. Veerle licked her lips, fighting down a rising sense of dread. *Don't lose it*, she said to herself. *You have to get to the bottom of this.*

'Could – I mean, are you sure about the name?' she asked at last. 'Kris Verstraeten? Are you sure it was that?'

'Yes,' said the old lady very firmly. 'My ears are my eyes, my dear. I heard the name very clearly.'

'I don't think this can be the same person I know,' said Veerle. Even to her own ears, her voice had a hollow ring to it.

'He said you had been at the village school, and while we were talking, I remembered. There was a Kris Verstraeten at the school, probably around about the same time you were there. A skinny boy, with very dark hair. So I asked him whether that was him, and he said it was.'

'That's the Kris I know,' said Veerle. 'But . . . I don't see how it could be him. It doesn't make sense.' She put up her hands and pushed back her hair with a long shuddering sigh. 'The person who called . . .' She couldn't say, *what did he look like?* 'How did he seem?'

'Not the way he said he was,' replied Mevrouw Willems. 'I gave him the same description I've just given you: skinny, with dark hair. I asked him whether he still looked like that, and he said yes, he did. But he wasn't being truthful.' She shook her head doubtfully. 'He wasn't a thin person. I could tell that from his footsteps, and from the sounds the chair made when he sat down in it. He sat in that same chair that you are sitting in.'

Veerle sat bolt upright at that and put her hands in her lap, as if the rose velvet upholstery and the ornate wooden arm rests were contaminated.

'He wasn't fat, though,' the old lady went on. 'He was tall and broad, and he was quite heavy, but I believe he was powerful rather than simply fat.' When Veerle didn't reply, she said, 'If I am quite candid, I didn't like him. I think if it was the Kris Verstraeten I remember, he must have changed a great deal.'

'I don't think it was the Kris you remember,' Veerle managed to say. The words came out unwillingly; her throat seemed to have constricted, as though someone had put a hand around it and squeezed.

After a pause Mevrouw Willems said, 'Do you think you know who it was?'

'Maybe,' said Veerle in a tight voice quite unlike her normal tone. 'What did you tell him? About where I was, I mean?'

'Well, I knew about your mother, of course. I was very sorry to hear that. And I knew you'd moved to Ghent.'

'Did you tell him that?' Now Veerle's voice was almost breaking with the tension. She thought, *If it was De Jager, if he starts looking for De Keysers listed in Ghent* . . . She thought about her father and about her tiny half-brother and something twisted inside her like a knife in a wound.

'No,' said the old lady firmly.

Thank God, thank God . . .

'As I say, I didn't like him. I wasn't sure you'd *want* to be contacted. I'm sorry if this was interference.' Mevrouw

Willems' shoulders sagged. 'I felt I had to say something, so I told him I thought you lived in the village, just with your mother, and – your mother's name was Charlier.'

A gasp burst out of Veerle. For a moment the shock was so great that it was as though a bomb had gone off: the bright light, the brilliant white of the walls, Mevrouw Willems' voice plaintively asking her whether she was all right, whether she had done the right thing, was all fading to nothing under the blast wave of horror that swept over her.

He knows. That was all she could think. *De Jager knows how to find me.*

31

De Jager had virtually abandoned any attempt to find either Kris Verstraeten or Veerle De Keyser by telephoning the numbers listed in the White Pages. His excursion to the house of Mevrouw Willems, the former headmistress, had proved far more fruitful. Now he had the correct name and he knew he had the right village; it was simply a matter of working his way methodically through all the possible addresses.

All the same, when he saw the advertisement for the maid service, he thought it worth making an exploratory call. The advertisement was being run in English in the English-language journals, because that was where much of the business was, but there was a Dutch version in the local paper too. De Jager was not attracted by the name or the type of business – his houses had always been ones where no maid or other visitor of any kind could be permitted to poke about – but the name printed across the middle of the advertisement caught his eye immediately. 'Talk to Manager Jeroen Verstraeten about your needs.'

There was a picture of Jeroen Verstraeten looking sleek and a little too well-fed. It was hard to tell from the monochrome photo whether he might be related to Kris Verstraeten or not, but it couldn't be ruled out: he didn't have the cheek-bones but he had the thick dark hair.

The thing that interested De Jager was the combination of the service being offered and the Verstraeten name. It might be coincidence, but his hunter's instinct said not. When you saw the spoor of deer, you didn't look for wild boar. The Koekoeken must have had ways of getting into the properties they visited, and ways of knowing that there would be nobody there. De Jager knew from the now defunct web forum that at least one member had been employed to water house plants while the home owners were away.

A relative who ran a maid service would be a very useful resource. Jeroen would have a register of expensive, opulent properties, and he would probably have keys and alarm codes for quite a few of them. Certainly he would know when the owners of the various houses were away because they'd probably cancel the cleaning service for that period. Perhaps Kris worked with – or for – Jeroen Verstraeten – or maybe he just used Jeroen's information, with or without his knowledge.

De Jager telephoned the number in the advertisement. It was a male voice that answered the phone, giving the name of the business and a brief greeting in both Flemish and English.

De Jager didn't bother to introduce himself. He said, 'Can I speak to Kris Verstraeten?'

'This is Jeroen Verstraeten. Kris doesn't work here,' said Jeroen, with a faint note of irritation in his voice.

'I'm sorry. Can you tell me where to find him?'

'Who's speaking?'

'I'm an old school friend of Kris's. I'm hoping to . . . get back in touch.'

'Well, give me your name and number and I'll pass them on.' Jeroen managed with his tone to convey both his self-importance and the fact that the caller was imposing on him.

'I'd rather call him myself. It's a surprise.'

De Jager heard Jeroen make a sound of real annoyance at this. He said nothing, waiting.

Eventually Jeroen said, 'I don't have his number here. You'll have to find it yourself in the White Pages. He's listed under Hemeleers, his mother's name.' Jeroen gave the first line of the address.

'Thank you,' said De Jager sincerely.

'Don't thank me,' said Jeroen tersely. 'Just tell Kris from me that I'm not his secretary.'

There was a click as he hung up.

32

Outside Mevrouw Willems's house, Veerle lurched over to a wall low enough to sit on, and sank down onto it, clutching at the front of her jacket for her mobile phone.

She could hardly recall the last few minutes of the interview. She had had to utter some mechanical words in response to the old lady telling her plaintively that she had thought the information she had given 'Kris Verstraeten' was harmless, since Veerle had moved away. Her main thought had been to get out into the fresh air as soon as possible, and call Kris. Now that she was trying to do just that, her hands were clumsy; she fumbled with the phone and almost dropped it.

Sitting out here in the open air, she felt horribly exposed. The space around her seemed to sing with tension, to stab with the gaze of a thousand hidden eyes.

De Jager knows how to find me.

He could be here, this instant, in the village, looking for her.

If he finds me . . .

Veerle had no illusions about what would happen then. In her mind she was running from him again, fleeing for her life down the dusty landing of the old castle, while the boards thundered under their feet and flames roared behind them. The blade had sliced through the air, cutting into her personal space, close enough to make her flinch and swerve. He had been a berserker then, raging after her in disregard of the heat and the dead end they were racing towards. Now he would be worse; he wasn't just hunting those who happened to cross his path, he wanted *her* and he wanted *Kris*, the two of them, personally. She thought that if he came upon her, here in the open street, sick and weak with horror, trembling too badly even to use her mobile phone, he would fall on her like an executioner's axe.

It was useless; her hands wouldn't do what she wanted them to. She put the phone back in her pocket and made herself stand up, her head turning as she scanned the street. There was one person some hundred metres away, but it was clearly a woman, skirted and dragging a wheeled shopping bag. Still, she couldn't feel safe. She glanced behind her at Mevrouw Willems's house, checking that the door had closed. The windows were opaque with reflections again; it was like looking at a face whose eyes were concealed behind reflective sunglasses, giving nothing away. The thought of De Jager inside, sitting on the very same rose velvet chair that Veerle had used, made her flesh creep. She put a hand to her mouth and stumbled away, heading blindly for home.

When she got to the end of Kerkstraat she stood by the churchyard wall, the great Sint-Pauluskerk towering over her, and stared at the front of the house. Such a short distance. She looked about her in every direction and saw nobody on the streets, but still she couldn't shake that terrible feeling of being watched. It *crawled* over her, like a swarm of restless insects.

Supposing he is watching me from somewhere I can't see? If I go straight to the front door, he'll know that's the house.

In the end Veerle made herself walk past the end of the street and climb over the wall at the back of the house, as she had once before. Even then she was horribly uneasy, thinking that she was making herself too obvious, too visible, in the moments when she was balanced on the top of the wall.

When she got inside, she locked the door behind her, checked it once and checked it again. She went through into the hallway, and as she reached out for the light switch she stopped herself.

The light will show from outside.

The sense of being trapped was suffocating. She could have put the shutters down – that would stop the light showing – but if there were anyone outside – lurking in the churchyard perhaps – the sight of the shutters being lowered would draw attention to the fact that she was at home.

Is he out there already? And if he isn't – how long?

The thick volume of the White Pages was lying in the hallway, just visible by the light coming through the open kitchen door. Veerle picked it up as gingerly as if she were handling a witch's grimoire. This was the book in which the forecast of De Jager's arrival was written. If there were twenty entries for *Charlier* before Claudine's, she might have a little time left. If there were only one or two, she could expect him at any moment.

She carried the directory upstairs, and as soon as she got to her room, where the light was strong, she flipped it open and began to search.

It didn't take long to find the entries for her local area. The listings for the village were included in those for the nearby town, so at first glance Veerle felt a huge wave of relief: there was a whole column of addresses for *Charlier*. But then she began to run her finger down the list and check which ones were specifically for the village, and now her heart began to sink; it began to drop like a lift disappearing into the black depths of a mine shaft.

She checked the list a second time but she already knew the result. Five listings ahead of *Charlier, C., Kerkstraat*.

Five listings. And it's been nine days, maybe ten.

She supposed even De Jager couldn't devote every night and every day to searching for his prey; if he had, he'd have been here by now. All the same . . .

I have to get out, Veerle thought. *He could be here at any time.*

The autumn school holiday had begun after school closed on Friday. A week wasn't nearly long enough to sort any of this out, but it felt a thousand times more possible than struggling within the straitjacket of the next ten minutes.

Veerle dropped the directory on her desk. She found the backpack she used for school underneath, hauled it out and upturned it unceremoniously on the bed. When all the files and pens had slithered out, she began to pack. Laptop, charger, a change of clothes . . .

Halfway through, she sat down on the bed next to the subsiding heap of school books, and phoned Kris's number. The call went straight to voicemail; either the phone was switched off or he was on a call. No matter; if she had to, she'd leave the house and call him afterwards.

She went into the bathroom and grabbed a handful of things, including her toothbrush. That felt very strange, as though she were packing for a holiday. It didn't feel like a holiday, though, unless it was one organized as a last wish for a dying person. Death was gathering about her; she could feel it, like the change in air pressure before a storm.

Veerle zipped up the bag, struggling a little, and then stood for a moment in the centre of the room, looking about her. So many familiar things. She couldn't take a fraction of them with her; there was nothing for it but to hope that she would be back again before too long. There was that stupid stuffed rabbit that her mother had given her, the one she had always hated but now no longer had the heart to throw out. She certainly wasn't taking it with her now, but all the same it gave her a pang to abandon even that. Would De Jager pick it up, touch it, as he ran his big hands over all her things, searching for a clue to her whereabouts? The thought made her shudder.

It also made her realize that she must make sure she didn't leave that clue for him. All her own contacts were stored on her laptop or her mobile phone, but Claudine's old address book was still there amongst the books neatly stacked at the back of the desk. She thought about De Jager sliding it out and leafing through the list of nearly everyone Claudine had known, and the sense of barely avoided danger was so intense that she could have sagged to the floor there and then.

It was no use collapsing. She thrust the address book into the front pocket of the backpack. Then she hoisted the bag onto her shoulders. All the time she was packing, the question of *what now?* had been nagging at her. At first all she'd been able to focus on was getting out of the house and away, *right now*, but she had to pick a place to go.

Not Dad's.

She was praying that nobody was watching the house. She'd have expected a direct assault if De Jager knew she was alone at home, and there hadn't been one. The street outside was quiet. If she left now she could probably get right away without being seen. All the same, she flinched from the idea of going to her father and Anneke. Adam was so tiny. If there was even one chance in a million that she might be followed . . .

No, she thought. *Not there.*

She had money, but not enough to spend more than a couple of nights in a hotel, even a cheap one. That wasn't the answer. She'd have to stay with someone. It had to be someone she knew and trusted, and that meant either Kris or Bram.

Veerle glanced around the room one more time, and then she left and went downstairs.

Out of the front or the back?

She went out of the front door in the end. She was going to have to take a bus anyway, and that meant standing within sight of the house. If anyone was watching they'd see her either way.

Veerle stood on the pavement with the old church at her back.

Which way?

One bus would take her to Kris, the other to the stop where

she could take the tram into Brussels and then a train to Ghent.

Think!

She looked down the street, and in the distance she saw a bus coming, the one that would take her to the tram stop. If she didn't take that one, she'd have to wait at least half an hour for the next one, or go in the other direction.

Think think think!

She remembered Kris, the time he had come to the house on Kerkstraat and said, *You have to go back to Ghent.* That had been one of the first things he'd said, after asking her why she hadn't answered his calls. He'd known about the danger, even then, and he'd wanted her out of the way of it.

She remembered Bram's words the last time she had spoken to him. *You could come back to Ghent,* he had said, and later: *You can come here, to my place, any time. No pressure. You can come here as a friend.*

No more time to think about it. Veerle leaned into the road and stuck out her arm to stop the bus. The indicator began to blink and the bus slowed, coming to a halt beside her.

A few moments later she was inside, swinging herself into a window seat, the bag on her lap. She turned her head as the bus pulled away from the kerb, wanting to get a last glimpse of Kerkstraat and the house she had grown up in. It was terrible to leave it, terrible to be driven by that overwhelming sense of impending danger, but worst of all, it was a relief to get away.

It was shortly after four p.m. on Saturday, and for now at least, she had escaped.

33

Veerle was at Brussel-Zuid when her mobile phone went off. She had arrived at the station a couple of minutes before the next train left for Ghent, so by the time she'd bought a ticket from the machine on the concourse, she'd missed it. The following one was due in about twenty-five minutes, so she went to sit in the burger bar. She wasn't hungry – at the moment she felt as though she would never want to eat again – so she just ordered an iced tea. The bar was nothing special but it was brightly lit and open. With her back to the wall she felt as safe as she could feel anywhere. She sat and watched people coming and going: a scruffy, skinny man who looked as though he might be sleeping rough, and paid for his order in small change; a dark-eyed mother in a hijab shepherding two small boys. There was nobody who looked anything like De Jager.

Veerle was trying very hard not to ask herself that question: *Am I doing the right thing?*

She hadn't called Bram yet. That probably didn't matter; he'd said she could come, and if he wasn't around when she got to Ghent she could always go to another anonymous place like this one and keep calling until she reached him.

She was putting off the moment because of the question she wasn't asking herself.

The ticket was in her jacket pocket, and that was reassuring because it meant a decision had been made. Besides, the other option – that of going back into the metro and then taking the tram back to Tervuren – was simply not sensible. When you thought about it (which she was trying not to), the idea was downright suicidal. Assuming she'd managed to get away without being tracked by De Jager, the only thing to do was stay ahead. She supposed Kris would be pleased when she finally spoke to him. She was doing what he had been telling her to do at the beginning – fleeing back to Ghent.

Veerle swilled the rest of the iced tea around the cardboard beaker, and decided she didn't want to drink it. Sitting here was making her fidget. Only ten minutes now until the next Ghent train left. She got to her feet and hoisted the backpack onto her shoulders. It was then that her phone rang.

Veerle slid it out of her jeans pocket. 'Hello?'

'It's me, Kris. Something's happened.'

Veerle strode out into the wide corridor that led to the main concourse, her head turning as she checked right and left. No sign of anything untoward. Into the phone she said, 'What's wrong?'

'It's Jeroen. My stupid, *verdomde* cousin Jeroen. He's given De Jager my address.'

Veerle stopped. For a moment she was speechless. The terror she had experienced when she realized that Mevrouw Willems had given away details of her own location to De Jager had been so intense that she thought it was impossible to dig any deeper into its toxic depths. Now she knew otherwise. She felt as though some mighty fist, the hand of a Titan, had tightened about her and was crushing her. She could barely breathe.

'Veerle?'

A small inarticulate sound broke out from her. She took a couple of steps and sagged against the wall. She put a hand up to her face, and the hand was shaking.

'Veerle?'

She forced herself to reply. 'I'm here,' she said in a taut voice. 'What happened?'

'Jeroen rang up in a stinking mood, and had a go at me for using him as a secretary. He said someone had rung the office asking for me. He was really pissed off. It was below his dignity as a manager or something. I told him I hadn't given the business as a contact number or anything. Then he said the caller was someone I'd known at school, wanting to get back in touch. So I asked who it was, and he said he hadn't left a name.' Kris sighed in exasperation. 'He was being really pissy about it so I pushed back and asked him why he hadn't asked for one. He said he *had* asked. The guy was evasive – at least that's how I'm reading it. He said he wanted it to be a surprise.'

'A surprise?' Veerle whispered into the phone.

'Yeah,' said Kris grimly. 'I can guess what kind of surprise. So I said, *Jeroen, you* klootzak, *tell me you didn't give him the address,* and he started blustering. Turns out he didn't just tell the caller where I lived, he gave him the name too. Hemeleers. So there won't be any confusion.'

'Shit.' Veerle was too shocked to find anything else to say. She gripped the phone, her knuckles white.

'Veerle?' Kris's voice spoke again in her ear. 'Where are you? It sounds like you're outdoors.'

'I'm . . .' Veerle made herself concentrate on what she was saying. 'I'm at Brussel-Zuid.'

'What are you doing there? Did you go into the city for the day? I thought you were going to see Mevrouw Willems.'

'I did,' Veerle managed to say. 'Kris – he knows how to find me too.'

'What? *How?*' Up till this point Kris had sounded remarkably calm, but now Veerle heard the urgency in his voice.

'He'd been to see her. Before I did. She thought it was nine, maybe ten days ago. Kris – he said he was you.'

'*Godverdomme.*' Now Kris sounded shocked.

'He said we'd known each other a while ago and he was trying to get back in touch. Just like . . .'

'Yes,' said Kris tersely.

'She's blind. I knew she'd retired early but I didn't know that was why. So she couldn't see him but she still didn't believe him when he said he was you. She got suspicious, but she didn't like to refuse to say anything.' Veerle shivered, thinking of the blind woman sitting in that bright white room with De Jager opposite her, slouched like a great toad in the rose velvet armchair, the hands that had lately been wet and red curled over the carved arm rests. She went on, 'She knew about Mum – I suppose nearly everyone in the village does – and that I'd moved away, so she told him that as far she knew I lived with my mother – whose name is Charlier. She thought she was protecting me, but . . . she told him how to find me.'

'And that's why you're at Brussel-Zuid,' said Kris slowly. 'Because you're going to Ghent.'

Verdomme.

'I had to get out of the house,' Veerle said. 'I tried to call you but I couldn't get through. And you kept telling me I ought to go back to Ghent.'

'Yes, I did,' said Kris in a flat voice. 'But I thought you didn't want to, in case your dad and his family got dragged into this.'

'I'm not—' Veerle bit her lip.

'You're not staying with him?' finished Kris. 'So you're staying with Bram?'

'Probably,' said Veerle reluctantly. 'I haven't called him yet. I wasn't sure what I wanted to do.'

'But you're at Brussel-Zuid?'

'Yes,' said Veerle curtly, stung by Kris's tone.

'When's your train?'

'In about five minutes.' Veerle hesitated. 'I don't have to get this one, though. There's another one in half an hour.'

'No, take it,' said Kris brusquely. 'You'll be safe in Ghent, at least for the time being.'

'What about you?' Veerle was walking again now, heading towards the platform where the Ghent train might already be waiting. She hated the feeling that Kris wanted her gone, but perversely it filled her with such a bitter emotion that she felt like going to spite him. 'What are you going to do?'

'I don't know. I was going to come to you, in Kerkstraat, but if De Jager knows about it, it's not safe, and you're not there anyway.'

'Shit, Kris, I didn't know . . .'

'Yeah. Well, the reason you couldn't get hold of me was that I was on the phone to Jeroen. Nothing we can do about that now. You were probably right to go.'

'Where are you now? You're not still at home, are you?'

'No. As soon as I knew what that *klootzak* Jeroen had done, I packed a bag and got out. I'm at a place in the town right now, in Overijse. It's safe here. He wouldn't try anything in a public place.'

I'm not so sure about that, thought Veerle.

'But where will you go?' she asked, stepping onto the escalator that led up to the platform. She glanced behind her quickly, but she couldn't see anyone resembling De Jager on the concourse.

'One of the houses,' said Kris. He didn't need to tell her what he meant by that. 'Probably the one with the pool. You remember that one?'

'Yes.' Of course she did; it had been the first they had visited together, if you excluded the dump where they had sealed the pact that drew her into the Koekoeken circle. 'How do you know it'll be empty? Did Jeroen tell you?'

'That idiot? No. I'm not telling him where I am. The less he knows, the better, in case De Jager decides to ring him up again. No, I know it's empty because he was whining about it last week. The owners have gone off for a month and they've cancelled the maid service. He tried to get them to carry on with it – told them it keeps the place in the best condition, stuff like that. But they cancelled anyway, and he was pissed off because of the lost revenue. So it's empty, all right.'

'That's good,' said Veerle. The words seemed a little lame, but what else was there to say? She had reached the platform now, and the train was waiting. She glanced at the clock and saw that it was due to depart in a couple of minutes. 'I'm on the platform,' she said.

'Well, I have to go anyway.' Kris paused. 'Good luck, Veerle.'

'Good luck,' Veerle started to say back, but Kris had broken the connection. She stared at the phone in her hand for a moment, and then stuffed it into her pocket.

The train was vibrating softly, the engine running. Veerle took one last glance around the platform, satisfying herself as far as possible that nobody was following her, and then she climbed aboard.

34

De Jager arrived at the house on Kerkstraat well after nightfall. He had driven from Overijse, where he had visited the
flat inhabited by Kris Verstraeten, and found it abandoned.
All the shutters were down, everything was switched off, and
there were signs of a hasty departure: drawers standing open,
the little fridge and the kitchen bin both emptied. He was
tempted to torch the place to relieve the unfamiliar and
infuriating sense of being balked, but he restrained himself. If
he failed to find Veerle, he might need to come looking for
Kris here again later. Instead he took a few things, to give the
impression that the broken lock was down to a simple
burglary, and then left without inflicting any further damage.

He made a mental note to call on Jeroen Verstraeten. It
was possible that Kris had gone there, and anyway, Jeroen was
clearly a relative of his, which meant that there was plenty of
leverage there.

Still, as he drove out of Overijse, his knuckles were white
on the steering wheel. To know that the prey had anticipated
his move and evaded him was almost more than he could
stand. Worse, if Kris Verstraeten had run, there was a good
chance Veerle would too – unless he found her first.

He'd checked out the first five addresses listed to Charlier in the local White Pages, and found nothing to connect any of them to Veerle. He would go to the sixth one, the place on Kerkstraat, now, immediately. If she wasn't there he'd try the next one. He knew he would get her in the end, even if she *had* run. She couldn't exist in limbo for ever: sooner or later she'd have to go home. But he wanted her *now*. He wanted to take her apart.

De Jager had dreamed of luring both of them, the girl and the boy, to the stinking tunnels under the city and making them die there, fighting him and each other. He had considered taking the girl first, of making her the bait. Now he was not sure he could wait that long. Let the boy come down into the sewers looking for her and find nothing but wet red remains.

The desire to hunt was sharp and urgent, and yet De Jager didn't lose his head; it was still necessary to approach the new address with caution, for fear of attracting attention. He drove once down Kerkstraat, marking the house he wanted, but he didn't stop there. He noted that the door had no cover of any kind – no porch or vegetation or anything to prevent curious eyes from observing an attempt to break the lock. De Jager went right past the house, and parked on another street some distance away. Then he went to the back of the row of houses via the alleyway Veerle had used, and scaled the brick wall into the garden. He was less agile than she was but he had the advantage of height and brute strength; he was over it very quickly and picking his way stealthily through the overgrown garden. The ebony-handled Japanese boning knife was inside his jacket. Soon, he thought, it would be sheathed in her flesh.

The shutters were down on the lower windows, but that meant nothing. If this *was* Veerle's house and she had a milligram of sense, she'd keep this back route into the house defended. The unshuttered back door was the weak point, though. He had to make a little noise to break in, but he waited until traffic passed along the main road nearby, trusting that it would help to cover the splintering sounds. At any rate, when he waited afterwards there was no sign that anyone inside the house or in the neighbouring properties had noticed anything.

De Jager entered Veerle's house.

He knew immediately that it was empty. The house was silent. Not only no sounds of anyone moving about, but no sounds of appliances running either. With most of the shutters down and the lights off, the interior was dim and cool. De Jager slid the boning knife out of his jacket and let it lead him around the house like a divining rod, the razor-sharp tip questing the air. He took the ground floor first, moving from room to room methodically. The floorboards creaked under his heavy tread. The sound of his breathing filled the silent air.

In the living room he found what he had been looking for: a framed photograph of the occupants of the house. He knew that this was what they were, and not distant relatives of the inhabitants, because he recognized one of them. *Veerle De Keyser*. She had an arm round the other person, a rather faded-looking older woman with a short, practical haircut – doubtless Madame Charlier, Veerle's mother. The two of them beamed out of the photograph, meeting De Jager's snarl with insouciance.

So they still lived here, Veerle and her mother. The presence of the older woman did not disturb De Jager. If necessary he would deal with her too. When he explored the rest of the house, however, he came to the conclusion that the mother was out of the picture. There was clearly only one person living here. Only one bedroom was furnished; the other upstairs rooms were empty. After looking into all of them, De Jager went back to the one that was Veerle's and switched on the light. Now it was apparent that Veerle had taken flight too. The wardrobe stood open; a T-shirt hung out of a half-closed drawer like a tongue drooping from a mouth. There was disorder on the desk too, and no sign of a laptop or tablet. De Jager went through the books and papers, pawing at them with his big hands, but he couldn't find an address book or planner, either. Veerle had been thorough.

After a moment, however, the frustration that had been building inside him gave way to the slow dawning of triumph. Veerle had cleared out her documents, but she hadn't thought to remove the photograph stuck up over the desk. De Jager pulled it off the wall, taking care not to tear it.

It showed a man and a very young child. The man was big, bear-like and amiable-looking, in his late forties or early fifties, with a shock of light brown hair blown back from his face by the breeze. The child, really just a baby, was bundled up in a blue padded jacket and fleece hat that did not obscure a very rosy and beaming face. In the background a row of ancient guild-houses with distinctive corbie steps could be seen, and a shining strip of water.

Ghent. The waterfront known as the Graslei. De Jager recognized it immediately.

Mevrouw Willems had told him that Veerle lived in the village with her mother *only*, the mother's name being Charlier. She had not said that the father had died, so it was a reasonable assumption that he was alive but elsewhere. *Elsewhere* perhaps meaning *Ghent*.

The mother's name was Charlier, but Veerle had taken the surname De Keyser. Of course, there could be any number of people with the surname De Keyser in the city of Ghent. If that was all you had to go on, it would take a long time to identify the one who was Veerle's father.

De Jager gazed at that amiable face for a moment longer, and then he turned the photograph over. Anneke had written on the back, perhaps wanting in some small and petty way to assert ownership before the photograph was surrendered to Veerle. Her handwriting was fussy but very clear. It read, *Geert and Adam.*

35

It was dark when Veerle reached her destination. The entire
time she had been travelling, she had been on edge, fidgeting
and shivering in her seat. It was impossible to shake the fear
of being followed, however improbable that might be, given
the changes between tram and train and bus she'd had to
make. She wanted to look out for De Jager every second of
the journey, but at the same time she was afraid to show her
face. If he were sitting in the carriage behind hers, or following the tram she took in his car, she had to know; it was her
only chance of keeping one step ahead of him. Still, if he were
looking out for her, turning repeatedly in her seat or letting
her pale drawn face be seen through the window was a sure
way to attract attention.

For a while she had seen an anonymous-looking silver
Toyota following her tram. She had felt her heart begin to
race and her hands had involuntarily curled into fists, the
nails digging painfully into her palms. Nothing could be seen
of the driver through the shifting reflections on the windscreen, but she had felt a sudden and terrible certainty that it
was *him*, De Jager. Veerle had begun to think about how she
might escape, running over the options with a queasy dread:

she could get off at her intended stop and run for cover; she could get off at a different stop and try to work her way back to the place she wanted to be; she could stay on the tram until the terminus and let it carry her back the way she had come. She worried at these ideas as her stomach turned over sickeningly, and then she glanced out of the tram window and saw the Toyota peeling away down a side turning.

Calm down, she thought. *It wasn't him.* But it was hard to do. Someone who could kill without a second thought, someone who had the intelligence and malevolence to track down people he barely knew, slaughtering others to get at them – that was someone to be afraid of.

When the tram reached the stop she wanted, Veerle decided to get off there rather than overshooting or continuing to the end of the line. She was tired from a mixture of travelling and tension, and she was hungry; she hadn't eaten anything for hours. There was nobody in the tram who looked remotely like De Jager, and as far she could tell there was no vehicle following it, but mainly she couldn't face any more evasive tactics. She wanted to get inside out of the dark and cold, and she wanted human contact. She wanted arms around her; she wanted warmth and life, because cold and dark and death were hanging over her like an evil premonition.

Veerle alighted from the tram into the sickly amber glow of streetlamps. She moved away as quickly as she could, wanting to vanish into the shadows. As she hurried away, she turned and scanned the tram stop, but the only other person who had emerged from the tram was a diminutive woman in her fifties or sixties. No men; definitely no one tall and broad-shouldered.

As she crossed the road she looked for cars slowing down or lurking at the kerb with the engine running, but she saw nothing suspicious. It was possible to take a bus from here but she didn't like the idea of standing about in the dark waiting; she felt too vulnerable. Instead she set off at a brisk pace, hoisting her bag on her shoulder. She had tried to pack lightly, concentrating on absolute essentials, but the weight that had felt manageable when she set off hours ago was now a chafing burden; her shoulders ached from carrying it.

Please God let him be there, she thought. That was the other thing, one she hadn't thought about enough – what she would do if he wasn't. Veerle touched the pocket where her mobile phone was. She'd thought about calling nearly the entire journey, but she hadn't done it, preferring to leave the explanations for later. It wasn't as though she could go home again. Better to present the whole thing as a *fait accompli*.

Still, it was unpleasant travelling alone through the dark with the knowledge that nobody you cared about knew precisely where you were.

De Jager could take me off this street and no one would ever know what had happened to me, thought Veerle. She stepped up the pace, glancing behind her. The street was empty, and quiet too; when she paused to listen there were no sounds of hurrying footsteps or voices. In so far as it was possible to be sure, she thought that no one was following her.

It took her a while to walk to the address she wanted, and the nearer she got, the more a new concern intruded. *Have I done the right thing, coming here?* She wasn't afraid of having the door closed in her face. It was knowing that she had made a choice that she had been deliberating for a long time, and when it finally came down to it, she had made it almost on a whim. Let yourself be carried in this direction to Bram or that direction to Kris – *decide now!* And she had.

Trouble was coming whatever she did, she knew that. It wasn't here yet, but it had appeared on the crest of the next hill and now it was cantering towards her, inexorably. Judging by what happened to most people who crossed De Jager's path, Veerle wasn't going to survive it, so what she did about her love life was probably irrelevant. Still, she was conscious that the decision she had made was a one-way exit from the dilemma. In her heart she was saying goodbye to someone with whom she had shared so much. Whether she had done the right thing or not, that still hurt.

After walking for some time, slipping into the shadows whenever she heard a vehicle approaching, Veerle came to the end of the street she wanted. She spent some time there in spite of the cold, which was becoming bitter; there would probably be a frost tonight. She wanted to observe for a while, to be one hundred per cent sure that she had not been followed. But in the yellow light of the lamps she saw that the street was empty, and the only sound was the murmur of distant traffic.

When she was sure that she was really alone, she went down the street until she came to the right building.

There were no lights on – at least, none that she could see – but all the roller shutters were down, so it was entirely possible that there was someone home and the place was lit – it was simply that it wasn't visible from outside. Veerle approached the front door cautiously and rang the bell. She thought she could hear it, a muffled sound deep inside the house. She waited, straining her ears for the sound of footsteps approaching the door, but there was nothing.

Veerle pushed the buzzer again, keeping her finger on it for longer this time. Again she waited. Again there was silence.

Shit. I should have phoned. Maybe he's not here.

She pulled her jacket closer around her body, shivering, and glanced up at the dark façade.

If he really isn't here, what am I going to do? I can't exactly go home.

Veerle took the backpack off her shoulders and put it down on the ground. She could feel the relief all through the muscles of her shoulders and down her spine.

I can't carry that any further. I have to go in.

She tried ringing again, but she wasn't surprised when there was no reply. Then she began to look for ways of getting in.

The front door was locked, obviously, but she tried it anyway, just in case. It didn't budge. It didn't even move in its frame. Veerle suspected it was fortified on the inside with deadbolts and latches.

Then she went all along the ground floor, checking for another way in – another door or an unshuttered window. That was in vain too; the only other door had a shutter on it as well, and none of the windows were undefended. Veerle shrugged. She wasn't entirely sure she would have risked breaking the glass anyway: if *she* got in that way, so could anyone else who turned up after her.

After that she tried phoning, but it went straight to

voicemail. Veerle turned off the phone and put it back in her pocket. No help there.

I'm going to have to get in by myself.

She went round the building a second time, looking up at the first-floor windows. They were all shuttered too, except for one circular window, which was glazed with coloured glass. It might not open at all, being ornamental. Still, it was the one weak point in the building's defences. The owners probably didn't bother about it because it was small and inaccessible unless you could climb like a monkey.

But I can, thought Veerle.

She thought it would be relatively simple to get to the right height. There were robust-looking metal drainpipes running from ground to roof level, and plenty of interesting architectural features, including a huge portico over the front door. The problem was getting at the window after that. There was no windowsill underneath it, no overhang above it. It was simply a glazed opening in the wall, flat as a button-hole. She would have to hang off one of the balconies and try to reach it one-handed. If it came to it, she could always try to break one of the panes. She might be able to reach in and undo the latch, if there was one. And if there was anyone in there, ignoring the doorbell, the sound of broken glass would probably bring them running.

Veerle rubbed her hands together and breathed on her fingers, warming them as much as possible before she began the climb. That was the danger – that her fingers would become too stiff from the cold before she reached the window. Still, she had climbed worse before, and in pretty cold weather too. She remembered the night she had climbed the façade of Tante Bernadette's apartment block in Montgomery. That had been cold too, and she had managed it. She could still remember the expression of astonished amusement on Kris's face.

Forget that. Concentrate.

Before she started climbing she put a couple of stones from the garden in her pocket. As an afterthought, she took a T-shirt out of her backpack too; if she broke the window she'd wrap it around her hand first.

Then she began to climb. It wasn't difficult to get onto the portico over the main door. Whoever lived there had put up metal brackets on either side to hold hanging baskets, although there were no baskets there now; cold would have shrivelled the flowers.

Veerle climbed from the ledge of the narrow window next to the door to the metal bracket, which was strong enough to take her weight but thin, so that it felt as precarious as a high wire. From here she was able to get onto the portico, and by standing on the apex of that she was able to swing herself up onto one of the first-floor balconies. She waited there for a few moments, catching her breath and watching every exhalation drift away like a white cloud.

The circular window was about a metre away, she judged. It was still not possible to see whether it opened or not. It was going to be a stretch to reach it at all, let alone climb through it, even if she could get it open.

What other option is there? Sleep in the shrubbery?

No point in hanging about up here until her fingers went numb. Veerle positioned her feet carefully between the metal bars of the balcony and leaned out as far as she could, one hand gripping the rail and the other running across the wall and onto the glass like a spider.

Extending herself like this, with most of her weight on one arm, put a lot of strain on her shoulder. It was hateful to think that some of the pain that was beginning its slow burn around the joint was the legacy of that night in the blazing castle, when she had tried to climb down the tower wall and had fallen from a height. It felt as if De Jager himself still had his hands on her, torturing the flesh. Soon she began to feel pain across her left hand too, the one that was gripping the balcony rail. *That* had been cut, right across the palm, by the man she had confronted in Ghent, the strange killer who had called himself Joos Vijdt. Veerle had the unnerving feeling that pieces of her were being sliced away by these encounters – that she was less than she had been. It was intolerable to think that the touch of those who had taken life was still on her. Veerle gritted her teeth and *forced* herself to ignore the pain.

She felt carefully around the window frame, probing with her fingers. The fit seemed pretty solid; either the window didn't open or it was fastened tightly. Veerle thought for a moment. Breaking the glass was drastic as a first measure. If she could clear every piece from the frame she thought she could just about get in through the hole, although it would be a risky manoeuvre: there were no footholds at all below the window so she'd have to rely on smearing with her toes on the rough surface of the wall. Not impossible, but risky. A worse danger was missing some of the glass. A single sharp shard sticking out of the window frame, and she'd cut herself to ribbons wriggling through it.

Veerle winced thinking about that.

Bang on the glass, she thought. *If there's anyone at home, they won't ignore banging on an upstairs window.*

She drew back her hand and tapped as hard as she dared – once, twice, three times. Then the pain in her left shoulder became so acute that she had to lean back towards the balcony and hold onto the rail with both hands to relieve the strain.

The cold was cutting into her. No time to hang about up here; she had to try again. Veerle let go with her left hand for a few moments so that she could exercise the shoulder a little. When she thought that it could take the strain again, she changed hands and leaned back towards the circular window.

Tap – tap – tap.

The sound was brittle and surprisingly loud in the cold night air. Veerle hoped it was as loud indoors. If anyone were inside the building, ignoring the doorbell, that knocking would probably bring them running.

The third time she leaned over and rapped on the glass was going to be the last, she could tell that. Her shoulder was hurting so badly now that it was becoming difficult to ignore, however much she gritted her teeth. Time to rest it properly, in case she had to try to climb through that window.

Veerle climbed over the rail onto the balcony. She waited, rotating the shoulder and watching the white cloud of her own breath dispersing into the night air. No sound was audible from inside the building. No approaching footsteps, no responding tap on the glass, no rattle of the latch or squeak of hinges as someone tried to open the circular window from within.

Perhaps he really isn't *in there,* she thought. *And if he isn't, am I still going to break in?*

She was still debating that point when the roller shutters on the window behind her began to rise up. They were electric ones – as you'd expect on a fancy place like this – and they moved upwards with smooth but agonizing slowness. Behind them was a glass door. As the shutters went up, Veerle saw a pair of scuffed boots, then dark jeans, and then a black leather jacket came into view. Then the shutters were the whole way up and the glass door was opening.

'Veerle,' said Kris.

36

As soon as they were both inside and the electric shutters were descending again, shutting out the dark garden and the road beyond, Kris said, 'I thought you were going to Ghent.'

It was dark in here; there was a light on somewhere outside the room, but not in here. Veerle guessed that Kris had put it out before he opened the shutters, not wanting to blaze his presence out to the whole street. As the shutters edged down, what little light came from the streetlamps outside narrowed to an ever-diminishing band. Finally it was gone altogether and she couldn't see Kris's face.

'I *was* going to Ghent,' she said. 'But I changed my mind.'

For a moment there was silence.

Then Kris said, 'So why *did* you come back?'

'To fight him.'

'Veerle—'

'To fight him with *you*, Kris.'

'Veerle, you can't do that. He's a monster. You know that. He's big and brutal and fast. You can't fight him.'

'You're going to, though, aren't you?'

'Yes. Look, Veerle, it's that or spend the rest of my life

running away. Where would I go, anyway? My life is here. But *you* have a whole different life in Ghent.'

'I've told you before, it's seventy kilometres. That's not going to stop him following me.'

'It might. Maybe it won't be worth his while when he finds you've moved on again.'

'Maybe? That's one hell of a gamble.'

'Better than walking right up to him and making him a present of yourself.'

'Oh—' Veerle stopped herself before she said something she regretted. Frustration was boiling up inside her. *How can I have been with him for thirty seconds and already be arguing?*

She felt like screaming. This wasn't the way it was supposed to go. With an effort she made herself calm down, and then she tried again.

'Kris, I agree with you. I don't think we can fight De Jager very well. We can try, but you're right: he's brutal and he's very fast. He's killed a lot of times and we've never tried to kill anyone. He thinks like a hunter, all right, and we don't. I'm not sure we could learn to think like that even if we had lots of time, and we don't, because neither of us can even go home now, and we can't live in other people's houses for ever.' She gave a shaky laugh. 'What are we going to do if there's a week when nobody's on holiday?

'OK, maybe if I went to Ghent I'd be safe for a while. Maybe for ever, though I don't think so. But . . .' Veerle paused. 'The very first time I saw him – on Silent Saturday – we were together. And that night the castle burnt down, when I saw him again, we were together then too.'

'I know, but—'

'Just *listen*,' insisted Veerle. 'In Ghent last summer, when we were on top of that building – that was terrible. That was the worst thing, Kris, even worse than waking up in hospital with a whole bunch of broken bones after I fell off the castle tower. I just kept seeing her face the moment before she went over the edge – you know?'

She couldn't quite bring herself to make it any clearer than that, to say the name *Hommel* out loud, not yet.

'I felt so bad. I felt *responsible*.'

'*You* did?' There was a brittle edge to Kris's voice. 'It wasn't down to you. I brought her up there. And I could have tackled him, that guy calling himself Joos Vijdt or whatever insane name that was. I could have tried tackling him, instead of . . .' Kris's voice trailed off.

'Instead of standing in front of me,' finished Veerle. She sighed. 'That was why I didn't return your calls after it happened. I couldn't bear it – the idea of being happy because someone else had died.' She stared at Kris in the darkness, wishing she could see his face. 'It's not like I can even say to myself, *Hmmm, it's what she would have wanted*. It *wasn't* what she wanted, us being together. She had a shit life, with that horrible stepfather and her mum not even caring enough to check where she'd gone when she left, and then she—'

She died. She was swept off the top of a building by a killer and died on the cobblestones all those metres below.

'You were probably the only good friend she ever had, Kris. So no, I don't think she would have wanted us to be together. And I felt so bad.'

There was a long silence.

At last Kris spoke in a very low voice. 'So what changed?'

Veerle rubbed uselessly at one eye in the dark. 'It didn't really change. I still feel bad. I just . . . I got onto the train just after you phoned me. I still have the ticket in my pocket. It was about to leave, and then . . . I just couldn't do it. I don't want to go to Ghent, Kris. I want to be here. With you.'

To her relief, Kris didn't ask her any more questions. Not, *What about Bram?* nor *It's more dangerous here – are you sure you want to risk it?* Instead he put his arms around her and pulled her close, holding her very tightly, as though he never wanted to let her go. Veerle put her arms around him too and rested her head against his shoulder.

Home, she thought, because she was. Her mother was gone; her father had another life that had little space for Veerle; she couldn't even go back to the house on Kerkstraat, where she had grown up. The landmarks of her own existence were dispersing, insubstantial as mist, leaving her isolated in a present time and place that felt lonely and dangerous. The one thing she had was Kris. He had known her as a little girl with a pale, serious face framed by dark hair pulled into two plaits; he had begun to love her as an almost-grown young woman. They had lived through the worst day of her village's history together; together they had faced the crossbow and the knife and the flames. She thought they might even face living with Hommel's death together – if they survived long enough.

Veerle looked up even though she could barely see Kris in

the darkness. She put up a hand and touched his face as she had wanted to do for so long, and when he began to kiss her she kissed him back with passion. For a while, at least, she was almost perfectly happy.

Home.

37

After a while they went downstairs to retrieve Veerle's back-pack from the front garden. Veerle had forgotten how large and opulent the rooms were. The hall was enormous, and dominated by a huge oil painting and a marble statue so tall that Veerle had to put her head back to look into its face. She remembered that statue from the last time she had visited the house; it was no less impressive on a second viewing. All the same, it wasn't exactly homely. Places like this always gave Veerle a feeling of unreality, as though she were exploring a stage set and not someone's house.

Kris turned off the hall light before he opened the front door, and even then he opened it slowly and carefully, check-ing that there was nobody passing who might glimpse the faint light from the rooms further back and realize that there was someone in the house.

As soon as she was able, Veerle slipped out through the widening crack and retrieved her bag. It felt as though it were stuffed with bricks. She tried hoisting it onto her shoulders again but there was an instant flare of pain in the left one. Veerle grimaced and carried it in by the handle instead.

Kris locked and bolted the door. He watched Veerle put the

bag down on the polished floor and then he said, 'Do you want something to eat?'

'Yes, I'm *starving*.'

Veerle followed him through the cream-and-green drawing room and into the kitchen. She remembered this room very clearly too; it was impossible to forget. A kitchen had to be really huge before you could decorate it entirely in scarlet and black; in a small room the colours would have been oppressive, like sitting inside an artery. The tiles were gleaming red and all the surfaces were made of cold black marble. There was a breakfast bar with a line of bar stools, all upholstered in red leather to match the tiles. What seemed like half a lifetime ago, Veerle had sat on one of those stools, watching Kris rewiring the plug on the enormous chrome toaster. That had been part of the deal, back when they and the other members of the Koekoeken were breaking into and exploring empty buildings: you did some small piece of maintenance to say thank you. Veerle wondered whether they would do that now, for this house. But this was not breaking in for fun; this was hiding to try to save your own skin.

She sat on one of the red leather bar stools and watched Kris moving about. He opened the gigantic stainless steel fridge and fetched cheese, sliced ham, unsalted butter. Then he brought out half a loaf of crusty bread and a little dish of olives. Veerle watched these things appearing with round eyes. Her stomach was aching with hunger.

Kris found her some pieces of gleaming cutlery and an outsize plate with a strident red glaze to match the kitchen. Lastly he fetched her a glass of wine. Then he sat opposite her. He didn't eat anything himself apart from a couple of the olives. Mostly he just watched her attacking the food, with a slightly amused expression on his face. Veerle didn't care; she was ravenous. She wondered whether Kris had bought all the food himself or pilfered some of it from the house, and found that she didn't care about that, either. They could always replace it.

She was beginning to warm up now, with the food and the comfortable temperature of the house. She finished the last olive and then took a sip of wine.

'How long did you say the people who live here are going to be away?' she asked, looking at Kris. She couldn't get enough of looking at him, now that she wasn't trying to pretend she didn't care.

'A month. But they've been gone about ten days.'

'So we could stay here for nearly three weeks?'

'Maybe. If we're sure nobody's noticed we're here.'

'And then what?'

'Well, by then . . .' Kris's voice trailed off.

Veerle looked down at her plate. *By then we may not need anywhere to hide, because either we'll have some real information we can take to the police, or we'll be dead, and I'm not sure the chances of it being the first option are all that great.*

After a while she said, 'Mevrouw Willems told me something. She remembered Joren Sterckx all right – I mean, not from the murder; everyone in the village knows about that – but from when he was at the school. She said he was troublesome but he wasn't very bright. She didn't really think he had the qualities to be a ringleader.'

She glanced at Kris and saw a dark eyebrow go up. 'He's changed, then.'

'I'm not so sure. Mevrouw Willems said she was surprised when the killing happened – you know, on Silent Saturday.' Veerle took a deep breath. 'But she said she *wouldn't* have been surprised if it had been his brother.'

Kris's dark eyes widened. 'He had a *brother*?'

Veerle nodded. 'About eight or nine years younger, she thought.'

Kris struck the black marble counter with his fist. 'The other bedroom – the kid's one. That was *his*.' He shook his head. 'But I still don't remember Joren Sterckx having a brother. What was his name?'

'Kasper Sterckx.' It gave Veerle a curious and not very pleasant sensation to speak that name aloud. Joren Sterckx, that was a name everyone knew. Everyone reviled it. Sterckx was a common enough surname, but Veerle doubted that any Sterckx would be calling their newborn son Joren any time soon; the combination was toxic now.

Kasper Sterckx, on the other hand, was a name still safely buried in obscurity. And yet . . .

Supposing it was Kasper who killed Karel Adriaensen?

That would turn everything on its head. It would be worse, far worse than if Joren Sterckx had committed the murder, as everyone thought he had, including the police and the courts. It would mean that the killer had started his career at *twelve years of age* – and had let his own brother take the blame. To be capable of that by the time you left primary school – well, where did you go from there?

Veerle thought she knew where you went from there. You went to hunting teenagers with a crossbow in empty buildings.

Kris was shaking his head. 'I still don't remember him.'

'He'd have been much further up the school than we were. Maybe even in the first year of secondary school by the time of the murder,' Veerle told him. 'I was seven, you were nine, right? And I worked out that Kasper would have been around twelve.'

'Does Mevrouw Willems know where he is now? Or the rest of the family?'

'No. She says she isn't even sure they're still alive. Joren's dad was a really old father, and his mother was sick. It was over a decade ago – they might be dead by now. And she said they didn't have many friends so there probably wasn't anyone who'd have a forwarding address.'

Kris considered for a moment. 'And Mevrouw Willems said she wouldn't have been surprised if it had been Kasper who did the murder?'

'Well, I guess she meant if he had been older at the time – based on what he was like as a kid. Twelve is young.'

'But not impossible.'

'No.' Veerle sighed. 'She said he was an unpleasant child, but she thought he was too young to do anything that brutal. She said that whenever there was trouble, he was on the edge of it, only it seems it was really hard to pin anything on him. There was one time she told me about, when a bunch of kids in the playground killed someone's pet rabbit—'

'What?! That's sick.'

'I know. Anyway one of the teachers caught them with it and Kasper was there in the middle of it, but afterwards another kid owned up. Mevrouw Willems wasn't convinced, though. The other kid wasn't the type to do something

322

horrible like that. So maybe Kasper did it and the other kid said it was him because he was afraid of Kasper.'

Kris exhaled slowly, pushing back the dark hair from his brow with one lean hand. 'That's a lot of *maybe*.'

'Yeah.'

'But supposing he *did* do it – that's brutal, a twelve-year-old killing a kid one year younger than him. And why on earth would Joren own up to something he didn't do, especially something as bad as that?'

'He didn't,' Veerle reminded him. 'He refused to say anything about it.'

'But he didn't *deny* it, either. Why not? I mean, he spent the last months before he died in prison, probably with all the other prisoners spitting at him.'

Veerle stared. 'That's probably it. He was going to die anyway.'

Kris's gaze met hers. 'Seriously? You think Joren Sterckx took the blame for something his twelve-year-old brother did, because he was going to die anyway?'

'I can't prove it,' said Veerle breathlessly, 'but it makes sense in a sick sort of way. If you're twenty and you're dying, how much worse can it get? And Mevrouw Willems said the reason she didn't think Joren was the type to hunt someone down like that was because he was easily led. He was in trouble quite a lot, but he was never the ringleader. She didn't think he was bright enough.'

'So you think Kasper talked him into taking the blame?'

'Maybe he didn't have to.' Veerle leaned forward over the black marble counter. 'The father was really old and the mother wasn't well. And Mevrouw Willems said the murder was the last straw – it broke them. Their oldest son was dying of cancer and if Kasper went to some juvenile offenders' place for murder, they'd lose their other son too. Maybe it was best for everyone if Joren took the blame.'

'That's hard to believe,' said Kris reluctantly.

'And impossible to prove,' added Veerle.

'But when did he decide to do that? And how come Joren was the one found with the body? I mean, he wasn't just *with* it, he was actually *carrying* it across the village.'

'Well, maybe Joren *did* do it. We can't exclude that. But perhaps he didn't – he just found it. He might even have known it was Kasper who'd done it. All the other kids had gone home by then, except Karel Adriaensen, because it was lunch time or whatever. So maybe Joren came looking for his little brother and found him with the body. He was completely horrified and so he picked Karel up and went to try to get help. Only it was already too late because Karel had bled to death. And he couldn't explain any of this to the police without dropping his little brother in it, so he said nothing.'

Kris was shaking his head. 'I can't take this in. When we saw him from the bell tower he looked *terrifying*. He had blood from here to here. It was raining and his hair was plastered down, and he had his mouth open, like he was howling. He looked like a monster.'

'Perhaps he wasn't howling out of – I don't know – blood-lust,' said Veerle. 'Perhaps he was howling because he was *horrified*.'

They considered this in silence for a while. Kris looked troubled and perplexed, as though he were trying to find the solution to an impossibly difficult puzzle. Veerle thought he was probably going over what he had seen from the bell tower in his mind, trying to decide whether it could be reinterpreted.

That wasn't the bit that was bothering *her*. Veerle was wondering whether Joren had indeed found his younger brother with the body, and as he stumbled back to the village with the bloodied child in his arms he'd had Kasper's words insinuating their way into his malleable psyche.

I didn't really mean to do it, Joren.

Tell them it was you, Joren.

Please, Joren, I'm so afraid.

Please. Please. Please.

She wondered whether Kasper had played that most atrocious of trump cards: *You're dying anyway, Joren, and if they take me away too, Mum and Dad will be all alone.*

Veerle shuddered.

You don't know that any of this is true, she told herself. *It might not have happened like that at all.*

But she was very afraid it had.

'Look,' said Kris after a moment, 'when you saw him – De Jager – in the castle that night, you recognized him, didn't you? Only you recognized *Joren* – the same guy we saw from the bell tower, carrying Karel's body. Not Kasper.'

'They're brothers.'

'That doesn't mean they look alike. Look at me and Denis.'

'Look at Marc and Jan – well, you don't know them. They're at the high school. Marc's two years ahead of Jan but they're so alike you could easily mix them up.'

Veerle sighed. 'I was one hundred per cent certain that the

man I saw was Joren Sterckx. The police think I'm mad because I kept insisting on it. But now . . .'

'You think it could have been Kasper?'

'I don't know.' Veerle pushed back her dark hair with one hand. 'He looked exactly the same to me – I mean, *exactly*.'

'Well, let's think about this. The night you saw him was well over a year ago but it was already a decade since the *last* time you saw him, assuming it was the same guy. So if he was about twenty when Karel Adriaensen was killed, by then he'd have been about thirty. Whereas Kasper, who was about twelve at the time of the murder, would be in his twenties by now. So *if* they look very alike . . .'

'. . . Kasper might look more like the man I saw on Silent Saturday now than Joren would, if he were still alive.' Veerle considered. 'You know, it's possible.'

'It's a better theory than the one that says Joren Sterckx managed to escape prison *and* his own death from cancer.'

Veerle put her elbows on the black marble counter and rested her head in her hands. So many possibilities – so many *maybes* – and all of them tenuous. And then there were things that didn't seem to fit at all, like the charred body found in the ruins of the burnt-out castle.

I heard him screaming in the flames, she thought. *If he was Kasper, surely he died there?*

But then, who was hunting her and Kris now? She was beginning to feel tired and frustrated, as though she had been stumbling for hours through an impossible maze.

'What are we going to do?' she asked in the end. 'Go to the police?'

'Yeah. We have to. It's that or turn up at one of the

rendezvous he sends us, and somehow I don't think that would be a good idea.' Kris paused, thinking. 'We'll have to get the story completely straight because I think we'll have a hard time getting them to believe us. I mean, Joren Sterckx went to prison for the original murder eleven years ago. It's been a closed case so long that the files have probably fossilized. We have to persuade them pretty well to get them to believe they had the wrong person, and actually *do* anything about it. You remember what happened when I tried to talk to them before? They thought I was wasting their time.'

'I wonder if they ever *did* check out that place in . . .' Veerle began. She was going to say, *Luik*, but suddenly she was ambushed by an enormous yawn. The discussion was important, she knew that, but she felt so very weary. The day had been long and tense, and now she felt safe, at least temporarily, not to say warm and pleasantly mellow after the glass of wine. She could almost have laid her head down on the black marble counter and closed her eyes right there.

'I'm sorry,' she managed to say.

'Don't be. We should leave this for the morning anyway. Come on, let's find somewhere for you to sleep.'

Veerle couldn't suppress another yawn as she slid down from the bar stool. She followed Kris back through the drawing room to the enormous hallway, where he picked up her backpack for her. Veerle wasn't about to argue with that; her shoulder was still aching in a vague but nagging way. She followed him up the stairs, looking wonderingly at the expensive décor in spite of her exhaustion. There were pieces of art displayed all the way up the staircase, and they looked original, even to Veerle's inexpert eyes. Some were very ugly too; she was reminded of the things she had seen on display in Fred's art gallery in Brussels the first time she had visited. She didn't really want to think about Fred any more than she wanted to think about what she and Kris were going to tell the police, so she pushed that thought away.

A shower, or maybe a bath, and then a long, long sleep, she told herself.

Veerle and Kris hadn't visited the upstairs the first time she came here. They had spent the evening messing about in the swimming pool and then sitting in the kitchen.

The upstairs landing was wide and long, with an ornate white-painted wooden balcony looking down over the hall below and the huge marble statue keeping watch like a sentinel.

Kris turned right, but Veerle could see that there was just as much corridor if you turned left. She'd known the place was enormous but she felt the scale of it all over again. They passed a number of closed doors – how many bedrooms did this place have? – before turning a corner.

Veerle found herself looking down another section of corridor and wondering just how long it would take her if she decided to go back down to the kitchen for a drink of water. The house was *huge*. To her relief it seemed they weren't going any further; Kris opened one of the glossy white-painted doors, and stepped inside to turn on the lights.

'Wow,' said Veerle as she followed him in.

The room was almost entirely decorated in cream and gold. It was very big – that went without saying – but every centimetre had been co-ordinated. The carpet was thick and creamy, and Veerle found herself stooping to unlace her boots before she dared take another step on it. There was a super-king-sized bed covered with a thick gold coverlet on which rested four plump cream-and-gold cushions, arranged with precision. The enormous bedside lampshades were gold too. The wall opposite the bed was dominated by a huge canvas, an abstract painting in shades of – yes, cream and gold, as well as everything in between: wheat, ivory, beige. Veerle wondered a bit about choosing art to match your gold bed-covers and lampshades, but she had to admit that the overall effect was impressive, if rather overwhelming.

There was a big window at the end of the bedroom, but of course the shutters were down. At any rate there was no danger of the light being seen from outside.

Kris went across the room and opened another door. 'Ensuite,' he said briefly.

Veerle went over and looked at that too. Predictably, the bathroom was one of the biggest she'd ever seen – the others had been in other villas the Koekoeken visited. For a change, the bathroom was decorated in cream, gold and turquoise. Even the towels matched. Veerle was pleased to see the row of gleaming bottles full of scented bath salts, shampoo, conditioner and body lotion; she hadn't been able to pack much of anything like that.

'Thanks,' she said. 'This is amazing. I think I'm going to have a bath and go straight to bed.'

'Good idea,' said Kris. He came up and put his arms around her. When Veerle turned her face up to his he kissed her goodnight and she felt his hand touch her hair, gently. Then he drew away a little, and said, 'I'm in the same room as this one, on the other side of the house – the mirror-image room, OK? So if you need anything, that's where to find me. I'm going downstairs again first, though, to clear up a bit. So if you hear someone moving around, it's me. Don't worry.'

'OK,' said Veerle. She didn't think she would have worried anyway. She thought she was going to sleep like the dead the instant her head touched the pillow.

After Kris had gone she went into the opulent bathroom and ran herself a hot bath, then lay in the water amongst clouds of fragrant steam, struggling to open her eyes each time they slid shut. When she felt boneless with relaxation and just a little *too* hot, she climbed out and wrapped herself in a couple of fluffy turquoise towels with embroidered gold motifs.

After she had finished in the bathroom she went to look for something to sleep in; she hadn't had space for a nightshirt in the backpack. The bedroom drawers and the walk-in wardrobe were all empty, however, and Veerle realized that this must be a guest bedroom. She tried not to get sidetracked into marvelling at anyone having a room like this just for guests; she really wanted to get to bed now. Eventually she dug out her spare T-shirt and wore that instead, with clean underwear. She was getting through her spare things too fast, but what the hell – she'd have a look in some of the other bedrooms tomorrow and see if she could find anything to wear.

A ballgown maybe, she thought, recalling the red silk dress she had worn once in another house.

Finally she was able to climb into bed, turning back the gold coverlet and sliding thankfully between the clean cool sheets underneath.

Veerle reached over to turn out the lights, then made herself comfortable, pulling the covers over her shoulders. She pushed her hair back from her face, closed her eyes . . . and utterly failed to go to sleep.

It was as though unconsciousness, which had been rising like flood water, threatening to suck her down into its murky depths, had suddenly drained away in an instant. Veerle lay for a while with her head on the pillow, expecting sleep to come, until she realized that quite some considerable time had passed, and she was no nearer dropping off. She was as tired as ever – she was *sick* with tiredness – but she couldn't get to sleep.

She turned over in bed, and now she became aware that she was not really relaxing. She tried to relax her limbs and it was like trying to unclench a fist. If she managed to relax a little, she was instantly restless, and as soon as she turned over she realized that she had tensed up again.

Veerle rolled onto her back and stared up into the dark. She wished she could open the roller shutters a little bit – just let in a tiny amount of light from the streetlamps outside. It was oddly unnerving being in a place you didn't really know, where the darkness felt unmapped and alien. The room she was in now was large and unfamiliar; she found herself trying to plan it out in her head, and that certainly wasn't helping her to feel sleepy.

Opposite the end of the bed was that huge painting, on one side of it the door that led into the corridor, on the other side the one that led into the bathroom. And then there was the walk-in wardrobe – and was there another door? Or was she remembering a built-in cupboard? She hadn't opened that one. Now she began imagining what might be inside.

Is it big enough for a person to hide in?

Veerle rolled over, restless, angry at herself for thinking of anything so stupid, even angrier that she couldn't shrug off the idea once she'd had it.

After a while she switched on the bedside light again, got out of bed and padded across the room to the last door. She looked at it for a few moments and then she opened it.

Linen.

Stacks of it, all neatly folded, and pillows too. There wasn't room for a cat to hide in here. Veerle shut the door and went back to bed.

Light out again. Now she heard noises.

The house was remarkably quiet compared to the one she had grown up in – the house on Kerkstraat was old and the floorboards used to make a sound like a sow in labour – but the noises she *could* hear were hard to identify. A ticking sound. A low hum that she didn't even know she was hearing until it suddenly cut out.

She heard Kris coming up the stairs – at least, she thought that was what she heard. Then the crisp sound of a door closing. After a few minutes of silence Veerle heard the ticking sound again.

It's probably the pipes. Just Kris taking a shower.

After a while she rolled over and turned the light on again so that she could look at her watch. She'd been lying there for over an hour.

What's wrong with me?

She knew what was wrong, though. She lay there for another ten minutes with the lamp glowing golden beside her, and then threw back the covers and got out of bed. The thick rug (gold and cream, of course, what else?) was very soft under her bare feet. Veerle crossed the room and opened the door to the landing.

It was quite dark out there, but not so dark that she couldn't see a thing. There was a light on somewhere round the turn in the corridor. She followed it, not without a wary glance into the black pit of the stairwell as she passed the head of it.

It wasn't difficult to find Kris's room. It was just as he had described, the mirror-image location of Veerle's, and a soft light was coming from it: the door stood ajar. Even so, Veerle didn't just barge in. She knocked on one of the glossy white panels and waited for a response before she went inside.

The room was every bit as luxuriously decked out as hers, but the colours were soft, natural ones with less of a film-star's-boudoir effect: pale green, cream and brown. Kris was sitting on the edge of the bed, bare-chested but wearing a pair of shorts, rubbing his damp hair with a towel. He turned to look at her and she felt that old familiar feeling, a *jump* inside, as though something were pulling her towards him inexorably. It was no use resisting it; she had worn herself out trying. Veerle looked at him – at the tousled dark hair, the bold eyes, the aquiline nose, the mouth that was a little too wide to be classically handsome but always seemed to have that ironic little pucker at the corner of it – looked and couldn't look away, even though she felt the blood coming to her cheeks. He was there in some of her earliest memories and now she couldn't conceive of a time when she hadn't loved him. She wanted to go over to him and push her fingers into that untidy dark hair – pull him to her and feel his lips on hers, his arms around her. She just didn't know how to do it.

Kris was looking at her, with one eyebrow slightly raised. She had to say *something*.

'I can't sleep,' said Veerle. 'I keep hearing noises.'

'Strange house,' said Kris, tilting his head to one side.

At last she said, 'Can I sleep in here . . . with you?'

'Of course you can.'

Kris threw the towel onto a chair and got into bed, pulling back the covers so that Veerle could climb in beside him. Like the bed in the cream-and-gold room, this one was a super-king-size, so wide that they could have lain sprawled out side by side without touching. It felt oddly formal too, as though they were some medieval royal couple, paired by arrangement and required to climb into the same four-poster after little more than an introduction.

After a while, however, they turned to each other. Kris's skin was warm from the hot shower; his touch was light on Veerle's face but her own skin seemed to glow where he had touched it. They gazed at each other for a long time without speaking. There was nothing to say anyway; neither of them wanted to conjure up the spectre of past or future danger or thoughts of those who were not here. Imperceptibly the world was turning, like a great wheel bringing them closer and closer to an uncertain tomorrow; best not to speak or think of it at all, but to live in the moment. So they were together in silence, until much later Veerle said *Yes*.

38

On the Sunday morning Veerle slept in. With all the shutters down on the windows there was no bright morning sunlight to wake her. The nightmares that had been dogging her – of being pursued by De Jager in some abstract form as she fled through a thorny maze or a complicated series of rooms – were completely absent. She slumbered on, curled up close to Kris, and when he slid out of bed to go and make some coffee she didn't stir.

Finally, when Kris sat down on the bed next to her and brushed her dark hair away from her face, Veerle opened her eyes, blinking lazily. Two mugs of coffee were steaming on the bedside cabinet.

'So,' said Kris. 'What do you want to do today?'

Veerle looked at him. After a moment she said, 'We ought to discuss what we're going to tell the police.'

'But?'

'But I don't want to. Not yet. Yesterday was' – her gaze slid away from Kris – 'horrible.' After a moment she looked back at him, not quite repressing a grin. 'Except the last bit.'

Kris grinned back. 'Let's take a day off, then. It's Sunday, anyway. Let's leave the crap for Monday morning.'

'OK,' agreed Veerle, without any further persuasion. The thought, *We really should talk to the police as soon as possible*, floated through her head but she pushed it away. Talking to the police meant taking a one-way trip to Planet Trouble, she could see that; there was nothing they could tell them that wouldn't lead to further and more difficult questions. Saturday had been long and horrific and exhausting; the thought of taking one day off and spending it with Kris was simply too tempting to resist. The house itself was a temptation too. It felt safe, with its shutters and deadbolts – in fact she *knew* it was safe because she had tried to break into it herself – and it was gloriously luxurious. It even had a heated swimming pool, for goodness' sake. You could spend much more than a day in the house and not run out of things to do.

One day, she said to herself. *Just one day before we nuke everything.*

In the end it all came down to the singleness of that day. Veerle had lost Kris twice in her life, and found him once more. She didn't want to lose him ever again. When she was with him she found herself thinking, *For ever*, and she knew that it was true. But she looked into the future, she looked into a time as close to now as tomorrow, and it was like looking out through a window into the endless dark of midnight, a frozen blackness in which nothing could be discerned, not the merest outline.

Can we make anyone believe us?

She really had no idea. And all the time he was out there, De Jager, circling silently like a great white shark, waiting for them to show their hand. Whether they were believed or not believed, a time was coming when they would have to face him, whether in the labyrinth of the legal system or the open hunting grounds of their lives. At best there would be months, years even, of questions, repercussions, accusations. At worst, the whole future that she might have shared with Kris would be snuffed out.

No – she had to have that one single day; that one chance to live all of it, before the world fell apart; a memory to hug to themselves for however long they had left, whether it was one day or a lifetime.

On Monday morning the world *did* fall apart.

Veerle awoke to the sound of Kris's mobile phone going off. He had left it on the glass-topped bedside cabinet, and as well as ringing it vibrated, so that it skittered about on the smooth surface.

She opened her eyes and found that Kris was sitting up in bed. His entire posture was tense and his face was a mask of horror.

'Slow down, Jeroen,' Veerle heard him say into the phone. He listened for a few moments and then swore loudly.

Veerle sat up too. She had a very bad feeling about this, whatever it was. She waited for Kris to complete the call so that she could ask him what was going on. It took a long time; clearly Jeroen was upset because Kris kept having to tell him to calm down and explain things again. Several times Kris exclaimed, 'No,' in a tone so bitter that it sounded as though he was in physical pain.

At last Kris pressed the END CALL icon and put the phone down. The face he turned to Veerle was terrible. She had only seen that look on his face once before, and that had been on the rooftop in Ghent, when he had looked over the parapet and seen what had happened to Hommel when she hit the cobblestones.

He said, 'Someone's taken Fien.'

'Fien? Who's Fien?' asked Veerle.

'Jeroen's kid. She's his daughter by his girlfriend, Ella. She's only four.'

'Oh God.' Veerle put her hand to her mouth. 'What happened?'

'Ella let her out to play in the garden. Fien has pre-school but she goes before Jeroen leaves for work. He was having a lie-in and Fien was making a racket so Ella told her to go outdoors and play for a bit. She didn't think anything of it. There's a wall the whole way round, and a gate, and Fien's not big enough to climb over, though an adult could.'

Veerle shuddered at that.

'She put Fien in her coat and hat too, so she thought she'd be fine for ten minutes while Ella made Jeroen his coffee. She took the coffee up, and when she came down Fien had gone.'

'Shit.' Veerle clasped her hands, squeezing them together as though she needed to hold onto something. 'She couldn't have got out by herself?'

'Jeroen says not. Anyway they checked the street outside and the neighbours' gardens.'

'Oh God. Poor kid. Her poor parents.' Veerle felt sick. It was impossible not to think the worst. She'd seen enough horror with her own eyes to know that there was nothing standing between that and even the most innocent. *She's only four.*

'Jeroen's called the police,' said Kris grimly. 'He wants me to go and help look for her. She knows me. He thinks if she's hiding somewhere – if something frightened her – she's more likely to come out for people she knows.'

'I'll come too.'

'Are you sure you want to? Jeroen lives pretty close to the village. That's not exactly lying low.'

Veerle knew what Kris was implying. If De Jager was out looking for her, the village was the last place she wanted to be. She stuck out her chin. 'Yes, I'm sure.'

Kris studied her for a moment. 'OK.'

'I'm going to get dressed,' Veerle told him. She slipped out of bed and went over to where her backpack lay on the carpet. She was dimly aware of Kris moving about the room behind her, gathering up his own things.

She tried not to give herself enough time to think. Get ready quickly, that was the thing to do. Think about getting out there and finding the kid. Don't think about *not* finding her, or about what might be happening to her while everyone's running around looking.

Veerle knelt by her backpack and began pulling out bits of clothing, and then she *did* think about what might be happening because the photo of Karel Adriaensen's startled-looking freckled face from the news articles flashed across her mind. She knelt on the brown-and-green rug with a T-shirt clutched in hands clenched so tightly that the knuckles were white, experiencing a paroxysm of horror so intense that it was like being electrocuted. *Please, no. She's only four.* The thoughts wouldn't go away, though. Veerle knew more than anyone that there was no inoculation against evil. You had to hope that you'd live your entire life inside the bubble –

because that was all it was, a bubble – and never see what was prowling around on the *outside*.

She forced herself to stand up and get dressed. The only thing she could do to help Fien and her parents was go and help search for the little girl. *Concentrate on that.*

Her boots were nowhere to be seen. Veerle recalled that she had taken them off when she first went into the cream-and-gold bedroom down the hall. She set off to fetch them, pulling her hair back into a ponytail and fastening it with an elastic band as she went.

The house was oddly dark with every single shutter down. The only natural light came from the circular window above the front door, the one that Veerle had considered smashing. The glass in that was coloured, so that the light that did come through had a greenish tinge to it, as though filtered through murky water. It was hard to believe that it was full daylight outside. But it was, and the day had started badly.

Veerle reached the cream-and-gold bedroom that had been hers. There were her boots on the opulent rug.

She knelt to lace them onto her feet and her hands were all fingers and thumbs. When she was finally done, she went into the bathroom, and just as she came out her phone buzzed in her pocket like an angry hornet trapped in a small space.

Veerle slid the phone out. She saw that an email had come in. She wasn't going to look at it now – but before she thought what she was doing she had pressed the icon to read the email.

A minute later, Veerle was *running* down the corridor, her eyes wide, the phone in one hand and the other hand pressed to her chest because the shock had hit her so hard that it was like an actual pain inside her – a crushing, twisting pain which made her think that her heart was actually going to stop, because surely nobody could have this feeling and carry on living?

She burst into the bedroom where Kris was standing by the bed, in T-shirt and jeans now, but holding his own phone, an expression of frozen agony on his face. His eyes were dark holes, and Veerle saw through them into the bleakness of death. The gaze of those eyes was so appalling that even in the midst of Veerle's own horror it stopped her in her tracks.

Kris said, 'I think De Jager has Fien.'

Veerle began screaming then. She threw the phone away from her as though it were a scorpion, and it bounced uselessly on the bed. She fell to her knees and pounded impotently with her fists on the rug, and all the time she was shrieking and shrieking, *No, no, no.*

The horror was like a black hole, dragging everything into itself so that the pressure built exponentially, until it felt as though something inside her would implode. Veerle pressed her face into the soft pile of the rug, and the agony poured from her throat until she was hoarse and scalding tears were running from her eyes. She had wrenched her shoulder from pounding on the floor but she barely noticed; it was a single drop in the ocean of affliction that had swept in on her.

Kris came and put his arms around her. He was gentle, but there was an urgency in his touch; he pulled her up to a kneeling position and pushed the dark hair back from her face, trying to make her look at him.

'Veerle, listen to me. I'm going to have to go.'

'Where?'

'I don't know yet. Look, he emailed me from Gregory's account again, with another of those grid references. I'll have to look it up online.'

'What did he say? Did he tell you to come?'

'No,' said Kris. 'There wasn't any message. Just the GPS co-ordinates, like the other time.'

Veerle clutched his wrist, her eyes bright with the evangelism of sudden relief. 'Kris . . . maybe it has nothing to do with Fien! She could just have wandered off – or be hiding or something – if he didn't say anything . . .'

She saw Kris's face change briefly, the sombre expression replaced by the pale ghost of hope. But then he shook his head.

'I hope to God you're right. But, Veerle, it *can't* be a coincidence. Fien disappears and I get another of those messages at virtually the same time? It's him. It *has* to be. He knows Jeroen and I are connected because Jeroen gave him my bloody address. He could have checked the flat out by now. Maybe he already knows I've gone – so he took Fien instead.' Kris looked down, his face etched with lines of anguish. 'He'd know we couldn't ignore that. I can't risk Fien . . . I have to go.'

'He'll kill you,' said Veerle in a voice that was choked with dread.

'What else can I do?' asked Kris grimly.

'We could call the police right now – we were going to talk to them today anyway—'

'No.' Kris was shaking his head. 'It'll take too long. Last time I reported one of these emails they thought I was wasting their time. And what if they do take us seriously this time? We'll be in there for hours telling them the whole story right back to the time I nicked the key to the bell tower on Silent Saturday. And all that time De Jager would have Fien. She's only *four years old*, Veerle. If he thinks I'm not coming, who knows what he'll do? If he has her, going to wherever it is is our only hope of getting her back, so I have to take it. It's not her he wants – it's me.'

Veerle looked at him then, and her hazel eyes were bleak. 'It's not just you, Kris.'

'What do you mean?'

'I got an email from Gregory's account too. That's why I ran down here.' Veerle's gaze slid away from Kris's and she put a hand over her face, her mouth distorting as she tried not to cry again.

'What did it say?' Kris's voice was urgent. 'Veerle, what did it say? Was it just numbers, like mine?'

'It didn't say anything. It was a picture.' Veerle glanced back at him, and now the tears *were* coming again. 'I was careful, Kris. I really was. When I left the house I took Mum's old address book with me. I thought, *If he breaks in, at least he won't find that.* But he found a photo of Dad and Adam. That's what he sent me, a scan of the photo. I forgot about that. It was pinned up on the wall over the desk, right where anyone would see it. You can see the Graslei behind them. Anyone would know it was Ghent. It won't take him any time to find them . . . if he hasn't found them already.'

'Shit. When did you last speak to your dad?'

'Saturday morning, before I saw Mevrouw Willems.'

'And he was OK?'

Veerle nodded. 'Yes.'

'And you haven't heard anything since then?'

'No. I haven't had any calls except the one from you.'

Kris was silent for a moment. 'Look, De Jager may be an evil murdering bastard but he isn't a magician. If he was here in Vlaams-Brabant this morning taking Fien, he can't be in Ghent. You have to try not to worry about your dad and your brother for the moment because I have to go to this grid reference *now*, otherwise . . .'

He didn't finish the sentence. Both of them knew the appalling truth: if De Jager had Fien, they might not see her again anyway.

Veerle wiped her eyes with the back of her hand. 'I'm coming too.'

'No,' said Kris instantly.

'Why not? Because it's dangerous?'

'Yes,' retorted Kris hotly.

'Kris, he's threatening my dad and my little brother. And anyway, you said it yourself. Your niece is only *four*. I can't just sit here doing nothing. I'm coming with you.'

'Veerle—'

'Don't tell me not to.' Veerle stared him down, her hazel eyes gazing into his dark ones. A tear still glistened on her cheek but now she wasn't crying. 'Look, shouldn't we find this place? Work out where it is, and then you can argue with me about who's going when we're on our way there.'

Kris didn't look happy at that, but Veerle had a point; time was sliding past while they were debating the matter. He fetched his laptop, booted it up and went online.

Veerle looked over his shoulder. Her mind kept ricocheting

like a ball bearing in a pinball game, from Karel Adriaensen to Egbert Visser and from Egbert to Valérie Renard, flinching back from each grisly scene before rebounding onto the next. A four year old in De Jager's hands it was unthinkable. Now that she had stopped screaming, her mind was struggling in other ways, probing the situation feverishly in an attempt to find the one flaw in the picture, the one fact that would make the whole horrible thing untrue. *It could be a coincidence. He didn't actually say he has Fien. He just sent a location, like he did last time. Maybe he's just fishing. Please God, let it be a coincidence.* It was no use; her mind kept stealing back to what the local Scouts had found at the first GPS location De Jager had sent – what the police *might* have found if they'd checked the one at Luik.

Kris was keying in the co-ordinates. A moment later the location appeared onscreen. There was a silence for a moment.

Then Veerle said, 'Are you sure you put in the right numbers?'

'I'll check . . . Yes. That's the place.'

They gazed at the map on the screen.

'It's going to be busy, even on a Monday morning,' said Veerle. 'You really think he wants to meet us there?'

'Who knows what he wants?' said Kris tersely.

'It's close. We can walk there.'

'I know.' Kris's tone was so ominous that Veerle glanced at him, her expression uncertain. He went on, 'He's probably guessed we've holed up somewhere around here, in one of the Koekoeken places.'

'Shit,' said Veerle. The back of her neck prickled, as though

De Jager might saunter through the open doorway behind them at any moment, the crossbow slung casually over his brawny shoulder.

'He doesn't know about this place,' said Kris, glancing at her. 'It's one of the ones I kept to myself, remember?' He closed the laptop and stood up. 'We should go.'

39

The intersection of Kastanjedreef – *Chestnut Way*, so named for the trees that grow alongside it – and Keizerinnedreef – *Empress Way* – is very seldom quiet. Drivers coming from the outlying villages to the tram stop at Tervuren often follow the picturesque route through the park, which takes them along Kastanjedreef. Expats park at the end of Keizerinnedreef and open the back of their 4X4s to let out their chocolate Labradors. Runners and cyclists planning a turn around the park congregate there, their breath hanging on the air in a silvery mist during the colder months. There is even a brasserie on the lakeside corner of the intersection, its decking looking out over the still waters of the Kasteelvijver.

Although it was a Monday morning, so none of the weekend strollers were about, the intersection was still relatively busy when Kris and Veerle arrived, on foot and looking about them warily. The parking spaces at the end of Keizerinnedreef were all taken. It was still early enough to see people cycling through the park to work in Tervuren. A group of runners were jogging on the spot, waiting for someone who hadn't turned up yet. The brasserie was closed but a lone tourist was eyeing it wistfully anyway.

Veerle kept close to Kris, who was grim-faced. She was doing her best to maintain a calm exterior but her heart was thumping so hard that she was afraid she might pass out; it felt as though some demented creature were banging on the cage of her ribs. She wanted to hold onto Kris, to clasp his hand in hers, but she was determined not to show weakness, however much she might feel it.

What can he do to us out here? she said to herself. This was not an abandoned building visited under cover of darkness; this was a public place in broad daylight. If a tall burly man appeared here with a crossbow and started shooting at people, there would be at least half a dozen witnesses. The police station was a stone's throw away, for goodness' sake.

Or was that the point of it? To make his move right under the nose of the police in the ultimate act of bravado?

Veerle could remember very clearly the tiny but distinct snapping noise that the crossbow made in the castle that night when De Jager had sent a bolt whizzing towards her, cleaving the air with brutal energy. She imagined hearing that sound again, hearing it too late, the bolt rushing towards them from some unexpected angle and burying itself in a shoulder or back – or worse, an eye. The thought of *that* made her almost nauseous with apprehension. Such a tiny sound it made; such a dreadful impact.

She tried not to think about it. *Look for Fien.* Veerle concentrated on that instead, scanning the scene for any sign of a small child. The only one she could see was a toddler dressed all in blue, made fat by layers of warm clothing. Kris's eye passed over the little boy without a pause.

There were the parked cars, of course. The windscreens

reflected the trees and the wintry-looking sky; it was impossible to see if there was anyone inside. De Jager might be sitting behind the wheel of any one of them – but if so, where was Fien? She knew Kris by sight – if she were in one of the cars she had only to look out and see him. It did not bear thinking about, how one might stop a lively little girl from banging on the window or jumping out of the car to run to someone she recognized.

Kris stopped at the corner between the two streets and Veerle pressed close to him.

'Where is he?' muttered Kris. He spoke in a low voice but there was an edge of urgency to his tone. He knew as well as Veerle what De Jager could do in the space of a single minute, let alone an hour, and yet the minutes were skittering past like a swarm of insects and there was no sign of Fien or her abductor. The waiting, the not knowing, was sending him into a state of feverish restlessness that had infected Veerle too. It was one thing to summon all your courage and make the grand gesture of offering yourself in place of an innocent victim; it was quite another to stand there for long, long minutes waiting to be taken. It felt as bad as standing by the scaffold waiting for your turn to meet the executioner.

The tourist hanging around outside the brasserie departed. The runners waited a little longer for their missing friend, then gave up and set off down Keizerinnedreef, shoulders hunched against the cold, breath steaming. Two cars left the parking area and another two came in. As far as Veerle could see, none of the drivers looked anything like De Jager; he could have concealed his face but not his build. Meanwhile cars were passing up and down Kastanjedreef. The sun was low in the sky and dazzlingly bright; it was very hard to see anything through the windscreens.

'*Verdomme*, I'm going to have to call Jeroen,' said Kris. 'I told him I'd come over. He'll be wondering where the hell I am.'

Veerle looked at him. 'What are you going to say?'

Kris grimaced. 'I don't know.' He had the phone out, in his hand, but he didn't make the call – not yet.

Veerle looked down, biting her lip. She felt slightly sick, wondering whether they had done the right thing coming here alone, instead of calling the police. She thought that Kris was right – if they reported what was going on, it would be a long time before anything was actually *done* – perhaps *too* long. And then there was still the possibility that Fien's disappearance and the email Kris had received were coincidental. In that case they might set a lot of useless hares running when everyone would be better searching for the little girl.

Please God let it be that, she thought. *Let them find her playing in a garden shed or something.*

Another car turned into Keizerinnedreef and continued for some distance, so that it was impossible for Veerle to see the driver when he or she got out. A cyclist went past on Kastanjedreef and Veerle turned her head to watch him go, but he was lean and light-boned, nothing like De Jager.

The air was cold, and Veerle realized that she was trembling, but not entirely from the chill. The strain of waiting for something to happen was almost more than she could bear.

More time slid by. Kris still hadn't made the call but he had the phone in his hand, and suddenly it went off with a shrill note that shocked both of them. Kris put the phone to his ear but his eyes stayed alert, his gaze warily roaming the intersection.

'Yeah. *Jeroen?*'

Kris listened in silence, and suddenly his gaze wasn't patrolling the end of Keizerinnedreef any more; it swung up towards the pale sky. He exhaled slowly, a great long shuddering sigh of relief. 'You found her. Where?'

Veerle wanted to grab his arm, to gasp out her own relief, but she made herself stay still and quiet, straining to hear what was being said. It was useless to try hearing what Jeroen was saying; the connection was crackly anyway and Jeroen was babbling with excitement. She heard Kris start to say, 'And did she say . . .' and then he fell silent again. A few moments later he said, 'What?' in tones of incredulity. Eventually he asked, 'Do you still want me to come?' but the reply was evidently in the negative. Kris ended the call and looked at Veerle. The colour had come into his face and his dark eyes were fever bright.

'They found her.' He put out his arms and pulled Veerle into a tight embrace, pressing his face into her hair. 'Thank God,' he said.

Veerle put back her head and looked up at him. 'Where was she? What happened?'

'They found her on the next street. Jeroen said they'd already looked there – they'd looked all over the place. The first time they checked, she wasn't there, and then Ella tried it again and there she was, sitting on a wall. It's strange because she'd been gone for well over an hour and they'd been up and down the streets around there for nearly all that time.' Kris recollected something. 'We should get away from here,' he said suddenly. 'If they've got Fien back, there's no reason for us to be standing around here. Let's go.'

He began to pull Veerle away from the intersection, and together they broke into a brisk walk, putting as much space between themselves and the meeting place as they possibly could. Kris was striding along so fast that pretty soon Veerle was half out of breath, but she didn't care. The relief was intense – not just the relief of knowing that Fien was safe but the blessed knowledge that they were no longer standing where De Jager had sent them, wondering whether they were in the crosshairs of some invisible weapon.

Instinctively they headed for the town centre, for the streets where it was impossible to be alone because there were shoppers and young mothers wheeling toddlers in pushchairs and deliverymen carrying things into shops and businesses.

'Are we going . . . back?' asked Veerle as she hurried along beside Kris.

'No. Not yet.' There was a grim edge to his voice.

In case we're followed, thought Veerle. The idea chilled her. She couldn't help glancing behind, but she could see nothing untoward, no bulky figure lurking there. Still, it was hard to shake the feeling of being stalked. Kris felt it too. He glanced into a bakery as he passed and then the bookshop, but he didn't duck into either; it would have taken them off the open street but they'd have been enclosed as surely as a lobster in a pot. Trapped.

They kept walking.

'Did Jeroen say anything else?' Veerle asked. 'I mean, I know she's only four, but did Fien say how she got out or anything?'

Kris nodded. 'Apparently she said she'd been for a ride with Sinterklaas.'

'What?' Veerle stared at him. 'Why would she say that?'

'Jeroen says she made it up as an excuse. I mean, she's four – she doesn't know Santa isn't real yet. She says Sinterklaas opened the gate and took her for a ride.'

'In what? A helicopter, like the one that always lands in the park?'

'He didn't say. He said Ella is as mad as hell with her, though.'

'I bet.'

When they had walked almost to the end of the town centre they turned into a side street, doubling back on themselves. A few minutes later when they looked round, the street was deserted. It did not seem possible that they were being followed, so they began to weave their way through the streets, heading back in the direction of the house.

Sinterklaas, thought Veerle. This was November, and the Christmas saint was due to make his annual appearance in Tervuren later in the month; it was not surprising that this event should be uppermost in a four-year-old's mind. *That was probably it. She can't wait to see him, so she made him up.*

Veerle wasn't entirely convinced, though. How had the little girl managed to vanish so completely for an hour or more and then be found in the next street? She wished she could have asked more questions – of Fien herself or the unseen Jeroen, whom Kris sometimes mentioned but Veerle had never met. Perhaps Fien habitually made things up; perhaps this was nothing new. All the same, she felt uneasy.

Supposing someone did *take her away for an hour? Supposing it was a big man – would she tell the difference between fat and jolly and broad and muscular?* That thought was chilling. *No*, Veerle said to herself. *It's not possible. De Jager couldn't pretend to be kind and jolly. He just couldn't. He'd frighten a kid half to death.*

'Kris,' she said aloud, 'do you think someone *did* take Fien, and then brought her back?'

Kris thought about that. 'I don't know,' he said finally. 'She's back, she's fine, and she didn't even seem upset, according to Jeroen. So maybe she was just playing about, and the Sinterklaas thing was a bit of fantasy. But it's a pretty big coincidence, those emails arriving at exactly the time she disappeared.'

Veerle couldn't help herself; she glanced round. The street was empty. She said, 'I don't understand the emails. I mean, why make us go somewhere and then . . . nothing happens?'

Kris looked at her. 'Well, *something* happened. Fien turned up.'

'That doesn't make sense,' said Veerle. They were walking more slowly now, feeling less anxious about being followed. 'Supposing the two things are connected, Fien vanishing and the emails, then wouldn't the whole point of it be to make us go to the place he told us?'

'Yeah. And when we were there, he didn't need Fien any more.'

'But nothing *happened* when we were there. I mean, I know Fien turned up, *that* happened, but nothing happened to us.'

They walked on in silence for a while. They passed out of the town centre and into the residential area that led to the house they had been staying in. They saw a single dog walker, female, diminutive and blonde, accompanied by a golden retriever. Other than that they saw no one on the street. When they approached the house they proceeded more cautiously, but when they were finally inside, the door closed and the code entered to disarm the burglar alarm, they both felt confident that they had not been seen. All the same, Kris took care to lock the front door and shoot all the bolts across.

'Do you want coffee or something?' he asked, and although she wasn't thirsty or hungry at all, Veerle said yes. It was something to do, something homely and reassuring.

They went into the red-and-black kitchen and Kris put the coffee maker on. Veerle looked around. They had cleaned up after themselves pretty well so far, but you could still tell that someone had been using the kitchen. There were smears and drops of moisture and a lone silver teaspoon abandoned on an expanse of black marble worktop. They would have to move on before the owners returned from wherever they had gone, and before they left they'd have to make sure that the house was spotless, with no sign they had ever been here.

Then what?

They could go to another house, Veerle supposed, assuming there was an empty one that Kris knew of. By then the school holiday would have been and gone and she'd be in trouble with the school for not attending. Kris might have been thrown out of his job. And then there was the possibility that De Jager would go for Geert and his family.

That was the only possible meaning of emailing her the photograph.

So we go to the police. Then we'll be in a different kind of trouble.

While the coffee was brewing she and Kris sat opposite each other on the red leather bar stools. Kris put out a hand and touched hers, his fingers warm. Veerle was glad of the reassurance – though it made her feel like crying, which she hated to do. She wondered whether he had taken her hand all those years ago when they had climbed the bell tower of the village church; whether he had helped her up the stone stairs and the wooden ladder. Here they were again, hand in hand, and yet she was afraid that there was a time coming, very soon, when her hand would be torn from his and she would drop into the dark.

The strangely pointless meeting in the park was on both their minds. Veerle could make no sense of it. Whether Fien's temporary disappearance was connected to it or not, why make Kris go to a particular place, seemingly for nothing?

'Maybe it wasn't for nothing,' she said suddenly. She looked at Kris and saw a question in his eyes. 'Look,' she said, 'did you ever reply to the other emails? The first one – you know, with the finger – and the one about the place in Luik?'

'No,' said Kris.

'Maybe that's it,' said Veerle. 'Those Scouts discovered the finger, right? And I bet the police never even checked out the place in Luik. We didn't go there, anyway. So supposing it *is* De Jager sending all this stuff, how does he know we're reading it?'

'He doesn't,' said Kris slowly. 'Unless he was there today, in which case he does know now.'

Veerle shivered. Was that it, and if so, where had De Jager been? Behind the wheel of one of those cars parked on Keizerinnedreef, invisible behind the reflective windscreen, or in one that had drifted past on Kastanjedreef?

'We were there for quite a while,' said Kris. 'Long enough for him to see us, and then drop Fien off in the village again, and Jeroen to ring me.'

'But he didn't follow us or anything,' Veerle pointed out, with more confidence than she felt. *At least I hope not*, she added silently. 'And he didn't try anything.'

'No,' said Kris. 'It would be a bad place to try anything, anyway. Too many people around.'

'But that was where he told us to go,' Veerle pointed out. 'If he'd said the middle of the woods we'd have gone there too.'

'Maybe he didn't think we would. Maybe he chose that place because it's busy. Easy for him to blend in and see if we turned up, and not too threatening for us. If he told us to meet him in the middle of the woods we might have thought better of it.'

They looked at each other.

'But what good has it done him?' objected Veerle. 'So he's seen us. Big deal. He knows we're getting his emails. But now we've gone again and Fien's back with her parents. He isn't much further on than he was before.'

Kris shook his head, his face grim. 'I think he is. He knows he has an open line to us now. And we know what he'll try next if he doesn't get what he wants. He knows where Fien and her family are. He knows your family are in Ghent.' He considered. 'I don't think this is the end of it. I think if he took Fien, he gave her back because he doesn't want a full-scale police hunt at this stage. I think he was just showing us what *might* happen, if . . .'

'If . . .?' repeated Veerle uneasily.

'If we don't do what he says . . . next time.'

40

De Jager reached the house that was not a home while Kris and Veerle were still walking through the streets, glancing behind them with unease.

He parked the anonymous-looking car at the side, where it was not obvious from the road. He stared at it with his flat gaze for a few moments before he went into the house. The car required some thought; if anyone were to go over it with sufficient care, it could cause him a considerable amount of trouble. On the other hand, there was no reason for anyone to do such a thing. The only significant risk was from Kris Verstraeten and Veerle De Keyser, and he intended to eliminate that risk within a span of days so short that it could be numbered in hours.

The means to do so was in his hands now.

He had always believed that Kris Verstraeten was receiving the messages that he sent from Gregory Verbruggen's email address; now he knew it for certain. The first time, things had gone awry by sheer chance. A bunch of Scouts had stumbled across the item he had left before Kris had a chance to look for it – assuming he *would* have looked for it. He hadn't turned up at the place near Luik, in spite of the tempting photograph that had accompanied the second message, and De Jager had wondered whether the messages were reaching him at all. Perhaps Kris had started using a new email address, disassociating himself from the disbanded Koekoeken. Or perhaps he had simply been too wary to respond.

Until now. It seemed that Kris was not to be provoked into action by a figurative gun to his own head, but a gun to someone else's had worked very efficiently. He'd come to the meeting place within the hour. And the girl, Veerle, had come with him.

De Jager had had one long clear view of them as he drove past the spot, the driver of another dull saloon car in a neutral colour, neither expensive nor unusual enough to attract attention. That was all he had needed, and that was just as well, since the situation inside the car had required containment. He could have achieved that instantly by killing his passenger, but he was unwilling to do that. The situation would have escalated and the police would certainly have become involved. Kris Verstraeten might have told them everything he knew, which was probably very little, but maybe enough to be a nuisance. No; better to take that one swift glance and then drive back to the village, where he was able to disgorge his passenger on a quiet street – all safe, no harm done, but the necessary warning delivered.

That one swift glance at Kris and Veerle was preserved in his mind's eye with photographic sharpness. He'd known them both immediately, from the night in the castle.

That night he'd studied Kris's features as they stared up at him from the ID card he'd filched from Kris's inside pocket.

Sealed behind clear plastic like an insect trapped in amber; De Jager had assumed that Kris would soon be just as dead, but he'd been wrong. And the girl, Veerle: he'd had a very good look at her as she leaned over the first-floor banisters, taunting him. There was no possibility of a mistake.

They'd stood out anyway amongst the mindless joggers and aimless tourists who crossed and re-crossed the intersection of Kastanjedreef and Keizerinnedreef. Kris Verstraeten had been all in black, and Veerle De Keyser, though not quite as funereal looking, had also worn mostly dark colours; they might have been a couple carved out of ebony. Even without that, their body language had betrayed them – a language in which a hunter is well versed. There had been a tension about them – an alert watchfulness. They had not been holding hands but had stood so close together that they were almost jostling, like animals backed into a small space. They made a very fine pair – Kris tall and broadshouldered but lean (and probably therefore no match for his own heavily muscled bulk, De Jager judged), Veerle smaller and lighter but athletic, her hair, caught back in a careless knot, almost as dark as Kris's.

A buck and a doe. De Jager would have liked to see them that way, magnificent to look at but with no more individual personality than the russet-coloured stag who snuffs the air suspiciously or the doe who crops grass by his side. *Prey* – to be hunted down and torn apart. The fact that he had become so closely associated with them that he'd had to learn their names – that he had visited their homes, tracking like a bloodhound through their pedestrian little lives – that he had become acquainted with their relatives – all that angered him.

They did not deserve such attention. And the anger fed on itself, because the emotion was a virus with which *they* had infected him. It was the offending eye that he wished to pluck out. He could not wait to exterminate them.

At any rate, he now knew that they were receiving the messages he sent them. The conduit was open; let Kris and Veerle beware of whatever came down it towards them.

41

That afternoon Kris and Veerle spent a long time discussing what to do. To go to the police right away, that was the obvious thing – but what to tell them? *Everything*, said Veerle at first, reasoning that no matter how much trouble it caused them and every other former member of the Koekoeken, it couldn't create any more trouble than it already had: at least two people dead and De Jager on their trail. But by the time she had talked Kris round, Veerle was beginning to lose confidence in the idea herself. She thought about that photograph of Geert and Adam with the Graslei in the background. How many De Keysers were there in the Ghent phone book? What if De Jager got to *De Keyser, Geert* before she and Kris had persuaded the police that they weren't just a pair of time-wasting fantasists? Maybe it would be better to take some other action, although she couldn't think what. Send an email back to Gregory's account? What would they say? She couldn't imagine bargaining with a killer, promising not to report him if he left her and Kris alone. Even if he agreed, she'd be looking over her shoulder for ever, and the death of anyone else De Jager attacked would be on her head.

Then she thought that perhaps they should tell Jeroen

everything, because he and his little family were between the dragon's talons. He had a right to know, so that he could be on his guard. But she and Kris had no actual proof that De Jager had had anything to do with Fien's disappearance at all. Jeroen himself thought she had made up the Sinterklaas story.

The discussion went round and round until it was growing dark outside and Veerle's head was beginning to ache. Then, just as she was opening her mouth to tell Kris that she didn't *know* what they should tell the police and perhaps they should just play it by ear, her mobile phone went off.

Veerle slid the phone out of her pocket and looked at it, seeing with an unpleasant frisson of dread that the caller was Geert De Keyser. This could be nothing good. She was seized with a sudden sick fear that the blow had already fallen; that her father was calling to tell her that this time it was her little brother Adam who had gone missing. When she pressed the green icon to accept the call her fingers were clumsy with nerves.

'Hello, Dad?'

'Veerle?'

To Veerle's relief Geert sounded angry and indignant, not upset.

'Yes,' she said, and waited.

'I'm still at work,' said Geert De Keyser, 'so I'll keep this brief. Anneke just called me. She's very upset.'

'She is?' said Veerle cautiously.

'Veerle, when you moved back to the village I asked you to make a promise. Just one thing. You remember that?'

'Yes,' said Veerle heavily. She remembered that, all right. *I promise I won't see Kris Verstraeten again.*

'I really hope you haven't been attempting to contact him,' Geert went on. 'I didn't make you promise because I want to make you unhappy, Veerle. I asked you to promise because I don't want to see you getting yourself into any more of these . . . situations.'

'Dad—'

'So please tell me the truth – *have* you been trying to contact Kris Verstraeten?'

'No,' said Veerle, closing her eyes and wincing at the half-truth. She hadn't *tried to contact* Kris, that was true, because *he* had contacted *her*, and now they were sitting across a narrow expanse of black marble breakfast bar from each other, with no need to make any kind of *attempt* to reach each other at all. She could have put out a hand and touched his face, or run her fingers through his dishevelled dark hair. She prayed that Geert would not ask anything more penetrating than that, since she really didn't want to have to start telling absolute lies. 'Has something happened?' she asked.

'Yes, it has,' said Geert tersely. 'Anneke called me – at work – to tell me that Kris Verstraeten had called the flat, asking for you. He was rude, and very persistent. Frankly, I want to know that you have nothing to do with this – that you haven't made any attempt to get in touch with him yourself or encouraged him in any way.'

'He called the flat?' repeated Veerle. A terrible suspicion was creeping over her, filling her with numb horror. 'Dad, when did he do that?'

Please let it be weeks ago, before Kris found me. But she

didn't really think it was, not if Anneke had suddenly rung Geert to complain about it today. And she didn't think Kris would be that rude, however provoking Anneke could be.

'Today, about an hour ago,' said Geert. He paused, waiting for Veerle to reply – to justify herself or perhaps admit something. When she didn't say a word, he said, 'Are you still there?'

'Yes,' said Veerle in a choked voice. She couldn't think what else to say.

'So tell me again,' said Geert. 'Have you tried to contact him?'

'No,' said Veerle.

Now it was Geert De Keyser's turn to be silent. Veerle said nothing. Horror had disorientated her, as though the world had suddenly turned on its axis, throwing her about like a rag doll in a tumble dryer. She saw Kris opposite her, telegraphing concern with his dark eyes, but then it was as though she had been swept past him and back into the maelstrom. Fragments of coherent thought came to her – *He didn't hurt Fien . . . He doesn't want Adam, he wants me* – but still she had no idea what to say, how to approach this. It was like an impossible climb, a rock face so sheer and so devoid of holds that you couldn't even get off the ground.

If Geert had hoped that his own silence would allow Veerle to tell him something, he was disappointed. At last she heard him sigh heavily into the receiver. He said, 'Fine. Look, if he does this again Anneke's going to report him to the police. She was really upset.'

'I'm sorry,' whispered Veerle.

'Well,' said her father heavily, 'if he's done this without any encouragement from you, it's not your fault.' He paused. 'I have to go. I'm calling from the office and I have a couple of things to finish before I go home. I'll speak to you later, OK?'

'OK,' said Veerle automatically. Then she started to say, 'Dad—' but Geert De Keyser had already gone.

Veerle put the phone down on the black marble counter. She didn't look up to meet Kris's eyes. She kept looking at the phone, a sleek compact shape sitting there on the reflective surface, inert as a pebble, poisonous as a cyanide capsule.

'Has he rung your dad?' asked Kris, and at first she didn't reply. She just kept on staring dully at the phone, as though her gaze could make it take back what she had just heard.

'Veerle? Has De Jager—'

'Yes,' she snapped. She put her head in her hands, thrusting her fingers into the strands of dark hair that overhung her face. 'Or at least – he's phoned Anneke, and Anneke phoned Dad.' Now she did look up, into Kris's eyes. 'He said he was you, just like when he went to see Mevrouw Willems.'

'Shit.'

'He was rude to Anneke, so she rang Dad to complain.'

'But she's OK?'

'Yeah. Pissed off, but OK. But, Kris, he knows where they are now.'

'Same as he knows where Jeroen and Ella and Fien live.'

They stared at each other.

'Oh shit,' Veerle burst out. 'What are we going to do?'

'Go to the police,' said Kris.

'And if they don't believe us?'

'We have to convince them.'

'That could take for ever! Look what happened last time you went.'

'Well, what else can we do?'

'He could be on his way to Ghent right now, Kris!' Veerle was almost beside herself. 'He could be *in* Ghent, going over to Bijlokevest right this minute.'

'Veerle – Veerle . . .' Kris reached over and clasped one of her hands in both of his. 'Calm down. Let's think about this.'

Veerle looked down at her own dim reflection in the black marble, not wanting him to see the treacherous tears forming in her eyes.

'It's us he wants,' said Kris. 'Not your brother or Fien. Otherwise – when he took Fien . . .' His voice trailed off. Neither of them wanted to contemplate what might have happened if De Jager had taken the little girl out of pure spite or revenge. After a moment he tried again. 'He wants to scare you, right? He was probably rude to your stepmother on purpose so that one of them, her or your dad, would call you up and complain about it. If he wanted them he probably wouldn't have bothered phoning. He'd just have gone round there.'

Veerle drew in her breath sharply at that.

'It was a message,' continued Kris. 'Same as the thing with Fien. He's trying to put pressure on us. Make us crack.'

'Why?' cried Veerle passionately. 'Is he just trying to torture us?'

'No,' said Kris. 'I don't think that's his style. He calls himself the Hunter and that's what he does. He hunts and kills. He doesn't piss about playing mind games for nothing.'

'For what, then?'

'So we do what he tells us, the next time he gets in touch.'

Veerle looked up then and they stared at each other. Into the silence came the irritable buzzing of Veerle's mobile phone.

'Talk of the devil,' said Kris grimly.

42

The email had been sent to both Kris's and Veerle's addresses. It was short and to the point. It contained a GPS reference, a date and a time – nothing more. No threat; there was no need for one. The consequences of not complying had been made perfectly plain.

All the same, it was a while before the full implications of the message sank in. Veerle looked at the date, and it took her a few moments to realize that it was *today*; that De Jager was summoning them to meet him *today*. Since she had visited Mevrouw Willems she had not looked at a newspaper or the television, and the marking of time was beginning to slide away from her. Before it sank in she thought that she still had a day or two, that there was still time to think about it. But no.

Then she looked at the time, and that made no sense, either. It was the middle of the night. As for the co-ordinates, those were just a string of numbers; whatever their significance, they meant no more to her than a random barcode or a stranger's telephone number.

Kris fetched his laptop so that they could check the location together. They stared at the screen.

'Why there?' said Veerle.

'Maybe I should enter the numbers again,' said Kris, but even when he did, the location was the same: a side street in the city of Brussels, in the Saint-Josse-ten-Noode area.

He zoomed in, then zoomed out again, checking the routes that led into and out of the street.

'There has to be something we're not getting,' he said, frowning with concentration. 'This is just a street, right in the middle of the city. It's not like he can sneak up on us here. He can't try any of that crap with the crossbow, either. He couldn't carry one in there without being seen.'

'It'll be dark,' Veerle pointed out.

'I know. But still. It's too risky for him.'

'That won't stop him carrying a knife.'

'It's still a bad place for him, if he wants to get at us. Even if it's late, it's the city. There will be a few people around. And look, it's not even like the street is a dead end. There are half a dozen ways out. He likes to hunt in enclosed spaces, like the Koekoeken house, not out in the open in the middle of a city.'

'Maybe it's going to be like last time,' said Veerle. 'We turn up and nothing happens. He's just trying to scare us. Or he missed us at the last place and he's still checking whether we'll turn up.'

Kris shook his head. 'That doesn't feel right, either. He wouldn't make a mistake like that. Fine, he's made a few false moves, like breaking into the wrong Kris Verstraeten's place, but those were things he couldn't control. If he meant to turn up this morning, then he *did* turn up. We just didn't see him.'

Veerle felt a chill at that, wondering at what precise moment De Jager's lizard-like gaze had slid over her and Kris as they stood there unconscious of his presence.

After a moment she said hesitantly, 'Perhaps he wants to negotiate.'

Kris looked at her. 'You mean . . . talk?'

Veerle grimaced. 'I know it sounds crazy.'

He sighed. 'Everything sounds crazy. Sometimes I think I'm going to wake up and find this was a bad dream. Who knows what De Jager wants? He's not normal.'

'It would sort of make sense,' said Veerle. 'If he's chosen a place where he can't hunt, he must want something else.'

'Maybe he thinks he *can* hunt there. He's killed people in a bunch of fancy expat houses, Veerle; places like this one. Who knows how many times he's done that? And he's got away with it every single time. Maybe the street is just a new challenge. And anyway, if the meeting place was an abandoned building or the middle of the forest, would we really go there?'

There was a silence. Then Veerle said slowly, 'Yes, we would. Because we don't really have a choice now.' She looked at Kris, at the face she loved so well, and her expression was bleak. 'We can't go home, either of us, and if we stay hidden someone else is going to pay. Either Fien or maybe Ella or . . .' She didn't want to come out and say it but in the end she finished, 'Adam. We can't ignore this.'

'We can go to the police. We agreed we were going to do that.'

'Look at the time, Kris. If we were going to the meeting place, we'd have to leave in a couple of hours. If we want to be there *before* the time he gave us, we'd be leaving a lot sooner than that. Maybe even now.' Veerle let out a long shuddering breath. 'He's done this on purpose. There's no time left to think about it. We have to choose. Either we go to the police right now, or we go to the meeting place. But if we go to the police and they don't believe us, or it takes too long, we'll miss the meeting. And then . . .'

She fell silent, looking down at the black marble worktop. It didn't take all that long to get from Tervuren to Ghent – she knew that because she'd made the trip herself a number of times. Take the tram into Brussels, take the train from there, and very soon you'd be getting off at Gent-Sint-Pieters. You could take a tram from there, but actually you could walk to Bijlokevest in about twenty minutes. If you had a car, you could get to the street where Geert and Anneke and Adam lived even more quickly. *If we don't turn up at the meeting, De Jager could be there before morning.*

It's not them he wants, she told herself, but that wasn't working. De Jager might well conclude that Geert or Jeroen had *information* he wanted – and then . . .

Veerle thought of Gregory, and the surge of dread she felt was so strong it was nauseating.

'So we go,' said Kris in a hard voice. 'We have to finish this one way or another.'

When Veerle heard him say that, it was almost a relief. She knew what Geert would say. He had forbidden her to see Kris again because he thought Kris was *trouble* – he thought Kris had a habit of leading his daughter into danger, ignoring the fact that Veerle had a habit of flirting with it herself. This probably *was* crazy, this decision to go and face De Jager, but some part of her was glad they had made it.

This has to stop, she thought. It wasn't possible to continue living her life wondering whether the next day or hour or minute would bring the call saying that the blow had fallen on Kris's niece or Veerle's father or little brother. It would never end, that insinuating fear that hung like a pall over everything. Supposing she and Kris went to the police, and were believed, and they warned everybody? Supposing they even gave Geert and Jeroen and their families protection, which Veerle didn't really think they would, not if they had dismissed Kris as a fantasist once before? De Jager had far more patience than the police; he had been stalking her and Kris for months. A week or two would pass without anything happening and then the police protection would be withdrawn, and it would be back to waiting for De Jager to make his move. She and Kris would have to move back into their homes because they could hardly tell the police they were camping out in some rich expat's villa. They'd spend the rest of their lives jumping every time the doorbell rang. Assuming they lived that long.

Veerle shook the hair out of her eyes and looked at Kris, her gaze level. She was still afraid. De Jager evoked a deep visceral fear in her, something instinctive and animal. She pushed it back, but it was like holding your breath underwater; the longer you did it, the more terrible the urge to give in, to open up and let the darkness in. Still, she made herself look at Kris calmly.

'What are we going to do?'

'We're going to get there before him, if we can,' said Kris. 'We don't want to walk into anything again.'

He meant the night in the castle, Veerle knew. Kris had gone there early, intending that they should hide and simply observe whoever turned up. Veerle had been supposed to arrive with him, but she had been held up, and by the time she got there, Kris was already lying on the dusty floorboards with a crossbow bolt through his shoulder. De Jager had anticipated that they would turn up early, and had been there even earlier himself, lying in wait.

It was a good idea to be there early, very early, to try to prevent the same thing happening again, but she doubted whether it was even possible. De Jager had left them virtually no time on purpose.

'Should we take something?' asked Veerle. 'To defend ourselves?'

'What, like a crossbow?' Kris made a face. 'I'm out of those. And I don't have a gun, either.'

He saw Veerle glance at the knife block that sat an arm's reach away on the black marble work surface.

'We could take one of those – but, you know, if we have to get close enough to fight with knives I think we're already dead. He's done this a lot more often than we have.'

'So what, then?' Veerle waited for Kris to suggest something, to pull a rabbit out of the hat. She couldn't see any way out of this herself. She had the feeling that they were walking right into a trap, that they were being guided inexorably into a space that was narrowing like the neck of a bottle. But for a long time Kris said nothing.

At last he sighed. 'I think we have to negotiate. We only have one thing we can really fight him with, and that's information.' Kris looked at Veerle. 'We know who he is. Kasper Sterckx.'

'But if he *is* Kasper Sterckx,' said Veerle slowly, 'he only has to get rid of us and no one's ever going to know.'

'So we leave the information somewhere somebody's going to find it, somewhere he doesn't know about. This house. If we don't come back from the city tonight, then in ten days or whenever the owners come home, they're going to find it. And they're going to hand it to the police, because even if they don't give a damn what happened to us, they're surely going to care about the fact that we broke into their palace and used their expensive stuff. We leave all the information and we tell De Jager we've done that. That's our leverage.'

'So we bargain with him? We say we're going to offer not to tell anyone who he really is if he agrees to leave us alone?'

'Yes.'

'And then we walk away and *trust* him not to try and get at us later when we're off guard? And let him get on with hunting people in the meantime?'

'Of course not. But we'll have bought some time. Which we don't have right now.'

'And what if we're wrong, and he isn't Kasper Sterckx at all?'

'I think he *is* Kasper Sterckx. It makes more sense than any other explanation. But if not' – Kris grimaced – 'then we're dead.'

43

They worked on it between them. Veerle did most of the writing, but they both signed the letter at the end. Kris had found some writing paper in a ground-floor room that served as an office. Like everything else in the house, it was expensive-looking: thick creamy-white paper sufficiently heavy to be slightly stiff to fold. They noted down everything they could think of: names, dates and addresses as well as their theory about Kasper, the younger brother of Joren Sterckx.

Both of them were conscious of the hands of the clock slowly stealing around the dial. Time was running out. Still, when the letter was finished and Veerle was folding it to slide into the envelope, she changed her mind and took a minute to unfold it and add her own message at the bottom: *Tell my father Geert De Keyser that I love him and I'm sorry. Veerle.* After a moment's hesitation Kris took the pen from her and added, *Jeroen – sorry. Please look after Mum. K.*

Veerle slid the paper into the envelope and sealed it. On the front she wrote: *Police.*

They left the envelope on the black marble worktop. When the owners came home, they might not go into the office right away, not if it were late at night, but they'd have to go into the kitchen if they wanted so much as a glass of water. The white rectangle stood out against the black marble; there was no way anyone could miss it.

Veerle gave it one last glance before she turned away and followed Kris to the front door. She was trying very hard not to calculate the odds of ever returning to retrieve the envelope and clear out of the house. If they didn't, who would pick it up, and when?

Stepping out into the darkness, she felt the evening air cool and slightly damp on her face. It wasn't quite raining, but there was a clinging clamminess in the air that threatened a deluge later. She didn't care; she turned her face towards the sky and breathed deeply, drawing the cool air gratefully into her lungs, savouring it as though it were deliciously perfumed. Everything seemed very clear and sharp, as though each of her senses were like the face of a loved one clustering close about her, saying *Goodbye, goodbye*. She had no idea whether she would be back here by sunrise or never see the sun again.

They set off for the town centre and the tram stop at a brisk pace. The pavements gleamed softly amber under the streetlamps. It was early in the evening and there were buses running, but neither of them wanted to stand and wait. Veerle enjoyed the feeling of striding along. She could have broken into a run; she could have shouted her head off. She slid her hand into Kris's and the touch was electric, as though a charge ran between them. She was tingling all over. She was as afraid as she had ever been, but she felt brilliantly alive, a falling star burning itself out.

When they got to the stop, there was a tram waiting, so they ran the last few metres, not wanting to wait for the next one. As it pulled away, Veerle stared out of the window at the lights of the town receding away from her. The tram rattled and lurched through the dark. A light rain began to fall, and the drops running down the windows turned the distant headlights of cars into yellow streaks. She could feel Kris's shoulder against hers as they sat on the narrow bench seat, and the warmth of his fingers enlaced with hers. It felt as though they'd had so little time together; she wished it had been longer. She thought fleetingly of Bram, too, safe in Ghent, and wondered whether he would ever hear from her again – whether he would ever know what had become of her, or whether he would shoot off into the future on his own trajectory, carrying fading memories of Veerle with him like a souvenir.

The tram ride passed quickly, and then they were disgorged into the metro with its faint ashy smell of grime. By now neither of them had the patience to sit still, so when the train arrived they stood together. At Botanique they got off and left the metro system, heading into the lamplit streets. Soft rain was falling here too. Soon damp tendrils of hair were sticking to Veerle's face. It was not very cold for November, but the rain was discouraging people from using the streets; a few pedestrians hurried past with umbrellas up, but most people seemed to be set on getting indoors as soon as possible. It was not a night for strolling.

After a little while they came to the end of the street that Kris had identified from the GPS co-ordinates. He and Veerle stood on the corner and looked down it. It was lit, with that same amber glow tinting the damp pavement, but several of the lamps were out, leaving pockets of seeping darkness. As far as Veerle could tell, there was nothing *open* on this street, no bars or restaurants. There were a couple of shops at this end with their security shutters down, but after that she couldn't see anything but shuttered windows and doors and garages. There were cars down one side only, the street being too narrow for parking on both sides. Veerle couldn't see anyone around. There were a few trees, frail-looking things in metal cages, dotted along the side of the road, but nothing big enough to hide behind. She felt fairly sure that there was nobody there.

Veerle let out a long breath; she had hardly been aware she was holding it.

Maybe he isn't coming. Maybe it's all just mind games.

Of course she knew that was a faint hope. It was hours before the deadline. But seeing the street so absolutely still and silent, inert as a deserted stage set, was comforting. She didn't see how anyone could enter it without them seeing or hearing him.

At the very far end she could see the lights of passing cars, and twice the black silhouette of a passing pedestrian crossed the intersection. So the road was not so lonely that a person could do *anything* to another person without risk of witnesses. It was the ideal place to meet someone whom you did not trust. *Perhaps*, she thought uneasily, *a little too ideal.*

Veerle heard Kris exhale beside her. She glanced at him. His sharp-boned face had a slight sheen on it from the rain. He seemed unaware of the wet, warily scanning the deserted street.

'Was it exactly here?' asked Veerle. 'Or isn't it that accurate – the reference, I mean?'

'No,' said Kris. 'I guess it would be about halfway down the street.'

Veerle followed his gaze. 'Round about where the lights are out?'

'Yeah. There.'

Kris felt inside his jacket pocket and brought out a small torch. It was something he pretty nearly always carried – that, and a screwdriver. In the Koekoeken days he'd used them when he was exploring empty buildings – or carrying out small acts of maintenance as payment. Veerle had carried those things too. She still had a mini torch on the keyring in her pocket, but the screwdriver with its set of interchangeable heads was back at the house on Kerkstraat, out of her reach.

Kris switched on the torch, and together he and Veerle began to follow the beam up the street. Veerle was aware that her heart rate had speeded up; the pulse was fluttering in her throat like an insect beating itself against glass. The sense of relief she had felt on seeing that the street was deserted had evaporated, to be replaced by an insidious feeling of dread. She did her best to keep it down, but her throat was tightening unpleasantly. She really didn't want to go into that black patch on the empty street.

The torch beam danced across slick yellow pavement, the wheel arches of the parked cars, a corner of kerb bordering the earth in which a sapling had been planted. Kris directed it at the fronts of the buildings they were passing, but mostly it revealed the grimy slats of closed shutters. The doors gave straight onto the street; there wasn't so much as a porch or a pillar behind which anyone could have hidden.

All the same, Veerle couldn't believe that De Jager would yield the advantage. He knew that they had tried to get to the old castle before he did that time; he must be expecting them to try the same thing. Was it possible that he was here somewhere, but that they simply weren't seeing him? Evidently the same idea had occurred to Kris; more than once he stopped walking and shone the torch up the façade of the building they were passing, checking for movement at a darkened window or on a balcony. There was nothing.

They were moving out of range of the last lit streetlamp before the broken one. It was darker here, but looking through the unlit section as through a dark tunnel, they could see the end of the street where headlights were passing. There was nobody on the pavement. There was nothing, in fact, to break the long stretch of slick paving stones except one small fenced-off area that looked as though it had been abandoned by workmen when night fell.

They were almost level with it when Kris said, 'This should be about the right place.'

Veerle shivered. She said, 'Now what?'

'I suppose we look around. I'd like to be sure he isn't sitting in one of these parked cars.' Veerle heard Kris make a hiss of frustration through his teeth. He said, 'This makes no sense at all. There's nowhere to hide here. I thought we'd find one of these places open or something, but there's nothing.'

He began to move about, shining the torch beam between the parked cars, peering into the dark interiors. Veerle stood watch, hugging herself against the cold. Even with a winter jacket on, she felt as though the damp were seeping into her bones. She watched Kris come round the end of one of the cars; this brought him right up against the plastic barrier that the workmen had left behind. They'd fenced off a tiny square in a rather rough-and-ready fashion, the ends of the barrier sections overlapping clumsily.

Kris had to manoeuvre his way round the obstacle. As he did so, he idly played the torch beam over it. After a moment he stopped moving. He stood where he was, holding the torch up so that one side of his face was faintly illuminated as he peered into the fenced-off area. Veerle had not taken her eyes off him, and she was becoming aware that his attention had been held by that particular point for longer than she would have expected. As the seconds slid by, her own interest was piqued. She put up her chin, watching alertly.

At last Kris said, 'Veerle, come and look at this.' He spoke quietly but she could detect the tension in his voice, like a false note played.

Veerle went over to the plastic barrier and looked in. She had expected a ragged earthen hole with a section of exposed pipe in it, something like that, but instead she saw a neat square opening. A manhole. The cover, she saw, was lying on the pavement beside it, which was odd: if the workers had replaced it, they needn't have bothered with the barriers at all. Kris shone the torch beam directly into the hole and she saw how it dropped away into the blackness below. The interior walls were slick with damp, and Veerle detected a distinct and unappealing odour seeping out of it. The torchlight showed the first of a series of metal rungs leading down into the malodorous dark.

Veerle leaned over the hole, trying to see further down – and then she saw what Kris had seen, and she jumped. The shock was like a sharp blow to the chest – an actual physical concussion. All of a sudden her heart rate had accelerated to a flat-out gallop and her lungs simply couldn't draw in enough air.

A face. There was a face down there, hanging in the slimy blackness like a pale lantern, disembodied and graven into stillness.

It took her several seconds to realize that it wasn't a *real* face she was seeing, but a mask. Then she took in the details and it was almost worse. Under other circumstances the mask might even have looked jolly, with its fatly bunched cheeks and smiling lips surrounded by moulded white curls. Now, however, it took on a sinister aspect. Thin words of denial slid unconsciously from Veerle's lips, but she knew what she was seeing.

Sinterklaas. Saint Nicholas, the Christmas saint – the one with whom Fien had taken her mysterious ride – hanging down there in the stinking dark. Veerle realized dimly that this was probably the actual mask he had worn, De Jager, when he lifted the little girl out of her front garden and carried her to the car.

She pressed a hand to her lips, afraid that she was actually going to vomit. It was too much – it was too close. Seeing the mask made it real.

Why? she thought, gazing into the hole with eyes that were wide and horrified, but almost as soon as the question crossed her mind she knew the answer. It was a message from De Jager. Sinterklaas was down there because that was where she and Kris had to go.

44

Veerle didn't cry this time. She didn't scream or shout or throw herself down and beat with her hands on the ground as she had when she received the email with the photograph of Geert and Adam. She stared into the hole from which the clinging smell of drains rose insinuatingly, and her eyes grew wide and glassy with horror. She began to tremble and her mouth worked uselessly, trying to express things too terrible to be said aloud.

All at once she felt unsteady on her feet. She put out her hands and clutched the plastic barrier. Kris was saying her name but she couldn't lift her head to look at him – couldn't reply. She just kept gazing at that hole, at the grinning white face down there in the blackness. It was dark up here, yes, but there were streetlights and the distant cars. Down there it would be pitch black, and the smell of festering detritus would be a thousand times worse; it would pervade everything, thick and greasy and disgusting. That wasn't the worst thing, though. It was the thought of being enclosed in a space that pressed in on you, that narrowed like a throttled throat.

It was the apotheosis of her dreams, she saw that now. The

nights when she had fled from De Jager through an endless series of enclosed places – thorny mazes, houses that were a series of wood-panelled rooms, each smaller than the last, so that by the end she was hauling her cramped limbs with difficulty through chambers that would hardly contain them – all of it had led to this. De Jager wanted her to go down there, into that black and stinking labyrinth, and however much she flinched from it, she was being driven towards it inexorably, like an animal being herded into an abattoir, because if she backed off, the blow would fall on Fien or Geert or Adam instead.

Kris was saying her name again, and now she *did* look at him, pleadingly, across the gaping mouth of the hole. She could see no salvation there. There were no answers in Kris's eyes, no last-minute rescue plan in his expression. He was as horrified as she was. Neither of them had foreseen this. The open street in the middle of the city, that was what they had thought they were getting. Not this.

Thinking about pushing aside the barriers and climbing down into that hole was like running full-tilt into a wall: you couldn't get past it, and the impact was stunning. Veerle tried to get to grips with the idea, with the limited options that were available, and failed; her mind was freewheeling, running mindlessly around a hamster wheel of panic.

She closed her eyes for a few moments, breathing deeply and trying to will herself into a state of calm. It hardly helped; even when she shut out the sight of that gaping black opening, she could still feel the cool damp air, and she could still *smell* it, that dank and rotten stink.

Veerle opened her eyes again and Kris was beside her. He

put his arms around her and hugged her to him fiercely. They held each other for a while, saying nothing. The sound of traffic passing on the busier street at the end of this one was like distant surf. Veerle pushed her face against the warm skin of Kris's neck and he pressed his lips against her dark hair.

After a while he said, 'You don't have to go down there, Veerle.' He spoke firmly and composedly. 'Calm down. You don't have to do it.' He touched her hair with his hand, caressingly. 'You don't have to,' he repeated.

Oh, thank God, thought Veerle, and suddenly she was weak with relief. The guillotine blade had been arrested in its descent; the last-minute reprieve had arrived when she had her foot on the very step of the scaffold. *Thank God, thank God.* Kris spoke with such conviction that she *knew* he had a plan – some way out of this trap – anything rather than descend into that black hole in the ground.

He *did* have a plan. Very gently he began to disentangle himself from Veerle. He pushed back a damp tendril of hair from her forehead, and then he leaned in and kissed her there, once. It was the way he did that – kissing her on the temple as though she were a child being told to behave while he was away – that made the alarm bells begin to ring again in Veerle's mind. Still she didn't want to consider what it meant – she wanted to push the thought away – until she saw Kris begin to move aside one of the plastic barriers at the entrance to the sewers. There was determination in the way he did it, and he wasn't looking at Veerle.

Veerle said, 'What are you doing?' and when he didn't reply, she said, more loudly, 'Kris, what are you doing?'

He did pause then, and looked at her. 'I'm going to settle this.'

Veerle's hands made fists in the empty air. 'You said we didn't have to go down there. You said we didn't have to do it!'

'I said, *you* don't have to go down there, Veerle. And you don't.'

Kris was circling the hole now, gauging the best way of lowering himself into it.

'Kris – don't . . .' Veerle stepped forward, frantic to stop this before it went any further. 'Don't go down there.'

'I have to.'

'Can't we just think about this for a minute?'

'No.'

'Why not?'

'If I think about it, I'll never do it. And I have to.'

'Then . . .'

Veerle thought about it, she really did, for one split second that felt very much longer – it felt like her idea of hell, a single moment of exquisite agony that lasted for eternity. Then she made her decision, and it was as icily refreshing and terrifying as launching yourself off a cliff to swan-dive into the sea below.

'. . . I'm coming with you.'

Kris, his feet on the topmost rungs now, looked at her grimly, the side of his face outlined by the torch he still held in one hand. 'You don't have to. I told you.'

Veerle took a deep breath. 'You think I'm letting you go down there on your own?'

'Yes,' he said firmly.

'No way,' said Veerle, and the words surprised her; they came out sounding strong and emphatic. She shook her head. 'No way on earth, Kris. Either nobody goes – or we both do.'

She meant it too. The thought of lowering herself into that dark and filthy and narrow space was appalling, but she knew that letting Kris do it by himself would be worse. She couldn't do it. She couldn't stand here in the half-lit street in the rain and watch him disappear into the darkness below; then stand and wait – wait for long enough to know that he was probably never coming back.

Kris was saying something, still trying to persuade her that she didn't have to do it, but Veerle was already shoving her way past the barrier. She stood over the hole and looked down at Kris, and although he could not have seen her face clearly unless he'd shone the light at it, the determination in her movements was plain.

'All right,' he said at last in a low voice. 'Look, I don't know what's down here. It could be anything. He might be there already. So come down slowly and wait for me to tell you it's safe.'

Veerle didn't bother pointing out that it wouldn't be safe, no matter what Kris did or didn't see. She simply said, 'OK,' with more confidence than she felt. Her heart was thudding almost painfully, and she felt lightheaded, high on barely suppressed fear.

Kris began to descend into the hole, moving with steady caution. He stopped once or twice and listened for any sounds indicating that there was someone waiting below. Once he let go of the rung with one hand and shone the torch into the darkness. There was nothing to be seen, nothing to hear except the occasional sound of water dripping into some unspeakable liquid below.

Veerle swung herself onto the first of the rungs. She tried to tell herself that the evil smell rising from the hole was becoming less noxious, that she was becoming used to it. Her shoulder brushed the wall of the hole, and that was un-nerving too because it reminded her of how narrow this space was, how little room there was to manoeuvre. She was keeping the desire to bolt back out of it very securely tamped down, but that didn't stop a swarm of tiny fears coming in to attack her, like a cloud of biting insects.

Veerle wasn't an expert on sewers – who was? – but she did recall a bit about them from a school visit to the Musée des Égouts, the sewer museum in Anderlecht. There'd been a few lively kids in the class, and the guide had evidently decided to warn them against exploring on their own. He'd told them that the sewerage system was one of the most hostile places you could possibly be. It wasn't just dark and mostly narrow and revoltingly smelly, making it an unpleasant environment for human beings; it was actually dangerous, because it wasn't designed for living people at all. It wasn't only the danger of the water level rising until it overwhelmed and drowned you. There could be pockets of poisonous gas down there. There were living things too: cockroaches, spiders and rats. And if you decided that you had had enough, that you wanted to get out by the nearest possible exit, then you probably couldn't: it was a lot harder to push up a manhole cover from underneath than it was to lever it up from above. You'd be trapped.

Trapped.

The effort required to suppress the fears that threatened to swamp her was so great that Veerle was almost rigid with tension. The fingers that grasped the metal rungs were hooked into claws. She was aware that the metal felt slimy in places, and forced herself not to think about that, either – about what the moisture might be.

Rats, she said to herself as she descended. *They're only mammals, like cats and dogs.*

Below her, Kris switched off the torch so that he could tell whether there was any other light source down there. Without its beam, blackness closed in. He waited for a little while in silence, listening, and Veerle waited above him on the ladder.

At first she heard Kris's breath shuddering in and out. He was breathing heavily, as she was; he was probably just as afraid as her, Veerle realized. After a few moments he got it under control sufficiently to hold his breath for a few seconds while he listened for the tiniest sound.

Drips of water falling into the wet at the bottom of the tunnel. That was all. Even the ambiguous sound of some sewer creature scurrying away into the dark might have been enough to make them think twice about descending any further, but Veerle couldn't hear so much as a beetle scuttling across the wall. If De Jager were waiting at the bottom of the ladder, he had stopped breathing altogether – or so she told herself.

Kris evidently thought so too, because after a while he switched the torch back on again and climbed down onto the wet floor of the sewer. He swung the light swiftly this way and that, raking both sides of the tunnel with its beams. Nothing moved.

He looked up. 'Veerle? You can come down.'

Veerle climbed down as carefully as she could. As soon as her boot touched the bottom of the tunnel, she found that she was standing in a few centimetres of water.

Rain, she told herself nervously, swallowing disgust, and then she thought about what would happen if the light drizzle above – barely more than damp air at present – were to turn into an actual downpour. *This is insane. We should climb back up and get the hell out of here.* But they'd had that discussion already. Veerle tried not to think about rain falling; it was just one more hazard to worry about and she was already overburdened.

'What now?' she whispered.

Kris had been raking the walls of the tunnel with the torch beam, and now he trained it on one place. 'Look.'

Veerle turned. There was something attached to the wall – at first she thought it was a cable of some kind, but looking more closely, she saw that it was a thin nylon cord. One end had been knotted around one of the metal rungs they had climbed down, close to the wall where it didn't interfere with your grip on the rung. The other ran along the tunnel wall, as far as the beam of light could reach, and vanished into the dark. Veerle didn't think it was standard equipment for sewers.

De Jager, she thought.

'At least we won't get lost,' commented Kris grimly. He reached out and rolled the cord between his fingers. He tightened his hold, taking a handful of the cord as though he meant to tug on it, but then he changed his mind abruptly and relaxed his grip. No sense in pulling on the line, not when you didn't know what kind of fish you might be reeling in on the other end.

He glanced at Veerle. 'Have you got a torch?'

'Yes.' Veerle began feeling for her keyring, but he shook his head.

'Save it. No point in using up both sets of batteries at once.' Kris had begun to turn away, looking down the tunnel, but he changed his mind. 'Look, Veerle, if this goes wrong . . .' He hesitated. 'If I can't make him talk to us, or if something happens to me, just go, OK? You have your own light. Get out if you can.'

There was nothing she could say to that. Veerle knew she wouldn't leave him; she knew her chances of getting out of here alone if she did were nearly zero anyway.

She waited for Kris to start moving down the tunnel, head bent, and when he did she followed him, doing her best to tread carefully. Noise was not good: it gave their position away and prevented them from hearing anything else; but not only that – the thought of any of the stinking fluid underfoot splashing up and running down inside her boots was appalling. She tried to hold her nose for a bit, but then she thought about the slick wet on the metal rungs and took her hand away from her face.

The tunnel was a strange shape. It was neither round nor square; it was more an inverted pear shape. The lower part was narrow and slightly rounded. With a tiny amount of standing water in it, it could be negotiated with care, but Veerle wondered how much rain would have to fall, how high the water level would have to be, before it became very difficult. Impossible, even. She remembered the damp air above, the light drizzle that had been enough to make her hair stick to her face. Veerle couldn't remember ever checking the weather forecast in her entire life – it was the sort of thing middle-aged people like Geert did. Now she wished she knew what was coming overnight.

They trudged on, and after a while Veerle realized that the stench had become bearable; she had become used to it.

I probably stink, though.

She imagined herself getting onto the tram home – the revolted looks people would give her – and an unstable laugh came bubbling up, then died before she gave voice to it. She probably wouldn't be taking the tram home, or anywhere.

The tunnel took several turns, so that sometimes Kris couldn't see very far ahead; then he would stop and listen again. Now there were not just occasional dripping sounds; there was a small but persistent trickling. It was impossible to say whether that was the sound of more rainwater flowing into the system, or simply the normal flow for this part of the sewers.

Veerle wondered how far they had come, but she had no idea about that, either. Distance was hard to measure when dim light and cramped conditions made progress difficult. It probably felt further than it was. Without the nylon cord they might not have tackled it; they were passing the openings to other tunnels and it was pretty clear that without a guide you'd never find your way back to the open manhole again.

As they progressed, she heard a faint and distant rumble, like the sound of an avalanche miles away; she supposed it was a train passing along the nearby metro line. They paused to listen, in case the sound masked anything in the sewer ahead of them, and when it had died away they went on.

At last Kris came to a halt, and pressed himself as close to the side of the tunnel as he could without actually coming into contact with the wall, so that Veerle could see what he was doing.

Up ahead, the pear-shaped section ended, opening out into what appeared to be a larger tunnel. The faint sound of running water could be heard; clearly this was a bigger conduit, with a greater volume running through it. And there was light – faint, but light nonetheless.

He's there, thought Veerle, and the adrenalin kick was like an electric shock. She was not sure what made her and Kris start moving forward again – perhaps it was no more than the desire to get the worst over and done with. Her legs felt oddly rubbery underneath her, as though she were staggering the last few metres of a marathon.

They reached the end of the tunnel and saw that the new one was indeed wider and more modern. There was a smooth walkway beside it and a rectangular channel below, with opaque dark water flowing through it. Before they had time to put their heads round the corner to peer cautiously at the source of the light, a voice said, 'Come out.'

Veerle had heard that voice before. It had told her with arrogant confidence, '*You won't do that*,' when she had threatened to throw a lighted match into the petrol that spread like a stinking lake over the floor of the old castle that night. It had said, '*You won't do it, because you're trapped up there. If this floor burns, you burn too. And so does Kris.*' She had screamed back her defiance at that, and the only other sound she had heard coming from his throat that night was the scream as the fire took him – or so she had thought. He had intended to let the knife he carried do the talking – he had tried to carve his intentions into Veerle's flesh, and he had come so close to achieving his aim that sometimes she could barely believe he hadn't done it.

Now he spoke again, more forcefully.

'Come out,' said De Jager.

45

Kris called out, 'We want to talk to you.'

There was a short silence. Veerle looked at the light that was coming from the tunnel where De Jager stood. It did not so much as flicker. She hoped this meant that he had not moved – that he was not inching his way silently towards them, armed with . . . what?

More than anything she dreaded hearing that sound again, the brittle snap of the crossbow firing a split second before the carbon bolt buried itself in its target. But surely he couldn't bring anything like that down here, and along that cramped tunnel?

Then she thought about the knife, that great gleaming triangular blade, and her stomach roiled with a cold and greasy fear.

'Come out,' repeated De Jager in that same tone, emphatic but devoid of emotion. There was a deadness in his voice that was chilling. There was not the slightest hint of human warmth you could work on, like the mortar between bricks that may be loosened with the point of a chisel. It was like a flat impregnable wall, forbidding as a castle keep.

'Will you talk?' called Kris. Veerle could hear his breathing when he was not calling out. It was rapid, as though he had been sprinting.

There was another brief silence, and then: 'Is the girl there?'

'Yes,' shouted Veerle.

'Then come out, both of you, if you want to talk.'

Veerle saw Kris put his head down for a moment, thinking. Then he called out, 'I'll come first. If you try anything, she's out of here.'

With careful deliberation he approached the opening that led into the larger tunnel. He put out his left hand. There was no brittle *snap*, no grunt as De Jager launched himself forward. Nothing. Kris leaned over and looked cautiously round the corner, then stepped out onto the concrete walkway. He didn't look at Veerle. There was a stealthiness to his movements, as though he was afraid that to move too abruptly might set off some catastrophe.

'And the girl,' said the dead voice.

'Not while you're pointing that thing,' said Kris coldly.

Shit, thought Veerle. She was trying to force down her fears, but it was like trying to prevent an angry swarm of wasps bursting out of a disturbed nest. The only thing that stopped her from grabbing Kris by the arm and dragging him bodily back into the feeble shelter of the tunnel was the knowledge that De Jager would surely react by firing whatever he was holding.

After a moment she saw Kris relax infinitesimally. Then De Jager said, 'Now the girl.'

Veerle approached the end of the tunnel. She did her best to peer round the corner, then stepped out slowly and cautiously. Nothing happened.

The light was behind him. De Jager was silhouetted against the bright glow of a halogen bulb, so that his face could not be seen clearly. There was no mistaking that hulking shape, though. There was something monolithic about De Jager. Other people moved subtly – they shifted their weight from one foot to the other, or cocked their head. De Jager just *was*. He was something human-shaped but seemingly made of stone, like an Easter Island statue.

Veerle was so far into fear now that she had almost come out the other side. She felt like an astronaut whose spaceship has been breached, who finds herself in space without a suit and knows that she has perhaps a minute of life at the most. No point in fighting the inevitable; simply marvel at how long sixty seconds can last when they are all you have left.

She looked at De Jager and saw that the silhouette of his right hand terminated in a shape she recognized, but small. If she had known anything about weaponry she might have identified it as a pistol crossbow. Veerle looked at it and saw slow death, Saint Sebastian style, half a dozen arrows sticking out of the victim's body. There was a cold tight feeling at the back of her throat as she imagined that arm swinging up, the trigger finger tightening, that sharp hard little snap. She didn't think the fact that the thing was pointing at the floor at present would stop De Jager shooting her or Kris, not for more than about two seconds. She wondered why he hadn't done it already.

'Talk,' said De Jager, and the hand that held the crossbow twitched.

'We wan—' began Kris, but De Jager cut him off.

'Not you. Her. Veerle. Talk.'

Veerle opened her mouth, and for a couple of seconds nothing came out at all. Her mouth was dry; her tongue felt like a dusty stone. That cold tight feeling in her throat threatened to choke her. When at last she managed to force words out, it was without thought of finesse and persuasion. It was as though she had vomited the words up.

'We know who you are,' she blurted out, and just that was enough. Speaking the words out loud steadied her, as though she had thrown up and rid herself of a nauseating toxin. She kept her eyes on the crossbow but now the words came readily.

'When I was seven there was a terrible murder in our village,' she said. 'A boy. Karel Adriaensen. He was hunted down and killed. And when he was dead, people in the village saw someone come walking in with Karel in his arms, and blood down his front, and they knew he must be the one who did it. His name was Joren Sterckx, and I saw him. So did Kris. We went up into the bell tower because it was Silent Saturday, and we wanted to see if the bells really had flown away. We looked down and we saw Joren Sterckx with the dead boy in his arms.'

Veerle was trembling, but now she could not stop the words; they came pouring out in a torrent.

'Joren Sterckx went to prison,' she said. 'And he died in there, of cancer.

'But something strange happened. Ten years later, Kris and I were part of a group who explored empty buildings. It was supposed to be an adventure, only people started disappearing. So we left a message for the person who was doing it. We arranged to meet him in a derelict castle. And when I saw him, I *recognized* him. I called him by name. *Joren Sterckx*. Only Joren Sterckx was dead . . .'

Still De Jager said nothing. The hand with the crossbow in it still pointed at the floor.

Veerle went on, 'We've done some research of our own since then, Kris and I. We found out that Joren Sterckx had a younger brother. The younger brother – he liked to hurt things. He tortured animals to death.

'I don't think it was Joren who hunted down Karel Adriaensen. You see, Joren was already sick with cancer – and if he took the blame, his parents didn't lose both sons.

'So it wasn't Joren Sterckx I saw that night in the castle. It was his brother, and . . .'

Veerle took a deep breath. 'He's you. You are Kasper Sterckx.'

Silence. What had she expected – that he would congratulate her? Veerle thought she saw De Jager's right hand move, that it was about to begin the upward swing that would bring her or Kris into range of the crossbow.

She blurted out, 'If something happens to us, the police will know—'

'We left a letter,' Kris cut in. 'It has everything in it, and it's somewhere you can't find it. If we don't go back to get it, then in a very few days the police will have it. They'll know who you are.' He spoke with increasing confidence. 'So this is the deal we want to make with you. You back off and let us walk out of here, and we'll go back and destroy the letter. We all walk away and forget we ever saw each other. We agree never to tell anyone what we know, and you promise to stop hunting us.'

Again that silence, as De Jager considered accepting their offer or rejecting it, or simply savoured the experience of prolonging their suspense. In the light of the halogen bulb, vapour swirled around his dark bulk. He looked like a brazen idol of the ancient god Moloch, devourer of children, from whose mouth came smoke and steam; he looked like no one to whom the concept of mercy was known.

At last he spoke.

'Kasper Sterckx is dead. I *was* him, you are correct, but now I am De Jager, the Hunter. I do not believe that you have left a letter . . .'

He ploughed on through their protestations with the brutal ease of a tank mowing down foot soldiers.

'. . . but it makes no difference. Kasper Sterckx no longer exists. There is no one for the police to find.

'You have told me your proposal. Now I will tell you mine. I offer you a choice. You cannot both escape.' Now the crossbow came up with a steady deliberation that made Veerle's stomach turn over sickeningly. 'So. You can try to run, and I will hunt you both, with this, and . . . this.' His left hand disappeared into his clothing and emerged with a blade in it, a great gleaming triangle. 'Or . . . one of you can survive. And here is how. One of you will kill the other.'

'*What?*' said Kris with horrified incredulity. He made a movement, as if to step forward, or perhaps to step in front of Veerle, but the crossbow swung round towards him and he froze.

'You kill her,' said De Jager in that flat dead voice which was like the dull ring of stone on metal, 'or she kills you. Whoever kills the other lives. That is my offer.'

Veerle stared at him, and all the air seemed to have been sucked from her lungs. She couldn't breathe. She tried to say *No*, but although her lips shaped the words, no sound came out. The pressure in her chest was like an actual pain.

De Jager was holding up the knife, the blade gleaming in the light from the halogen lamp. 'Which of you wants to live? You, Kris Verstraeten? Do you want to live enough to kill her?'

The blade glittered as he turned it this way and that.

'You could do it easily.'

Now something *was* creeping into that dispassionate tone: a persuasive, gloating note.

'Or you, Veerle De Keyser? He's taller than you, but you're fast. You're agile. You can take him down, if you want to badly enough.'

'Fuck you,' Veerle tried to say, but the words dissolved to a whisper in her mouth. The light sparking off the blade was mesmeric. She felt as though it had already passed through her limbs, hamstringing her. She could have fallen to the floor. Only the fear of provoking De Jager into striking kept her on her feet.

'Come on,' said De Jager, and the gloating in his voice was audible. 'One of you – or both. Isn't it better that one of you lives?'

'This is shit,' Kris burst out, his hands balling into fists. 'You think we're stupid? You'd kill us both anyway. Because if either of us gets out we're going straight to the police.'

'No you won't. If you went to the police you'd have to tell them you killed your girlfriend yourself. Are you going to do that, Kris?' De Jager shook his head slowly. 'I don't think so. You're going to put it behind you and walk away.' He hefted the knife in his hand. 'A few minutes' work that you're going to want to forget, Kris. And then the rest of your life to live.' The blade turned over, glittering. 'Or you, Veerle. You could be the one to walk out of here, all alone.'

De Jager looked from one to the other. 'A minute to decide. And if neither of you steps forward, I shoot one of you. The other can try running, but it will not be for long.'

There was silence then, silence that stretched out, taut and deadly as a tripwire.

One of you will kill the other.

It was there in front of Veerle, like a big red-and-white STOP sign. She couldn't think about what De Jager was suggesting – couldn't evaluate it as a real possibility. The knife in his hand was enormous – she would have used it with caution even in a kitchen. The idea of taking the handle of that great blade in her fist and attacking someone with it – hacking and slashing – was so terrible that when she looked into her imagination for it, she came up with a blank space. She knew Kris wouldn't think about it for an instant, either. He'd stepped between her and Death that time on the rooftop in Ghent. She knew he'd die for her, that he'd die rather than hurt her.

So she was completely unprepared when Kris looked levelly at De Jager and said, 'I'll do it.'

46

Veerle hears Kris say *I'll do it,* and for a moment she isn't shocked, she isn't afraid – she just doesn't process what he has said because it simply isn't *possible.* The words seem to tumble down a deep dark well inside her, turning over and over as they fall, echoing more faintly as they plummet away from her until the final and sudden impact, which is as brutal as a slap in the face. She realizes what he has said.

Veerle stares at Kris and her eyes widen. She is open-mouthed, shock spilling across her face like a bright stain. For a moment she forgets to breathe. Then she sucks in air in a great sobbing gasp and screams at him.

'*Kris – what are you doing?*'

She keeps screaming his name. She wants him to look directly at her, to show by the expression on his face that he didn't mean what he just said. He *can't* mean it. He won't kill her to save his own skin.

But Kris isn't looking at her. They're so close that she could reach out and touch him, but a chasm has opened between them. Kris won't catch her eye and he isn't even looking at De Jager. His face is turned aside.

Veerle sees shame in that posture. She wouldn't have said

what he has just said. She would have taken her chances – died beside him. Kris wants to live at any cost.

She sees determination too. He isn't going to look at her because if he does that, he will be tempted back into feeling for her. If he doesn't look, he can distance himself. He can step into De Jager's universe. Then Veerle becomes less than human. She becomes prey, a running thing to be cut down.

Veerle knows all this instinctively. There is no time to analyse what has happened. She simply sees that what was one against two has become two against one.

Still she doesn't want to believe it. In the scorched landscape of her mind, hope blooms. Kris is bluffing. He *must* be bluffing.

She looks at him. She calls him by name: *Kris, Kris.* He only has to look her way once. If she sees the message in his eyes, if she knows this is a ruse, she can face anything. She calls again. 'Kris!'

He doesn't react. There's no sign that he's even heard her. Veerle might as well be screaming at him from the other side of soundproof glass. She can't understand it. For a moment she wonders whether she has gone completely insane and she imagined shouting his name. Then she cries out again, and this time she tries to grab his arm, to shake him into reacting.

Kris shoves her away with such force that she slams into the wall of the tunnel and the breath goes out of her. She stumbles and her hands slide uselessly across stone slimy with unspeakable wet that runs down it like rank perspiration.

'Shut up,' he snarls, and Veerle has one glimpse of his face, set into a grotesque mask of ferocity. She hardly recognizes him. She is bewildered and outraged. She staggers back, strands of dark hair hanging over her face, her breathing ragged, dimly aware of a dull pain where her shoulder connected with the wall.

She says, 'Kris, don't do this.'

Her voice is still strong. She isn't pleading yet. She is telling him not to do it. This is still Kris, after all. She has known him since they were both children, she a little pale-faced girl with her hair pulled into two plaits, and he a sharp-faced boy with a shock of hair as dark as her own. They have spent the night together; she has laid her cheek on his bare chest and listened to his heart beating. She has to get through the desperate need for self-preservation with which he has armoured himself, and make him stand with her again.

'Kris,' she says, and although she hesitates to touch him again, she tries to get between him and De Jager, daring even the threat of the crossbow at her back, just so that she can look into his face.

'I said, *shut up.*'

This time Kris doesn't just shove her. He takes her shoulders with both hands and slams her into the wall.

Veerle begins to fight him. It goes against the grain to go for him, someone she loves, trying to hurt, but she has no choice now, any more than she could stop herself clawing her way towards the surface of the water if she were drowning. She twists in his grip, kicking out with her right leg, trying to wrest her arm free so that she can aim a punch at him. Kris parries the blow easily, and then Veerle loses it altogether and flings herself at him, trying to scratch and bite. She doesn't care that this is exactly what De Jager wants, that he is standing watching this display with undoubted pleasure, though his expression is still hidden in shadow. She has some idea of forcing Kris over the edge of the walkway and into the filthy water below, and she puts such desperate energy into the attempt that she almost succeeds. Kris steps back and his heel is a centimetre from the edge.

Veerle batters at him, sobbing, and then suddenly her head is wrenched back so hard that she stops trying to do anything except go with it, to stop the instant pain as her hair is almost ripped out by the roots.

Kris has his fist in it, twisting it. Veerle screams, her hands flailing the air. Then she hears something that makes the terror inside her explode like a bomb.

Kris says, 'Give me the knife.'

She thought she had put everything she had into fighting before, but now she becomes an animal. The pain in her scalp when she tries to pull herself out of Kris's grip doesn't stop her. She screams and bucks, tearing at his face with her nails. She would gouge his eyes if she could. Panic has given her the strength that allows people to lift entire cars off loved ones after an accident. She no longer cares if she hurts herself, so long as she gets away. Kris holds her with great difficulty.

'Give me the fucking knife!' he shouts hoarsely.

'No,' says De Jager.

The word falls on them like the tolling of a bell, penetrating even Veerle's fog of panic. Reprieve? No. De Jager is too cautious to risk his own neck by coming in close to hand over the knife. It could too easily be turned against him, and that is not part of the plan. Instead he puts it down on the concrete walkway and steps back, levelling the crossbow at Kris.

'Come and get it.'

Kris hesitates for a moment, his fist still entwined in Veerle's dark hair. Perhaps he is considering the risks of coming within close range of the crossbow. Small though it is compared to the one De Jager used that night at the castle, one of those bolts could still cause horrific damage, especially at close quarters – through the eye socket, for example.

Then his excruciating grip on Veerle's hair relaxes and he lets go of her. Disoriented, Veerle swings at him and meets only empty air. She screams at him, calling him the worst names she can think of, but after that she doesn't waste any more time. Kris is going for the knife, and once he has it in his hand she doesn't want to think about what is going to happen.

Veerle lunges towards the black opening that leads back into the tunnel shaped like an inverted pear. A two-second start without a light in her hand and no time to fumble for her torch is not much but it's all she has – she'll take it.

But water is running freely out of the opening now. It's not deep – not yet – but it is running fast enough to bring with it the slimy detritus of the tunnel. Veerle's boot slides, her arms wheel in the air, and then she goes down like a felled tree, down into the stinking mess. There is a crack as the torch in her pocket splinters into fragments underneath her. Her fingers, clutching like claws, sink into something gelatinous and unspeakable. Veerle fights for purchase, trying to lever herself up out of the filthy muck, and then she looks over the edge of the walkway and screams.

She sees now what she did not see before, because she looked left when she came out of the tunnel, not right. Down in the water is a body, half submerged – the body of Maxim, although Veerle doesn't know that. He has been in the water for several days, but even she can tell that it isn't just the water that has done this damage. Bone is showing, and teeth gleam whitely through the ruined flesh. The thing lists in the water, because it no longer has even the basic symmetry of the human body. An arm has gone altogether. Fluids spread from the carcass in a murky cloud, tainting the already filthy water.

Kris stands behind her, the knife in his hand now, and for long moments he does nothing except stare at what is left of Maxim. He seems mesmerized. An oath drops from his mouth like a toad, almost unnoticed.

De Jager's harsh voice saws through the rank air like the serrated edge of a knife. He says, 'Do that to *her*, Kris. Make *her* like that.'

His voice is commanding, and it holds a threat. *The crossbow is here waiting, and unless you do it, unless you make the girl who is shivering in front of you into a thing like the one in the water, a bolt will shoot out of it and bury itself in your neck or your eye.*

Veerle reacts first. She pushes herself up, mindless of the filth under her hands, and lunges for the tunnel opening. It is as black as death in there but she doesn't care. She would burrow into the earth itself to escape. Water splashes under her boots and she struggles to keep her feet. The floor of the tunnel is slightly curved, and slippery with things she does not want to picture. Maxim's ruined head fills her mind's eye.

Make her like that, De Jager said.

Light illuminates the passage ahead of her. Kris is in the mouth of the tunnel, torch in one hand, knife in the other.

Veerle throws a long shadow, and beyond that the tunnel is a faint grey outline fading to black where the beam fails to reach. Water is flowing down it, more than before. She hears it, the trickling, running sound of distant drains. The rain is still falling.

Something comes down the tunnel towards her, a tiny shape moving rapidly on the water. A rat, swimming on the filthy tide, its fur in wet spikes, black eyes intent.

Veerle doesn't bother to scream. She doesn't care about the rat, about a thousand fleeing rats, as long as she can keep out of range of the knife. She staggers onwards, heedless of the stinking water soaking the legs of her jeans and seeping into her boots, desperate to keep ahead of the coming light.

Kris roars like a berserker, driving her on. The dim grey tunnel ahead of Veerle flickers as the torch beam moves. She isn't going fast enough – the floor is too slippery, the water at her ankles hampers her. She doesn't know what she will do if she gets far enough ahead to outrun the light. One false turn in these tunnels and she will die slowly in the freezing dark instead of quickly and painfully.

She hears De Jager's voice in the tunnel behind them now, booming like a cannon. He wants to see it, of course – the kill. He wants to see Kris carve the life out of Veerle. He wants to see Veerle's face before it is obliterated – as she sees what love has turned to, as Kris tries to buy his own life by taking hers.

Veerle has one advantage. She is smaller than the others, but strong and agile. She is a climber, after all. She can move through the tunnels more easily than De Jager, whose bulk almost fills the width of one, whose height requires him to stoop.

Veerle knows that Kris is gaining on her in spite of this. Perhaps if she can draw him far enough ahead of De Jager she can plead with him. If De Jager is at his shoulder urging him on, aiming a carbon bolt at his head, she hasn't a chance. De Jager won't be satisfied with anything less than slow and bloody agony. With Kris alone she might stand a chance.

Please don't do it, Kris. You have the knife. Let's fight him.

Or even: *Please – make it quick.*

That idea flashes through Veerle's head, and she thinks she may vomit. The tunnel curves round a corner, and as she follows it, she stumbles and then slips. She falls to her knees in the water that is now flowing so fast that she can feel it gushing around her hands. Rain. Still rain. If it continues, sooner or later she will be unable to make any more progress against it. She will be washed back towards Kris and De Jager.

It is harder to stand up this time, but somehow she manages it. Her right knee flares with pain; she has banged it in the fall. She limps on anyway, forcing herself into a half-run.

She thinks that De Jager *has* fallen behind them. His voice still booms through the tunnel but it seems to her that it has a more distant, echoing quality. Hope, that irrepressible emotion, flares suddenly and painfully. Maybe she can get away. Maybe she can outrun them both. *There* is the cord running along the tunnel, almost in the water; she could follow that with her hands, even in the pitch dark, if she could only get away from the others. That is how she thinks of them now, as a pair, as separate from her. The enemy.

Veerle rounds another bend, and here there is the mouth of a second tunnel emptying into this one. A wash of filthy water comes down it, swilling into the stream already running over Veerle's boots. Down she goes again, feet skidding in the slime, and this time the impact on her knee is appalling, a bright explosion of pain. In spite of this she struggles to rise, and then Kris is on her, slamming her into the wall.

47

Veerle screams as though the knife is already buried to the hilt in her flesh.

'No – no – no – no!'

'*Shut up.*'

Kris's dark eyes are centimetres from her shock-widened hazel ones. They blaze into hers. His grip on her arm is vice-like. He presses against her, preventing her from wriggling free.

'*Godverdomme*, Veerle, shut up.'

Veerle draws breath to scream again anyway, and then she realizes that he has not done anything. The torch is still in his left hand. It is digging painfully into her upper arm where he is holding onto her. Where is the knife? For one long and grisly moment she thinks that perhaps he has already thrust it into her, that she will look down and see the handle protruding from her bloody T-shirt, that the pain kept at bay by shock will slam into her like a tidal wave. But there is nothing.

Kris speaks rapidly. 'He's coming, Veerle.' He shows her what he has in his right hand, the one that isn't holding onto her. The knife. Veerle flinches. 'I'm going to be there.' He nods

at the adjoining tunnel, the wet tongue of running water spilling from its mouth. 'You take this.'

Kris presses the knife into her hand. Veerle's fingers curl around the handle. She holds the knife, she doesn't drop it, but her face is the face of a sleepwalker. She is still assessing the fact that she is alive. Kris has not hurt her. He never meant to hurt her. It was a ruse, a convincing ruse, and it worked because now they have the knife.

Relief is short lived, barely experienced. Death is still coming. She looks at Kris. He holds out the torch. 'That too. If I have it he'll see me.'

There is a bellow from the part of the tunnel they cannot see, somewhere round the curve, and the sound of someone splashing through the filthy water. Close. Too close. There is no time to discuss what to do.

Kris says, 'Tell him you killed me. Bring him this way – past that.' He glances at the dark opening again. Then he glances back at Veerle. He says, 'Shit. No blood.' He takes the knife out of her hand again.

Another bellow. De Jager can only be round the last bend, only seconds away from them. Kris looks down at himself, hesitating. He is not a surgeon. He has no idea where to cut to cause bleeding without doing terrible damage, perhaps slashing an artery. Not the leg. He needs to be able to move; he can't risk laming himself. He turns over his left hand, looks at it for a split second and then slashes it across the ball of the thumb. As always, there is a slight delay before the pain cuts in, a moment when he feels only the sharpness of the knife, like a needle sliding through the fabric of his skin, and then it is agonizing. He cries out, not bothering to stifle it, because

if De Jager thinks he has been wounded, so much the better. He presses his hand to Veerle's face, wincing, and now she is marked with his blood too. He holds out the knife again and she takes it.

'For God's sake convince him,' Kris tells her, and then he pushes past her, towards the dark opening in the tunnel wall.

Veerle's hand tightens to a fist around the handle of the knife.

Don't think. Just do it.

She hears the splashing mere metres away. Light is visible round the corner. She shouts, 'Jager!' and her voice is an angry roar. A war cry. Then she goes to meet him.

Veerle rounds the curve of the tunnel. She moves slowly and deliberately. If she charges at him, he will shoot.

She wants him to see that it is her and not Kris, bloodied and carrying the knife. Her heart is racing; the blood sings in her veins. A lock of hair, lank with filth, hangs over her blood-streaked face, making her unkempt and savage.

There he is, filling the tunnel with his solid bulk. The troll. The ogre. The deadly thing is in his hand, ready to fire sixteen centimetres of carbon bolt into her. In this cramped space De Jager cannot stand upright, which will hamper his aim, but it probably won't stop him hitting her if he tries.

'Jager!' she shouts again. 'I killed him!' She brandishes the knife, the once-bright blade now tainted with drying gore, and her eyes glitter fiercely in the torchlight. 'You think I couldn't? He's dead, you bastard. So now back the fuck off.' She shakes back the hair from her face, which is striped with dirt and blood like warpaint, and glares at him.

De Jager looks at her. In the torchlight his expression is as

impassive as ever, the heavy features graven in cruel lines. Then he comes on, not bothering to hurry, covering Veerle with the crossbow.

'Stop!' screams Veerle hoarsely. 'I did what you wanted, so back the fuck *off*!' She holds up the knife, the point towards him, her knuckles white around the handle, but at the same time she takes a step backwards.

She sees De Jager pause, and thinks for a second that he really is considering what she has said, but then she sees him look down. The water running along the bottom of the tunnel is flowing freely over his feet, bubbling up around his ankles. He is beginning to notice it as he moves; it is becoming just noticeably more difficult to make progress against it.

Veerle can feel it too, the current tugging at the sodden legs of her jeans as the water flows past. Alarm bells are ringing at the back of her brain about that; she knows that the tunnel doesn't have to be full to the ceiling with water for it to be lethal. The floor is polished with the passage of water, and slippery in places with the unspeakable residue of the sewers. Once the water reaches a certain level, if she or Kris or indeed De Jager falls over, it will be impossible to stand up again.

She files this hazard away for future reference. The next few minutes are going to be taken up with trying not to be shot and then carved into pieces.

She takes another step back. She does not dare turn her back on him. She makes herself maintain eye contact, although it is as repellent as looking into the black eyes of a shark. Her heart is thudding so hard that passing out altogether seems a real danger.

'I did what you said!' she screams, hitting a convincing

note of wavering confidence. 'One kills the other! You said I could go!'

The tip of the knife trembles in the rank air.

De Jager looks at her with those dead eyes. He doesn't bother to point out that he was lying – that his aim was to luxuriate in the gorgeous pleasure of watching either Kris or Veerle kill the other before he finished the survivor off. Hitherto he has enjoyed the physical aspects of the hunt most: the tracking, the chase, the bringing down of the prey and the inflicting of physical pain. He finds this new psychological element exciting – the idea of bending someone so hard that they will break; that they will do anything to anyone in order to save their own skin. He could go a lot further with this. It has potential. He thinks that he will begin by applying more pressure to Veerle. She hasn't been out of sight long enough to do much more than cut Kris's throat; he will make her mutilate the body too. Then, when there is nothing left to do, or she is unable to go any further with it, he will kill her. Slowly.

He moves towards her again, his feet dragging slightly against the current of water at his feet, driving her back towards the spot where he believes the body lies.

Veerle backs up. There is water all around her; she feels it running over her boots, she hears it trickling down from the drains that run into this sewer. There is wet on her face too; red wet. And yet her mouth is dry. She licks her lips and there is a foul taste on them. Corruption. If De Jager wins, if she dies down here, she imagines herself dissolving into this appalling organic muck, becoming part of it. Despair sucks at her like a hungry mouth.

Back another step. She is at the bend in the tunnel. At some point she has to break and run, so that when he passes the spot where Kris is hiding he will be going too fast to check the opening. Veerle steps back again, and this time she feels her heel slide over the slippery floor. She keeps her balance with difficulty.

'Listen,' she says to De Jager, remembering her role as lure. 'You don't have to do anything to me. I won't tell anyone. I *can't* tell anyone, not now.'

Abruptly, De Jager loses patience. He isn't interested in talking to Veerle. He wants to hear her scream. He aims the crossbow. Veerle sees this and tries to lunge away. She hears the brisk *snap* as the bolt is released.

What saves her is the slippery floor underneath. Her feet slide out from under her and she goes down, this time on her hip. The bolt passes uselessly over her head. The torch goes into the water and winks out. Now there is only De Jager's light, illuminating her pitilessly. The knife has gone. By some miracle she has managed not to fall on it, but she can't waste time fumbling for it in the murky water. She has to get away.

De Jager is reloading and she has seconds before he can fire again; this is not like the other crossbow, the one he used before – this one can be loaded in mere moments.

It is harder to rise this time because the water is deeper and faster and her clothes are becoming waterlogged. Sheer self-preservation makes her do it. Veerle stumbles round the curve in the tunnel, spraying filthy water with every step. With no light of her own, the darkness closes in. She wonders how far she will get if the next bolt hits her. The rasping of her breath fills the tunnel.

Then at last she is level with the opening where Kris should be hiding. Veerle doesn't turn to look. Light is blooming behind her, and that means De Jager is going to have a clear line to shoot at her at any moment. The running water churns under his feet as he pursues her. She prays that Kris will be able to stop him but the thought seems increasingly unreal. The thing behind her is like a raging bull, solid with muscle, unstoppable. Fists won't drop him in his tracks, and what else is there? She has lost the knife, and there isn't so much as a loose pebble in the tunnel, let alone anything they can use as a weapon.

Veerle is past the opening now, and De Jager is close behind. He has followed her round the curve, and now the tunnel ahead is illuminated – apart from her own shadow, which flees ahead of her. She can't help it, she has to look back, but while her head is still turning she hears a grunt and a splash. Kris has attacked De Jager with the only weapon he has to hand: the screwdriver he always carries when they go exploring.

Kris is determined but he isn't as savagely brutal as De Jager. He doesn't go for the eye socket or the throat. The steel shaft buries itself in De Jager's shoulder. De Jager lets out a roar of pain and fury that is cut off as he loses his balance. Now it is his turn to fall, and with Kris's weight on his back he goes down with bone-jarring force, his skull connecting with the stone wall. The crossbow goes off, the bolt firing uselessly into the wall. The light he was carrying, the only light left working between the three of them, goes into the water, and instantly they are plunged into almost complete darkness. It doesn't stop working – this one is waterproof – but most of its light is subdued by the murky liquid into which it has vanished.

'Veerle – the light!' yells Kris, and then he is fully occupied with the heavy body beneath him, which convulses like a shark with a hook in its mouth. He tries to wrench free the screwdriver and succeeds, but the next moment it is lost in the dark. If De Jager rises, Kris will have lost the fight; he cannot compete in weight or sheer savagery. He pounds with his fists at the blunt head, gritting his teeth against the searing pain in his left hand. He fights blindly in the near-dark and the filthy foaming water.

Veerle is on her hands and knees in the water, groping for the torch. The water is flowing from behind her towards the struggle that is going on in the darkness, a battle that sounds as though it is being waged by nothing human. She sees the dim glow that is the torch moving away from her, nosing along in the current like a fish, but when she grabs at it, it seems to dart away from her. If it disappears into the churning water ahead, she will never get her hands on it. The darkness will close in for ever. How will they fight De Jager then? He will have the advantage when they cannot tell enemy from friend.

Veerle throws herself full-length into the water, reaching for the space just ahead of the light. Water splashes up all around her; it soaks through to her skin. The smell of it fills her nostrils revoltingly. Her fingers close around the torch, and for a moment she almost fumbles it because the casing is slick with slimy wet. Then she has it.

Now she has to try to get up, but that is easier said than done because her clothes are sodden and heavy with filthy water and one hand is clutching the precious light. She wallows in the water and the beam of light veers drunkenly about, illuminating first a section of curved wall, then a muscular shoulder outlined in wet fabric, then the water that bubbles along the bottom of the tunnel. For a moment Veerle thinks she is not going to make it, that she will drop exhausted back into the water and be carried into the mêlée ahead as though shooting along a slide. But then, miraculously, she manages to sit up, and then haul herself upright in defiance of the flowing water that strives to suck her back down.

Veerle staggers but keeps her feet, shivering uncontrollably. She shakes back tendrils of wet hair and spits, trying to rid her mouth of the evil flavour of the sewers. Then she raises the light and trains it on the darkness where she knows Kris and De Jager are, although she cannot tell whether the struggle is still going on because now the tunnel is filled with the sound of rushing water.

In the wavering beam De Jager rears up, bleached by the light, and it is her childhood horror again: his hair is plastered to his blunt wet head, his mouth is a cavern rimmed with teeth. Blood runs down his face, mingling with other, filthy fluids. His eyes are screwed into tiny specks through which nothing human looks out.

Veerle experiences a savage adrenalin kick, a biochemical grenade that almost unhinges her. She thinks she is dead, that De Jager has her, and—

Where is Kris where is Kris where—

Then Kris is there, the beam of the torch slashes across him as he clings to De Jager's back, struggling to keep a grip with one hand while battering at the monstrous head with his other fist. He might as well try to ride a snarling tiger; it is obvious that he cannot win this one, not now that De Jager is back on his feet. De Jager is heavier and stronger and there is no limit to his brutality. He will do *anything*; he will tear Kris apart with his teeth and his bare hands if he has to, and then he will do the same to Veerle.

De Jager turns in the narrow space like an enraged bear, trying to throw Kris off, trying to ram him into the tunnel wall, and now Veerle sees her chance. She throws herself at the struggling figures with all her weight and as much momentum as she can. Under the weight of both of them, De Jager goes down again like a tree being felled, the terrible shark-like face slammed into the water with enough force to break his nose on the tunnel floor.

If he rises again it is all over. So Kris and Veerle beat his head and shoulders, Kris with his fists, Veerle with the butt of the torch, hammering him down into the muck. Underneath them the prone body writhes and bucks, and Veerle, who is astride him, blinded by the stinking water and the strands of filthy hair that hang over her eyes, feels the animal power that courses through De Jager like an electric current. Terror fuels strength, and she brings the torch down so hard that for a moment the light goes out altogether and they are plunged into darkness.

Veerle feels a single moment of sharp and terrible panic, and then the light flickers back to life. She grips it, panting and coughing, racked with tremendous shudders. She is afraid to strike again in case the light goes out for ever, and it is several long moments before she realizes that she doesn't have to.

De Jager has stopped struggling. He lies in the fast-flowing muck, massive and ominous as the toppled statue of a deposed dictator.

Veerle looks at Kris and he stares back at her, his face drawn and terrible in the beam of light. There is a bloody contusion on his upper lip and everything sticks to him – hair, clothes – all of it sodden, as though he has been vomited up from the slimy throat of a sea monster.

They stand up, the body unmoving in the flowing water at their feet, and Veerle says, 'Is he . . . ?'

Kris crouches and grasps the shoulder, turning De Jager over so that he can see the bloodied face.

He says, 'No. Still breathing.' He stands up again.

Veerle sees that Kris is beginning to shiver. It is cold down here, very cold, and the stinking dark presses in from all sides, held back only by that one single remaining light in Veerle's hands. The water churns around their calves. Unless they get out of the sewers very quickly, they will never get out at all.

Kris reaches out and touches Veerle's shoulder, as though he wants to reassure himself that she is really there, that they have both survived, at least this long.

'Go,' he says, pushing her gently.

Both of them glance back at the fallen colossus in the tunnel. There is no decision to be made. There is only one light, only one slender chance of escape. They turn away and begin to fight their way up the tunnel, following the torch's wavering beam.

The nylon cord is still there, low on the wall, leading them out of the labyrinth where the Minotaur lies with no sound but the rasping of his breathing, which will soon be bubbling and then nothing. Kris and Veerle do not speak as they follow it. They both know that if the cord is torn from its anchor at the bottom of the manhole, or if the water rises too much or too quickly, they won't get out of here, either.

The journey back seems to take much longer than it did when they first came down. They are soaked, filthy and exhausted. Veerle's teeth are chattering. She feels the nylon cord running through fingers that are numb with cold, and her imagination throws up nightmares of it continuing for ever, never reaching the way out at all, leading them on and on into the dark until the light fails and the water rises to engulf them.

At last, though, they come to the spot where the cord is attached to the metal rungs that lead up to the street. Veerle is almost too exhausted to climb, but faced with the stark choice of that or drown, she finds the strength. She goes first, Kris following, and the cramped space is filled with the painful gasps of their breathing as they haul themselves gratefully up into the fresh air.

It is cold up here too, and raining heavily now. They lie on the pavement next to the open hole, and the rain sheets down on them, actually running down their faces in streams, but Veerle thinks that however much falls, it can never get rid of the stink of the sewers. She coughs and shivers, hugging herself, and then rolls over and puts her head over the edge of the hole, gazing into the darkness below.

Veerle hears rushing water; she hears the splatter of rain all about her. She hears nothing else – no sound of someone splashing through the water below, or dragging himself heavily up the ladder. There is a distant boom and she remembers a storm several years before, when the drains had flooded so quickly and violently that a drain cover on her street had been blown up. She holds the torch over the hole with trembling hands and directs it downwards, into the dark. She sees the gleam of fast-flowing water down there. The tunnel has flooded. Nobody is coming out of there. Another five minutes and she and Kris would not have made it.

After a while Kris raises himself up, and with an effort he pushes the manhole cover back into place over the hole, sealing the tomb.

The time after that is miserable. They cannot lie for long on the wet pavement; they are already risking hypothermia. They have to get into the warm and dry as soon as possible, but it is after midnight, and the metro and trams have stopped running. Tervuren is twelve kilometres away; the distance is not impossible to cover on foot if you are warmly dressed and well rested, but Kris and Veerle are exhausted, shocked and soaked to the skin. They find a taxi stand, but the single driver still waiting there takes one look at the pair of them, filthy and dripping, and worse, inhales the appalling scent coming off them, and shakes his head firmly.

Kris takes out his mobile phone, but it is damaged beyond repair. The screen is cracked and water has seeped inside. Veerle's is no better. She presses the buttons with fingers that are white with cold, but the screen refuses to light up. The phone is dead, drowned.

Eventually they find a bar. It has closed for the night but the owner is still inside. It takes all the cash in Kris's wallet to make him agree to let them use the telephone; one whiff of the odour that clings about the pair of them makes him react much as the taxi driver did. But he lets Veerle stand inside while Kris calls Jeroen, because she looks half dead with the cold and wet – like a girl who has barely been rescued from drowning.

Jeroen rants a bit and tells Kris he is a *klootzak*, but he agrees to come and get them. Kris tells him to bring the old car. He doesn't think Jeroen will want them sitting on the upholstery in the BMW, and indeed when his cousin arrives he looks revolted and indignant in equal measure. He lets them get into the car, though.

'This is Veerle,' says Kris as they slide into the back seat. 'Veerle, Jeroen.'

Veerle takes in brown eyes and that same thick dark Verstraeten hair, and a face that is considerably rounder and better fed than Kris's. She does her best to smile at Jeroen, but mostly she hugs herself and shivers uncontrollably. Kris holds her, but he is as cold as she is; he has no warmth to lend her. Jeroen puts the heater on full blast, although he looks as though he would prefer to open all the windows and let in some fresh air. The car pulls away from the kerb.

'Where to?' says Jeroen ironically, playing the taxi driver, and Kris does not know what to say. He cannot ask Jeroen to drop them at the villa and he has no idea what they will find at his own flat or the house on Kerkstraat, given that De Jager has almost certainly been inside both. In the end Jeroen takes them home with him. Veerle crouches under a hot shower for a long time, while Kris and Jeroen argue, keeping their voices down because of Fien, and Ella stuffs their clothes into the washing machine, looking all the time as though she is trying not to throw up.

Veerle is not interested in what Kris does or does not tell Jeroen. She pulls on one of Ella's nighties, cleans her teeth with a blob of Jeroen's toothpaste on her finger, and collapses into the bed in the spare room. When Kris joins her much later, smelling now of Jeroen's shower gel, she is too soundly asleep to stir. Her sleep is dreamless. De Jager no longer chases her through endless labyrinths.

48

Twelve months later

The bistro was full, as usual, and noisy – this was a university town, and most of the clientele were students. Still, the layout was sprawling and there were still one or two spots at the back where you could sit if you wanted peace and quiet to talk or read or get a little romantic with someone. One of these alcoves contained a circular table currently crowded with perhaps two too many students for the available space. The tabletop was equally crowded with beer glasses.

Someone was talking – a pale, heavy young man with blue eyes, rather red lips and a beard. He leaned forward earnestly.

'So these two guys are working the sewers, right? There's been a lot of rain recently or something, a lot of rubbish washed down there. And they find this body, down there in the tunnels. Really badly decomposed. I mean, it stinks down there anyway, but this is something else. Even these two guys, who've seen it all before, and probably smelled it all before too, are trying not to puke.'

'Gross, Matthias,' says someone.

Matthias continues unperturbed, gratified to have the floor. 'So they have to notify the police and all that, and nobody's all that thrilled because it's going to be a really nasty job getting the body up to the surface. I mean, it's falling apart. And it's kind of odd too because the guy is quite well equipped – he has waterproof boots on, and some kind of jumpsuit thing to keep the wet out – but he doesn't have a torch with him. Who goes down into the sewers without a light? It's suicide, but if you want to do that there are quicker ways, and anyway, why bother with the boots and stuff?

'Anyhow, after that the sewers are crawling with people for a while and it's not long before they find something else. Another body. This has been down there just as long as the first one, so it's also pretty rotten, but when they do the autopsy they find out this one's been cut up pretty badly. Someone killed him with a knife and left him down there in the dark.

'So there's a mystery. What happened to those two guys? And what were they doing down in the sewers in the first place? I mean, supposing the one they found first murdered the other one with a knife and left him down there, how did he lure the guy down there in the first place? I mean, if you have bad blood with someone, you're not going to go some-where like that with them. And where was the torch – and the knife the guy used?'

'Maybe they got washed away,' someone suggested. 'I mean, if there'd been a lot of rain.'

'Maybe,' said Matthias darkly. 'Or maybe there was some-one else involved – someone they never caught – who took the stuff away with them.'

'Like who?' asked someone else.

'Like the Burnt Guy.'

There was a short silence and then laughter.

'Come on, Matthias. The Burnt Guy's just an urban legend. He doesn't exist.'

'Well, you know,' said one of the girls slowly, 'I think the thing about the body in the sewer is true, Milo. I'm sure I read something about that last year.'

'Where?' said Milo sceptically. 'In the newspaper?'

The girl shrugged. 'I don't read those. I get the news online.'

'Online? Well, don't believe everything you read on the net.'

'I don't.'

The atmosphere had become markedly less genial, so when the waitress passed the alcove where they all sat, Milo called her over.

'Who wants another beer?'

They ordered, and the girl went off to get the beers. She was pretty in an understated way, with clear hazel eyes and dark hair swept back into a loose knot; her figure was slender but toned, a climber's figure, and Milo watched her go with ill-disguised interest. He wasn't having much success with the girls in the group and he wondered what the waitress would say if he waited for her later and asked her out.

'Don't bother,' said Cas, who was sitting next to Milo. 'She won't be interested.'

'You know her?' asked Milo.

Cas shrugged. 'Slightly. She's a student too. Works here some evenings. The rest of the time she just studies. Miss Sensible. People ask her out and she always says no.'

'A waste,' said Milo.

'I guess.'

At the bar, Veerle De Keyser loaded beers onto a tray. She worked swiftly but deftly. She never dropped a glass, and rarely spilled a drop. The job was important to her, and not just for the money, which wasn't all that good anyway. It meant stability; it showed she had her life under control. She was studying at the university; she worked in the evenings; she kept house for herself and she kept her nose clean. Once a week she called her father, Geert, in Ghent, and every so often she took the train there and visited him and his girl-friend and her half-brother, Adam. Veerle was very fond of Adam. She still disliked Geert's girlfriend, Anneke, but she took care not to let this show.

Veerle thought about Geert as she carried the drinks back to the table where the students sat. She was impervious to the looks some of the male students gave her. She was thinking instead that soon she might take the plunge and introduce Geert to the guy she was seeing.

Veerle anticipated some awkwardness, but she'd stayed out of trouble for a long time now, and besides, she was more than old enough to make her own decisions. She loved Geert, even when he was doing his over-protective father routine, but he had to accept that she wasn't a kid any more. She was pretty sure she could win him round in the end.

As she walked back to the bar, Veerle glanced at the clock on the wall.

Half an hour to go, she thought. The bistro wasn't taking food orders any more. It wouldn't be long before that group of students left, shrugging on coats and winding scarves around their necks against the chill night air.

Twenty-eight minutes later, when Veerle was clearing a table, the street door opened. In came a tall young man with handsome aquiline features and unruly dark hair falling over his eyes. Unlike the students, with their colourful scarves and novelty ski hats, he was dressed all in black: leather jacket, jeans, boots. He stood on the doormat stamping slush from his feet.

Veerle looked up and felt that familiar feeling: a kind of *jump* inside, as though something were pulling her towards him.

Kris.

She took the last few things on the table back to the kitchen as quickly as she could, and grabbed her coat on the way back out. She was still wriggling into it when she reached Kris. He kissed her on the lips, deliciously but briefly, and then he took her hand and they went outside, into the night. It was dark, but most of the shop-window displays were still lit up and there were still people on the streets, holding their collars closed against the cold.

When they were a little distance from the bistro, Kris stopped and put his arms around Veerle, pulling her to him. He kissed her again, lingeringly, pushing his fingers into her dark hair.

When at last he broke the kiss, Kris said, 'Do you want to go somewhere?'

Veerle looked up at him, into his bold dark eyes, and her own eyes were shining. 'Of course I do. Where?'

Kris grinned. 'There's a choice. There's an old place, not all that far from here; it's abandoned so it'll be freezing, but the interior is amazing. All old stuff. The last people just walked out and left it. Or there's a house. A big one. With a pool.'

'Hmmm. Tough choice. What do you think?'

'Let's toss a coin for it.'

Kris dug in his pocket and came up with a fifty-cent piece. He glanced at Veerle, his eyes full of amusement. 'Heads, the old place. Tails, the one with the pool.'

They stood together and watched the coin rise and fall in the air, golden and glittering as it turned over and over in the light from the streetlamps, and waited to see which way it would fall.

ACKNOWLEDGEMENTS

Once more I would like to thank Camilla Wray of the Darley Anderson Agency for her enthusiasm and honesty. I would also like to thank Annie Eaton, Ruth Knowles and the team at Random House for the vision and energy that have made this book and indeed this trilogy a reality.

Special thanks are due to the friends in Flanders who have helped and advised me and offered accommodation and transport during my research trips, including Gaby Grabsch and the Lindsay family.

I'd like to express my undying appreciation of the music of Flemish band Clouseau, which featured as the backdrop to many hours of plot development!

And as ever, I would like to thank my husband Gordon.

'She couldn't take her eyes off him. He was coming closer . . .
Veerle began to scream.'

The FORBIDDEN SPACES trilogy, now available . . .

 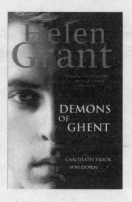 

'For something so chilling, it is terrific entertainment'
Sunday Times

'Gripping and atmospheric . . . shades of Larsson'
Guardian

'Grant has established herself as a major talent . . .
this confirms that'
Daily Mail

If you've enjoyed Helen Grant's books you might enjoy these other thrilling reads . . .

To catch a killer, Finn Maguire had to become one . . .

A page-turning trilogy of secrets and danger
from Niall Leonard

From the pen of bestselling crime author, **Jane Casey** . . .

If you love *Veronica Mars*, you'll race through the
unputdownable thrillers featuring Jess Tennant.

A chilling and bloody tale for older readers from the master of horror . . .

'*Red Rain* is a slam-bang, stay-up-all-night, leave-the-lights-on thriller'
Harlan Coben

'Leave the lights on and the door locked'
Kathy Reichs